For the
Love of Mike

Also by Rhys Bowen

The Molly Murphy
Mysteries

Death of Riley

Murphy's Law

The Constable Evans
Mysteries

Evan Only Knows

Evans to Betsy

Evan Can Wait

Evan and Elle

Evanly Choirs

Evan Help Us

Evans Above

For the
Love of Mike

Rhys Bowen

 St. Martin's Minotaur ✖ New York

www.minotaurbooks.com

Library of Congress Cataloging-in-Publication Data

Bowen, Rhys.
    For the love of Mike / Rhys Bowen.—1st ed.
       p.   cm.
    ISBN 0-312-31300-4
    1. Murphy, Molly (Fictitious character)—Fiction. 2. Women private investigators—New York (State)—New York—Fiction. 3. Irish American women—Fiction. 4. Women immigrants— Fiction. 5. New York (N.Y.)—Fiction. 6. Missing persons— Fiction. 7. Clothing trade—Fiction. I. Title.

PR6052.O848F67 2003
823'.914—dc21

                            2003046819

First Edition: December 2003

10 9 8 7 6 5 4 3 2 1

This book is dedicated to the memory of
my great aunt Sarah, who shared Molly's spirit
and also survived working in a sweatshop, going on
to become a teacher and woman of letters.

Acknowledgments

With thanks to New Yorkers S. J. Rozan and Annette and Marty Meyers for believing in my books, to Rochelle Krich for attempting to set me straight on all things Jewish, and as always, special thanks to John, Clare, and Jane for their great suggestions and for making me work hard.

For the
Love of Mike

❧ One ❧

J. P. Riley and Associates,
M. Murphy Notes:
Monday, Oct. 14, 1901
Followed JBT from his office at 38 Wall Street. Observed him
entering 135 E. Twelfth Street at approximately 7:40 P.M.

Actually I had been guessing at the time. I heard the clock on Grace Church, a couple of blocks away at Tenth and Broadway, chiming the half hour and it hadn't yet chimed the three quarters, but in my profession guessing wasn't really good enough. I'd just have to get myself a watch. I sensed my mother turning in her grave at the thought of such presumptive ideas. No one in Ballykillin had ever owned a watch, apart from the family at the big house, and they didn't count, being English. It was a pity I hadn't managed to get my hands on Paddy Riley's pocket watch before the police took his body away. Now it was probably on some sergeant's watch chain, where it was going to stay put, and as for myself, I wasn't making enough money to indulge in luxuries. If you want a real confession, I wasn't making any money at all.

After a rather eventful summer during which I found myself without an employer, I had decided to run J. P. Riley and Associates (I being the associate) without him and had taken over

1

a couple of the divorce cases that were still on his books. The first of them was resolved by the parties in question, who reconciled during a romantic summer encounter at Newport, Rhode Island. I learned this from the wife, who sent me ten dollars, "for my time and trouble." Since I'd been tramping all over the city, locating the different actresses and brothels that the wandering Mr. Pfitzer had been visiting, the ten dollars hardly covered my time and trouble, but there wasn't much I could do about it. These society people knew each other and I'd not be likely to find any more clients if I aggravated the few I had. But the cheek of it still rankled. I wondered if she'd send her doctor ten dollars for his time and trouble if the patient recovered after his ministrations!

But I was learning to hold my tongue when necessary nowadays and sent the good lady a receipt for her donation. The other investigation was still ongoing, which was why I was spending a long, dreary evening on the sidewalk of East Twelfth, between University Place and Broadway, observing the brownstone opposite. I hadn't yet discovered who lived there, but I knew it was a woman, as I had heard the man I was following, Mr. John Baker Tomlinson III, ask the maid if her mistress was at home. Her mistress, mark you, and no mention of a master. Maybe this time I had struck gold. No man of quality would visit an unchaperoned woman after dark without jeopardizing her reputation.

By 11 P.M. my suspect still hadn't emerged and I began to wonder if he was intending to stay the night. Not a happy thought for him, having to face an angry wife tomorrow morning, nor for me. It had begun to rain around nine and I had forgotten to bring an umbrella. I could feel my bonnet becoming soggier by the minute. My cloak was beginning to smell like wet sheep.

I stamped my feet and walked up and down a little, before I remembered that I was supposed to be invisible. My departed employer, Paddy Riley, could remain motionless, blended into

2

the shadows for hours. I would never learn his patience; in fact I was beginning to question whether I was cut out for this line of work after all. I liked the excitement all right and it beat working in a sweatshop for eighteen hours a day or gutting fish at the Fulton Street market, which seemed the only other options for an Irish girl fresh off the boat. There had been a companion's position, but we won't go into my reasons for leaving that. It was still too painful to think about. Even after three months the ache wouldn't go away. Let's just say that proving I could do quite well without Daniel Sullivan was the main force that drove me to stand on a wet, windy sidewalk when most respectable folk were already in their beds.

There was a light on in the upstairs bedroom—a soft glow which hinted at a gas bracket turned down low, and not the harsher brightness of a new-fangled electric bulb which seemed to be the rage in this city—but the blinds were drawn. Was it too much to hope for that the wicked couple would come to the window and be silhouetted in passionate embrace? In fact, so far I had not managed to catch Mr. Tomlinson doing anything that might be grounds for divorce. I had loitered outside his Wall Street office. I had followed him to lunches at his club (all male) and dinners at restaurants (with respectable companions), but not a single hint so far to confirm his wife's suspicions that the illustrious Mr. Tomlinson was carrying on an illicit amorous liaison.

And if I now could provide proof that Mr. T had been straying, what then? I'd earn myself a big fat check and Mr. Tomlinson would be out on his ear—which was a shame as I rather liked him. In observing him from afar I had seen him to be polite, courteous, and with a good sense of humor. Again I asked myself whether the private investigator's life was really for me. What I wanted was something other than divorce cases, although Paddy had maintained they were his bread and butter. And bread and butter were surely needed at the moment.

The rain was now driving from the East River, forcing me to move into the comparative shelter of a flight of steps leading up to a front door. My back pressed against the brickwork of the house, I tried to look on the bright side of things. At least I wasn't starving. I had a splendid place to live and the chance to carve out a real profession for myself if I could only stand the elements!

I glanced up as the light in the upstairs room was extinguished. The curtains remained drawn. I watched and waited. Nothing moved, no door opened, no wandering husband slunk out of Number 135. I wasn't sure what to do next. Would I really have to hang around until morning? Not a pleasing prospect, given that the weather was getting worse by the minute. Fortunately Mr. Tomlinson had chosen his dalliance in my own corner of the city. My own room was but a ten-minute walk away down Fifth Avenue. I could slip home to change my clothes, have a bath and a good sleep and be back in position before dawn broke, this time equipped with an umbrella. Of course, Mr. Tomlinson could emerge from the house at any time during the night and I'd miss my opportunity. If I left my post, he'd undoubtedly slip out while I slept and I'd have to conduct a nightly vigil all over again. Besides, Paddy would never have left his post and I was trying to live up to his example.

I resolved to stick it out a little longer. If anyone could endure wind and rain, then it was surely I—having been raised on the wild west coast of Ireland where the rain usually fell horizontally and was whipped so hard by the driving wind that it stung like a swarm of bees. And nothing more than a shawl to wrap around me in those days either! Nothing like this long warm cape I had inherited from Paddy. I pulled it more closely around me and stuck my hands into the pockets to keep them warm.

Down at the other end of the block, on Broadway, the city was still awake. I heard a hansom cab clip clop past, the clang of a trolley car bell, raucous laughter, shouts, running feet. The city was never peaceful for long, but at least it was alive, which was more than I could say for County Mayo.

I stiffened as I heard a police whistle blowing, but the gale picked up and sounds were muffled again. Then I saw two figures coming along Twelfth Street toward me. I froze and stepped back behind the flight of steps, hoping they would pass by without noticing me. It was at times like this that I realized being a woman alone was a distinct disadvantage. Although I was still in a highly respectable neighborhood, only one block from the patricians of Fifth Avenue, things went downhill pretty quickly in the other direction and Broadway was not a street on which I'd feel comfortable walking alone at night. The footsteps came closer—a heavy measured tread of boots. I held my breath and pressed myself against the railing. They were almost past me when one of them turned. Before I knew what was happening, big hands reached out and grabbed me.

"Well, lookee what we've got here, Brendan!" a deep Irish voice boomed. "One of them did get away after all. And she's a little wild cat all right!" This last comment uttered as I tried to wriggle free from his grasp and swung a kick in the direction of his shins.

"Let go of me this instant!" I sounded less rattled than I really felt. "I'll call the police. I heard a police whistle just down the block. They'll be here in a second."

"Call the police—that's a good one, eh, Brendan?" The big man who had hold of my wrists chuckled. His taller, skinnier companion laughed too—a higher hee hee hee followed by a snort through his nose which I found very annoying.

"You don't think the New York City police can deal with the likes of you?" I was still attempting to remain calm and haughty. "Now unhand me immediately."

"A proper little firebrand, and Irish too," the big man said, as he attempted to bring my hands behind my back and I attempted to stamp on his toes. "We are the police, as you very well know."

Relief flooded through me as I recognized the familiar uniforms under their rain capes. "Then you're making a terrible mistake, officers. I am no criminal. I'm a respectable citizen."

This caused them more mirth. "A respectable citizen—and my father's the pope in Rome! You did a bunk through the back window when my partner and I raided Tom Sharkey's saloon a few minutes ago. So where did your fancy boy get to? Left you to face the music alone, did he?"

It was just beginning to dawn on me that they thought I was a woman of a very different occupation. "Jesus, Mary, and Joseph. I'm thinking the pair of you are in need of glasses," I said angrily. "Look at me. Do I look like a woman of the streets?"

"She is kind of dowdy looking and she's not even wearing any rouge on her cheeks," Brendan commented. "Maybe we have made a mistake."

I decided to ignore this unflattering assessment of my charms. "Of course you've made a mistake. But I'll accept your apology, given that the light is so poor," I said.

"So maybe she wasn't the young girl who escaped from the bawdy house," the larger officer conceded, "but she's still up to no good. What would a respectable woman be doing out alone at this time of night?"

"If you really must know, I'm a private investigator, out on a case," I said. "I'm observing a house opposite."

If they had been mirthful before, then this time their jollity positively overflowed. They nudged each other in the side and staggered around guffawing while I gave my impression of Queen Victoria not being amused.

"If you don't believe me, I have my card in my purse," I said. "I am a partner at J. P. Riley and Associates. You must have met Paddy Riley."

"Paddy Riley?" The large constable gave me an incredulous glance. "Paddy Riley? You're not expecting me to believe that he'd ever work with a woman, are you? He hated women. Couldn't stand the sight of them. And anyway, Paddy Riley's dead and buried, in case you didn't know."

"Of course I know. I'm carrying on the business without him, or I would be if you two great clodhoppers would just leave me in peace."

He still had hold of my arm and I tried to wrench myself free.

"Oh no, you're coming with us, my dear. Whatever you were doing, I'll wager you were up to no good."

"Observing the house opposite, she says," the skinny one called Brendan commented, looking smug. "Do you think she could be working with the Dusters, scouting out places to rob?"

"Holy Mother of God! Of course I'm not scouting out places to rob. If you'll just let go of me, I can produce any number of respected citizens who will vouch for me. In fact if you take me to your police station, I'm afraid you're going to look very foolish because I happen to be a good friend of—" I bit my tongue and left the rest of the sentence hanging. I was dying to see their faces when I told them that their own Captain Daniel Sullivan could vouch for me, but I wasn't going to use his name every time I was in a jam. He'd be only too delighted to remind me yet again that I was playing with fire and no good would come from trying to be part of a man's world.

"A good friend of whom, my dear?" the large officer asked. "The mayor, was it? Or the governor? Or maybe our new president Teddy himself?" He grinned at the other policeman again and dug him in the ribs.

"You'll see," I said, determined not to lose my dignity. Then I added, as they began to manhandle me away, "And please put me down. I am not a sack of potatoes. I have two good feet and can walk on my own."

"Just as long as you don't try to do a bunk on us," the large officer said.

"Do the Dusters ever use women?" Brendan asked we started to walk away. "I know the old Gophers had some terrible fierce women working with them, but I don't know that much about the Dusters."

"They're getting very tricky these days. No knowing what they'll try next," the other officer said.

The rain had eased off and the street lamps were reflected in puddles.

"Who are these Dusters?" I asked.

"The Hudson Dusters? You've never heard of them?" Brendan sounded surprised. "This is their territory, west of Broadway all the way to the Hudson."

"Are they some kind of gang then?"

"One of the biggest—along with the Eastmans and the Five Pointers, of course."

"That's enough, Brendan. She knows very well who the Dusters are. I'll wager one of their squealers will identify her for us in the morning."

I heard the sound of a front door slamming behind us down the street and looked around to see a tall figure in a long greatcoat and top hat hurrying in the direction of Fifth Avenue. It looked like Mr. Tomlinson but I had now missed seeing him come out of the house. Since one of my captors liked to gab, I couldn't resist asking, "So that house I was watching, the one with the two bay trees in pots beside the front door—you don't happen to know who owns it?"

Brendan took the bait right away. "That's Mrs. Tomlinson's house, wouldn't you say, Brian?"

"Your mouth's going to be the death of you, boy," the older policeman snapped. "You should know better than that. Next you'll be lending her your nightstick to break in with."

"I wasn't doing no harm . . ."

I hardly heard this exchange. My brain was still trying to digest what Brendan had said. "Mrs. Tomlinson?" I said, looking appealingly at him. "You don't mean the wife of John Baker Tomlinson, do you? I've been to her residence. It's on Fifty-second Street on the East Side."

"No, this is an older woman—a widow. Maybe it's your man's mother."

Terrific, I thought as we sloshed our way down Sixth Avenue toward the Jefferson Market police station. I had spent an entire evening risking pneumonia, getting myself arrested, and all to watch Mr. John Baker Tomlinson III visit his mother! As a detective it appeared I still had a long way to go.

❧ Two ❧

The Jefferson Market police station was in the triangular-shaped complex that also held a fire station, a jail, and the market itself. It was a mere stone's throw from my house on Patchin Place and I looked longingly as we crossed Tenth Street.

"Look, Officers, I live just across the street," I said. "If you'd just take me home, my friends will vouch for me."

"You're not going anywhere till morning," the brusque constable said, giving my arm a warning squeeze. "We've been instructed to bring in any individuals behaving suspiciously and a young woman, out alone late at night, counts as suspicious in my book."

"But I've explained what I was doing."

"You can explain it to my sergeant." I was shoved into the police station. "When he gets here in the morning," he added.

"You mean I have to stay here all night?" For the first time I began to feel alarmed. I had been in jail once before and I had no wish to repeat the experience. "You can't keep an innocent person in jail with no cause."

"You watch your mouth or I'll have you for resisting arrest," the constable said. "Go on. Down to the lockup with you."

Oh, but I was so tempted to call upon the name of Captain Sullivan. Watching their faces when they realized their mistake would have been worth any lecture that Daniel might give me. But as my mother always told me, I was born with too much pride. I pressed my lips together and said nothing.

I was manhandled down a dank, echoing hallway that smelled of urine and stale beer. I passed a cell full of dark shapes. The shapes stirred themselves as we passed and ribald comments from crude male voices were hurled after me.

"Shut your mouths in there." The constable rattled his nightstick along the bars. We paused in front of the next cell. It too was fronted with bars instead of a wall and full of more shadowy figures. My heart leaped in fear that I might be locked up with men like those we had just passed. Before I had time to voice these fears, a key was produced, a door within the bars swung open, and I was shoved inside. I half stumbled and was grateful to see myself staring at a delicate foot and a skirt.

"Over here, dearie," a rasping voice said from the darkness. "Move yer bum over, Flossie. The poor thing looks like she's about to faint."

I wasn't really the type who fainted, but this was not the moment to protest my apparent frailty. I gave a grateful smile and sat on the few inches of bare wooden cot that had been offered to me. As my eyes accustomed themselves to the gloom, I saw that my cellmates were indeed of the profession I had been accused of pursuing. There were five of them and they were rouged and powdered with bright red lips and hair piled in ridiculous pompadours. One was wearing a black French corset that lifted her bosoms like overripe melons. No dress over the corset, mind you—just the corset and a shiny black skirt beneath it. The skirt was hitched up as she sat on the floor to reveal black fishnet stockings and high-heeled boots. Flossie on the bench was in a low-cut red satin dress. The other occupant of the bench had her shawl pulled around her and was trying to sleep. In contrast to the others she looked young and innocent, apart from the circles of rouge on her cheeks and the bright lips. I tried not to stare too obviously.

"So what you in for, honey?" the coarse voice asked again. It belonged to the large woman sitting on the floor in the corner, legs spread apart in a most unfeminine pose. She had an ostrich feather sticking from her hair and a feather boa around her neck.

I thought it wise not to say that I was a detective. That might cast me with the enemy and I had a whole night to spend in their presence. In the months since I had fled from Ireland and come to New York I had become adept at lying without so much as batting an eyelid. When the police officers had grabbed me, I had tried telling the truth for once and look where it got me.

"I'm afraid the officers have made a terrible mistake," I said, trying to sound sweet and demure. "Just because they found me sheltering from the rain on my way home from a tryst with a young man, they thought that I was—one of you."

This caused great merriment. "Thought you was one of us— that's a good one." The large blowsy woman's breasts heaved as she laughed. "You wouldn't get many clients dressed like that, dearie."

"They must have wanted their eyes testing," the one in the corset agreed. "Look at you. Anyone can see you're a proper young lady and not riffraff from the streets."

"Getting too big for their boots, that's the trouble with coppers around here," Flossie in the red dress chimed in. "A girl's not safe even when she's paid her protection money. Just because there's a Tammany mayor in city hall, the police think they can do what they damned-well like and nobody's gonna stop them."

"Language, Bessy, there's a young lady present," the blowsy one reminded her. She leaned across and patted my knee. "Don't you worry yourself, dearie. You'll be out of here in the morning and this will all seem like a bad dream."

I looked around the cell and found the young girl awake and staring at me. She had big dark eyes and was looking at me with such a wistful expression that it almost broke my heart. It will seem like a bad dream for you, the expression said. For me there will be no waking up in the morning.

13

I shut my eyes, leaned against the cold brick, and tried to sleep. But sleep wouldn't come. Now that I was over my initial fear, I was so angry I felt I could explode at the unfairness of it all. This would never have happened if I'd been a man. Men were free to walk when and where they chose in this city. But a lone female, out unchaperoned at night, was immediately suspected of being up to no good. I had already realized that there were many things that Paddy Riley had been able to do that were just not open to me. He had contacts with gangs, and with the police. He frequented various taverns. He could move freely and unobtrusively through the worst areas, and could change his appearance easily by means of a beard or a moustache. I had tried disguising myself as a young boy once and was amazed at the freedom it gave me. Of course, Paddy had seen through it right away, but maybe I should consider using such a disguise again, if I wanted to avoid more embarrassing encounters with the police.

And then again, maybe I should give up the whole idea of trying to carry on Paddy's business. Divorce cases may have been Paddy's bread and butter, but this short acquaintance with them had made me decide that they were not for me. I found them small, mean-spirited, and sordid. If I was going to stay in this business at all, then I should take up my original plan—finding immigrants who had lost touch with their families back in Europe. At least I'd be doing something positive then.

I should never have started along this train of thought. My mind moved from immigrants, to Ellis Island, to my own unpleasant experience there, and then to the little family I had brought with me when their mother couldn't travel with them. I wished I hadn't rehashed that particular worry. When I delivered them to their father, I had thought that my job was complete. It wasn't. The father, Seamus, had not been able to work since he almost lost his life in a collapse of the new subway tunnel. They had been evicted from the flat I found for them and the latest I had heard, they were back rooming with relatives on the

14

Lower East Side. The fact that I wouldn't wish those relatives on my very worst enemy and that I had grown remarkably fond of the two little ones nagged at my conscience. I knew I should be doing something to rescue them, but I also knew it would mean leaving the most delightful circumstances in which I now found myself. My big room on the top floor of my friends' house on Patchin Place was little short of heaven. Living in a house full of artists and writers and thinkers had made it one step better than heaven itself.

I had been putting off making any decision, hoping that Seamus would be fit enough to return to work and that he'd find a good place for his family. Now it seemed that he might never be fit enough to return to hard manual labor. Which meant it was now up to me to rescue them from a Lower East Side hellhole and a dragon of a cousin. I gave a big sigh. Life seemed to be one perpetual roller-coaster—up on top of the hill one minute, then rushing downward to the depths the next.

I should never have started thinking about roller-coasters either. Instantly my mind whisked me back to happier times, when Captain Daniel Sullivan had taken me to Coney Island. I smiled now at the memory of it. Daniel had expected me to scream, faint, or cling onto him as we rushed down into the depths. Instead I had laughed, loudly. The next time we began a descent, he had kissed me and we had hardly noticed when the car reached the bottom. I turned off that memory hastily. No good would come of dwelling on that part of my past. Besides, it all seemed blurred and dreamlike, as if it was something I had read about in a book.

I glanced around the cell. Quiet had fallen. The young girl beside me slept like an angelic child. Heavy snores were coming from the bosomy lady on the floor. I closed my eyes and drifted into uneasy sleep.

The rattle of a billy club along bars woke me. First gray light was coming in through a high window. It was cold and drafty in the cell. The door was opened briefly and a tray of tin mugs full of a hot dark liquid was shoved inside. I took the mug handed to me. It was coffee, at least I think it was. I longed for a warming drink, but my gaze fell on the bucket in the corner, which one of the women was now using noisily. There was no way on God's earth that I was going to follow suit. I put the mug down untouched and wondered how long it might be before the sergeant arrived and I would be released. I opened my purse, which I had clutched in my arms all night, and took out my comb. At least I would try to look respectable when they came for me.

A little later I heard deep voices and the tread of heavy boots echoing as they came down the hall.

"The house behind Tom Sharkey's saloon, you say. They work for the Dusters then, Harry?" I heard a voice saying.

"Couldn't say, sir. Nobody's questioned them yet. You can take a look for yourself and see if you recognize any of them. Down here on the left."

The footsteps came closer. A balding uniformed sergeant stood in front of our bars and behind him stood a taller, slimmer man with unruly dark curls that escaped from under the derby he was wearing. If I'd have had time, I would have pulled my cape over my head. His gaze fell on me as I shrank into the corner and wished myself elsewhere. "Holy Mother—what about this one, Harry? What's she in for?"

"Not sure, sir. Found loitering on the street, late at night, as I understand it. Couldn't give a proper explanation of herself. My boys thought she might be a lookout for the Dusters, seeing as where she was stationed."

"Did they now? Well, isn't that interesting?" The man's dark eyes flashed with amusement. "Bring her out, Harry. I'll question this one myself."

"Out you come then." The sergeant motioned me to the door. "Not you girls. Stay well back or you'll get my nightstick on your knuckles."

"Good-bye, dearie. Good luck. Don't let that scum scare you."

The wishes echoed after me as I walked beside the sergeant down the hall. Another door was opened. I was shoved inside.

"Now behave yourself and answer the captain's questions and you'll come to no harm."

The door shut behind us and I looked up into the captain's face.

"You hear that," he said, his eyes holding mine. "You'll come to no harm if you just obey me."

"Very funny, Daniel," I said. "I suppose you think it's most amusing that I had to spend the night in a room full of loose women."

I watched him suppress a chuckle. "No, I'm sure it wasn't funny at all for you. You do get yourself into the most impossible circumstances, Molly. What was it this time?"

"I was minding my own business, observing a house on East Twelfth Street, when two of your great clodhopping constables grabbed me and hinted that I was an escaped prostitute."

This time Daniel Sullivan did smile.

"As if I look like a floozie!" I snapped. "I told them I was an investigator, observing a house, but they wouldn't believe me. They laughed in my face. They thought I was working for some gang, scouting out a place to rob, if you please. I've never been so insulted in my life."

Daniel put his hands on my shoulders. "Hold your horses, Molly. They were quite within their rights, you know. They have orders to bring in any suspicious persons and I'm sure you seemed suspicious to them."

"If I'd been Paddy, they'd have turned a blind eye and walked on past."

"Of course they would. Everyone knew Paddy."

"And he was a man."

"That too." Those big, reassuring hands squeezed my shoulders. "Molly, when will you give up this stupid idea? Women just can't be investigators. You've seen for yourself now that it doesn't work. Last night was just an embarrassment for you. Next time it could be worse—the rumors about the white slave trade are not all exaggerations, you know. Prostitutes don't have very long lives and replacements don't exactly line up to volunteer for the job. A young woman alone on the streets at night is just what they are looking for." A picture flashed into my mind of that young girl, looking at me with sadness and longing. I shuddered. "And then there are the gangs," Daniel went on. He paused, still holding my shoulders, still looking down at me gravely. "Right now there is a war going on between two of the worst gangs in the city. The Hudson Dusters and Eastmans are fighting over territory and control of the cocaine trade. And the third gang, the Five Pointers, are hoping to expand their activities while their rivals are at each others' throats. A nasty business. There were two men lying dead in the alley behind Tom Sharkey's saloon last night. Neither gang admits knowing either of them. They've no identification on them. If some family member doesn't report them missing, they'll be buried in the potter's field and we'll never know their names. They might have been gang members, or they might have been innocent men, caught in the crossfire in the wrong place at the wrong time. Do you understand what I am telling you?"

"You're saying I shouldn't be out on the streets alone at night."

"Precisely. And why in heaven's name didn't you have me called when they brought you in last night? I could have had you out in seconds, rather than spend the night in jail."

"Because I have my pride," I said. "Because I knew you'd behave exactly as you are behaving right now." I took a deep breath, "And because I can mean nothing to you."

"Nothing to me—how can you say that?"

I had been so strong all night. Now I was weary, relieved, and Daniel's hands on my shoulders were unnerving me. I had a horrible feeling that I might break down and cry at any minute.

I fought to master myself. "I haven't read in the *Times* that Miss Norton has broken off her engagement," I said stiffly.

"Not yet, no."

"Then I can be nothing to you, Daniel. We've been through this before. Now if you'd just let go of me, I want to go home."

"I don't want to let go of you, Molly," he said, with a look that made me feel even more unsteady. "You know that. I want you to have patience until I can get things squared away."

"You won't ever break off your engagement," I said coldly. "Not while your career is at stake."

"Give me time, Molly, I beg you. I do love you, you know."

I held his gaze. "Not enough, Daniel."

His hands slid from my shoulders. "You're free to go," he said.

I left the room without looking back.

❦ Three ❧

As I closed the front door at 9 Patchin Place, a voice yelled out, "She's here, Gus, she's here!" and Sid came flying down the stairs toward me, wearing kingfisher blue silk pajamas, followed by Gus wrapped in a large scarlet Chinese robe. Their faces were a picture of relief and joy.

"Molly, where have you been? We've been worried sick," Gus exclaimed over Sid's shoulder. "We've been out half the night, tramping the streets, looking for you."

"I'm so sorry to have caused you such worry," I said. "I'd have let you know if I could. I got myself arrested and spent the night a mere stone's throw away at the Jefferson Market police station."

"Got yourself arrested?" Sid asked, looking amused now and not horrified as a more respectable woman would have done. "Molly, my sweet, what had you been doing?"

"Nothing. That was the annoying part of it. I was minding my own business, standing on a residential street and observing a house. I was picked up by the police because no decent young lady should be out alone at night."

"The nerve of it," Sid said. She helped me off with my cloak which was still damp and still smelled of wet sheep. "Your clothes are completely soaked," she added as she hung it up. "You'd better let Gus run you a bath and I'll go along to the kitchen to make us all some strong coffee. We were so worried we didn't even think of going to the bakery for rolls yet, but I'll remedy that as soon as I've put the coffee on."

"Come on, Molly, up the stairs with you." Gus shepherded me up the stairs and by the time I was out of my wet clothes and into my robe, the steam was rising from the mammoth claw-footed tub that was the pride of our bathroom. "I'll even let you use my Parisian soap to make you feel lovely and decadent," Gus said with a wicked grin as she closed the door.

I eased myself into the water and lay back, thinking how lucky I was to have such wonderful friends. Their names, of course, were not really Sid and Gus. They had been named by their parents, rather more conventionally, Elena Miriam Goldfarb and Augusta Mary Walcott, but around Greenwich Village, where we lived, they were always Sid and Gus. They were also, for all intents and purposes, a couple—something I had not come across in my sheltered Irish existence before. At home this would have made them social outcasts, to be whispered about behind closed lace curtains. In the society in which Sid and Gus moved, there were no rules. I found this delightfully refreshing and had become very fond of them both. They, in their turn, treated me as an adored child who could do no wrong.

By the time the water had begun to cool I was feeling relaxed, energized, and ready for anything again. I came downstairs to find fresh rolls from the French bakery around the corner on the kitchen table and the wonderful aroma of Sid's Turkish coffee. I can't say I had ever learned to love Turkish coffee as much as they did, but at this moment it was clearly a symbol of home and everything being all right after all.

"So do tell all, Molly. We're quite agog," Sid said, pulling up a chair beside me and breaking open a roll. She had changed out of the silk pajamas into dark gray trousers and an emerald green gentlemen's smoking jacket which offset her black, cropped hair wonderfully.

"Not until she's had something to eat, Sid. The poor lamb has been through an ordeal," Gus said, taking the basket of rolls

from Sid and handing it to me. "They're still warm. Heavenly."
She was still in the red robe, her light brown curls still wild and
untamed around an elfin face.

I sipped the black syrupy liquid and then took a big bite of
warm roll, with melting butter and apricot jam. It felt good to
be alive again.

"You'll never guess why they apprehended me to begin with,"
I said, looking up from my roll with a grin. "They thought I was
a woman of the streets."

"You? Were they particularly nearsighted policemen?" Sid
asked.

"It was dark and apparently they had just made a raid on a
nearby bawdy house."

"Then why didn't they release you the moment it became
obvious that you were not that type of woman?" Gus asked.

"They decided I had to be up to no good, loitering alone in
the middle of the night. They thought I might be a lookout for
a gang."

"Molly as a gangster's moll! This gets better and better," Sid
spluttered through a mouthful of crumbs.

"I'm sure it wasn't very amusing for poor Molly." Gus patted
my hand. "A night in a dreadful jail cell. How horrid for you,
my sweet."

"It wasn't too bad. The cell was full of prostitutes, but they
couldn't have been kinder to me. They knew as well as I did that
I'd been wrongly arrested."

"So presumably someone with sense came on duty this morning, took one look at you, and realized a terrible mistake had been
made." Sid reached over to refill my coffee without being asked.

I made a face. "The person who came on duty was none
other than Daniel Sullivan—the last person in the world I wanted
to see in such circumstances."

"Daniel the Deceiver, you mean?" Gus asked. They were well
aware of my story and thought very poorly of him for his actions.
"Why didn't you use his name to get yourself released last night?

It's the least he could do for you, after trifling with your affections like that."

"I refuse to ask Daniel Sullivan for help. My pride won't let me. And besides, I knew he'd only say I told you so—which is exactly what he did."

"I take it he still hasn't broken his engagement then?"

"Let's not talk about it," I said. I helped myself to another roll. "And do you want to hear the ultimate annoyance of the evening? I found out when the police were leading me away that I had tailed my erring husband to his mother's house, not his floozie's."

They both burst out laughing.

"You spent the evening spying on him visiting his mother? Oh, but that is rich."

I had to laugh with them. "How was I to know? All I knew was that he was visiting a woman. It never occurred to me that the woman could be his mother."

"Poor, sweet Molly," Gus said, still smiling. "I wish you'd stop this highly dangerous life and become something sensible like a writer or a painter."

"I made up my mind to stop last night," I said. "Stop doing divorce cases anyway. I find they leave a bad taste in my mouth. I know they were Paddy's bread and butter, but . . ."

"But they're not your cup of tea!" Sid finished for me, delighted with her own wit.

"Precisely. I'm going to go back to my original intention of helping to reunite families. I've decided to place an advertisement in the Irish newspapers, and see if that brings any customers. If not, then I'll start thinking about a change of profession."

Sid jumped up at the sound of the morning post landing on our doormat. She came back with a big smile on her face. "Look at this. Postcard from Ryan."

This was, of course, our friend, the delightful, flamboyant, annoying Irish playwright, Ryan O'Hare.

"Where is he?" Gus leaped up, peering over Sid's shoulder to see the postcard. "The postmark is Pittsburgh."

"That's what he says. Listen. 'Greetings from the land of smoke and fume. We open in Pittsburgh tonight, although what these Vulcans will think of a wickedly urbane satire, I shudder to think. After Cleveland I have come to realize that I was right. Civilization does cease outside of New York. The air here is quite unbreathable. My coughing at night rivals that of La Dame aux Camelias, indeed I may well return consumptive . . . Yours in great suffering and tribulation, Ryan O'Hare, playwright extraordinaire.' "

Sid and Gus looked at each other and laughed. "Typical Ryan. Everything has to be dramatic," Gus said. "Now he's dying of consumption."

"Of course I do feel for him," Sid said. "It was most unfortunate that President McKinley died just before his play was due to open. It wasn't his fault that the theaters were all closed for a month of national mourning. So it makes sense to take the play on the road before tackling New York, even if that road includes Pittsburgh."

"Let's hope he returns to triumph at Daly's Theater, just like he planned," Gus said. "Is there a tad more coffee in that pot do you think, dearest?"

I listened to them chatting merrily but my thoughts had moved elsewhere. Something about Ryan's postcard had left me feeling uneasy. We had, of course, been together when the president was shot. That would leave anyone feeling uneasy, but it was over now. The poor president was dead and buried and life had gone back to normal again. Then I realized what it was— Ryan's mention of consumption. My nagging conscience came back to me. Poor Kathleen O'Connor was dying of consumption, back home in Ireland while I had been neglecting her children more than I should. I resolved to pay them a visit this very morning. If their conditions were not satisfactory, then I'd do something about it, however much I hated to leave this wonderful life of bohemian ease.

I got to my feet. "I should go out," I said.

They were instantly at my side, the postcard from Ryan forgotten. "You'll do no such thing," Gus said. She could be quite forceful in spite of her delicate appearance. "You've just spent a night in damp clothing in jail. You need a good long rest."

I tried to protest, but Sid took my arm. "No arguing. Now up you go and we'll wake you for lunch."

I thought it best not to protest further. I went up the two flights to my room, opened the windows, and lay down on the bed. Delightful autumn sunshine streamed in through my window, along with the chirping of busy sparrows in the bushes outside. I could have been miles from the city. How could I possibly give this up? I tried to sleep but my mind was coiled tighter than a watch spring. In the end I gave up, put on my business suit—since my dark skirt was still sodden around the hem—then crept down the stairs like a naughty child. Out of Patchin Place, diagonally across Washington Square until I met the Bowery. Then I headed south to the Lower East Side where Seamus and his family were now again living.

I stopped at a butcher to buy a chicken, and at the greengrocer to buy grapes, remembering how Seamus had enjoyed them before. Then I added two lollipops from a street stall. If you're wondering where the money came from, seeing that I wasn't making any yet, I was paying myself a modest salary from the money Paddy had left in the business—or more accurately, the money I had found hidden in the bottom of a filing cabinet drawer. I had not been naïve enough to hand it over to the police but had opened a bank account with it until a next of kin claimed it. So far no next of kin had come forward.

As I went on my way, the streets became noisier, dirtier, and smellier, the buildings taller, crammed together, shutting out the sunlight, giving me the feeling of being hemmed in. Memories of my own arrival in New York and my first unpleasant days on

26

these streets came flooding back to me. How long ago it seemed. Was it really less than a year ago that I was walking these streets, penniless, afraid, with nowhere to go? I took stock of how far I had come and felt more cheerful right away.

As I passed through the Jewish quarter, crossing Hester Street then Rivington and Delancey, the streets became clogged with humanity—pushcarts everywhere, laden with every kind of merchandise. Vendors shouted their wares in tongues I couldn't understand. Chickens and geese hung by their necks in rows. Strange foods sizzled on makeshift stoves giving off exotic, spicy smells. I looked with interest at a pickle vendor, producing fat green pickled cucumbers from a barrel like a conjurer bringing rabbits from a hat. I wondered what they tasted like and was tempted to stop and buy one. There were so many things in the world that were still new to me. One day I should take the time to try them all. But the suspicious looks I was getting from bearded men in tall black hats, from women who passed me with baskets on their arms, dragging serious, dark-eyed children let me know clearly that I was an outsider with no business in their territory. My bright red hair and Irish complexion were definitely a disadvantage for a budding detective. Paddy could blend in anywhere. I'd find it hard to look anything but Irish.

It was the same as I moved into the Italian section to the south. Streets echoed with men in animated conversation, laundry flapped above our heads, old women in black sat on stoops in the morning sunshine, babies cried, children played, more pushcarts with different wares—jars of olives, jars of olive oil, jars with what looked like thin sticks in them which I guessed might be uncooked spaghetti—and me with the definite feeling of being the outsider.

A group of street urchins with dark, close cropped hair came running past me, the steel tips on their boots creating sparks on the cobbles. They leaped up at me and tugged at my long red hair. "Hey, where's the fire, lady?" one of them shouted in accented English. He grabbed at my hair ribbon. I had grown up with brothers. I reacted instantly, caught him off guard and sent him sprawling backward. They didn't bother me again.

There was no mistaking when I came to Fulton Street. The fish market announced its presence long before I was anywhere near it. The smell of fish was heavy in the air, making me bring out my handkerchief and hold it to my nose. There were fish scales floating in the gutters and men hurried past pushing carts piled high with boxes of fish. I passed the market itself and was glad to turn onto South Street where a good, strong breeze from the East River made it possible to breathe again. Out of all of New York City, why on earth had they chosen to live right here?

Of course, I had to grant them the view. Over our heads the Brooklyn Bridge soared majestically across to the far shore, suspended, it seemed, by the frailest of strands. The East River was dotted with sails, ranging from tall-masted ships from across the ocean to squat, square-sailed barges going upriver. It painted a charming, lively canvas and I would have lingered longer to admire, had not the whiff of the fish market caught up with me. I crossed South Street and passed open shop fronts where sailmakers and woodwrights plied their trades before I turned into a narrow side alley and found the building I was looking for.

It was another dreary tenement building, even worse, if anything, than my first home on Cherry Street. The dark, narrow staircase smelled of urine, boiled cabbage, and fish. I made my way upstairs, past landings cluttered with prams and old boxes, hearing crying babies, voices raised in anger, a woman singing. I started when something scurried across the floor in front of me. Too big for a mouse. It had to be a rat.

I was out of breath by the time I had reached the fifth floor and prayed that Seamus would be at home. How did he manage to climb so many stairs with his damaged lungs? I knocked on the door and prayed this time that Nuala might not be at home. I had no wish ever to see her again. My prayer was not answered. Nuala herself opened the door, her bloated shape blotting out any light that might have come from the room behind her.

"Saints preserve us," she said. "Would you look what the cat dropped on our doorstep."

"Lovely seeing you again too, Nuala." I tried to get past her and into the apartment but she remained blocking the doorway.

"I didn't think you'd be turning up again, like a bad penny. So your fancy man finally threw you out, did he? I knew it would happen in the end—didn't I tell you so, Seamus? Wasn't I saying that she'd come a cropper, for all her airs and graces? Well, it's no use thinking you're going to bunk here—packed like sardines, we are."

"I have absolutely no wish to move in with you, Nuala," I said. "I have a very comfortable apartment, which I share with two female friends and not a fancy man in sight. I came to see how Seamus was getting along."

Grudgingly she stood aside and let me enter. It was a hell-hole of a room with no windows, lit by one anemic lamp. Seamus was sitting in the one armchair and the lamplight made him look like a pale shadow of himself.

"Molly, my dear," he said, rising awkwardly to his feet. "It's so good to see you. How kind of you to come and visit us."

"I was concerned about you, Seamus. I heard that you'd found a new place so I thought I'd come and pay you a call."

"Yes, well it's not exactly what you'd call homely, is it, but it will have to do for now, until I can get back on me feet again."

"Why on earth did you choose to live here of all places?" I blurted out before I realized it wasn't exactly a tactful remark.

"Beggars can't be choosers, can they?" Nuala answered for him. "And seeing as how I'm the only breadwinner in the family and I'm working at the fish market there, I'm not risking walking home alone in the dead of night past all those drunken men. This city's not safe for a woman."

I thought privately that the men would have to be very drunk indeed to have intentions on Nuala, but I nodded agreement.

"So Finbar isn't working?" I asked.

"That idle, no good bag o' bones? Who would hire him?

29

When he worked for the saloon he drank more than he earned. I tried to get him a job as porter at the market but he couldn't lift the loads." She sniffed in disgust. "He's sleeping in the next room."

"I heard that," came Finbar's voice and the person himself appeared in the doorway, looking like Marley's ghost in a white nightshirt and nightcap, his face pale and gray as the cloth he was wearing. "And if I've told you once, I've told you a hundred times, woman, I've got meself a fine job lined up for the election." He smiled at me, revealing a mouth of missing teeth.

"The election." Nuala sniffed. "We'll believe that when we see it."

"Ask the Tammany boys yourself," Finbar insisted. "They told me they'd pay me for every man I lead, push, or drag to the polling place—who puts his cross for Shepherd, of course."

"Pay you in liquor," Nuala said. "You'll drink yourself stupid and then be out of work again."

I shifted uncomfortably at this brewing fight. "And where are the children—in school?" I turned to Seamus.

"We haven't got them into a school yet," Seamus said. "Bridie's out running errands, and the boys—well, I don't quite know where they are."

"Speaking of errands, I stopped off along the way and brought you a chicken and some grapes." I found space for them on the table between dirty dishes, yesterday's *New York Herald* and some socks that Nuala had been darning. "I thought you maybe could use some nourishment."

"Most kind of you," Seamus said. "You're a good woman, Molly Murphy."

I watched Nuala sidling up to whisk away my offering.

"Any news from Kathleen?" I asked, beating Nuala to the grapes and handing them to Seamus.

"Yes, but it's not good. She's fading, Molly. She keeps up a brave front, but I can tell she's fading. If only I could be with her. It fair breaks my heart. I tell you, Molly, there are times when I'm ready to take the risk and borrow the money for a passage home."

"It must be very hard for you," I said, "but you know you'd be thrown in jail or even hanged if you go home. Think of the children. What good would it do to have a father in jail and a mother who's deathly sick?"

"What good am I here to them?" he said. "Another useless bag of bones like Finbar. Not able to earn my keep at the moment."

As he spoke I heard the sound of light feet running up the stairs. The door burst open and Bridie stood there. When she saw me, her face lit up. "Molly. You've come back to us. I was praying in church on Sunday that you would."

I put my arms around her thin little body. "How have you been keeping? And how's your brother?"

She looked up, a big smile on her face. "He's become a junior Eastman."

"A what?"

"He and our cousins. They've joined a gang. They're called junior Eastmans, and they go around busting stuff up. And sometimes they get to do stuff for real big gang members and the big guys give them a quarter each."

"Seamus, did you know about this?" I asked.

He shrugged. "There's no harm in it. Just talk. Boys always run in herds, like young ponies, don't they?"

But I couldn't take this news so lightly. I had heard enough last night about violence and protection rackets to make me believe that there was indeed harm in young Shamey running with a gang. And I knew it was up to me to get him out of it. I'd just have to find a place of my own and bring them to live with me, at least until Seamus was on his feet again. I felt deep depression settling over me at the thought of leaving the little heaven on Patchin Place, but it had to be done. I was only alive now because the children's mother had given me a chance to escape. Giving up a few months of my life was the least I could do in return.

❧ Four ☙

I walked home with heavy steps, deep in thought. How could I afford a place of my own, big enough to take in Seamus and the children? I wouldn't want it to be in a neighborhood like this, either. I wanted to stay in Greenwich Village, where I had made friends and where I loved the exuberance of the life-style. Somehow I needed to make money. I did have the means in front of my nose—I'd just have to overcome my repugnance and get on with the Tomlinson divorce case—if I wasn't arrested every time I tried to follow Mr. T.

I gave a big sigh. I wasn't the sort of person who liked going against her principles, which was the reason that I was not prepared to spend the tidy sum of money that I'd discovered in Paddy's filing cabinet. It was sitting in the bank, waiting for an heir to claim it. So far no one had, which probably meant it was my money. But I still couldn't bring myself to use it for anything but official business.

I stepped back from the curb, hastily, as a carriage went past, its wheels and the horses' hooves spraying up muck from the gutter. I supposed I'd have to go back to spying on Mr. Tomlinson. I just prayed he didn't have aged female relatives all over the city. Next time I'd find some excuse to check out who owned the houses he visited. It was all so complicated. Why couldn't the wretched man just agree to give his wife a divorce and save me all this trouble? I was half tempted to go to his office and beg him to grant her wish, so that I was spared any more of this sordid business. I paused on a street corner, one foot in midair. Why not? Why did it always have to be furtive and sordid like this? We were, after all, civilized human beings.

Having made up my mind, I turned on my heels and instead of catching the trolley up Broadway, I went in the other direction, down to Wall Street. I knew where Mr. Tomlinson worked. I had stood outside waiting for him enough times now. It was right next door to the magnificent columns of the stock exchange where there was always such a hustle and bustle that I could blend nicely into the crowd. This time I didn't lurk in the shadows. I went up the steps, through the front door, and up a flight of marble stairs. I passed an impressive mirror and glanced at myself. I was glad that I had elected to put on my one respectable garment, a beige tailored business suit which had been made for me when I decided to become a female investigator. But I wished I'd put my hair up. With it tied back in a ribbon I looked ridiculously young and most unprofessional. I stepped into a recess and attempted to twist it into a knot. If only I could learn to wear hats like other women, then I'd never be caught out like this. But I'd grown up without wearing a hat and only wore one when strictly necessary. I didn't like the feel of my head being restricted any more than I liked the restriction of a corset on my body.

J. BAKER TOMLINSON III, STOCKBROKER, was on the second floor. A hollow-eyed young man wearing a large starched collar greeted me and tried to wheedle out of me why I wanted to see Mr. Tomlinson. I was suitably enigmatic and, shortly afterward, I was shown into a tastefully furnished office with mahogany desk and thick carpet on the floor.

"Miss Murphy?" Mr. Tomlinson waved me to a leather padded armchair. "My secretary didn't make it clear what your manner of business was. Are you here for financial advice?" I saw him summing up the quality of my costume and the hair, which was probably already escaping from its makeshift bun.

"I'm here on a very different sort of matter, Mr. Tomlinson," I said. "One which causes me considerable embarrassment."

"Really?" He was looking interested, not guilty. "Please proceed. I am quite intrigued."

I handed him my card. "My company was hired by your wife." I met his gaze. "She wanted us to provide proof for her to file for divorce."

Mr. Tomlinson sat back in his chair with a thump. "Good God." He hadn't even noticed the profanity spoken in my presence. "Lillian wants a divorce? I can't believe it." His eyes narrowed. "So if you are working for my wife, why exactly have you come to see me?"

"Because I don't like it, that's why," I said. "I'm not the sort of person who enjoys snooping for sordid details. I've been watching you for a couple of weeks now, and you seem like a gentleman to me. Quite the opposite of another chap I was watching who was with a different floozie every night. So it seemed to make sense to lay it out straight in front of you. If your wife wants a divorce, why not behave like a gentleman and agree to give her one? That way we will all be spared a lot of embarrassment."

He continued to look at me through narrowed eyes then he started laughing. "You're a rum one all right, Miss Murphy. I have to admit you've caught me completely off guard. I had no idea that Lillian wanted a divorce. We haven't had the happiest of marriages for some time, owing to her illness, of course."

"Mrs. Tomlinson is ill?"

He sucked through his teeth before answering. "She thinks she is. She takes to her bed at the slightest excuse and we have a constant procession of doctors coming to the house. I know she thinks I'm not sympathetic enough but God knows I've tried. She complains I'm never home, but who'd want to stay home with a wife who spends the evening taking patent medicines and then retires for the night at eight?" He stopped suddenly, as if he realized he had said too much. "I've stuck it out so far because I was raised to do the right thing, but by God, if she wants a divorce, I will be happy to grant her one."

"Is there anyone—another woman?" I couldn't resist asking. "I've been following your movements and I've not found one yet."

"So now you're getting me to do your work for you?" A spasm of annoyance crossed his face, then he laughed again. "You really are delightfully refreshing, Miss Murphy. They always say your countrymen have a touch of the blarney, don't they?" He straight-ened a pile of papers on his desk before he looked up again. "If you really want to know, there is one young woman I would have approached, had circumstances been different. But, as I say, I was brought up to do the right thing. I have thrown myself into my work and put thoughts of other women aside."

I left John Baker Tomlinson's office with a warm glow of success. Now both the Tomlinsons would get what they wanted. Lillian would be free of a husband who paid no attention to her and John would be able to court the woman he admired. I always knew that the forthright approach was best. All that time Paddy had wasted, lurking in dark alleys and trying to take incriminat-ing pictures, while I had brought my first divorce case to a happy conclusion without any effort!

I stopped off at the post office on the way home to buy a stamp, so that I could send my advertisement to Dublin. I was about to leave when the postal clerk, a florid man with mutton chop whiskers, called me back. "Aren't you the young woman who worked for Paddy Riley?"

"That's right."

"Letter just came for J. P. Riley and Associates," he said and produced it. I thanked him and put it in my purse, although I was dying to open it. Once I was safely in the street, I ripped it open.

The letter was typewritten. "Mr. Max Mostel requests that

you call on him at your earliest convenience, regarding a matter of great delicacy and confidentiality."

The address was on Canal Street—a seedy area of commerce, factories, and saloons. Another divorce case? In which case, a strange address for a client. But he had called it a matter of some delicacy. The difference was that a man had written to me this time. And in all the other divorce cases in Paddy's records, the clients had been women. This in itself made it appealing. More appealing was the fact that it represented the possibility of enough money to rent a place of my own.

Sid and Gus were out when I returned to Patchin Place, probably doing the morning shopping at the Jefferson Market opposite. I hurried up the stairs with a sigh of relief. I sat at my desk and wrote a letter to the *Dublin Times*. "Lost touch with your loved ones in America? Private investigator will make discreet inquiries. Reuniting families is our specialty." I didn't mention the sex of the private investigator, nor that I had never actually reunited a family. I asked for long-term advertising rates and promised to send payment by return of post. Then I went downstairs again and deposited the letter in the mailbox at the end of the street. I looked up to see Sid and Gus bearing down on me. Gus's arms were full of flowers. Sid carried two overflowing baskets.

"Look, Gus, she's up and awake and looking so much better. We have been having such fun, Molly. Gus has been buying up the entire market."

"I wanted oysters, but Sid wouldn't let me, even though I told her there was an R in the month so it should be fine."

"They didn't look fine to me, they looked decidedly peaky," Sid said. "I had an uncle who died after eating a bad oyster. I'm not taking any chances with you."

"So I had to settle for lobster instead. Even Sid had to agree they were still swimming around with great vigor and positively radiated health. So I'm going to prepare a true Boston lobster feast tonight. Whom should we invite?"

"Someone who won't mind plunging the damned things into boiling water," Sid said, laughing.

They swept me along Patchin Place, caught up in the excitement of frivolous living. It was moments like this that reminded me how very hard it would be to leave them and move to a place of my own.

That afternoon, while Sid and Gus were in a flurry of preparation for tonight's lobster feast, I made myself look respectable and businesslike, secured my hair in a bun with twenty or more hairpins, perched my one respectable hat on top of it, and set off to present myself to Mr. Max Mostel. As I followed the Bowery southward, and then turned onto Canal Street, my confusion and curiosity grew. This was not a respectable residential area—it was full of factories, run-down saloons, the occasional seedy boarding house. Certainly not the kind of area in which I expected my clients to live. When I came to Number 438 it wasn't a residence at all. The bottom floor was half open to the sidewalk and I could hear the sounds of hammering and sawing going on inside. A newly made chair was being varnished just inside the doorway. I asked for Mr. Mostel and was directed up the staircase around the corner. A business then, not a home. I went up the dark and narrow stairway, one flight, two flights, then a third, until I came to a doorway with a sign on it: MOSTEL AND KLEIN, LADIES FASHIONS. I knocked and entered a packing and shipping area. Men were staggering around with large boxes and depositing them on a primitive platform outside a back window to lower to the street. I asked for Mr. Mostel.

"In his office. Up two more flights. Go through the sewing room and you'll find the stairs at the end," an elderly man gasped as he paused to mop his brow.

Up another flight that ended in a closed door. I knocked on this and eventually was admitted into a long gloomy room full of young women sewing, row after row of them, their heads bent low over their work. I had been in a room like this before, when I had briefly tried my hand at any job I could get. I hadn't liked it then and I didn't like it now. The room resounded to the clatter of the machines. A hundred pairs of feet worked the treadles while one hundred needles flew up and down. There were bolts of cloth piled along walls. It was airless and lint rose from under my feet, causing me to sneeze. This made several of the girls glance up, look at me, and then go back to their sewing again, as if they begrudged the second they had wasted. Nobody said a word as I walked the length of the room until a male voice roared out, "Hey, you—where do you think you're going?"

I imagine that every sweatshop employs at least one male bully to strike fear into its female workers. This one—sallow, sagging, and with the sort of face that had a perpetual leer—was rather more repulsive than the one I had encountered before. Luckily I was in a very different situation this time. I eyed him coldly.

"I am on my way to see Mr. Mostel. Would you kindly find out if it is convenient to see me at this moment?"

"You want to see Mr. Mostel? Miss Hoity Toity, ain't we! If it's about a job, I'm the guy you see. The boss don't see no stinking girls."

"Fortunately I bathed this morning and don't happen to be a stinking girl," I said, hearing the titter of laughter from some of the workers who understood English. "But I received a letter from him this morning, asking me expressly to call upon him." I was about to hand him my card, when I remembered that I should be discreet and confidential. No need to let this greasy man or any of these girls know who was calling on the boss. "If you would direct me to his office, please."

"Follow me," he said, "and don't blame me if you get your head blown off."

He led me up another flight of stairs, negotiating boxes of

thread and trimmings on almost every step. He knocked on the door and opened it gingerly. "Young lady to see you, sir. Says you wrote her a letter."

I stepped past him into a cluttered little office. There were more bolts of cloth stacked in the office and a dressmaker's dummy displaying a frilled blouse and black skirt. Max Mostel was seated at a cluttered desk. He was a big podgy man with heavy jowls, sweating in a pinstriped three-piece suit. A cigar stuck out of one corner of his mouth.

"Yeah? What do you want?"

I handed him my card. "You wrote to me. Here I am."

He looked at it, glanced up at his foreman. "What are you hanging around for?" he growled in heavily accented English. "Get down there again before one of those girls shoves a few yards of my ribbon into her blouse. Go on. *Raus!* And shut the door behind you."

The foreman went, closing the door none too gently. Max Mostel continued to scowl at me. "You're the one I wrote to?"

I nodded. "I am Miss Murphy. Junior partner. I'm sorry if you were expecting a man, but I assure you I am most efficient and do excellent work."

"No, I wasn't expecting a man," he said. "It's a woman I need for this job. I was asking around and a little bird told me that you were doing this kind of thing. Am I right?"

"What kind of thing was that, Mr. Mostel?"

"Snooping. I need someone to do some snooping for me."

"I see. Would you care to elaborate?"

He leaned across the desk toward me, even though the door was shut and we two were alone in the room. "We've got a plant."

I looked around the room, also, trying to locate this particular piece of flora.

"A plant?" I asked.

"A spy in the camp, Miss Murphy. A traitor in our midst." He looked around the room again. "You see this design"—he

40

handed me a page from a catalog showing a sleek, long dress with high collar and sweeping skirt.

"It's very nice," I said.

"And it was on the racks in all the major department stores a week before ours was finished, with the Lowenstein label on it. My design, mark you. My garment. With his filthy label on it."

"Are you sure that it wasn't an unhappy coincidence?"

He shook his head so that his chins quivered. "Stolen, from under my very nose. And not the first time it's happened either. Someone in this building is a plant, Miss Murphy, secretly working for Lowenstein. Getting their hot little hands on my latest designs and running them across town for him to copy in a hurry."

"And you would like me to discover who this person is?"

"Exactly. Have you ever been involved in the garment industry, Miss Murphy?"

"Only very briefly."

"But would you know how to operate a sewing machine?"

"With only moderate success. I haven't had much practice."

"No matter. We'll take you on here and train you, until you get up to speed. Then I want you to apply at Lowenstein's. Keep your ear to the ground in both places and see who turns up where he or she shouldn't."

I nodded. "I can do that. Who has access to your designs?"

"Not many people. The cutters and finishers would see them when they are in the process of being made, but the girls at the machines—they only do piecework, whatever is put in front of them. Their only concern is a sleeve or a pocket or a collar. They never see the finished garment." He tapped the side of his nose. "That's not to say that a smart girl couldn't do some snooping if she'd a mind to, but I don't see how. I'm usually here in my office most of the day. The designs are kept in this drawer. And I lock my office when I go out."

"Are you the only one with an office up here? What about Mr. Klein?"

"Mr. Klein?" He looked surprised. "Dead, Miss Murphy. Dropped dead two years ago—may he rest in peace."

"I'm sorry to hear it, Mr. Mostel. So who might come up to your office during the course of the workday?"

"My foreman. My two sample hands—who are completely trustworthy, by the way. The samples are made in the little back room up here, behind me, so nobody has a chance to see the garments before they are ready to be shown. Apart from that—I usually come down if there is a problem with an employee. They don't come up here."

"And buyers?"

"I go to them, Miss Murphy. Buyers are not going to climb up five flights of stairs."

"Could anyone get in when everyone has gone home at night?"

"I take the designs home with me."

"So it has to be someone who works here during the day."

He nodded. "A nice little problem we've got for ourselves, eh? So will you take on the job, Miss Murphy? I'll make it worth your while."

"This could require several weeks of work," I said. "Shall we say a retainer of one hundred dollars, plus the regular wages I would earn if I worked here?"

He put his hand to his chest. "One hundred dollars? Miss Murphy, I asked you to help me, not bankrupt me."

"I assure you this is the sort of fee my clients expect to pay, Mr. Mostel. If you think you can find someone who can do the job more cheaply . . ." I got to my feet.

He shrugged. "If it will allow me to sleep soundly in my bed at night, then I suppose I have no choice—even if the children will have to live on rye bread and cabbage soup for a few months."

42

"I understand cabbage soup is very healthy, if properly prepared," I said and I saw a smile twitch his cigar up and down.

"So it's a deal then, Miss Murphy." He held out a meaty hand. I shook it.

"I will enjoy the challenge, Mr. Mostel."

✄ Five ✄

I came home bubbling with enthusiasm. Now this was a real case, one I could sink my teeth into with no twinges of conscience about catching illicit couples. It would be easy enough to blend in and pass as an ordinary working girl, since I was one. Not in such dire circumstances as most of them, but still struggling to earn my way in a new country. Of course learning to be an efficient seamstress was another matter. Skill with a needle has never been one of my greatest attributes.

The front door at 9 Patchin Place was open, revealing a veritable hive of enthusiasm and industry. Exotic, herby smells wafted down the hallway toward me. Gus was studying an enormous cookery book in the kitchen, while Sid was stringing paper lanterns out in the garden. The kitchen sink teemed with scrabbling lobsters. I didn't even have time to spill the news of my new commission before Gus pounced upon me.

"Molly, you're just in time. I need someone to slice onions."

I was given an apron and dragged into the frantic preparations. By eight o'clock the house was ready and started to fill with writers, painters, poets, and freethinkers. There were many more people than there were lobsters, but it didn't seem to matter. There was plenty of wine and ale, so a good time was had by all. Myself, I was content to sit back and take it all in. I was still such a newcomer to the world of artists and freethinkers that

I felt a little awkward taking part in their witty badinage, but I soaked it all in like a sponge. The discussion moved from women's rights to birth control to anarchy. Then the talk moved on to New York politics and the upcoming mayoral election.

"It really seems that Tammany might be losing its grip," Lennie, a painter friend, said, waving an ear of sweet corn—a delicacy I had just discovered. "There's little love for this Shepherd fellow. Everyone says Seth Low is the man to get rid of Charlie Murphy's corruption."

"I see little point in discussing an election in which half of us can't participate," Sid said angrily. "Whoever wins it will be the same—more jobs for the boys, more kickbacks under the table."

"And what do you say, Mr. Clemens?" Gus asked an elderly gentleman with bushy white hair and a drooping mustache who had come to join the group. He looked too old to be part of Sid and Gus's artistic set and I wondered how he had been invited.

The old man smiled. "It should be perfectly obvious what you have to do. Give women the vote. That will do away with tyrants and dictators instantly. Women will always opt for sensible and compassionate over warlike and corrupt."

There was loud applause from the whole room. I began to think that he must be a politician of sorts. I nudged Gus who was standing beside me. "Who is that man?"

She looked at me in amazement. "You haven't heard of Samuel Clemens?"

I shook my head.

"He's one of our most distinguished writers. He's just come back from Europe and he has chosen to live in our little neck of the woods. Isn't he magnificent?"

I had to agree that he was and resolved to go out and buy one of his books forthwith. Any man who was a champion of votes for women was definitely worth reading.

As the talk went on late into the night, I found myself becoming philosophical. This group and those factory girls I had witnessed just a few short blocks away were so far removed from each other that they might have been circling two different suns. I knew that some of these people also struggled to survive. That chubby painter in the corner only ate when he sold a painting. And yet survival was not at the core of their existence. If they had to choose between paint and food, they would choose the former. Whereas those girls at the sweatshop worked their lives away in those dreary conditions to pay for food and rent and probably thought that they had no choice. But didn't each of us have a choice in what we did? Then I decided that it was the unaccustomed wine that was making me think this way.

The last reveler didn't leave until the wee hours of the morning. We collapsed into our beds, only to be woken at first light by a hammering on the front door. I heard Sid's slippers flip-flopping down the stairs, a conversation, then up again, calling softly, "Molly, are you awake? A man is outside with a message for you."

My head was throbbing from the effects of alcohol. I reached for my robe and hurried downstairs. A young boy grinned at my disheveled appearance. "Compliments of Mrs. Tomlinson," he said and handed me a letter. I had to race upstairs again to find a dime to tip the boy, then I opened the note. I hoped it would contain her check and grateful thanks. Instead it requested that I present myself in person at the Tomlinson house as soon as possible. Obviously the good woman wanted to pay me and thank me in person.

So after breakfast, suitably businesslike in my attire, I made my way to the East Side. I was shown to an upstairs room where Mrs. Tomlinson reclined on a daybed. She looked pale and languid, but she sat up easily enough as I came in.

"Miss Murphy," she said.

"I came as soon as I got your message, Mrs. Tomlinson."

"You went to see my husband yesterday—"

"I thought it better for both parties. Your husband seemed

like a gentleman. I didn't feel right trying to expose him. So he agreed to do the gentlemanly thing, did he? That must be a relief for you."

"A relief? You stupid girl! I asked you to find me facts, not to interfere. Now look what you've done!"

"He won't grant you the divorce?" I was puzzled.

"Of course he'll grant me the divorce." She spat the words out. "He came to my room last night and told me he'd be only too happy to set me free from a restricting marriage."

"But isn't that what you wanted?"

She glared at me. "It is not at all what I wanted. I had no intention of actually getting a divorce. I hoped my actions would spur my husband into paying me more attention and realizing how shamefully he was neglecting me. But now—" she put her handkerchief up to her mouth and gave a little sob "—now he sees a divorce as a liberation for both of us. I've lost my husband, Miss Murphy, all because of you and your meddling ways!"

"I'm truly sorry, Mrs. Tomlinson," I said, "but I was instructed to find evidence for a divorce case. And if you really want to know, I came up with no blot on your husband's character."

This only made her cry harder.

"If you tell him your true motive, maybe there will be a hope of your reconciliation," I suggested. She didn't answer. I thought it best to make a retreat, and I hadn't the heart to ask her for my fee. That's it, I decided. The last divorce case that I shall ever tackle. I resolved to do a better job when I went spying at the factory.

A loud jangling noise woke me. I sat up in darkness, my heart thumping. Fire. It must be a fire bell ringing. I had to get out. Then my foot touched the cold oilcloth and I remembered that I had borrowed Sid's alarm clock to make sure I woke at six A.M. I had to report to work at Mostel and Klein by seven. As I went down the stairs to the bathroom I remembered that I had been dreaming about a fire before the bell woke me.

I came back upstairs, shivering in the early morning chill and dressed with care in my old white blouse and the plaid skirt that I had worn when I fled from Ireland. I tied my hair back instead of putting it up. I had to look as if I was a newly arrived immigrant. I would have to watch my mouth too. Last time I had worked in a similar sweatshop I had told the foreman what I thought of him, which had brought me dismissal within a week. That and having sewn a whole pile of sleeves inside out.

I tiptoed down the stairs, trying not to wake Sid and Gus, and helped myself to some of yesterday's stale bread and jam. As the reality of what I was doing hit me, I began to question yesterday's enthusiasm. Stale bread and twelve hours of toil ahead of me instead of a leisurely breakfast of fresh hot rolls and Sid's strong coffee—if this was what an investigator's life was like, couldn't I find a more civilized job?

I let myself out into cold gray dawn. The Jefferson Market was in full swing, but as I crossed Washington Square it was still deserted. Too early for students or artists! But as I followed the Bowery southward, the city came to life—trolley cars clanged as factory workers dodged past them to cross the street. Delivery wagons rumbled past, pulled by huge stocky horses. I reached Canal Street with ten minutes to spare and had time to collect my thoughts before I entered the building. Mr. Mostel had given me my instructions. Nobody was to know that I wasn't an ordinary worker. I was to blend in and keep my eyes open. But not at the expense of my work. I couldn't be seen to be minding other people's business. And I'd be treated just like any other girl—not a pleasant prospect when I remembered the leering foreman. Still it was only for a few weeks. I could stick it out for that long, couldn't I?

A parade of girls was now making its way up the stairs. I joined them, getting some odd stares. I listened to the conversation going on around me and realized I couldn't understand a word of what was being said. The girls in front of me were speaking Yiddish, those behind me were gabbing away in Italian. It suddenly hit me that this assignment was not going to be easy. If there were any kind of conspiracy, I'd have no chance of overhearing any whispered messages. I'd just have to rely on using my eyes and my instincts.

The other girls hung up their hats and shawls on a row of hooks then took their places at their machines. I stood looking around, not knowing what to do next.

"You are new, *ya?*" one of the girls asked in broken English. I nodded, shyly.

"You must wait until Seedy Sam gets here," another girl said. She was tall, slim, and attractive with a smart white blouse and a cameo at her neck. "He'll tell you where to sit."

"Seedy Sam?" I asked innocently.

She grinned. "It's what we call Sam Walters, the foreman. Only don't let him hear you call him that, or you'll be out on your ear." She looked at me with interest. "You're not Jewish or Italian—are you English?"

"No, I'm Irish."

"That's very funny."

"What is—being Irish?" I stuck out my chin and felt my fists clench. Nobody made fun of the Irish when I was around.

"Sorry. I don't mean funny. Strange. It is strange. The girls who speak good English don't stay long, and they talk back to the bosses. That's why Sam likes to hire newniks like us who can't talk back. I'm Sadie. Sadie Blum."

"Molly Murphy," I said, shaking her hand politely. "Pleased to make your acquaintance. You seem to speak pretty good English," I added.

"Yes, well I'm here two years now and I learn quick."

Several other girls had clustered around listening to this exchange. One of them tapped my shoulder. "Weren't you here the other day, visiting the boss?"

She was eyeing me suspiciously.

"That's right. I was bringing him a message from an old friend in Europe. Then I decided I might as well ask him for a job while I was here." I saw a glance pass between two of them. "Oh, don't worry," I said. "The boss made it very clear to me that I could expect no special treatment if I worked here, just because my great uncle knew him."

"Whassamatter, did they declare a public holiday that I didn't know about?" a big male voice boomed and Seedy Sam came into the room.

"If they did, we wouldn't get it off," Sadie muttered in my ear.

"Get to it then. It's already one minute past seven. To your machines and no talking. You know the rules!" Then he noticed me. "And what have we here?"

"My name's Molly Murphy. Mr. Mostel said I might start work today."

"I remember you, all right." Sam sneered. "All that garbage about delivering letters to the boss, when you were really after a job here!"

"That was true," I said. "I was delivering a message from an old friend. I just decided to ask him for a job when I was talking to him."

"Don't think you're going to be treated any different from the rest of these girls," Sam said with his usual leer.

"Why would I be? I have no connection with your boss, other than delivering him a message. Now where would you like me to sit?"

"What skills do you have? You know how to sew, don't ya?"

"I can operate a machine, but I'm a little out of practice. Mr. Mostel said I could start out on something simple until I get up to speed."

"Collars then. Go and sit next to Golda. She's in charge of our learners. She'll show you what to do."

A large middle-aged woman in a high-collared black dress

beckoned and patted a stool beside her. "Sit your heiny down there and we'll get started," she said, giving me a friendly smile. "Did you bring your needle?"

"Needle?"

"Oh yes, girls have to supply their own sewing needles in this shop. And your own thread too. You can start off with one of mine, but during your lunch break you pop across to the dry-goods store and get yourself a medium-point needle and a spool of white thread."

"They make us buy our own needles and thread?" I burst out before I remembered that I was supposed to be shy, withdrawn, and not attract any attention to myself.

Golda looked shocked. "But they do at all the shops. Where were you working last?"

"At a little place in Ireland," I said. "It was different there. Just a few girls. Friendly atmosphere."

"How nice," she said wistfully. "You won't find the atmosphere too friendly here, thanks to Seedy Sam over there. He makes sure we're always miserable. We're not supposed to talk at all. If a girl is found talking, he docks five cents off her wages. We get away with it now, because I'm showing you what to do. Now watch carefully." She took two pieces of collar, put them together, and the machine clattered as it flew around the edges of three sides. "Smooth sides facing out. Get it?"

I nodded and demonstrated for her, rather more slowly.

"*Ach ya*, you'll do just fine," she said, a short while later. "She's a quick learner, Sam. She's ready to start out on her own."

Sam motioned me to an empty place beside Sadie, who gave me an encouraging grin as I sat down. A large pile of pre-cut collars was put on my right side. I started sewing. As I finished each piece a small girl darted up with a large pair of scissors to cut the ends. As fast as the pile went down, Sam was there with another huge pile. It was never ending. I thought I was doing well until he said, "If you go at that speed, you'll be here all night. Step it up, will ya?"

I glanced at my fellow workers. Their needles were positively flying up and down. How was I going to be able to observe who might be sneaking around when I obviously wouldn't have a moment to breathe? The morning dragged on. Nobody spoke, unless Sam left the room and then there were whispers. One girl got up and walked down the room toward the door.

"Where do you think you're going?" Sam demanded.

"Washroom," the girl said. "I need to go."

"You were up and down all day yesterday," Sam complained. "Think you've found a way to slack off, do ya? Well, I'm docking ten cents from your pay packet. That'll teach you."

"Give her a break, Sam," Sadie said. "She's expecting. Everyone knows you have more calls of nature when you're in that condition."

"You girls should think more about your duty to your boss and less about populating the world with more stinking kids," Sam growled. "Go on then. Go to the washroom, but you're staying late if you don't meet your quota. I don't care how many brats you got squalling for you."

Sadie looked at me and shook her head.

At last a bell rang and everyone jumped up.

"Half an hour, remember," Sam yelled. "Not no stinking thirty-five minutes. We don't pay you good money to waste the boss's time."

"They don't pay us good money, and that's a fact." Sadie fell into step beside me as she reached for her shawl.

"You talking again, Sadie Blum?" Sam's voice echoed down the room. "Better watch that mouth or you'll owe me more than you earn by the end of the week. Okay, line up for inspection if you want to go out."

"What is this, the army?" I whispered to Sadie.

"He has to inspect our bags and pockets to make sure we're not stealing any of the trimmings," she whispered back. "Sometimes they even lock the doors when we're using expensive stuff."

Sam came charging up to us. "Some people never learn, do

they, and now you're teaching the new girl bad habits. I'm docking you each ten cents from your pay packet. And next time you talk, it will be a quarter. Your fancy airs and graces don't work around here."

He searched my purse then he put his hands on my waist and ran them down my sides. "Hey, watch it!" I said, slapping his hands away from me. "You can search my purse if you like, but you're not touching my person."

"I'm only checking your pockets, sweetheart. Nothing to get your dander up about." He grinned at me with that insulting leer. "If I was really feeling you up, I'd do a much better job of it."

At last he opened the door and we filed down the stairs. "That man is awful," I muttered to Sadie as we passed through the door and started in a procession down the stairs. "Why doesn't somebody do something about him?"

"Do what? If we complain, we're fired. The boss doesn't care how we're treated as long as the work gets done. And there are plenty of girls stepping off the boat every day waiting to take our places."

"And it's better than some of the shops," another girl commented, coming up to join us as we stepped out into the fresh air of the street. "My sister only gets five dollars a week if she's lucky, and they dock her pay for the use of the firm's power supply, and an extra five cents for the use of the mirror and towel in the washroom. She says the mirror is so small you can hardly see to powder your nose. She tried bringing her own towel from home too, but they still docked her the five cents a week."

"None of these bosses care about their workers, Sarah. It's all about money," Sadie said. She turned back to me. "Girls are always getting sick because there's not enough air to breathe and too many of us crammed into one room, but they won't let us have the window open, even in summer."

"So why do you stay?" I asked.

"What else can newnik girls like us do?" Sarah, the second girl said with a shrug of her shoulders. In contrast to Sadie, who was tall and carried herself with a certain air of grace, Sarah was frail and hollow looking, as if she hadn't had a good meal or been out in the fresh air recently. "Nobody's going to hire immigrant newniks outside of the sweatshops."

"I'm educated, but it don't matter," Sadie said. "Back at home I had a good life. I was taking piano lessons and French. Too bad it wasn't English. Now I just pick up gutter English." She slipped her arm through mine. "You speak nice. You help me to speak more educated, okay?"

"So why are you here, if you had such a good life?" I asked.

Sadie and Sarah looked at each other as if I was rather stupid. "When there's a pogrom, they don't care which Jews are rich and which are poor. They destroyed and burned our house. They threw my piano out of the upstairs window." She turned away, biting her lip. "And what they did to my big sister was unmentionable. My mother was thanking God that she died. I was hiding under the straw in the henhouse, but we could hear her cries for help." She pressed her lips together and turned her face away from us.

"They killed my father," Sarah added. "They ran a bayonet through him while we watched. My mama brought us to America with money she had sewn into the hem of her skirt."

I had had no idea that such things went on in the world. I looked at tall, elegant Sadie and frail little Sarah and was amazed how calmly they were telling me this. No wonder these girls put up with such bad conditions in America. At least they didn't have to fear for their lives every day.

I should do something to help, I thought. I speak English. I could make the bosses listen. Then I reminded myself that this was not my struggle. I was only here as a spy. In a few short weeks, I'd be gone again.

❧ Six ❧

B y the time I had been at the garment factory a week, I
had almost come to believe that I really did work there
and that this terrible life of drudgery was all I had to
look forward to. My feet ached from working the treadle. My
fingers were raw from handling the cloth. I prayed to get the
assignment over quickly, but my sewing still wasn't good enough
to guarantee that another firm would hire me. In addition to this,
the designs for the new spring collection wouldn't be ready until
the middle of November, at least three weeks away. The plan I
had hatched with Max Mostel was as follows: I should work for
him until I was up to speed, which would give me time to observe
his workers. I would then apply at Lowenstein's and start work
there at least a week before Max Mostel finished his designs and
passed them to the sample hands, so that I was familiar enough
with the routine at the new factory to be able to know who was
who and what was what. That meant about two more weeks at
this hellhole.

I think it was the lack of air that got to me most. That and
the lack of light. As the autumn light faded and one gray day
followed another it became harder to see what we were sewing.
The row of girls closest to the window had a slight advantage,
but not much because the windows were small and badly needed
washing. Those of us three rows back had to rely on anemic gas

lamps. No wonder the girls bent low over their work and several of them were wearing glasses.

And of course for me the hardest thing of all was holding my tongue and not getting myself fired. Those girls were so submissive and browbeaten that it riled my fighting spirit. Every time one of them was docked money for going to the washroom too often, or coming in one minute late from lunch I was itching to jump up and tell that leering monster Sam what I thought of him. On the last day of my assignment I'd let him have it all right! I spent those long hours at the machine thinking up choice phrases to hurl at him when I made my grand exit.

By the end of a week I had received a pay packet containing four dollars and ninety cents. The other dollar and five cents had been docked for various sins—twice back late from lunch, once whispering, once dropping a collar on the floor and once getting up to stretch out my back. On the way home I thought gloomily that I hadn't foreseen how hard this assignment would be. I couldn't imagine any of those downtrodden females having the nerve to slip upstairs to the boss's office and steal his designs from under his very nose, even if they could ever get past the fearsome foreman.

A whole week had gone by and I hadn't even started my investigation. At this rate the new designs would come and go and I'd still be trying to get up to speed on collars! I should be sounding out the other girls with cleverly phrased questions. If only Paddy had still been around, he would have known what to ask. Why did he have to die before I had had a chance to learn from him? There was so much I still didn't know. In fact every time I set out on a case, I felt like a lone traveler, floundering through a blizzard.

My only chance to talk to the other girls was at lunch, when some of them went to the little café across the street and got a bowl of stew or at least a coffee to go with their sandwich.

"So what are we actually making here?" I asked, like the bright new learner that I was. "I only get to see collars."

"Right now it's ladies dresses—latest fashion for the big stores," someone said.

"Latest fashion, eh? That sounds very exciting," I said. "So I'll get some tips on what to wear if I see what comes out of this shop?"

"You won't ever see the finished garment," Sadie said. "They have finishers who put the pieces together."

"So who designs these latest fashions? Do they come from Paris or something?"

"Listen to her! Paris? Such ideas."

I laughed. "Well, I don't know anything about it. I'm new. I always thought that fashions came from Paris."

"I think old Mostel designs his own, doesn't he?" The girls looked at each other.

"Yes, and he thinks he's the cat's whiskers too."

"I can't imagine him designing ladies dresses." I grinned at them. "He doesn't look like a fashionable kind of man."

"You should see his family," Golda said, leaning confidentially close. "Oy vay, but do they live like kings. He's here working away at the business every day, making sure nobody steals a yard of his precious ribbon and his wife and children are out spending his money as fast as he can make it. And when you see them, they go around with their noses in the air, like they were born aristocrats and not just arrived from a stadtl, like the rest of us."

"They're immigrants too?"

Golda nodded. "Only they came here twenty years ago. He arrived with nothing but the sewing machine from his father's tailor shop—and look what he's made of himself. You have to hand that to him."

"On whose backs, though, Golda?" Sadie asked. "With our sweat and our labor."

"Hush, Sadie, you shouldn't talk like that. You never know who might be listening," Golda said.

"You mean there might be spies?" I asked innocently, looking

59

around me for any face that might have betrayed shock or embarrassment. "Tattletales who report back to the boss?"

Golda touched the side of her nose. "You never can tell."

What did that mean, I asked myself as we went back to work. Did she know that one of the girls present was a spy for the boss—in which case did she have any idea if any of the girls might be a spy for someone quite different? I'd have to make friends with Golda and see if she'd divulge any of her secrets.

At home in my room that night I made a list: Befriend Golda. Get to know the sample makers. They have the means—see designs first. But motive? Old women. Rheumatism. One is Max's cousin.

The trouble was that stealing designs from under Max's nose required courage and bravado. I couldn't picture any of those downtrodden girls taking such an appalling risk. Of course, the most likely suspect was our foreman Seedy Sam. He looked to be the type who wasn't above shady behavior and he had access to Max's office. Maybe I'd eat my sandwiches at my machine in the future, so that I could keep an eye on him.

The sweatshop had become my life so completely that I had almost forgotten the advertisement I had placed in the Irish newspaper. I was therefore stunned when, in the middle of my second week, I received a letter from Ireland.

> *Collingwood Hall*
> *Castlebridge*
> *County Wexford, Ireland*

Dear Sir,

I saw your advertisement in the Dublin Times. *I am trying to locate my only daughter Katherine. The foolish child has run off with one of our estate workers, an undesirable young man called Michael Kelly, and it appears that they took a ship to New York. Naturally I want her found and brought home as soon as possible,*

although I fear it is already too late where her reputation is con-
cerned. As you can imagine, this is breaking her mother's heart.
My wife is bedridden and of very delicate constitution. I cannot
leave her or I would have undertaken this assignment myself. Please
advise by return of post whether you will take on this commission
and the fee you would require.
   Yours faithfully,
   T. W. Faversham, Major, Retired

Now this was just the kind of job I had imagined when I made the absurd decision to become an investigator. I wrote back immediately to Major Faversham, telling him that I would be delighted to find his daughter for him, that I needed as many details and photos as he could send me, the amount of money she might have taken with her, plus the names of any friends or relatives she might contact in the United States, and that my fee would be one hundred dollars plus expenses. My conscience got the better of me and I had to add, "In matters of extreme delicacy such as this, our junior partner, Miss Murphy, usually handles these cases with the required finesse and discretion."

It was only when I posted the letter that I stopped to wonder how I would manage to juggle these two assignments. If I was in a sweatshop from seven until seven every day except Sundays, I wasn't left with any time for finding missing heiresses. I didn't actually know whether she was a heiress, but the English who had settled in Ireland had mostly done very well for themselves—unlike the Irish who had either starved or been driven from their homes during the potato famine.

I decided to start making inquiries right away. It should be possible to find out when a Mr. and Mrs. Michael Kelly had arrived in New York. I presumed they would claim to be married. I'd have to find out if the records were kept over on Ellis Island, and if they'd let me go over there to check them. But in the meantime a splendid notion had come to me. If Miss Faversham had any connections among New York society, then my acquaintance Miss Van Woekem would hear about her. I resolved to visit her this coming Sunday and sent her a note to that effect. Miss Van Woekem liked things to be done correctly.

On Sunday morning, at an hour when all good Christians would have returned from Sunday services and less good Christians like myself had finished taking coffee and pastries at Fleischman's Vienna Bakery, I took the trolley car up Broadway, alighted at Twentieth Street, and walked to the charming brownstone on South Gramercy Park. In case you are wondering how an Irish immigrant girl like myself should have friends who live in such exalted parts of the city—I had briefly held the post of companion to Miss Van Woekem. For once I was not fired, but resigned from the position myself, for personal reasons. We had sparred considerably, the old lady and I, but had forged a mutual respect. She admired my decision to strike out on my own and had invited me to drop in from time to time.

The maid showed me into the first-floor drawing room, overlooking the park. Miss Van Woekem was sitting in the tall-backed armchair by the fire.

"Ah, Miss Molly Murphy, what a delightful surprise." She held out her hand to me. "To what do I owe the honor of this visit? Not coming to reapply for the position, I fear. My current companion is a feeble little creature who cringes when I shout at her. No fun at all." Her beaky, birdlike face broke into a wicked smile. "Come, seat yourself. Ada will bring coffee, or would you prefer tea?"

I took the armchair indicated on the other side of the fireplace. "Coffee would suit me very well, thank you."

She was looking at me, head cocked to one side in another remarkably birdlike posture. "You're looking well," she said, "and more . . . established. You're more sure of yourself since the last time we met. So tell me, is your detective business flourishing?"

"Hardly flourishing yet, but I am currently engaged in two interesting cases."

She leaned forward in her chair. "Do tell me—all the details."

She listened attentively while I told her about the garment factory, making annoyed tut-tutting noises as I described the conditions there. "If anyone can sort them out, then you can," she said, "Now, about this missing girl."

"Her name is Katherine Faversham. English landed gentry, living in Ireland. I thought that if she was staying with society friends anywhere in the city, you might hear of it."

Coffee arrived and was poured. Miss Van Woekem took a sip, then looked up. "Faversham," she said thoughtfully. "Faversham. The name doesn't ring a bell. Of course, if she has married a penniless scoundrel, she might not wish to make her presence known to friends of the family. Although if she is married, her family presumably has lost authority over her and can do nothing."

"My job is to locate her," I said. "How they persuade her to come home is not my concern. When I find out under what financial circumstances she left Ireland, I'll know where to start looking, but in the meantime I decided it couldn't hurt to put my spies to work."

Miss Van Woekem cackled. "Your spies. I like that. I have always wished to be a spy. In fact, if I had not been born a woman, I might well have volunteered my services to the government. I will keep my ear to the ground, my dear, and report back to you."

"Thank you," I said. "I knew I could count on you. I am really glad that—"

I broke off at the sound of voices in the hallway outside. Before I could finish my sentence the door was flung open and a young woman burst in with a great rustle of silk.

"I've caught you at home, how wonderful!" She stood with arms open, a vision of loveliness in lilac silk, with a white fur wrap flung carelessly around her shoulders and an adorable little bonnet, also fur trimmed. "I wasn't supposed to come to town this weekend, but Alicia Martin dragged me to a concert at Carnegie Hall last night and I'm so glad we went because it was an

Italian tenor. You know how I feel about Italian tenors because you've promised to take me to hear Mr. Caruso the moment he comes to New York—and then we spent the night with Alicia's aunt in a really interesting apartment in the Dakota. I'd always thought only poor people lived in apartments, but Alicia's aunt isn't at all poor and summers in Paris. Then this morning we were about to go strolling in Central Park but I said that I had to surprise my darling godmother first—are you suitably surprised?"

"Oh yes," Miss Van Woekem said. "Most surprised."

"You don't seem overwhelmed with delight at seeing me." The young woman pouted.

"I am very pleased to see you, of course, Arabella, but, as you may notice, I already have company."

"Oh." The girl's mouth formed a perfect circle and she appeared to notice me for the first time. I saw her taking in the cut and quality of my clothes. "Oh, I didn't realize. Have I burst into the middle of an interview for a position in your household? I'm awfully sorry."

"I am entertaining a good friend," Miss Van Woekem said calmly. "Allow me to introduce you. Miss Murphy, this is my goddaughter, Arabella Norton. Arabella, this is Miss Molly Murphy, a famous private detective who was actually trying to capture that odious man when he shot President McKinley."

"Really? How amazingly exciting. I think I've seen you before, haven't I?"

"Maybe." I knew exactly where I had seen her before but I didn't trust my mouth to utter more than one word. Luckily she kept on babbling.

"A woman detective—how frightfully interesting and brave. You should meet my intended. You two would have a lot to talk about, although I don't know what he will think of a woman doing his job."

Then, to my horror, she turned back to the door. "Daniel, do stop sulking out there and come and say hello. I promised you we'd go walking in two seconds, but you have to meet this fascinating female detective."

I took a deep breath as Daniel Sullivan stepped into the room. He was wearing a smart black-and-white check suit I hadn't seen before with a white carnation in his buttonhole. His unruly dark curls were slicked down and parted. His derby was clutched in his hands. His face said clearly that he also wished himself anywhere else but here at this moment. "Miss Van Woekem," he said, bowing slightly. "I trust you are well."

"In better health than you at the present, I surmise, Daniel." Although I had told her nothing, the old lady had been very quick to grasp the situation when I left her employment. "And this is Miss Murphy."

"Miss Murphy." Daniel's eyes didn't meet mine as he bowed.

"And she's a detective, Daniel. Did you ever hear of such a thing?" Arabella slipped her arm through his and drew him close to her. "You two must have a lot to talk about."

"Arabella, we are interrupting a private conversation," Daniel said. "I really think we should be going."

I got to my feet. "No, it is I who should be going. We have already concluded a most delightful coffee hour and I have friends waiting for me at a restaurant. Please excuse me." I took the old woman's hand. "Thank you for the coffee and for an enjoyable morning."

"Do come again soon, my dear." She patted my hand, a gesture which was most unlike her. "I hope to have news for you."

I stumbled from the room, down the hall, and out of the front door. Arabella's high, clear voice floated after me. "Where on earth did you meet her, Aunt Martha? What extraordinarily dreary clothes."

I kept walking fast until I came to Park Avenue, then I turned and started walking south. The wind in my face was bitter, but I kept on walking. If I slowed down then I'd have to think, and if I thought, then the conclusions I'd come to would not be pleasant. I knew that Daniel was engaged to another woman, but he had sworn that he loved me and planned to break that engagement as soon as possible. And so I had kept hope in my heart. Now, seeing them together, I was forced to admit that such hope was ill founded.

❧ Seven ❧

I came into the front hall at Patchin Place to find most of it taken up by an enormous hat stand made of the antlers of some unknown giant beast.

"What in heaven's name?" I asked.

Sid poked her black, cropped head around the drawing room door. "Don't you adore it?" she asked. "Mrs. Herman across the street is going to live with her sister in South Carolina and was getting rid of items that were too big to move. This was so wonderfully ugly that we just had to have it. Gus is going to hang her painting smock on it up in the studio."

My mind was already moving beyond painting smocks. "Across the street, you say?"

"Yes, you know, the old lady at Number Ten. With the cats—who are all travelling to South Carolina in baskets, you'll be pleased to hear."

"So Number Ten will be vacant? Will she be selling it, do you know?"

"I don't think she owns it. Gus will know better than I. She's the one who takes an interest in the neighbors. Help me carry the monstrosity up to her studio and you can ask her."

We picked up the hat stand between us and womanhandled it up two flights of stairs.

"Look what your devoted servants have done for you," Sid

said, pushing open the studio door. "We have risked life and limb bringing the monstrosity up the stairs for you. I hope you are duly grateful."

Gus looked up from her painting. To me it was a lot of red streaks and black dots, but then I hadn't yet learned to appreciate the intricacies of modern painting. Sid went over to it and put an arm around Gus's shoulder. "It's one of your best yet, Gus dear. It speaks to the heart. A true representation of the chaos of war."

I smiled and nodded agreement without actually having to say anything.

"Do you know what is going to happen to the house opposite when Mrs. Herman moves out?" I asked, before I was drawn into a discussion on the merits of the painting.

"It will be rented to someone else, I imagine." Gus slashed another great daub of red across her painting.

"You don't happen to know who the landlord is, do you?"

"What is this?" Gus laughed. "Have you tired of our company and are seeking to make an escape?"

"Not tired of your company," I said, "I could never do that, but I have been plagued with guilt about the little family I brought over from Ireland. I can't leave them living in deplorable circumstances any longer. Now that I have two commissions and I'm well on my way to becoming a successful businesswoman, I could consider renting a place of my own if the rent were not too high."

"We would hate to lose you, Molly," Sid said. "But across the street would be better than nothing. And I have to admire your philanthropic attitude."

"Across the street would suit me just fine," I said. "It would be perfect, in fact. I could wave to Gus as she does her painting, and come over for Sid's Turkish coffee."

"Of course you could," Gus said. "And we can help you look after those two poor, dear children."

It was sounding better by the minute. I resolved to write to the landlord immediately. As yet I had no money of my own, apart from the pittance being paid me for my work at the sweatshop, but J. P. Riley and Associates had money in the bank, from which I could loan myself an advance on my salary. It would be an enormous risk, renting a whole house on such a flimsy promise of future income, but if worse came to worse, I could always take in boarders or even start my own small school. There was no limit to the things I could do with my talent and enterprise! I was resolved to forge ahead with my life without Daniel Sullivan, one way or another.

I dropped the letter in the mailbox on my way to work on Monday morning and got a reply on my return home the very next day. The landlord was prepared to rent the place for forty dollars a month. Forty dollars a month was twice as much as I was making in the sweatshop right now. Although I had the expectation of a handsome fee at the end of my assignment, I had come to realize that not all cases were resolved successfully and not everybody paid. In my case nobody had paid so far! Four hundred and eighty dollars a year—I went hot and cold all over at the thought of it. My family had never owned that much money. I wasn't at all sure I could earn that much in a year, but I wasn't about to let this chance slip away. I wrote the check with trembling hand to pay the deposit. I had already taken some fairly large risks in my life, but this counted among them. Like most of my risks, I had little choice if I wanted to rescue Seamus and his family. Afterward I was so excited and full of nervous energy that I went straight to Fulton Street to deliver the good news.

Nuala let me in, grudgingly, her eyes darting to see if I had come with more chickens or grapes. The children had already bedded down for the night, curled up like puppies on top of some crates that still smelled of their fishy origin. They all scrambled up as I came in and Bridie ran to my side.

"Greenwich Village," Nuala said with a sniff as I told them my news. "No respectable person would want to live there—a lot of students and rowdies and Negroes and anarchists from what I've heard."

"Which suits me just fine, because you surely won't be welcome, Nuala. Not you nor your children." You don't know how long I'd been waiting to say something of the kind. It gave me enormous satisfaction. I looked at Seamus, sitting pale and white in his chair. "So it's up to you, Seamus. If you want to move into your own room, with heat and running water, then I'm offering you a place. But no relatives. Take it or leave it."

Bridie rushed to hold my skirt. "I want to go and live with Miss Molly," she said.

Seamus smiled weakly. "We'd be honored," he said, then turned hastily to his cousin. "No offence, Nuala, but I have to do what's best for the children."

Nuala smoothed down her apron over her wide hips. "You don't see me crying my eyes out, do you? Crammed in like sardines we were with the three of you. I'll be glad to see the back of you and that's God's truth."

I beat a hasty retreat from what could turn into an ugly scene.

I arranged with the landlord to take up residence at the end of the week. In the meantime my days would be more than full with twelve hours spent at the sweatshop, and hopefully enough time and energy to pursue my first inquiries into the whereabouts of Katherine Faversham. I was really rather annoyed that I found myself trapped in such a lengthy and demanding assignment when this Irish case was just what I had dreamed of when I decided to become an investigator. How would I possibly be able to comb New York when I was chained to a sewing machine until dark?

I hadn't yet heard anything from Miss Van Woekem, so my first step was to ascertain that Katherine and Michael Kelly had indeed come to New York. If they had access to Katherine's money, they could have crossed the Atlantic in a second- or third-class cabin, which would mean that they stepped ashore with little or no formality and might well have already left the city. If they were penniless, on the other hand, they would have entered through Ellis Island and there would be a record of their arrival.

I wasn't sure how to go about checking the Ellis Island records. I knew a record of each ship and its passenger manifest must be stored on the island, but I didn't believe I'd be allowed to look at them. The general public was kept well away from the island buildings. Relatives who came to meet their loved ones were kept waiting at the dockside. If things had been different with Daniel I could have used his influence, but there was no point in thinking about him anymore.

Then it occurred to me that bribery and corruption had been very much in evidence when I came through Ellis Island. One of the inspectors or watchmen might do the job for me, if I offered to make it worth his while. Which was why I was standing on the dockside long before first light the next morning, waiting for the six o'clock government boat that would take the day shift over to the island and bring the night guards back. Several watchmen were standing together, impressive in their blue uniforms. I hesitated to approach a group such as this. The fewer people who knew of my plan, the better. Then I noticed a young inspector, dressed in a dark suit and stiff white collar, heading for the boat slip alone. I hurried to intercept him.

"If I might have a word with you, sir?"

He stopped and regarded me nervously. I could see him trying to decide if I was a criminal or a woman of the streets about to accost him. I gave him a big smile. "I'm Molly Murphy just come over from Ireland, and I'm trying to trace my cousin Katherine. I know you're an inspector on the island and I wondered if you'd know how to look up the records and find out if Katherine ever got here."

"You could write a letter to the governor, requesting such information," he said stiffly. Wonderful—out of all the corrupt inspectors on the island, I had picked the only stiff shirt.

"I daresay I could, but it would take so long," I said, "and I'm worried about my poor cousin Katherine, who may be living in a slum with no money when I could be helping her get a good start." I gazed up at him appealingly. "If you'd be willing to put yourself out, I'd make it worth your while. I'm not rich, but I do have a little put by, and my cousin is very dear to me."

I saw his Adam's apple go up and down. "What exactly would you require me to do?"

"Nothing illegal. Just check the entries for the last few months to see if a Mr. and Mrs. Michael Kelly from Wexford arrived in New York. She ran off with this Mr. Kelly, you see, and the relatives at home suspect that they headed for America." I touched his arm lightly. "If you are prepared to do that for me, I've got five dollars saved up that I'm willing to pay you for your trouble."

I saw him glance around. Other inspectors were now hurrying past us to the dock. I heard a boat give an impatient toot.

"I have to go," he said. "How will I find you again?"

"I'll meet you here, shall we say on Friday morning, to give you enough time. And I'll have the money with me."

He glanced at the men now boarding the government launch. "I don't know . . ."

"Do your best anyway," I said. "I'll understand if you can't go through with it, but I'll be forever in your debt if I can find my dear cousin. Michael and Katherine Kelly. They would have sailed from Queenstown."

He nodded and had to sprint to jump onto the boat as the gangplank was being pulled away.

On Friday morning I was up before dawn, and waited in swirling fog for the young inspector. I cursed myself that I hadn't thought to find out his name. If he hadn't managed to do what I asked, then I'd have to start all over again, or I'd have to write to the governor and wait for the wheels of bureaucracy to turn. Then at last I saw him, hurrying through the fog.

"Miss Murphy?" he said with a little bow. "This is for you."

He handed me an envelope.

"Thank you kindly. And this is for you." I, in my turn, handed him an envelope. Neither of us checked our envelopes as we went our separate ways. Once around the corner, however, I ripped it open.

Michael and Katherine Kelly. Sailed from Queenstown on the S.S. *Britannic. Admitted to the United States August 18, 1901.*

A big smile spread across my face. I had bribed an official, passed money, and got information I wanted. I was turning into a real investigator!

❧ Eight ❧

That Sunday I took up residence in my own home across the street. Even though the houses looked the same from the outside, my new abode had not benefited from Sid and Gus's loving and artistic care, or from any of their modernizations. There was no beautiful claw-footed bathtub and the W.C. was in a little room outside the back door. The old lady had lived there for thirty years without giving anything even a lick of paint—or a good spring cleaning. So Sunday was spent with sleeves rolled up, scrubbing linoleum so dirty that the roses on it only came to light after hours of elbow grease. Seamus and the children arrived early in the morning and tried to help with the cleaning, but to be honest I'd have done a better job on my own. Seamus was weak after pushing their belongings from the Lower East Side and the two little ones saw an opportunity to play with water.

After we'd moved my meager possessions across the street, we had an impromptu party. Sid and Gus brought over food and wine and we ate at the kitchen table by candlelight (the gas having been turned off when Mrs. Herman left).

"To Molly's ventures, may they all flourish, and may she stay in one piece," Sid said, raising her glass. I fervently seconded this. If my current ventures didn't end in success, I'd not be able to make the rent.

Now that I had good reason to believe that Katherine and Michael Kelly might indeed be in New York City, I had no idea how to start looking for them. Talk about looking for needles in a haystack! How many Irish lived in the Lower East Side alone, not to mention over in Hell's Kitchen or any of the other tenement districts? And how could I begin to hunt for them in the dark, at the end of my working day? I'd discovered already that being out alone after dark was not wise for a woman. For a lone woman who would be asking questions in run-down boarding houses and taverns in the worst slums of town, it would indeed be asking for trouble. I've attracted enough trouble in my life so far, but I've never actually asked for it!

Of course I could do nothing until I knew who I was looking for. I had to wait to receive full descriptions from Katherine's father. In the meantime, I would just have to be patient and concentrate on the bird in the hand and Mostel's spy.

That Tuesday was election day in New York. I made my way to work through a city draped with bunting and banners. Men I passed in the streets were wearing rosettes with the likeness of either Edward Shepherd or the Fusion party candidate, Seth Low. I knew little of what either of them stood for, and cared even less. If I didn't get a say in choosing them, then what did it matter?

When I came out of the garment factory twelve hours later, I found the streets full of drunken men singing, laughing, and fighting. It seemed that both parties had lured voters to their side with the promise of drink, or even of a dollar, which had now been spent in the nearest saloon. I passed a polling booth, still in operation. It was decorated with American flags and it looked decorous enough, but the area outside was patrolled by the toughest-looking louts I had ever seen. They swaggered around, swinging blackjacks and pouncing on any unsuspecting man who came past them.

"Have youse done yer votin' yet?" I heard one of them growl at a thin little fellow in a derby hat.

"Not speaking good English," the fellow replied, spreading his hands imploringly.

"No matter. Youse go in there and put yer X next to Shepherd, you hear? The one that starts with S—dat's the one. And when you come out, there will be a whole dollar for ya. If you vote for the wrong one, I'll break yer head. Understand?"

The little chap scuttled inside fast. I passed the polling booth without meriting a second glance. I was a woman and therefore no use to them. I did, however, have to fight off several amorous attempts as I made my way to the trolley.

The next morning the *New York Times* proclaimed that the Tammany candidate had lost, in spite of the bully boys' intimidation and bribery tactics. The editorial hoped for a brighter future in a city free from corruption. Unless they'd elected St. Patrick himself, I doubted that would come to pass. The gutters were full of discarded rosettes and trampled bunting.

The world went back to normal and work went on at Mostel and Klein, one day blurring into the next. Each night I came home wondering how much longer I could keep going and why the heck I was putting myself through this torture. Then the next Monday's post brought a second letter from Major Faversham (retired). It was a fat packet containing a photograph of a lovely girl in a ball gown. The photo had been tinted so that the gown was light blue and her hair was a soft light brown. The gown was low cut and she wore a locket on a velvet ribbon at her neck and carried a fan—every inch the daughter of privilege. Another photo fell out of the envelope, this time of Katherine in hunting attire, on horseback. The young man holding the bridle was looking up at her—a good-looking example of Black Irish, not unlike Daniel's appearance. He was younger, taller, and skinnier than Daniel but with similar unruly dark hair and rugged chin. It didn't take a genius to guess that I was looking at Michael Kelly.

I read the accompanying letter:

*I have enclosed two good likenesses of my daughter. The groom
is, of course, the scallywag Michael Kelly. He is the most repre-
hensible young man. When he was caught poaching on my estate
I took pity on his youth and had him trained to work in the stables.
He proved himself good with horses and could have made something
of his life if he had learned to be content with his station. Instead
he became a rabble-rouser, a so-called freedom fighter, and was
arrested for attempting to blow up the statue of Queen Victoria in
Dublin. Again I spoke for him, and hoped that my lecture would
make him mend his ways. It did not. Again he was implicated in
civil unrest and, not content to flee the country, persuaded my
young, impressionable daughter to flee with him. Heaven knows if
he plans to make a respectable woman of her or if she is ruined
forever.*

*You can see why my case is so desperate. If we could bring her
home and manage to hush up this whole sordid business, she would
still have a chance of a normal life in society. She is but nineteen
years old.*

*I can only presume that he took her with him, hoping to get his
hands on her fortune. She will, indeed, inherit a considerable sum
when she turns twenty-one, but at present she is as penniless as he
is. If she has any money at all with them it would be from the sale
of some minor pieces of jewelry she took with her.*

*As to friends in America—we have none. Most of Katherine's
life has been spent in India, where I had the honor to serve Her
Majesty in the Bengal Lancers. She is completely unused to fending
for herself and I am in grave fear for her. I urge you to put the
full facilities of your enterprise to this commission and find our
daughter as soon as possible.*

I am in this matter, your obedient servant,
Faversham

I reread the letter with satisfaction. At last I had something
to sink my teeth into. Katherine had come to New York penniless. That meant there was a good chance that she was still

here in the city. Now that I had photos I would start to track her down. My main problem was when. How could I track down Katherine Faversham if my days were still spent in a dreary sweatshop, with no end yet in sight? Indeed Max Mostel hadn't even completed the designs in question, so there was nothing to steal. And every day my frustration was boiling up, ready to explode. I wasn't at all sure how much longer I could continue to hold my tongue.

That very day Paula Martino, the young pregnant woman, had risen from her chair and was creeping toward the exit when she was spotted by Seedy Sam. "Where do you think you're going now?" he demanded.

She gave him a shrug and an apologetic smile. "Sorry. I gotta go."

"You gotta go, all right," Sam bellowed. "Get your things. You're outta here. The boss don't pay no stinking girls to waste his time powdering their noses."

"No, please," she begged, her face white and strained. "I'm sorry. It's only until the baby—it presses down so and then I can't help it."

"Listen, kid, I'm doing you a favor," Sam said. "You wouldn't be allowed to bring no squalling baby in here anyway. Buy yourself a machine and start doing piecework from home."

"Buy myself a machine?" Paula demanded, her face flushed and angry now. "How you think I buy myself a machine, huh? You think I got gold hidden under my bed, huh? I got two kids to feed and a husband who can't find work and you say buy myself a machine?"

I could stand it no longer. I jumped up and grabbed Sam's sleeve. "You can't fire her for heeding the call of nature. That's just not fair. And it's not as if she's paid by the hour, so she's not wasting your time. She's paid by the piece and she stays late to finish her work if she has to."

Sam shook himself free from my grasp and eyed me with a distasteful leer. "I remember now why we don't hire no Irish.

They stir up trouble. Ain't none of your damned business. Go and sit at your place and get on with your work if you don't want to follow her out of the door."

The encounter might well have ended with my being fired but at that moment there was a diversion. The door opened and a young man swept into the room. He was wearing a top hat and a silk-lined cape and carried a silver-tipped cane. He looked at our little scene with amusement.

"Are you bullying people again, Sam?" he demanded. "What's the poor girl done this time—dared to sneeze when the filthy lint got up her nose?"

Sam managed a weak smile. "I'm just trying to keep 'em in line, Mr. Benjamin. Making sure they don't waste your pa's time and money, that's all."

"My father's in his office, is he?" the young man said, his amused gaze sweeping the room until his eyes rested on me. I saw him register surprise at my Irish freckles and red hair. When I didn't look down demurely, as most of the girls here would have done, he gave me an outrageous wink. Fortunately I was used to winks too. I smiled politely, nodded my head graciously, and didn't blush. As he walked toward the doorway that led to the stairs I saw him glance back at me. "I hope he's in a good mood," I heard him say to Sam. "The automobile just had an unhappy meeting with a streetcar and the front fender is no more."

Sam turned back to us. "Well, what are you waiting for, get back to work. The boss don't pay you to sit around gawping." He jerked his head at Paula. "You, out."

I went back to my machine wondering what I could do. The boss's son had seemed interested in me. Could I appeal to him to override the foreman's decision? Then I had to remind myself that I was not here to make trouble. I was just playing a part. I would help nobody by getting myself fired. When the boss's son came down from his father's office again, he walked waked past us as if we didn't exist.

"I expect he got a ribbing from his old man for denting the automobile," Sadie whispered to me.

"That's Mr. Mostel's son? Is he part of the business too?" I whispered back.

She shook her head. "Goes to some fancy university—studying to be a doctor." Her eyes became dreamy. "Imagine that—less than twenty years in this country and already a son who'll be a doctor. We should all be so lucky."

"Sadie Blum and Molly Murphy—five cents docked for talking," came the voice from the other end of the room.

I sat, treadling away furiously, and fumed. Somebody should do something for these girls. Their lives shouldn't be like this. At the end of the day, we took our wraps from the pegs on the wall and I walked down the stairs with Sadie and Sarah.

"I could hardly wait for seven o'clock to come around," Sarah whispered, even though work was officially over and we were allowed to talk. "I was near to bursting, but I was too scared to ask if I could go to the W.C. after what happened to Paula. In the future I'm just not going to drink anything at lunchtime."

"You wouldn't have a problem, Sarah." Sadie looked at her kindly. "You're quiet and shy and you do what you're told. And you're a dainty worker too. It's girls like you that they like."

"That's my aim," Sarah said softly, "to stay invisible and pray to get through each day."

My annoyance boiled over at the thought of little Sarah, too frightened to ask to relieve herself.

"It's not right," I said. "Why doesn't somebody do something? If you all got together, you'd have strength."

They looked at me with pity. "You think nobody has tried?" Sadie said. "We've had girls here who are all fired up like you and try to do something to make things better, and what happens? They disappear. One day they are here, next they don't come to work. And if we all joined together and demanded better treatment, Mr. Mostel would just fire us all, send Sam down to the docks and pick new girls straight from the boats. We are at the bottom of the heap, Molly. We have no one to speak for us. We work here with one thought in mind—that one day there will be something better."

I should be doing something, I thought. I could speak up for these girls. Then I had to remind myself severely that good investigators do not allow themselves to become emotionally involved in their cases. So far I wasn't being too successful in this area. My assignment, for which I was being paid, was to find a spy—and the sooner the better, as far as I was concerned. I wanted this assignment to be over for various reasons, not the least was the bad taste it left in my mouth.

But I was also itching to move on to my other case. How could I track down Katherine Faversham and her scallywag companion while they were still in the city when I had no time and no energy? As things stood, I only had Sundays to devote to finding Katherine and Michael. If I didn't find them soon, they might be out of the city and far away and I would have lost them for good.

I stood in the cold, dank street as the other girls wrapped their shawls around their heads and scurried off into the night. I hesitated on the sidewalk. This is ridiculous, I thought. The Katherine Faversham case was important to me, important to my whole future as an investigator. Was I going to let it slip away because I was sewing collars all day? I'd just have to take some risks and find enough energy to hunt for them at night. I wrapped my shawl around my head and started toward the dock area.

I only got as far as the first corner tavern before my resolve faltered. A couple of drunken men staggered out and made a grab at me. I fought them off easily enough and crossed the street with their ribald comments and laughter ringing in my ears. The next street was dark and I was scared to enter it. I hated to admit I was giving up, but clearly this wasn't going to work. Reluctantly I made my way back to Broadway and the trolley, trying to put my racing thoughts in order. Exactly why was I slaving away at a sewing machine all day? I was proficient enough now, so what could I achieve until Max's designs were ready? By the time I reached the trolley I had come to a momentous decision. I had wasted enough time working for Max Mostel. I was going to take a few days off.

As soon as I got home I sat at the table and started to write a letter.

> Dear Mr. Mostel,
>
> I have been at your garment factory just over three weeks. This has given me ample opportunity to observe your workers and to get my sewing up to speed. I now plan to apply at Lowenstein's, so that I am completely familiar with his workers and operation by the time your designs are complete. Please keep me apprised of the status of your designs and send me a copy of them by messenger the moment they are complete. You can always leave a message for me at my new address, 10 Patchin Place.

Bridie came to look over my shoulder. "You write pretty," she said. "All curly."

"You'll learn to write like that too if you study hard at school," I said. "Your pa should enroll you in a new school this week—one close by."

"I ain't going to no school," Shamey said, standing in the doorway and scowling at me. "School is for sissies."

"You're going whether you like it or not," I said. "Everybody needs to know how to read and write."

"I know how to read and write already," he said. "My cousins don't go to no sissy school and they earn money."

"Running errands for a gang, Seamus? I don't think your father would want you doing that."

He glared at me defiantly. "I want to earn money too so I can take care of my pa and my sister."

I looked at his skinny young face and realized that the scowl had not been of defiance, it had been of worry. He had decided that he must take over the duties of head of the family. I went over to him and attempted to put an arm around his shoulder. "That's a very noble thought, Seamus," I said, "but you'll be able to take care of them much better if you educate yourself first."

"I don't have time." He shook himself free from me. "I can get a job as a newsboy right away."

"Of course you have time. You have a place to live and enough to eat."

He looked at me scornfully. "Nuala says it's accepting charity."

"Charity? Of course it's not charity."

"You ain't a relative. Only relatives are supposed to help each other. That's what Nuala says."

"Your Nuala talks a lot of rubbish." I smiled at him. "But I'll tell you what—if you need to earn money now, then I'll employ you. Promise me you'll go to school and then you can run messages for me when school is out. I need a messenger tomorrow morning, as it happens."

"You do—where?"

"To take this letter to an address on Canal Street."

"I know where that is." His face had lit up.

"Good. Then you're hired. When you take it, make sure it goes directly to Mr. Mostel. Tell them it's important. Oh, and Shamey—don't tell them it's from me."

I finished the letter and addressed the envelope from J. P. Riley and Associates. When I handed it to Shamey the next morning, I felt a great sense of freedom and relief. No more sweatshop for a few days. I was off to find a missing heiress!

❧ Nine ❧

I started the trail for Katherine and Michael at the very tip of
Manhattan Island where the ferry from Ellis Island lands the
new immigrants. If they were penniless and knew nobody,
then their first priority would be finding themselves a place to
stay. I remembered clearly my own arrival from Ellis Island. I had
been with Seamus, of course, and he had led me directly to his
apartment on Cherry Street, but we had run the gamut of touts,
waiting to prey on the newcomers. Those same touts were already lined up, bright and early in the morning, waiting for the
first ferry from the island. Some of them clutched signs, some
wore sandwich boards: The messages were written in Italian and
Yiddish and Russian and God knows what else. A few, however,
were written in English. MRS. O'BRIEN'S BOARDINGHOUSE, CHEAP
AND CLEAN. ROOM TO LET. GOOD SAFE NEIGHBORHOOD . . . as
well as the more ominous, PETER'S PAWN SHOP, 38 THE BOWERY,
GOOD PRICE PAID FOR YOUR VALUABLES. Some men carried no
signs. They lurked in nearby saloon doorways and watched and
waited. Maybe they were hoping to find unaccompanied young
girls, or even young men, but you could tell just by looking at
them that they were waiting to prey on the weak and the un-
protected.

I walked among the signs, taking down the addresses of the
various boardinghouses and rooms for let. Then I started to visit

them, one by one, beginning with those closest to the ferry dock. If they had arrived late in the day and were tired, they'd have chosen the closest.

Several hours later I was tired and footsore, and none the wiser. I had visited ten boardinghouses, God knows how many rooms for let, and none of them had heard of Katherine and Michael Kelly.

From what I knew, the Irish slum areas were along the waterfront, facing the East River, stretching from Cherry Street, where I had first lived with Nuala, down to Fulton Street where she now lived. There was also an area on the other side of the island, also along the docks, where my former employer, Paddy Riley, had lived, and then further up there was Hell's Kitchen— although I didn't look forward to going back there. I'd just have to start on the Lower East Side and work my way around. A daunting task, but I couldn't think of any way around it. Again I was reminded how little I knew about being an investigator. Paddy would have probably been able to locate the missing couple with a few well placed questions. He had the contacts on both sides of the fence—the police and the underworld. I had no contacts, anywhere. Everything I did was by trial and error.

I decided to start on Cherry Street and comb the area methodically. It was now midday and commerce was in full swing. The saloons were open and a parade of men drifted in and out. It was likely that Michael Kelly had slaked his thirst in one of these. He was, from his photo, an attractive young man, with the ability to charm both Major Faversham and his daughter. He'd have been noticed. But women did not go into saloons. Again I was reminded how much easier this job was for a man.

I had to be content with stopping women on the street and asking about local boardinghouses or landlords who let cheap rooms. At each of these establishments I gave the same emotional plea about my dear lost cousin Katherine and her husband Michael. I asked about other boardinghouses nearby. Usually the answer was similar, "There's herself down at Number Eighty-nine on the corner. Calls herself a boardinghouse but it's so dirty even the mice won't stay there." I worked my way down Cherry Street, up Water Street, and then I moved inland—Monroe, Madison, Henry, and their cross streets. It was hopeless. In this area of crowded tenements almost every building had rooms that were let, sublet, and sub-sublet. Half the families took in boarders. And there were enough people called Kelly to send me on several wild-goose chases.

In the end I gave up and went back to the ferry dock, realizing that I should have questioned the touts and shown them the photos. They were a striking couple. Someone might well have remembered them. I came back to find a three-ring circus in full swing—a boat was just unloading, children were screaming, touts were shouting and trying to herd hapless immigrants in the direction of their establishment, small boys were trying to earn some coppers by carrying baggage which the frightened owners were not going to release, and among the crowd I spotted enough criminal element to make the immigrants' fears justified. Pickpockets were doing a lively trade in the crush and some more brazen crooks were simply snatching bundles and boxes and dodging off with them into back alleyways. What a welcome to the land of the free! And where were New York's finest when you needed them? I'd have to tell Daniel—forget that right now, Molly Murphy, I told myself. I wouldn't be telling him anything again.

I was cursing myself for coming all this way for nothing when I saw something that made me grin from ear to ear. At the far side of the crowd a tall lugubrious fellow was walking up and down with a sandwich board with the words, MA KELLY'S BOARD-INGHOUSE. JUST LIKE HOME. CHEAP AND CHEERFUL. The address was on Division Street, a mere half block from where I had stopped my search.

Of course they would have gone there if they'd seen the sign. How could Michael Kelly have resisted going to someone who might even have been a distant relative? I hurried to the

Third Avenue El and rode it up to Canal Street where it was a mere hop, skip, and jump to 59 Division Street. A dreary tenement like all the rest—five stories of dingy brown brick. I knocked on the front door and it was opened by an enormous woman wearing a dirty white apron over a faded black dress. "Yes?" she asked, folding her arms across the monstrous shelf of bosom.

"I'm looking for my cousin and her new husband who recently arrived from Ireland. I'm wondering if they might have stayed here, seeing that their name is also Kelly." I gave her a hopeful smile. "Michael and his wife Katherine—a young couple, just married, they are."

I had hoped that her granite face might have softened when she heard the Irish accent, but she continued to glare at me. "Don't mention them to me, the no-good pair," she said.

"Then they were here?"

"They were here all right. Treated them like me own son and daughter, didn't I? Him with his blarney about us being related." She hoisted up the bosoms and sniffed. "No more related to him than the man in the moon."

"So they're not here any longer?" I asked cautiously.

"Upped and left without a by your leave or a thank you, didn't they?" she demanded. "Waited until I was doing me shopping then simply upped and left. When I came back there was no sign of them, and they left owing a week's rent too."

"How long ago was this?"

"Going on for a month, I'd say. Good riddance to bad rubbish."

"I'm sorry they treated you so badly," I said. "It's Katherine who's my cousin, not this Michael Kelly. I understand from the folks at home in Ireland that he's a bit of a rogue."

"A bad lot if you ask me." She bent toward me. "I think your cousin married beneath her. Always behaved like a real lady, that one, and talked all highfalutin too—although she could be a proper little madam if she'd a mind to. Had the nerve to criticize my housekeeping, she did. She told me her dogs at home wouldn't want to eat off my floor. Can you imagine? The nerve of it."

I swallowed back the smile. From what I could see of the grimy lace curtains and pockmarked linoleum, Katherine was quite right. I nodded with sympathy. "She was brought up rather spoiled," I said. "But she's a sweet nature and I'd like to help her if I can. You've no idea where they went, have you?"

She shook her head. "It wasn't as if they said more than two words to me. Kept themselves to themselves, they did."

"Were they around the house much when they lived here? Did they find jobs?"

"She did. She was out all day and every day, but that great lummox of a husband of hers, he lazed around doing nothing half the day. He didn't perk up until the saloons opened and then he was out half the night."

"So he could have been working a night shift then?"

She leaned closer to me again. "You don't come home from the night shift on unsteady legs, smelling of beer."

"Do you happen to know where Katherine was working?" I asked. " "Maybe I could trace her through her job."

Ma Kelly sniffed again. "Like I told you, we hardly exchanged more than two words. Kept herself to herself, that one, but with her fine airs and graces you'd have thought that she'd have had no trouble landing herself a refined job."

I tried to think of more questions to ask, but couldn't. "I'm sorry to have troubled you then, Mrs. Kelly. If any post arrives for them from home, maybe you could have it forwarded to my address. It's Ten Patchin Place, in Greenwich Village. Molly Murphy's the name."

"I can do that," she said. "I hope you find your cousin. Like I said, she was no trouble at all. He was a typical Kelly. Just like my late husband—couldn't trust him farther than you could throw him. Went and inconvenienced everybody by dying when all he had was the influenza." She sniffed again.

"If you do hear anything about Michael and Katherine, please let me know then," I said. "I'll be offering a small reward for information."

"I've just given you information," she said, a gleam coming into her eyes.

"So you have." I reached into my purse. "Here's fifty cents for your trouble. If the information leads to finding them, it will be more, of course."

"I'll keep me eyes and ears open for you, my dear," she said, smiling at me most benignly now.

I left Ma Kelly's unsure what to do next. Katherine and Michael had been living there until recently. Then they had left in a hurry. Had they found a better place to live—a room of their own? If Katherine was working, then it was entirely possible. But how would I ever trace them in a city this size? Paddy's words came back to me—always start from what you know, however unimportant you think it is. What did I know? I knew that Katherine had found a job, and that Ma Kelly had suggested it might be a job suiting her refined airs and graces. A shop maybe? I knew that ladies sometimes worked in hat or dress shops, but how many of them would there be in the city? Too many for me to check out all of them.

I knew that Michael lounged around most of the day and came back at night smelling of beer. So the next step would be to find out where he did his drinking. If his step had been not too steady, then the saloon wouldn't be far away. I'd start with the saloon on the corner and work outward.

I knew I'd be asking for trouble if I went into saloons, but I had to follow up on my only lead at this point. I'd just have to put on my most haughty expression and keep a hat pin ready. I slipped it out of my hat, held it between my fingers, and made my way to O'Leary's Tavern on the corner of Division and Market. It was now around one thirty and the lunchtime trade was in full swing. Through the open door I could see men lined up at the bar, each with a bowl of hot food and a roll in front of him—all for the price of a beer. These free saloon lunches were most popular, especially with single workingmen. At least this looked like an honest workingman's bar and I thought I'd be fairly safe.

I had scarcely passed in through the open door when one of the wags at the bar called out, "Careful, boys, here comes someone's old woman, wanting to get her hands on his wage packet."

The bartender came hastily around the bar to me. "Sorry, Miss. No women allowed."

"I'm not intending to stay, sir," I said. "I'm trying to locate a missing cousin of mine and I understand he might frequent this saloon. I wonder if you might have seen him."

"Lady, I get a hundred men a day in here. Unless they get rowdy and smash up the furniture, I couldn't tell them one from another and that's the truth."

"I just thought you might have noticed this young man. He lived just down the street, until a couple of weeks ago. His name was Michael Kelly—tall, dark haired, good looking, straight from Ireland, had the gift of the blarney, so they say."

The barman shook his head, then I saw his expression change. "There was one fella used to come in here for a while. Liked to talk big. Boasted about blowing up things and escaping from under the noses of the English police."

"That would be the one," I said. "Any idea where I might find him now? He left his boardinghouse a few weeks ago."

The man shook his head. "I can't help you there, I'm afraid. Some of these gentlemen are in the bar of an evening—they might know more than me." He raised his voice. "Young lady here is looking for her cousin. Remember that young fellow name of Mike Kelly—did a lot of talking about being a Fenian and a fighter for home rule? Whatever happened to him?"

An older man in dirty overalls looked up from the roll he was eating. "Last time I saw him, he was talking to Monk."

"Monk?" I asked.

"Monk Eastman," the man said, lowering his voice so that the words were barely audible.

"And who's he?" I asked.

Some of the men looked at each other. "He's the local gang boss, Miss," one of them said, lowering his voice and his gaze.

"You think Michael might be involved with a gang?" I looked directly at the older man. He shrugged.

"I mind my own business, miss. I don't get mixed up with the likes of Monk Eastman. I'm just telling ya what I saw. I saw him in front of the Walla Walla, talking with Monk."

"He better have been in Monk's good books, because if not he'd be floating in the East River by now," someone else chimed in.

"What is this Walla Walla?" I asked.

"It's the nickname for the Walhalla Hall—a local social club."

"A social club? And where would that be?"

Again I saw the men exchange glances.

"Just around the corner on Orchard Street, just off Canal, but I wouldn't go there yourself, miss. It's a regular gang haunt. Not a place for nice young ladies, like yourself."

"Don't worry, I don't intend to do anything stupid," I said. "Thank you for your time and trouble, gentlemen."

"Not at all, miss." Several hats were raised. I left like departing royalty. I stood on the street corner, enjoying the sun that had appeared from between the clouds. Several men followed me out of the saloon and one of them took off at a run. I wondered if I had made him late back to work.

My, but that stew smelled good. My growling stomach reminded me that I hadn't eaten since breakfast. Yet another disadvantage of being a woman was that I couldn't get myself a nourishing lunch for the price of a beer, but would have to seek out a café. Not wanting to stop when I was now hot on a trail, I bought myself a bag of hot roasted chickpeas from a pushcart. I had never tried them before, or even heard of them, but they were salty and crunchy and satisfied the hunger pangs very nicely.

I was in a quandary about what to do next. I knew that it would, indeed, be foolish to go asking questions at a gangland haunt. I needed to tread very carefully. But what harm could there be in walking along Orchard Street in broad daylight, just to get a look at the place? Mostel's factory was only a block or so around the corner, on Canal Street and I had never felt myself in danger when I walked from the Broadway trolley car. I picked up my skirts, stepped off the curb, and struck out along Canal Street, looking a good deal more confident than I felt.

The Walhalla Hall was a solid-looking brick building with an imposing front door and marble ornamentation. It was, unfortunately, completely deserted, closed and shuttered at this time of day. I even crossed the street and examined it. From the outside it looked respectable enough, apart from the bars over the downstairs windows. There were posters on a billboard in front, advertising coming dances and social events. A perfectly respectable community hall, by all appearances.

I wasn't sure what to do next. Clearly there would be no activity at the building during daylight but coming here at night would be a big risk to take. I surely didn't fancy myself coming face-to-face with Monk Eastman or one of his cronies in the dark! I walked up and down the block once more and was wondering whether I might show Michael's picture to any of the neighbors on the street when I heard the clatter of boots on cobbles. Three small figures came hurtling down Orchard Street and dodged into an alley on the far side of the Walhalla Hall. I thought I heard a police whistle blowing in the distance. With grim determination I set off after the boys down the alleyway. And in case you think I needed my head examined, let me just say that there was more at stake here than just getting information. I had recognized one of the boys. In fact I had put that black cap on his head myself this morning.

✂ Ten ✂

The alley was dark, narrow, full of garbage, and stank. I picked up my skirts to negotiate rotting food and turned the corner with heart pounding. I heard a scurry of boots and a voice whispered, "Someone's coming."

"Someone's coming all right," I said, loudly. "Come out here this instant, Seamus O'Connor, or you won't be able to sit down for a month."

"It's her," I heard a small voice whisper and by and by three small faces appeared from out of a coal bunker. They belonged to Shamey and two of his cousins, Malachy and James. I grabbed Shamey by the neck before he could escape again. "Holy Mother of God, I thought you and I had a bargain," I said. "I thought we agreed no more hanging around with the cousins, no more gangs. You promised you'd go and enroll yourself in school."

"She's not your mother," Malachy said. "She can't tell you what to do."

"No, I'm not your mother," I replied, "but we both know what your dear mother would think of the way you are behaving right now, don't we? She'd want you to be doing the best for yourself. Do you want to make her worry if she hears that you're getting yourself into trouble? Do you want to break her heart if she finds out you've got yourself killed or thrown into jail?"

Shamey's lip quivered. "No," he said, looking down at his boots.

"Well then, remember in the future that a promise is a promise," I said. "You're coming home with me right now. And these boys better run home to their own parents if they've any sense."

I took him by the hand and led him away.

"I'm sorry, Molly," he whispered when we were clear of the cousins. "I came down here to deliver your letter like you said and I met them. They told me I was a sissy and they said that the men would give us a whole dollar for going to smash up a fruit stall on the Bowery. A whole dollar, Molly."

"A whole dollar—is that a good trade for a life in jail? It's a crime you know, breaking up someone's property. Is it a gang member that's telling you to do these terrible things?"

"It's the Eastmans." He looked proud and defiant. "They rule this part of town. They're going to rule the whole of the city when they've shut down the Dusters and the Five Pointers. They're going to take me on when I'm bigger. I'm going to be a junior Eastman. They say I'm a fast runner."

"You are not joining any gang, Seamus, so put that out of your mind right this minute. People who join gangs wind up dead. If you really want to help your family, you go to school and study hard and better yourself. And in the meantime you can make yourself some money by being my messenger and right-hand man."

This perked him up a little. "I delivered your letter, just like you told me," he said. "I told them I had to hand it straight to the boss because it was important so they took me up and I gave it to him."

"Did he say anything when he saw who it was from?"

"No, but he nodded and put the letter in his jacket pocket right away."

"You did well, Shamey. I can use you again, if you're going to be trustworthy. But if you think of running off with those no-good cousins, then forget it."

96

"You can use me again," he said. "Are you really a detective?"

"How did you know that?"

"Nuala said. She said you told her but she didn't believe you. She said you had a fancy man who beat you up."

"Like I said, Nuala talks a lot of rubbish."

We had reached Broadway and joined the line waiting for a trolley car.

"If you're really a detective, I could help you," Seamus whispered. "I could go and find out things for you."

A thought had struck me. I tried to dismiss it. I wrestled with it. Seamus knew the Eastmans. They had employed him. Would I be putting him in harm's way if I sent him to ask a simple question of them? I pulled him back from the trolley queue into the shadow of an awning.

"Could you do a real job for me? I don't like to ask you, but I don't have a way of finding out myself. It's about the Eastmans."

His eyes lit up. "I know plenty of Eastmans."

"Listen, I don't want you to get yourself into any danger, but I need to know if a man called Michael Kelly is part of the Eastmans gang. Could you find out for me? Tell them it's his cousin from Ireland who wants to know. A girl cousin. I'm trying to find him."

"I can do that. Easy as pie. Do you want me to run down there now?"

"Is anyone around during the day? The hall was closed up."

"I know where to find them." Shamey looked grown up and proud. "They're only around the hall when there's a dance or something going on. Otherwise they're at their headquarters."

"Which is where?"

"On Chrystie Street, around the corner."

"I don't want you going to any gang headquarters," I said. "Forget that I even asked you."

"Some of the Eastman guys might be at the saloon," Shamey suggested. "I've been there before with my cousins, delivering messages."

"I'll come with you then. I'm not having you going to any saloon by yourself."

He looked horrified. "They wouldn't tell me nothing if you came along. It's a saloon. Full of people. I'll be safe as houses."

"Very well," I said hesitantly. "Ask the question and come straight home then. Here." I reached into my purse. "Here's a quarter. That will take care of your trolley fare and in case you get hungry."

"Gee. Thanks." His eyes lit up.

"Be home before it's dark, and no running off with your cousins again."

"I will. Bye, Molly." He waved and set off back in the direction we had come. I watched him go with considerable misgivings. I had just used an innocent child to do work I was afraid of doing myself. That couldn't be right—what had I been thinking of? I started to run after him, but he had completely vanished.

I went home on the trolley and prepared a big plate of sausage and mash, which I knew was Shamey's favorite. The dinner was ready, it got dark, and still he didn't come.

I told myself it was early yet. He may have had to wait around until some of the gang members showed up. I told myself that he was accepted by them. He ran their errands. But none of this took away the worry that gnawed at the pit of my stomach.

"That smells good," Seamus Senior said, looking more sprightly than I had seen him recently. "I think I'm getting my appetite back. Where's the boy? Out running around again?"

"He'll be back soon," I said. "I'll put this in the oven until he gets here."

Darkness fell. I served the food to Seamus and Bridie but I was too sick of heart to eat it myself. At last I could stand it no longer. "I'm going looking for him," I said. "That young scallywag has no idea of time." And I tried not to let my face betray my worry to them.

Back down Broadway on the tram, then along Canal Street.

It was poorly lit after the bright lights of Broadway and the Bowery and seemed empty and deserted. No pushcarts here, no street life going on—no movement at all except for figures who slunk through the shadows and men who emerged from corner saloons. Why hadn't I thought of changing into boy's clothes? I had done this once and was delighted how I could pass invisibly through the city. Now I felt horribly vulnerable and was annoyed at myself. I was no better than the helpless females I so despised. I'd be reaching for my smelling salts and wearing a corset if I wasn't careful! I pulled out my trusty hat pin and curled my fingers around it. Now ready and armed I turned onto Orchard Street.

The front door of the Walhalla Hall was still closed, but I could see some lights on inside. I hesitated, unwilling to rap on that formidable door. I walked past, trying to find a window I could peek through, but they were all too high. I crossed the street to observe it from the other side. Nothing much seemed to be going on. I continued down the street, annoyed with myself that I had not asked Shamey the name of the saloon the Eastmans were known to frequent. I really had no idea where I was going or what I was looking for. On the corner I paused and spotted the street sign. Chrystie Street! That name rang a bell. Shamey had said that was where the Eastmans had their headquarters. I was about to take the plunge and walk in that direction when I heard footsteps behind me.

I tried to remain calm and nodded a civil good evening as a man passed me. Instead of passing, however, he stopped.

"Can I help youse, lady?" he asked in a strong Bowery accent. "Dis ain't no neighborhood for a lady like yourself to be out alone. Youse lookin' for someone?"

He was young and skinny, a harmless looking little chap with a fresh, clean-shaven face, dressed in a smart black suit with a jaunty derby on his head.

I felt a sigh of relief escaping. "Why, thank you, sir. Actually I'm looking for a small boy. I sent him to this neighborhood before dark to run an errand for me and he hasn't returned. He's nine years old—Irish like me. Skinny and dark haired. You wouldn't have seen him by any chance, would you?"

"You know I tink I did," he replied. "A whiles ago now."

"Oh, thank heavens. If you could show me where you last saw him . . ."

"He was talking to some guys outside the Walhalla Hall. Come on, let's go and see if he's still there."

He gave me a reassuring smile. We crossed the street together and headed back to the Walhalla. The area around the hall was still deserted.

"Dey might have gone in," my rescuer said. "Let's go ask inside."

He pushed open the front door. I hesitated. "Are you sure it's all right to go in there? I mean, isn't it a dangerous place where gangs hang out?"

He laughed. "It's just a neighborhood social club, miss. They hold parties here—weddings and wakes, all that kinda stuff. Even church socials. And you'll be safe enough wid me."

I stepped inside. He closed the door behind us. We found ourselves in a large, dimly lit room with chairs around the walls and a large expanse of floor.

"Not much happenin' tonight, is there?" he asked. "Dead as a doornail. Let's check the back."

He strode across that big floor, his boots making loud tapping noises on the wood floor, his white spats flashing. Beyond the hall was a long dark hallway. Light was coming from under a door at the far end. The young man sauntered ahead and confidently rapped on the door, opened it, and went in. Emboldened by his apparent lack of fear, I followed.

"Hey, Monk," he said. "You know that dame you wanted? I got her for you." And he shoved me inside, slamming the door shut behind us. The man standing in front of me was no thin and harmless-looking little chap this time. He was also quite young, big-boned but not very tall, with a large pudgy round face, a lot of dark hair on top of it, and a derby a couple of sizes too small for him perched on top of the hair. Where the other fellow was neatly dressed, this one was scruffy, with suspenders over rolled-up shirtsleeves and—I started in surprise as my eyes took in the shape—a live pigeon sitting on his shoulder. His appearance verged on the comical until I noticed some kind of club sticking out of his waistband. "Who's dis dame, Kid?" he demanded, also with a strong New York accent.

"You know how Bugsy said some redheaded dame was asking questions at O'Leary's today and then she was poking around the hall? And you said we should bring her in. Well, I tink she's the one what you want. I caught her snooping around again now—says she's looking for a kid dis time."

I had recovered from my shock just enough to realize that I was face-to-face with Monk Eastman himself. Not a pleasant thought. I just hoped he had a finer nature I could appeal to. "Yes, sir. I'm only trying to find my lost nephew, sir. Seamus O'Connor. I sent him down to this part of the city with an errand and he should have returned hours ago—but he's very smitten with your gang and I know he's hung around you in the past, with his cousins, that is." I knew I was babbling, but I was watching his face for a sign that he might be softening toward me.

"And today you wanted to know about Mike Kelly, right? Doing too much snooping altogether, if you ask me." He stepped toward me, eye to eye with me, but intimidating in his bulk. "Okay, so who sent ya? Because whoever it was is going to find out dat Monk don't like no snoops."

"Nobody sent me," I said.

"Then youse don't got nothing to worry about, have ya?" He opened the window behind him, brushed the pigeon from his shoulder, and it took off into the night with a loud flapping of wings. I saw the flash of something bright on his fingers. A lot of rings, maybe?

"Whatta youse want me to do wid her, Monk?" Kid asked.

"Take her to my place. I'll be along as soon as Lefty gets

back from dat little errand." He grinned. It was in no way a charming grin.

"Okay, girlie. Get going and no fuss." Kid went to grab one of my arms. I am not used to doing anything without making a fuss. I twisted sharply and stuck at him with the hat pin.

"Will you let go of me! This is no way to treat a perfectly respectable lady." Kid yowled and sucked at his hand. For a moment I had broken free. I grabbed the door handle.

"Watch her, she's got a knife," I heard Kid shouting.

Before I could wrench the door open, Monk had grabbed me and held me with one giant paw. "Youse is lucky I don't use me nucks on women, or you'd be lying dere with a smashed face," he said, pleasantly enough.

"It wasn't a knife, it was just a hat pin, like any lady would use in her own defense," I said. "I don't know what's the matter with you people, but if this is the way you treat ladies then I'm glad I'm not married to one of you." The words came out as an angry torrent, masking the fear that was rushing though me. All of Daniel's warnings about white slavery had come back to me. I was determined not to let them see I was afraid. "And if you can't answer one simple question about a little lost boy, then in heaven's name just let me go."

"Youse ain't going nowhere," Monk said. "Not until you tell us who sent ya. Coppers or Five Pointers or Dusters? Which one youse working for, huh? Take her upstairs instead, Kid. I'll get to her in a minute."

I was vacillating between playing the weak and helpless female and doing my Queen Victoria impersonation, haughty and aggrieved. I thought the second might have more chance.

"Will you get it into your heads that nobody sent me? You are making a horrible mistake," I shouted as Kid twisted my arm behind my back and shoved me out of the door. "I'm an ordinary Irish girl—the name is Molly Murphy. I was asking about Michael Kelly because he's married to a sort of cousin of mine and I understood they had arrived in New York recently, and the young boy who lives with me, Seamus O'Connor, offered to come down to this part of town and try to find Michael for me. That's all. Nothing complicated about it."

We were halfway along that hallway when doors burst open. Whistles were blown and suddenly the hall was full of blue uniforms. "Cops!" I heard someone shout. I could hear the crash of chairs turning over and hasty footsteps up above our heads.

The hand released my twisted arm.

"What the hell do youse tink you're doing busting in like this?" I heard Monk behind me shouting. "Dis is a respectable social club."

"And I'm the president of the United States," the policeman said. "The chief would like a word, Monk, if you can spare the time. All nice and friendly like."

"Your chief is asking for trouble." Monk almost spat out the words. "Youse guys know youse can't touch me. Bring me in and Tammany's going to hear about it, I promise you. Then you'll see what heads are going to roll."

"I told you, it's a friendly chat, Monk. Nothing more. Nobody's talking about arrest."

"Then get the damned cuffs off me."

"Just making sure you don't do a bunk on us. Now into the wagon nice and easy and you'll be back home in no time at all."

Monk was manhandled out the front door, followed by a squirming Kid. I heard feet on the stairs and saw officers bringing down more men. It was only then that they appeared to notice me.

"What about the dame?" one of them asked.

"Bring her too."

"I'm not one of them," I said angrily. "In fact you've just rescued me. They dragged me in here."

I saw two of the constables exchange a grin. "Out you go, girlie, and no tricks."

I was escorted out to a waiting paddy wagon and shoved into the back with five or six members of the Eastmans.

"Whoever did this is going to be very sorry," Monk said as the horses got up to speed and we were thrown around. "Who do they tink they're messing with? Why do they tink I pay them protection money, huh?"

It was a mercifully short ride. As we were taken out, I saw that we were at Mulberry Street headquarters. Up the steps and into the building.

"What have we got here?" a bewhiskered sergeant asked.

"Five Eastmans and one of their molls. Chief wanted a word."

"I am not anyone's moll," I said, stepping away from the column of men. "They dragged me into their building and the coming of your men actually rescued me." I weighed up whether to use Daniel's name, and decided that he owed me a favor. "You can ask Captain Sullivan if you like. He'll vouch for me."

"Is Captain Sullivan in the building?" one of the arresting officers asked.

"I think he just stepped out for a bite to eat," the sergeant said. "Put her in a holding cell until he gets back. Oh wait, speak of the devil . . ."

Daniel Sullivan had come in through the front door. "What's going on here, O'Malley?" he asked. He recognized the largest of the prisoners. "To what do we owe this honor, Monk? Gracing us with your presence?"

"Go to hell, Sullivan, and tell your chief he'd better watch the way he picks on innocent citizens or he's going to be sorry. Tell him next time to send a hansom cab for me. The seats in your Black Maria are too hard—besides, I got my reputation to consider!"

"Please escort Mr. Eastman and his friends upstairs and let the chief know they're here," Daniel said.

"And the girl, sir. Says she knows you."

Daniel looked at me and I saw his eyes open wide in astonishment. "Molly—what in heaven's name have you been doing with yourself now?"

"Minding my own business, until these gentlemen pounced on me and dragged me into their building."

"You know her then, sir?" the sergeant asked.

"Oh yes, I know her," Daniel said, glaring at me angrily. "Take her up to my office. I'll talk to her later."

I tried to protest. I was escorted up the stairs and sat on the hard chair in Daniel's glass-fronted cubicle, waiting for him. At least Monk Eastman and several of his men were now in custody. Maybe they could be persuaded to reveal if they had done anything with Shamey. I tried not to think what might have happened to him. Now that all the excitement was over, I found I was shivering. I had never seen Daniel look so angry.

At last he came storming up the stairs. "What in God's name have you been doing, woman?" he shouted at me. "Do you know who those men are?"

"Yes, I do. Monk Eastman and his gang."

"And didn't I warn you about gangs? Didn't I tell you about the turf war going on at this moment and the struggles for the cocaine business, not to mention the white slave trade? What on earth possessed you? You're lucky to be alive."

"I know that," I said.

"If you don't give up this absurd notion of yours, I'm going to have you arrested and shipped back to Ireland as a public nuisance—do I make myself clear?"

I knew this was a threat he wouldn't carry out but, all the same, it brought me up with a jolt. I could never go back to Ireland, where there was a price on my head.

I decided to try humility for once. "I'm sorry, Daniel. I knew I was asking for trouble, but I was looking for young Seamus O'Connor. He's been running errands for the Eastmans and I was worried about him."

"Seamus O'Connor—the boy you brought over from Ireland?"

I nodded. "His no-good cousins got him mixed up with a gang."

"And Molly, the champion, took it into her head to go and find him, single-handed? Sometimes I think you were born with a death wish."

"I had no option, Daniel. I acted because I thought the boy was in danger—the boy is probably still in danger."

"You could have come to me." His voice was quieter now. He was gazing at me steadily.

"When will you get it into your head that I cannot keep running to you for help?"

"Are we not still friends?" he said. "And friends can ask each other for a favor."

"Oh yes, and I can picture Miss Arabella allowing you to have friends like me," I said angrily. "For one thing, I don't wear the right sort of clothes."

I saw him try to stifle the grin. "I'm really sorry about the other Sunday," he said. "It must have been very unpleasant for you."

"No more pleasant for you, I'd warrant," I said, smiling also now.

"You behaved perfectly. I was most grateful."

"And you could have taken the opportunity to tell Arabella the truth. You could have said, 'This is the woman I love. I can't marry you.' But you didn't."

"No, and I despise myself for it. I suppose you are right. My career does mean a lot to me. If Arabella felt I had betrayed her, she would not rest until she had ruined me completely."

"And yet you could end up married to such a woman? Certainly a pleasing prospect."

He shrugged and looked away. "I will tell her, I promise. The time has to be right."

"This is no time to be discussing our unhappy situation," I said. "Not while young Shamey O'Connor may be in danger." I got up from my hard chair. "I must go, Daniel, if I'm permitted to do so and not to be charged as a gangster's moll. I must continue looking for the boy."

He put his hand on my sleeve. "Molly, I thought we'd been through this before."

"All right," I said. "Seeing that you owe me a favor for my good behavior and for holding my tongue that Sunday—you find the boy for me."

"I will do that. Where was he last seen?"

"He went to get some information from the Eastmans for me."

"You sent a child to the Eastmans?"

"Hold your horses—all right, I'm not feeling so wonderful about it myself now, but it seemed like a good idea at the time. This child has been used by them as a messenger. I thought he'd come to no harm and he might get more out of them than I would. I've been trying to locate a man called Michael Kelly, newly come from Ireland. I have reason to believe he may have joined the Eastmans. Young Shamey was going to find out for me, seeing that he knew about their haunts."

Daniel made a tut-tutting noise but said nothing and got out his pad. "Description of the boy?"

I gave it to him. "And while you're about it, I've got a picture of Michael Kelly. You could make inquiries about him too—find out if he is known to the Eastmans."

I fished for it in my bag.

Daniel studied it. "Not unlike me," he said. "Not quite as good looking, of course." I went to slap him playfully and withdrew my hand at the last second. "And why are you looking for him?"

"Part of my missing person's business," I said. "He ran off with a girl of good family. Here is her picture—her name is Katherine Faversham, or was before she married Michael Kelly. The father wants her found."

"I'm not surprised if she's run off with a gangster." He took the portrait from me, stared at it for a moment, then handed it back. "Not a bad-looking girl either. A little haughty for my taste."

I was about to remind him that Arabella Norton spent her life looking down her nose at the rest of us, but I decided to concentrate on more important matters. "All I've been able to trace so far is that they lived on Division Street until about three weeks ago, when they did a bunk, leaving rent unpaid. I heard a rumor that he might have joined the Eastmans."

"And how did you hear that?"

"Local tavern," I said breezily and watched Daniel sigh again.

"All right," he said. "I'll do what I can. I don't think the Eastmans would stoop to killing children—although who knows? They've been pretty violent in their actions recently. We've had a body brought into the morgue almost every day, although they've all been men. They have a different fate for women." He frowned at me again. "But for that police raid, you might never have been seen again, my dear." He turned away. "Can I make you swear to me that you will never do such a foolish thing again?"

"I'll try to behave more sensibly," I said, moved by his emotion.

"I couldn't bear it if anything happened to you." He reached out and stroked my cheek. I wished he hadn't done that. Any other gesture and I could have handled it. This was so tender that tears welled to my eyes. Instinctively I covered his hand with my own and held it to my cheek. Then I controlled myself, brushed his hand away, and rushed from his office. "I've got a lost boy to find," I said.

❦ Eleven ❧

I was not looking forward to going back to Patchin Place and telling Seamus that I had lost his son, but I didn't want worry him just as much by staying away.

I turned back to Daniel, who was guiding me down the stairs. "You will do what you can, won't you? He's just a little boy. He may think he knows his way around the city but he really hasn't been here long and . . ." I let the "and" hang in the air.

Daniel put his hand on my shoulder. "I'm sure he'll be all right. You know boys. He's found a pal and gone off with him, or he's gone back to his cousins' place."

The latter hadn't occurred to me. Nuala's place was not too far away. If Shamey had found himself in a spot of bother, he might well have run there for protection. I should have thought of that.

"I'll try the cousins myself," I said. "I can do that without getting myself into any kind of trouble."

Daniel's lips twitched in a smile. "Yes, I imagine so. I'll put men out onto the streets straight away, and I'll have a little talk with Monk and his friends too, just in case they know something they are not telling you."

"Thank you," I said.

"And Molly, please—" Daniel began.

"I know, take care of myself," I finished for him. "I'll have to, won't I, since I've no one else to care for me."

At that moment a great voice boomed up from the basement beneath us.

"Why don't you pick on someone your own size, you big bullies? Frightening tender young children to death like that!"

I recognized the voice and broke away from Daniel, hurrying down the stone stairs into the darkness. I heard a policeman shout, "Hey, you, where are you going?" but I didn't stop.

At the end of a dark, dank hallway Nuala was standing, arms folded in defiance over a considerably smaller police constable.

"Let them out of there this minute, or I won't be responsible for me actions, so help me God," she said, unfolding her arms and giving every indication of winding up to take a swing.

"Nuala!" I called, relieved for the only time in my life to see her. "Have they got the boys down there? Is Shamey with them?"

"Locked them away like hardened criminals and all for a bit of boyish fun," she said.

I ran toward her. Shamey's scared face peered out at me from behind the bars.

"What's all this about?" I asked the constable, who now looked doubly scared at having to confront two angry women.

"They were identified as the gang that broke up a fruit vendor's stall this morning," he muttered.

"A gang you call them?" Nuala's beefy arm tensed again. "Nothing more than boyish high spirits. Have you got nothing better to do with your time or are you afraid to go after the real criminals?"

Daniel had come to my side. "What's going on?" he asked.

I pointed to the cell. "Shamey is in there," I said. "Apparently he helped his cousins to smash up a fruit stall."

"We didn't mean no harm," Malachy, the oldest cousin said.

"Honest, Officer, we was just foolin' around," James, the second cousin added.

"Of course you meant harm," Daniel said coldly. "You were

being paid for it, weren't you? You don't have to tell me. I know. The Eastmans like to pay kids to do their dirty work, then you get caught, not them. They had you smash up the stall because the owner wouldn't pay his protection money, didn't they?" He walked up to the bars. "Take a good look around you, boys. Do you like the look of this place, because it's not half as bad as some of the cells in the Tombs down the street, and that's where you'll be spending most of your lives, if you are foolish enough to mix with gangs. If you live long enough, that is. Would you like to see how many bodies I've got lying on a marble slab in the morgue right now? Gang members, every one of them."

He nodded to the constable who produced a key. "I'm going to let you out this time, but if I find you in here again, then you'll be very sorry."

The door was opened. Nuala's two boys ran into her arms. "He said he'd throw away the key, Ma," Malachy sniveled.

Nuala hugged them fiercely. "Let's go home, boys, before these no-good bullies change their minds. But if I ever hear about you working with a gang again, I'll knock your blocks off, so help me God." She drove them like sheep ahead of her up the stone steps. Shamey stood there outside the cell, looking up at me with big, frightened eyes.

"And as for you, Seamus," Daniel said, glaring at him. "You remember me, don't you?"

Shamey sniffed and nodded. "You're Captain Sullivan. You used to come visiting when we lived with Molly before."

"I'm a very important policeman, Seamus, and I've got my spies all over the city. If I ever hear that you've had anything to do with gangs again, then you're going to be very sorry indeed. We've even worse prisons than this, you know. This one's like Coney Island compared to the Tombs. So do I have your word that you'll not make Molly worry about you again?"

"She asked me to go and talk to the Eastmans," Shamey said, a hint of defiance returning.

"She didn't realize how stupidly dangerous that was. Now

she does. She'll not be asking you to do a foolish thing like that again, I can promise you. Now go home, the both of you, and let me get on with my work."

"Let's go, Shamey," I said gently. "There's sausage and mash keeping hot in the oven."

He nodded. I spared his dignity by not taking his hand as we walked up the stairs. At the top I looked back at Daniel. He was watching me with such an intense look of longing on his face that it gripped at my heart. For once he was the one suffering. Good.

Once outside I put my arm around Shamey. "You've had quite a fright, haven't you?" I said. "I blame myself for sending you to do something that was stupidly dangerous. I'll never do that again. I'm sorry."

"The police were watching the place and they grabbed us," he said. "I'm sorry I didn't get to ask about that guy for you, Molly." Then, a few steps later, "Does my father have to know?"

"I don't think we need to worry him, do you?" I said. "We'll tell him that you went home with the cousins and Nuala invited you to stay to supper."

A beaming smile spread across his face. "And it was so good I forgot to come home," he finished for me, then burst out laughing. It is hard to keep the young downhearted for long. I, on the other hand, had some serious thinking to do. My thoughtless behavior today had brought me to the notice of the Eastmans. They had been looking for me, maybe they'd come looking for me again. I would have to tread very carefully in the future.

The next morning I took Shamey and his sister and personally enrolled them in the local school. "And if I hear you've been playing truant, it will be bread and water for a week," I said, giving Shamey my severest stare.

As I walked home, I was unsure what to do next. I had to hope that Daniel would keep his promise and find out about

Michael and Katherine for me. Until then, I had nothing to do. After those weeks at the sweatshop, it was a strange feeling. I went to have coffee and rolls with Sid and Gus and recounted my adventure with the Eastmans. They were suitably impressed.

As the weekend approached and still no word from Daniel, I realized that I could wait no longer—I would have to apply at Lowenstein's on Monday morning, or I'd miss the crucial moment when the new designs were finished. And if Daniel hadn't found out any more about Michael and Katherine for me, then I'd just have to do it for myself, even if I was putting myself in danger.

I was walking the children to Washington Square on Saturday afternoon to play with a new whipping top Sid had bought for Seamus when I saw a young police constable striding up Patchin Place.

"Miss Murphy?" He stopped and saluted. "I was told to deliver this by Captain Sullivan. He told me to apologize that he hasn't the time to deliver it himself, but he said to tell you that he's had no sleep all week, what with this gang business." He handed me a slim envelope, saluted, and went back the way he had come. I stood fighting back the disappointment that Daniel himself hadn't delivered the note. I kept making splendid resolutions never to see Daniel again, then was down in the dumps when I didn't. This had to stop.

I tore open the envelope. It contained a few lines scrawled in Daniel's sloping script, obviously written in haste:

> *Sorry that the news is not happier for you: Michael Kelly was indeed loosely connected with the Eastmans for a short while. They claim to have no knowledge of where he is now or what happened to him. However, one of the cadavers found in a gangland back alley certainly bears a resemblance to your photograph. I cannot give you positive proof, as the skull was smashed with great force, but he was of the same height, build, and coloring. Of course he had no identification on him and nobody has come forward to claim the body.*

I fear the news on Katherine is no better. A young woman was pulled from the East River three weeks ago. She also had no identification on her, but was described as fair skinned, light brown hair, blue eyes, about five feet, four inches. She was also pregnant— do you know if this was the case?

It seems likely that Michael was killed and Katherine threw herself into the river in a fit of despair. Both were buried in the potter's field so we have no way of verifying either identity.

It was signed simply, Daniel.

I stood staring at it until Shamey pulled at my jacket. "Aren't we going to play in the square, Molly? You promised to show me how to make my top go fast."

I came out of my reverie. "Yes, of course. We're on our way." I thrust the letter into my pocket and took Bridie's hand as we crossed the street. So the case was closed. I was not looking forward to writing to Katherine's father with this worst of all news.

We reached the park and I demonstrated how to whip a top with great expertise.

"There. Now you do it," I said.

"Let's play tag, Molly," Bridie yelled. "You catch me!"

"Not right now, sweetheart," I said. "Molly doesn't feel like playing at this moment."

I stood watching them run through dead leaves, hearing their whoops of exuberance and started the letter to Major Faversham in my mind. "It is with deep regret that I have to inform you that your daughter appears to have met an untimely end."

It was a pity that I couldn't confirm the awful truth. It would leave the parents never being completely sure. It did seem to be the most logical answer, however. Either Michael had crossed the Eastmans or run afoul of a rival gang and wound up dead in an alleyway. But I couldn't believe that Katherine had drowned herself in despair. That girl in the photograph with the proud stare and determined chin didn't look as if she would give in so easily. She had, after all, dared to leave a life of privilege to run off with a family servant. That took spunk. Being pregnant and alone in a strange city, and in grief for her new husband too, might have driven her over the edge, but I just couldn't see Katherine flinging herself into the East River. If she truly had wound up in there, then somebody else threw her in. Which meant that I should look into this a little further.

Hold your horses, I told myself severely. I had promised myself never again to get involved in a criminal case. I was not the police. I could share my suspicions with Daniel and he could look into it or not as he chose. My work on this case was done. I had located Michael and Katherine and now I all had to do was report the sorry news and collect my fee. It left a bad taste in my mouth, but that was that. On to Lowenstein's in the morning and back to a life of drudgery.

"You're no fun today, Molly," Shamey said, tugging at my skirt.

❧ Twelve ❧

Whereas Mostel and Klein's garment factory had been in a loft, up several flights of narrow stairs, Lowenstein's was in a basement just off Houston Street, at the northern boundary of the Jewish quarter. From the heights to the depths, I thought as I stood outside the building on a cold, damp morning and peered down into a narrow well area. The first chill of winter was in the air and the horse that pulled a wagonload of barrels past me was snorting with a dragon's breath. I felt frozen to the bone and wished I had worn Paddy's lovely long wool cape. But sweatshop girls couldn't afford capes. They wore shirtwaists and skirts and wrapped themselves with whatever might pass as a shawl.

I picked my way down a flight of broken steps and ducked in through a low doorway. I found myself in a long dark room with a low ceiling, lit only by two high windows up at street level, through which some railings and the base of a lamp were visible. The ceiling was strung with pipes and festooned with cobwebs. There were gas mantles hissing away, but they did little to dispel the gloom. The clatter of fifty sewing machines echoed back from the brick walls. I had arrived just after seven and it looked as if everyone here had been working away for hours. Not a good sign. I had thought that Mostel's had crammed in as many machines as possible into that one room, now I saw I was wrong. The girls here were working, crammed so closely to-gether that they could barely move their arms without hitting each other, and there was hardly any space between the tables. It suddenly occurred to me that there might not be a vacancy for me after all, in spite of Mostel's insistence that I'd get a job here with no problem.

I stood in the doorway and looked around for the boss. Not one of the girls looked up from her work to notice me, but a little child—a thin little scrap who couldn't have been more than ten, who was squeezing her way down the table, cutting off threads from finished piles with an enormous pair of scissors—looked up, saw me, and reacted with a start, jogging the elbow of the nearest girl.

The machinist yelled something in Yiddish, and slapped the child around the head. The child started to cry and pointed at me. Heads turned in my direction.

"Hello," I said brightly. "I'm here about a job—whom would I see?"

It turned out I didn't have to ask. At this outburst of noise a man had come out of a room at the far end. "What is it now? Can't I leave you lazy creatures to work for five minutes while I get the books done?" he shouted. He had a heavy European accent but he spoke in English.

"It's a new girl, Mr. Katz," someone at my end of the room said.

The man forced his way toward me. He was younger than Seedy Sam, thin, angular, good looking almost in a depraved sort of way, with heavy-lidded dark eyes, a neat little black beard, and a sort of half smile on full lips. He was wearing a formal black suit and white celluloid collar, although the black suit was now well decorated with pieces of lint and thread.

"So this young lady thinks she can disrupt the work of a whole room, does she?" He stared at me. "And for why should I hire you?"

"The child was startled when she looked up and saw me,

that's all. And I'm here because I'm a good worker and I was told you are about to hire more workers for the busy season."

He was still gazing at me with a hostile sneer. "What accent you speak with? Irish? And for why should I want to hire an Irish girl when most of my workers speak Yiddish?"

"Since we're not allowed to talk when we're working, what difference would it make?" I demanded, looking him straight in the eye. "And if you're not hiring, just say so, and I'll take myself elsewhere." I turned to go.

"Wait," he shouted. "I didn't say we weren't hiring. I can always use a good worker. Where have you worked before?"

I had decided it would be wise not to mention Mostel and Klein. "I'm just arrived from Ireland, sir. I worked for my auntie who ran a dressmaking business. We did everything—bride's dresses, latest fashion, and always in a hurry. I'm used to hard work, sir."

It was hard for me to address this obnoxious fellow as sir, but it obviously worked, because he nodded. "I'll give you a trial. You'll get five dollars a week if you do your quota. You bring your own needles and thread."

I nodded. "I have them with me."

He looked annoyed that he hadn't had a chance to catch me out. "You pay us ten cents a week for the use of power."

Power? I thought. Those pathetic gas brackets counted as power? I certainly couldn't feel any form of heating.

"And five cents for the use of mirror and towel in the wash-room."

It struck me that I had heard that one before. Someone at Mostel's had told me about it. I wondered if it was common practice in the garment sweatshops.

"The rules are simple," he said. "Do your work on time and you get paid what you're due. You don't leave your seat without permission. You don't talk. Obey the rules and you get your full paypacket. Got it?"

"Yes, sir." I looked suitably humble.

"All right. Get to work then. What are you working on, Lanie?"

"Sleeves," a voice from the middle of the room said.

"Start her on sleeves too then. What's your name, girl?"

"Molly, sir."

"Go and sit next to Lanie. She'll show you how we do things around here. And the rest of you, get on with it. Mr. Lowenstein is not going to be happy if he comes in and finds you're behind with this order. If those dresses aren't ready to be shipped by Friday, I'm docking everyone a dollar's pay. Understand me?" For the sake of those who didn't, he repeated the whole thing in Yiddish. I then heard someone passing it along in Italian, then maybe Russian or Polish, with a gasp each time.

I squeezed my way between the rows of girls until I came to a plump girl with a magnificent head of dark hair, coiled around her face. She looked at me with big, sad eyes and a rather vacant expression.

"I'm Lanie," she said. "Pleased to meet you, I'm sure."

I squeezed myself onto the vacant chair beside her. The chair had a broken back and rickety legs. I hadn't been told to remove my shawl and now I was glad to notice that most of the other girls wore theirs too. Some of them wore gloves with the fingers cut out. The atmosphere was decidedly damp and chill. From the depths of the room came the sound of coughing.

"You've worked a machine like this before?" Lanie asked over the noise of the treadles.

Luckily I had. It was identical to the ones at Mostel's. I nodded.

"We're doing sleeves," she said, pointing at the huge stack of dark blue bombazine. "All you have to do is the side seam, then pass them on to Rose. She's setting them in the bodice."

I turned to the girl on my other side. She was petite with red curly hair and she gave me a bright smile. "Another redhead. Now I won't feel so much like a freak."

I smiled back. "We redheads must stick together."

I started sewing. By the time the clock on the wall rolled around to lunch, my fingers were stiff and cold and my back was aching from sitting on the uneven chair with no support. A bell rang and chairs scraped as we got to our feet.

"Did you bring your lunch with you, Molly?" Rose asked as we joined the throng of girls making their way to the exit.

"Not today. I wanted to see what the other girls do."

"As you can see, we all leave," Rose said. "Nobody wants to be down here, breathing this rotten air, for a second longer than necessary. When it's nice we eat our sandwiches in a churchyard—only don't tell my father. He's a rabbi. He'd die of shock to hear that his good Jewish daughter was hanging around a church."

I laughed. "And when it's not nice, like today?"

"Then we go to Samuel's Deli on the corner over there. You can get a bowl of soup with matzoballs or liver dumplings for a nickel. It's good and filling."

We joined the line waiting to be served, then carried bowls of clear soup with what looked like three small dumplings in it to the counter that ran around the wall. It was already lined with girls standing and eating.

"Can you make room for two hungry people, Golda Weiss?" Rose said, shoving another girl in the back.

"There's no room, Rose. We can hardly breathe here."

"Then hold your breath, we're hungry and there's nowhere else to go." Rose elbowed her way in to a few inches of counter, then grinned at me.

"So how do you like it so far?" she asked. "Isn't it fun? Like being on holiday, huh?" She rolled her eyes.

"Beggars can't be choosers," I said.

"Ain't that the truth. I tell you, Molly, if I could find something else to do, I'd be out of here like a shot."

"What else is there for poor girls?" I asked.

"Only walking the streets, which makes more money, so I hear, and I understand it may even be more pleasant."

"Rose Levy—if your father could hear you talking like that!" The girl Rose had elbowed aside spun around to look at Rose in horror. "You ask for trouble, you know. You and your mouth."

"Just joking, Golda. For God's sake we need to joke sometimes, don't we?" Rose rolled her eyes again and looked back at me. "They all take life too seriously. Most of them just try to keep going until their parents make a match for them—hopefully with a guy who can afford for them not to work."

"Their parents make a match for them? They don't choose their own husbands?"

"That's how it's done in the old country."

"So will you marry someone your parents choose for you?" I shuddered as I thought of the great, clodhopping louts that my parents would have chosen for me.

"Not me," Rose said with a look of bravado, "only don't tell my father. I aim to be a lady writer and support myself."

"You do? Then you must—" I had been about to say that she must come and meet my friends in Greenwich Village, before I remembered that nobody must know I wasn't a poor Irish girl just off the boat.

"I must what?" she asked with interest.

"You must keep going until you succeed," I said lamely. "Have you written anything yet?"

"Lots of things, but mostly just for me. But I'm hoping to get a weekly column in the *Forward* someday soon. I'd like to write articles exposing the injustices in this city."

"Like the treatment of girls in sweatshops?"

She looked at me curiously. "You've only been here one morning and already you notice that we're not justly treated?"

"Paying for the company's power and the use of the company's mirror?" I said. "And that cold, damp room. Do they bring heaters in when it gets really cold?"

"They brought in two oil stoves last winter, but what good were two stoves for a room that size? The W.C. froze. That's how cold it was. I tried complaining to Mr. Lowenstein himself, but it didn't do any good. He told me if it was too cold, he'd shut down the place until the weather warmed up again. None of us can afford not to work." She chopped off a big piece of matzoball and chewed it with satisfaction. "I'm the only bread-winner in my family."

"Is your father sick?"

"No, just religious." Again that wicked smile. "I told you, he's a rabbi. In the old country he was well respected. He ran a big shul and we lived well. Here there are too many rabbis and no one earning enough money to make donations."

"So he won't try and get a real job, just until you're settled here?"

"You haven't met my father. God will provide, like Moses in the desert. I tell you, Molly—if I didn't work, we'd all starve and God wouldn't care."

I looked at her with admiration. She was clearly younger than I, probably still not even twenty and yet she had taken the responsibility for her family on her young shoulders.

"I'm just not good at keeping my mouth shut," she went on. "This is the third shop I've worked in. I can't seem to shut up when the foreman is being mean to a girl or they are cheating us again."

I found that I was staring at her in amazement. It was like looking at myself.

"What?" she demanded. "Have I spilled soup down my chin?"

I laughed. "I think you and I are going to get along just famously."

On the way back from lunch, our stomachs satisfied and our bodies warm, I had to remind myself that I must not become too intimate with any of the girls, even Rose. Least of all Rose. Because one of them could be a link in the chain that smuggled designs out of Mostel's and into Lowenstein's and I ultimately would have to expose her.

As we made our way down the slick, crumbling steps and ducked into the workroom the foreman was waiting for us, hands on hips and an indignant expression on his face. "Late again! Won't you girls ever learn?" He pointed at the clock on the wall behind him. It showed twelve thirty-three. "That will cost you ten cents. At this rate you'll end up paying me by the end of the week."

"We can't be late," I blurted out. "I looked at the clock at the deli and we had five whole minutes to cross the street."

I felt Rose dig me in the ribs.

"Late on your first day and argumentative too? Dear me, that's not a good sign, Miss Murphy. I'll have to dock you twenty cents so that you learn to keep your trap shut. Now get to your machines, all of you!"

As Rose and I made our way down the line of machines she whispered to me, "I should have warned you—if you oppose him, he fines you, so it's not worth it."

"But I'm sure we weren't late. How can we have taken eight minutes to cross one street?"

"We weren't late. He puts the hands forward on the clock. He does it all the time. And he turns the hands back when we aren't looking so that we work later at night."

"Jesus, Mary, and Joseph. That's disgusting. Does the owner know?"

"Oh, I'm sure the owner knows all about it," Rose said. "He turns a blind eye, if he didn't order it in the first place."

"It's terrible. We should do something. They can't treat us like that. It's just not fair."

Rose smiled and shook her head. "You're new," she said. "You'll learn that a lot of things aren't fair." She leaned closer to me. "Oh, and another word of warning—don't let Katz get you into the backroom alone. He'll claim there is something wrong with your work, or pretend he needs to give you a talking-to. All he wants to do is to force himself on you. He's tried it with a lot of girls."

"I still hear talking!" Katz's voice shouted. "Someone want no pay this week?"

We got down to work. I watched the clock carefully all evening to make sure that Mr. Katz didn't try to move the hands backward. I was dying to catch him at it. But he didn't go near it.

It was raining and a cold wind was blowing as we staggered up into the fresh air at seven o'clock.

"I'll see you bright and early then," Rose said. "He likes us in our seats at six thirty, although our day officially starts at seven."

"If that was one day, I don't know how I'll manage a whole week," I said. "My back is so stiff from that broken chair. I pointed it out to Katz and he told me I could bring my own if I wanted."

Rose waited for a group of girls to go past, then pulled me closer to her, under an awning out of the rain. "If you really want to help change things, some of us are trying to get a union going. There's a meeting on Wednesday night."

I had promised myself I wouldn't get involved. I shook my head. "I'd really like to, but . . ."

She nodded. "I understand. It's a big risk. If someone snitches on us and the bosses find out, nobody would hire us again, but I'm willing to take the risk. I'm educated. I can think for myself. If someone doesn't speak out for these girls, nothing will ever change."

"You're very brave."

She laughed. "Maybe I'm just stupid. Me and my big mouth, huh? But I feel it's up to me—most of these girls are peasants, they can't even read and write. They don't speak English well, and their families are desperate for money. So they shut up and put up with all of this. We won't get nothing unless we unionize. My brother was with the Bund in Poland."

"The Bund?"

"It's a radical socialist group, working to change the old or-der—justice, freedom, equality for all people. Many Jewish boys were involved, even though it meant possible prison or even death. My brother had to keep his work secret from my father—my father would never have approved."

"What does your brother do now?"

"He lies in an unmarked grave. He was executed when one of their group betrayed them to the secret police."

I touched her arm. "I'm so sorry. So many tragedies in the world."

"That's why I'm doing this work with the union. Someone has to make sure my Motl didn't die for nothing. Someone has to make sure this country is better than the last one." She draped her shawl over her head. "Think about it and let me know if you change your mind. You'd be a real help, because you speak good English."

"So do you."

"*Ya*, but I sound like a foreigner—a newnik. Nobody's going to take me seriously. The union loves English-speaking girls. There was this English girl who came a few times. You should have heard her talk—*oy*, but she talked real pretty. Just like the queen of England. 'We're going to make these petty tyrants sit up and listen to us,' she said." Rose did a fair imitation of upper-class English speech. Then she laughed. "Real hoity-toity, she was. I got a kick out of her."

"She's not there anymore?"

Rose shook her head. "Nah. She only came for a few weeks, then she didn't show up no more. I expect she'd found something better—a girl like her from good family. I don't know what she was doing working in no lousy sweatshop to start with."

I was getting a chill up my spine and it wasn't from the drips that were falling on us from the awning.

"What was her name?" I asked.

"Kathy," Rose said. "I remember it because none of us from Europe can say that 'th' sound proper. We called her Katti and she kept correcting us."

"And when did she stop showing up?"

Rose put her hand to her mouth, thinking. "Must have been about three, four weeks ago."

"I've changed my mind," I said. "I think I will come to this union meeting with you after all."

❧ Thirteen ❧

There were lots of girls called Kathy in the world, I told myself. I shouldn't read too much into this—but it did sound a lot like her. I would try to ask for a description, without seeming too interested, of course. And at the union meeting maybe I'd find out more. In the meantime I had to remind myself that I was being paid to discover a spy. Sometime in the next few weeks, someone was going to deliver stolen designs to Lowenstein's.

By the time Wednesday night rolled around, I was more than ready to attend the union meeting, and not just because I wanted to find out if the English girl called Kathy was the Katherine I was seeking. As I watched injustice after injustice going on at Lowenstein's, I realized that I couldn't just sit quietly and do nothing. I had promised myself that I wouldn't get involved, but I wasn't very good at following my own advice. Someone had to do something and that someone was me.

If Mostel's had been purgatory, then Lowenstein's was hell itself. The dark, dank cold went right through clothing and bones to the very soul. To sit hunched over machines, eyes straining in the gloom, fingers numb and chilblained, with the constant sound of coughing over the clatter of the treadles was enough to break even the bravest of spirits, and these girls had been through so much before that their spirits were already broken.

On Friday evening the bully Katz wound back the clock hands twenty minutes so that we'd stay to finish the workload and he wouldn't have to pay us overtime. I saw him. So did several other girls, but nobody said a word. I also watched him smirk to himself as he passed by to his office. I sat there fuming, longing for a chance to get even with him. I'd help get these girls unionized if it was the last thing I did!

The bell rang to signal seven o'clock, which was really seven twenty. Tired girls stood up, stretched cramped limbs, stamped cold feet, snatched up belongings, and got out of there as fast as they could. As I followed Rose to the door, a hand grabbed my arm. "Not you, Murphy. I want a word with you."

I looked around to find Katz smirking at me.

"What have I done?"

"These sleeves," he said. "Call yourself a seamstress, do you? I don't know what the standard of work is like in Ireland, but it must be pretty bad."

"There's nothing wrong with my sleeves," I said angrily. "I stitched a nice straight seam and I finished my quota."

"Not what I've been seeing," he said. He turned and disappeared through the door into the back room. "Call this a nice straight seam?" He held up a sleeve and waved it at me.

I stomped into the back room after him. "Let me see that. I'll tell you if it was my work or not."

I snatched the sleeve from him. "Why, this isn't even my sleeve. I don't start my work that way, and look, the threads aren't even cut. Little Becky cut every one of my threads today."

I looked up and he was still smirking. I realized then that I had been tricked. The sounds in the workroom were dying away.

"I like 'em feisty," he said, coming toward me. "A good fight makes the conquest all the sweeter, and you look like a lusty girl who enjoys it, am I right?"

I was so frozen in horror that I didn't react quickly enough.

He pushed me against the cold wet brick wall and pinned me with his body, his knee thrust between my legs. As I opened my mouth to scream, he forced his mouth onto mine, his tongue into my mouth, his hands groping at my body.

I didn't know what to do. I hadn't believed he could be so strong. I tried to shake myself free from him, but he held me pinned like a butterfly to a board. Revulsion flooded over me as I felt him getting excited and impatient but I fought to remain calm. If he wanted to take this amorous attack one stage further, he'd have to move to lift my skirt and then I'd go for him where it hurt. I was finding it hard to breathe. Then I felt him trying to shift me along the wall to where bolts of cloth lay piled on the floor. If he got me that far, he could throw himself on top of me. I wasn't going to let that happen. I managed to get my hands up to his face. I couldn't reach his eyes, but I grabbed his long, curling hair, and I yanked as hard as I could.

He reacted just enough for me to break free of his mouth.

"Let go of me or you'll be sorry!" I gasped. "I killed the last man who tried to rape me."

"I don't kill so easy," he said, laughing. "Like I said—the harder the struggle, the sweeter the conquest."

"Molly? I've been waiting for you. Are you ready yet?" Rose's voice echoed behind us, unnaturally loud.

Katz spun around. "What the hell are you doing here?"

"Keeping an eye on Molly and making sure she gets home safe and sound," Rose said calmly. She walked over to me, linked her arm through mine, and dragged me away. "Let's go home now, Molly," she said. Then she walked with me calmly out of that door and down the long, empty workroom.

"Thank you," I stammered. "If you hadn't come back for me, I don't know what might have happened."

"I hung around," she said. "I thought he might try it. I've noticed him looking at you. He tries it with all the pretty new girls."

"He's disgusting," I said, wiping my mouth with my hand and

fighting back a desire to vomit. "The owner should be told. He shouldn't be allowed to get away with it."

"Mr. Lowenstein doesn't care about anything except quick profits," Rose said. "How often do you think he even shows up here? Hardly ever. And Katz gets the work done on time for him. That's all he cares about."

"I'm putting a knife in my skirt pocket in the future," I said, "in case he tries it again."

"He won't," Rose said. "He'll go on to someone who's easier. That's one thing you can count on around here—a never ending supply of girls."

"Not when we get the union going," I said.

Rose chuckled. "Another redhead just like me. We're all born fighters, Molly. I'm so glad you came here. We'll show 'em; won't we?"

"We'll set the dogs on Mr. Katz!"

We linked arms and left the building smiling.

On Monday morning an old gentleman with a neat white beard came into our workroom. He wore a long black coat and top hat and he carried a silver-tipped cane. The effect was rather like an elderly wizard.

"*Guten Morgen,*" he said in German. "Everyone working hard. That's good. Where is Katz?"

Katz came flying out of the back room at the sound of the voice.

"Mr. Lowenstein—such a privilege that you should visit us," he said, groveling. "Everything is going well, sir. The order will go out today like you wanted."

"*Gut. Gut.*" Lowenstein rubbed his hands together. "And think about taking on some more girls. Busy season coming up. I should have the new designs in the next week or so and then it's full speed ahead, *ja?* A bonus for everybody if we get the first batch of new dresses in the stores two weeks before Christmas."

He rubbed his hands together again. "It's cold in here, Katz. How can these girls do their best work if it's cold? Get the oil stoves out, man."

"Papa, are you coming?" A slim, dark-haired beauty made her way gingerly down the outside steps and poked her head through the door. She was wearing a fur-trimmed bonnet and a big blue cape, also trimmed with white fur. The cape was open and she wore a black velvet ribbon around her throat on which hung a silver locket, sparkling with precious stones. She posed in the doorway, conscious that all those eyes were on her.

"It's too cold waiting out in the carriage," she said. "Hurry up, please or we'll be late for our lunch appointment."

"Coming, my dearest." Mr. Lowenstein looked up at her and smiled. "Sorry I can't stay longer. Keep working, everyone. Good-bye."

He waved and joined his daughter.

"How about some of us help you carry the oil stoves, Mr. Katz?" Rose asked, not wanting him to be able to wriggle out of it while the boss was in earshot. "Come on, Molly and Golda and Lanie. Let's help him."

"Very well. Come on, then." He stomped into the back room and finally unearthed two oil stoves from a storage closet. We picked up one between two of us and carried them out.

"So that was the boss?" I whispered to Rose as we staggered out with the stove.

She nodded. "He might look like a nice old gentleman, but he's hard as nails. When Gussie died of consumption right before he gave out the Christmas bonus last year, he wouldn't even send the bonus to her family. And how do you think she got sick in the first place? Sitting in this damp hole, that's how."

"And that was the boss's daughter, I take it?"

She made a face. "Letitia, her name is. Only child. Spoiled rotten."

We set down the stoves and waited for Katz to come with the can of kerosene. I couldn't get the picture of the boss's daughter out of my mind. There had been something disturbing about her, something that made me uneasy. I thought some more, but couldn't put my finger on it.

"Be happy that the boss has such a kind heart," Katz announced as he poured in kerosene and got the stoves going. There was no room for them between the rows of girls so one stood at the doorway to the street and one at the doorway to Katz's back room. Most of the girls felt no effect at all.

I was looking forward to the union meeting on Wednesday. I had written a list of grievances that I couldn't wait to share with union organizers. Maybe with two of us, Rose and myself, we could light a fire under those girls at Lowenstein's and get them to speak up for themselves.

Rose and I had a bowl of soup together at Samuel's and then we made our way to Essex Street where we went down the steps into another basement. This one was quite different— brightly lit, warm, and filled with benches, most of them already occupied.

"Here's Rose, at last," one of the young women called as we stood hesitantly in the doorway. "I thought things had been too quiet until now."

"Yes, and look what I've brought with me," Rose said, dragging me inside. "A new warrior for our struggle. This is Miss Molly Murphy, come from Ireland."

"Welcome, Molly. Sit yourself down." A place in the back row was indicated for me. I sat and looked around the group. I was interested to see an equal number of men and women in the group—serious young men in worker's garb, with dark beards and dark eyes. There were plenty of young women like ourselves, dressed humbly in shirtwaists and skirts with shawls around their shoulders, but one or two stood out, the cut and fabric of their dress announcing them to be not of the working class. What were they doing here?

Three men and two women sat at a table in front of us. The women were better dressed than the rest of us and one of them looked familiar. I stared, trying to place her. Had I seen her picture in a newspaper? She had dark and rather angular features, a long thin nose, and hair swept severely back from her face. She wore a black fitted coat, trimmed with astrakhan, and a neat little black velvet bonnet sat on the table beside her, decorated with a stunning black ostrich plume. Obviously not one of us, then.

"Right then, let's get started." A young man banged a gavel on the table. "For those of you who don't know, I'm Jacob Singer of the United Hebrew Trades, and we're here to help you form a ladies garment workers union." He spoke with the slightest trace of a foreign accent. He was slim with a neatly trimmed beard and expressive dark eyes, framed with round wire-rimmed spectacles which gave him a boyish, owlish look.

A slim girl in black rose from my left. "We've had such a union for a year now, Mr. Singer."

"Yes, I know that, Miss Horowitz, but it has only existed on paper, hasn't it? It hasn't sprung into action yet." Jacob Singer smiled. His face had been so grave and earnest before that it came as a shock to see his eyes twinkling. It quite changed his appearance.

"No, but it will." The girl thrust out her chin defiantly.

"I don't doubt it, but first it needs members. How many members are on your books so far?"

"Twenty-five." The girl's voice was little more than a whisper. There were some titters from around the room.

"So it would appear, ladies, that our first task is to grow your membership," Jacob said.

"How do we do that?" Rose got to her feet. "How can we persuade girls to join us when they fear for their jobs? Where I work, at Lowenstein's, we are treated worse than animals. We have no rights. There are constant abuses. But if a girl speaks up, she is dismissed. So all remain silent and the abuse goes on."

Jacob nodded his head gravely. So did the others at the top table. "We can do nothing without solidarity," another man at the top table said. He looked more like a student, with straggly beard and Russian worker's cap on his head. "I represent the cloak-makers union, and we have had some small successes with strikes in the past. But only if we get one hundred percent participation. All for one, one for all. We cannot hurt them until we are united. If there is to be a walkout, then all must walk out."

"If we walk out, then they just hire new girls," Rose said.

"If the walkout is only at one shop," the straggly young man agreed. "If all shops walk out at the same time, then they have a problem."

"It will never happen," a voice behind me said.

"We have to let them see that it can happen," the slender young woman at the top table said. "Maybe there will have to be some sacrifices, but we must let the owners see that we are prepared to strike and lose our jobs if we want progress."

"Begging your pardon, miss." A girl with a luxuriant coil of hair, wound around her head like a halo, rose to her feet. "But you keep on saying 'we' and 'us.' It won't be you who loses your job. You have a nice house uptown to go home to after these meetings. I know you mean well, but you can't know what it's like to live in a stinking tenement and never have enough to eat."

The girl at the top table flushed, then nodded gravely. "You're right. I can't know exactly what it's like for you, but I do have some experience with confronting the enemy when it comes to the suffrage movement. I have been to jail twice, and believe me, I was not treated like a lady there. There are many of us, all of good families, willing to go to jail, to make nuisances of ourselves, if we can obtain the right to vote for our sisters."

There was scattered applause from the audience. The young woman from uptown bowed her head again. "But I admit that I know I will have a home to go to and food on the table when I am let out of jail. I know you will be asked to make enormous sacrifices, but somebody has to, or nothing will ever improve.

Every generation of immigrants who steps off the boat will go into conditions like the ones you are enduring right now."

"So what can we do?" Rose asked.

"You must recruit members where you work," Jacob said. "Plant seeds in the minds of your fellow workers that you can change things, that you can make your employers fear you. I know that for many of you the busy season is approaching—the rush to get items into the stores for the holiday shopping and then the new spring lines after the January sales. This is when the shops make their biggest profit. If you walk out now, you will cost them valuable time while they find and train replacements. Maybe they are not so willing to lose that time. Maybe they are willing to negotiate."

Rose looked at me, her eyes shining. "It might just work, Molly. If we walked out the moment Lowenstein wanted us to start on the new designs, maybe he would listen."

"It's worth a try," I said.

Rose got to her feet. "We are willing to try. Mr. Lowenstein prides himself on getting his garments into the store first. Maybe this will be a way for us to make him listen."

"Good for you, Rose," the dark girl at the table said. "Do you have someone to work with you?"

"I have Molly," Rose said. "She has just arrived from Ireland. Stand up, Molly, and let them see you."

I rose to my feet.

"Two redheads, *oy vay*," someone near me said. "I pity poor Mr. Lowenstein."

There was good-natured laughter.

The meeting progressed. It was decided that Lowenstein's should be a test case. We would try to bring all of the girls into the union so that we could conduct an effective walkout the moment the new designs were produced. I knew better than any of them that this might work. Lowenstein counted on getting his stolen designs into the stores before Mostel had his ready. If he couldn't corner the market first, then he would lose. A good bargaining tool indeed.

When the meeting concluded, refreshments were served—cookies and hot tea and a big plate of sandwiches. The girls fell upon them with gusto. I took a cup of tea, then joined a group of girls.

"So you're from Ireland, are you, Molly?"

I agreed that I was. "And I understand that there was another Irish girl here not too long ago? Didn't you say so, Rose? By the name of Kathy?"

"Kathy? But surely she was English," one of the girls said.

"I thought someone said she was from an upper-class English family, only she lived in Ireland."

"I don't think she ever said where she was from, did she?" The girls looked at each other.

"No, very tight-lipped about herself, she was. But outspoken when it came to union matters. You should have heard her talk. My, but she could have talked the hind leg off a donkey."

"Remember you told her that, Fanny? And she laughed and said something about being good at blarney, whatever that means."

"Too bad she stopped coming to meetings."

"So where did she go?" I asked. "Did she move away?"

The girls looked at each other and shrugged.

"I don't know what happened to her," one said.

"Which company did she work for?"

Again the girls shrugged. "She only came a few times, then she stopped. Too bad because I'd have loved to hear her tell those bosses what she thought of them. Real haughty she was, and kind of looked down her nose when she spoke to you."

"Did she have light brown, sort of wispy hair and very light eyes?" I asked.

"Yes, did you know her?"

"I thought she might have been a friend from back home," I said.

"So you just arrived from Ireland, did you?"

"That's right." As I said it, I found myself looking at the upper-crust young lady from the top table. She was standing with a sandwich in her hand, staring hard at me. Then she put down the plate and came straight toward me. "Now I know where I saw you before," she said coldly. "What exactly are you doing here?"

✦ Fourteen ✦

hat do you mean?" I asked.

"You're not one of us," she said. "So what are you doing here? Spying for the bosses, perchance?"

"Of course not," I said angrily. "What on earth makes you say something like that? I'm from Lowenstein's, with Rose. Ask her."

Then suddenly I remembered where I had seen her before. She had worn her hair differently, and the light had been dim, but I had once sat across a table from her in a Greenwich Village café, at a meeting of anarchists that had almost cost me my life.

"And I could ask you the same question," I said to her. "The last time I saw you, you were plotting to bring down the government at an anarchists' meeting with Miss Emma Goldman."

"Not I. I am a socialist, not an anarchist, Miss Murphy. I was there to support Emma Goldman because she represents change—empowerment of the masses, birth control. Anything that can improve the condition of women—that is my personal quest."

"Then you and I have no quarrel," I said. "You know my name, but I don't know yours."

"It's Nell," she said. "Nell Blankenship."

I held out my hand. "We are on the same side, Miss Blankenship, both working to right injustices."

She took my hand reluctantly, but still looked at me quizzically. "And is your name really Molly Murphy, fresh off the boat from Ireland?"

I decided to take a gamble.

"If I could have a private word, then some things would become clear."

"Very well." She moved away from the crowd around the food table to the far corner of the room.

"You are right that I am not really a garment worker," I said in a low voice, even though the other occupants of the room paid no attention to us. "I am actually a private investigator."

"An investigator—is that not the same as a spy?" she asked, still frowning at me. "Were you not spying at Emma's meeting? You clearly were not in sympathy with our cause."

"I came to your meeting with Ryan O'Hare," I said. "He insisted that I meet Emma Goldman."

"And that was your only reason for being there?"

"No, not my only reason," I said. "When you met me before I was on the trail of the man who killed my employer. I caught up with him, only too late."

She looked at me quizzically again. "A lady detective," she said. "I didn't realize that such things existed. The only question is for whom are you working this time? The sweatshop owners, so that all this will be reported back to them?"

"Of course not," I said angrily.

"Then why throw yourself into a cause that is clearly not your own?"

"I could ask you the same thing," I said, staring her down. "You are not a garment worker either. Why waste your time on the lower classes when you could be dining at Delmonico's?"

"Precisely because I have the luxury of time," she said. "These girls are ill equipped to speak for themselves. If I can make their lot better, I shall have accomplished something worthwhile. This and getting the vote for my sisters—these have become my life's work."

"Then I commend you, Miss Blankenship," I said.

"And I hope I can equally commend you, Miss Murphy." She still didn't smile.

At that moment a shadow fell between us. Jacob Singer, the young man in the wire-rimmed spectacles, approached with a plate of cookies. "Are you bullying our newest recruit, Nell?" he said, giving me a friendly smile. "I am Jacob Singer and we have not been introduced yet."

"How do you do, I'm Molly Murphy," I said.

"I am pleased to make your acquaintance, Miss Murphy." He clicked his heels and gave a little bow in a charmingly foreign fashion. "I hope Nell was not putting you through a grilling? She can become a little too passionate about her causes, I'm afraid." He chuckled. Nell didn't return his smile.

"Just sounding her out, Jacob," Nell said. "Just trying to find out whose side she is on, because she is not a garment worker fresh from Ireland. She is a lady detective—so beware what you say."

"A detective?" he looked at me with concern. "Not a garment worker then?"

I looked around to see who was within hearing distance. "I took on a job that necessitated my posing as a sweatshop girl. While working under such conditions, I decided I could not sit idly by. That's one of the reasons I'm here tonight. I want to help."

"Excellent," Jacob said. "Just the sort of recruit we need, wouldn't you say, Nell?"

Nell looked at him, then at me. "Perhaps I owe you an apology, Miss Murphy."

"But I'm also here for another reason." I looked around again, then moved closer to them. "The English girl called Kathy you heard me asking about earlier. I have been asked to trace such a girl by her family in Ireland. This Kathy sounds very much like the Katherine I was asked to find."

"I don't think anyone knows where she is now," Nell said.

"She came to meetings for several weeks and seemed fired up with enthusiasm. We were hopeful that she would be a real force for change because she was so articulate and unafraid to speak her mind. Then one week she didn't come."

"I'm afraid I might know where she is now," I said. "A body, resembling her description, was pulled from the East River."

"Oh no. A victim of foul play?" she asked.

"The police are of the opinion that this girl took her own life."

Nell shook her head. "Then it is not the same person. Kathy would not have given in to despair any more than you or I would have done."

"My feelings exactly," I said. "I never met her, but the face in the photograph I have is not of a weak character."

"You have a photograph? Then I can verify that it is the same person."

"I don't have it with me," I said. "And I don't know if there is any point in taking this matter any further. If she is dead, then I can't bring her back to life again."

"But if she is dead, then someone is responsible and should be brought to justice," Nell said.

It was strange to hear my own sentiments echoed back to me. "I agree. But I am not the police. I have so little to go on and no way of investigating further."

"You could be of help, Nell," Jacob said. He turned to me. "Nell is a reporter by profession. She writes articles for the major newspapers to expose the corruption and abuse in this city. She has made some useful contacts in many strata of this city. And this is just the sort of challenge you enjoy, is it not, Nell?"

I sensed that Nell was not really inclined to put herself out on my behalf, that she still had not warmed to me, but that she didn't want to turn me down in front of Jacob. "I suppose I might be of some help, it is true," she said.

"Splendid." Jacob smiled at me again. "Then why don't we

continue this conversation at another time? Where do you live, Miss Murphy?"

"Patchin Place."

Finally Nell looked interested. "Patchin Place. How extraordinary. I have friends there. Do you know two delightful women called—"

"Sid and Gus?" I asked. "I lived with them until a week ago. Now I have taken up residence across the street."

"What an amazing coincidence. I should most like to renew their acquaintance," she said. "Tomorrow then?"

I shook my head. "You forget. I am employed in a sweatshop from dawn until night and have little energy for good conversation afterward. How about Saturday night? I don't have to rise early on Sunday morning."

"Saturday it is then."

"Am I to be included in the invitation?" Jacob asked. "Perhaps I may also be of use in your inquiry."

"Of course you are most welcome, Mr. Singer."

He bowed again. "I shall look forward to it then."

"Miss Blankenship? Could you come over here for moment? Bella has a question for you." One of the girls approached Nell hesitantly.

"Of course," Nell said. "Excuse me."

I was left alone with Jacob Singer. "Have you had a cup of tea, Miss Murphy? Or one of these cookies?" He held out the tray to me. I took one.

"I've never been known to turn down a cookie," I said. "Or a biscuit as we say in Ireland, where they were luxuries reserved for special occasions."

"One of the best things about America, wouldn't you say? We didn't even have such luxuries at home in Russia. Sugar was kept hidden away in a little wooden box for special occasions."

His eyes, ringed by those wire spectacles, lit up with amusement. Such a pleasant face. Quite a handsome face too.

145

"I am very glad that you'll be joining us," he said. "As you can see, we need all the help we can get."

"Are you involved in the garment industry yourself, Mr. Singer?" I asked.

"He is involved in no particular industry," Nell said, coming back to join us and slipping an arm through his. "He is a professional rabble-rouser."

Jacob Singer laughed. "I am employed by the United Hebrew Trades to help fledgling unions get off the ground. I was active in the Bund before I left Russia, so I have experience in civil disobedience to share. But you must excuse me, you probably have not even heard of the Bund."

"Oh but I have," I said. "Rose's brother was a member. He was executed."

Jacob nodded. "An all too common fate, I'm afraid. That or Siberia, which was often a death sentence in itself. I had to flee for my life when they came for us. I escaped by swimming across an ice-filled river. Not a pleasant experience, I can assure you."

"How terrible. I've heard so many tragic stories."

"But your country is no stranger to tragedy either," Jacob said. "How many of your countrymen died in the great famine?"

"That's true enough. Everyone in our village had a story of lost relatives, including my own family. Apart from my father and my brothers I don't think I've a living relative in the world."

"Then we are united in a struggle to make things better, are we not?" He smiled at me. His eyes held mine. I flushed and looked away.

"Jacob is a photographer, as well as being a rabble-rouser," Nell said. "He and I work together. I fish out the facts, he takes the pictures. Together we have been into the most disreputable parts of the city."

"Then I am indeed fortunate to have met both of you," I said. "I can't tell you how much it riles me to have to abandon my search for Katherine."

"Let us hope you will not have to abandon it," Jacob said. "If

Nell recognizes your photograph, then we can start to trace what happened to this unfortunate Katherine. All will be made clear on Saturday."

"And in the meantime," I said in a low voice, "please don't give away that I am not just an ordinary sweatshop girl. I am with them heart and soul in this struggle and I fear they would not trust me if they knew I was not really one of them."

"You can count on us to say nothing," Jacob said and glanced across at Nell for agreement. Her face remained impassive.

"At what time do you expect us on Saturday?" she asked.

"Shall we say eight? We are supposed to leave work at six on Saturday, as a special gesture of beneficence."

Jacob laughed. "She has the Irish gift of the gab, does she not? I am so glad that your investigation brought our paths to cross, Miss Murphy."

"Eight o'clock on Saturday then," Nell said. "That will work out splendidly. We'll have time to go to the opening of that art exhibition first, Jacob. Are we done here, do you think? I am suddenly tired and would like you to walk me home." She had her arm through his and she steered him away from me, toward the door.

They must be sweethearts, I thought, and was surprised at the rush of disappointment that I felt.

"I wondered where you'd got to, Molly. Have you tried these little cakes yet?" Rose took my arm and dragged me back to the group at the table.

❧ Fifteen ❧

On Saturday Sid and Gus insisted on preparing a feast at their house.

"But it's so long since we've seen Nell," Gus said, when I tried to protest, "and we've been dying to meet this Jacob Singer, so you can't be selfish and keep them to yourself."

"All right, if you insist," I said, "but you have already done so much for me. Let me at least provide the food."

"Nonsense. You know how we love trying new recipes," Sid said. "And we have just been reading a book about a woman who traveled alone through North Africa, disguised as a male Bedouin. Doesn't that sound like a simply marvelous thing to do? We were all set to try it when we finished the book, but then we decided we really couldn't abandon dear old New York and Patchin Place. So we've settled for the food. We shall cook couscous and kebabs—although I don't think we can procure camel's hump."

I laughed. "Camel's hump. Now I've heard everything."

"It is considered a great delicacy among the Bedouin," Sid said, attempting not to smile. "But you may bring the wine and the grapes, if you insist."

So when I was finally released from work at six thirty-five on Saturday I wandered among the Italian food shops south of Washington Square and chose a jug of robust red wine, enclosed in a neat raffia basket. I felt very worldly carrying it home. If they could see me now in Ballykillin, I thought with a smile of satisfaction. When I arrived at 9 Patchin Place I found that Sid and Gus had been up to their old tricks—they had transformed their parlor into an Eastern boudoir, with the walls draped in velvet and gauze and the floor strewn with Oriental carpets and large pillows. They had even produced an Oriental water pipe which they insisted we should smoke later.

Nell and Jacob arrived at eight and we had a messy meal, eating with our hands, while perched on cushions.

"Now I know why they always have dogs around in such scenes," Nell exclaimed, wiping a sticky chin with her napkin. "It is to clean up the food that falls around them. I feel revoltingly primitive."

"But remarkably free, wouldn't you say?" Sid asked.

I glanced at Jacob and found that he was watching me. We exchanged a smile.

I looked at the plates, still piled high with food. I ate another grape and felt instantly guilty.

"Doesn't it worry you sometimes that we can go home to eat like this while those girls at the sweatshops probably go to bed hungry each night?" I looked across at Nell and Jacob.

"I can't let it worry me," Nell said. "I do what I can to improve the lot of women. If I didn't get enough to eat, I wouldn't have the energy to accomplish what I do. And I see no sense in pretending to be poor."

"And I only eat such meals as this when decadent friends invite me, Miss Murphy," Jacob said. "Then I return to starve in my garret."

"Only because you choose not to make money from your photographs," Nell said, slapping his hand and laughing. "You know very well that you could be rich and famous and dine at all the best houses in town if you chose. You are a brilliant photographer. You just choose to photograph slums and strikes."

"You're right. We Russians don't know how to live without

suffering," Jacob said, also smiling, and again his gaze strayed across to me. "Miss Murphy understands. She comes from Ireland where suffering is also the way of life."

"Not exactly," I said. "We are under the yolk of the English and live in squalor, but we still like to enjoy life. As long as we've music and a good swig of liquor, then we're happy."

"Is that all it takes to make you happy?" he asked. "Music and a good swig of liquor."

"I didn't say me," I said, blushing at his teasing gaze now. "But we like good friends and good company too, and I'll say amen to that."

"When are you going to show us your photographs, Jacob?" Gus asked. "I've been dying to see inside a photographer's studio."

"You must come tomorrow then," he said. "All of you. I shall be honored."

"What fun. We accept," Sid said. "Now, shall we try the hubble-bubble?" She indicated the water pipe.

"We have to work while our brains are still clear," Nell said. "It was the reason we came, after all."

I opened my purse and took out the photos.

"This is the Katherine I was looking for," I said.

Nell studied it. Jacob came to look over her shoulder. They looked at each other and nodded. "It is the same girl," Nell said.

I produced the picture of Katherine with Michael at her stirrup. "And this is the man she ran off with. His name is Michael Kelly. I have learned that he was involved with the Eastmans gang. But he too disappeared and the police think he might have been one of the unnamed men who have been killed in recent gang wars."

"All too probable," Nell said. "They lead violent lives. What else do you know?"

"Very little. I traced them to a boardinghouse on Division Street. They left that address without paying their rent about the same time that they disappeared."

Sid came to join us. "If this Katherine is dead, as Molly has told us, then why are you still searching? Shouldn't she just write to the parents and tell them the sad truth then forget the matter?"

"Nell and I believe, as Molly does, that Katherine would not have taken her own life," Jacob said, glancing across at Nell for confirmation.

She nodded. "I only met her on a few occasions but I came to admire her. She had zest and fire. She was not going to let her current circumstances browbeat her."

"Then I think we owe it to her to find out how she met her end," Jacob said, "and who better to find out the truth than you, Nell? You know every back alley of this city."

Gus put a hand on my shoulder. "Oh dear, Molly. You should never have met these people. Now you've found someone to encourage your wild schemes."

"I don't know that I agree with this one," I said. "I can't see how we can find out more than we know right now. The young woman pulled from the river is already buried in a pauper's grave. And it would be impossible to find out if she went into the river willingly or was pushed."

"Not impossible," Jacob said, leaning closer. "If we know where the body was fished from the river and about how long it had been in the water, then we should be able to guess where she was thrown in. And if she was thrown in, then someone might have seen it happen."

I looked at him with admiration. "And I thought I was supposed to be the investigator. You are far more suited to it than I, Mr. Singer."

"Why so formal?" Gus said. "This is Greenwich Village. In this house we are on a first-name basis—no need for the restrictions of polite society. So it is Molly and Jacob and Nell. Is that clear?"

Jacob glanced across at me and smiled again. "If you permit then, Molly?"

"I shall be charmed, Jacob. And you too, Nell?" I included

her hastily, just in case she thought I had any designs on her young man.

"Absolutely. I have never been one for the conventions of polite society, which is why I have been such a trial to my parents. Twenty-eight years old and still unmarried. What is more, I told them that I see marriage as a legal method of condemning women to a life of subservience. But don't let me start on that topic—let us get back to our foul play, which is more interesting than my lack of nuptial bliss. How do you propose we tackle this, Molly?"

"I can ask the police if any records were taken of where the body was fished from the water and what kind of state it was in. I suppose they recorded what she was wearing, although if she wore any jewelry which might identify her, it will be in some policeman's pocket by now."

Nell laughed. "I can tell you have had experience with our delightful police force since your arrival here."

"Including three different occasions in jail," I said. "But I do have a—" I was about to say friend. I corrected myself "—a person I can contact who is a police captain."

"Splendid," Nell said. "So you will find what details the police have on this woman. I will attempt to find out everything I can on Katherine's life here—where she worked, whether she had a confrontation with her boss there . . ."

I caught her gaze. "You don't think—" I began "—she might have made a nuisance of herself at the sweatshop?"

"Some of the sweatshop owners are in cahoots with the gangs," Jacob said. "In the past when there have been walkout attempts, the shop owners have hired starkes—strong-arm men—to intimidate the strikers. If they had an employee who was likely to create too much trouble, the simplest thing would be to pay a gang to get rid of her."

"Holy Mother of God." I put my hand to my throat. "That had never even crossed my mind. Are they that ruthless, do you think?"

"Definitely," Jacob said. "Profit means everything. Anyone who stands in the way of profit must be eliminated."

"In that case, finding out what happened to Katherine is all part of the same fight," I said. I didn't add that I was now taking over Katherine's role. I might soon be seen as a nuisance who should be eliminated.

Jacob looked from Nell to me. "Now that I think about it and have heard the circumstances of her disappearance, my advice to you is to let this lie," he said quietly. "I have seen much tragedy in my life. You can't bring this Katherine back to life. Do not risk your own lives for something that can't be undone."

"Who's talking about risking lives?" Nell demanded. "A few carefully phrased questions in the right quarter, that's all we're talking about. My first task will be to find out where she worked, and then to ask some discreet questions about that particular shop owner and his foremen."

"You will never be able to prove anything," Jacob said. "And the deeper you delve, the greater the risk you take."

Nell patted his arm. "You are such a fussbudget, Jacob. Molly and I are intelligent, sensible women."

"I worry because I have met too many people who do not play by the rules," he said.

"Enough of such gloomy talk. Not allowed in this house," Sid said firmly. "I shall now produce the hubble-bubble and we will transport ourselves into a Bedouin black tent. And since you are the only male here, Jacob, you may be the sheik!"

We concentrated our energy on the water pipe with hilarious results, and the next morning, after our Sunday ritual of coffee and pastries at Fleishman's Vienna Bakery on Broadway, we headed for the Lower East Side. I realized that I had become accustomed to it, as Sid and Gus pointed out sights that they found strange and exotic. "Flavors of the Levantine, Gus dear. Does this not make you want to travel there after all? We could take in the Holy Land and Egypt and then on to Morocco and the Bedouins."

"Think of the dirt, though," Gus said, picking up her skirts to avoid the rotting fruit, horse manure, and other debris that cluttered the street. "The smell of this is bad enough. I do not think I have the stomach for Oriental alleyways."

Jacob's atelier was in a loft on Rivington Street, which was in the more prosperous side of the Jewish quarter. Here the houses were built of solid red brick, trimmed with white brick around the windows, and there was a lively trade going on in the many stores that lined the street. I was about to ask how they could be allowed to open on Sundays when I realized that Saturday was the Jewish Sabbath and Sunday only another ordinary day. I found myself wondering if Jacob observed Jewish rituals and went to worship at a temple.

He came down to greet us and escorted us up the stairs, past doors from which came the smells of fat frying and the sounds of a violin being played and up to the top floor. His studio was stark but neat, with a kitchen sink and scrubbed pine table at one side, a bed behind a screen, and the rest of the space taken over with photographic equipment and photographs he had taken.

"I am so glad you could come too, Miss Murphy," he said after he had greeted Gus and Sid. He was dressed in a Russian worker's garb, a high-buttoned black tunic that suited him well. His black curly hair was freshly washed and slicked down in an attempt to tame the curls.

"We must be outside Greenwich Village, since I have reverted to being Miss Murphy, or have I in some way offended you?" I said, and was rewarded by his blush.

"You must forgive me. I was raised to a strict code of behavior. My parents lived by every rule society ever invented."

"Your parents are still in Russia?" I asked, expecting to hear that they were dead.

"No, they are here. I managed to bring them to the New World soon after I arrived here. They live a street away on Delancey and think me a bad son and a terrible sinner because I do not choose to live with them. That an unmarried son should branch out on his own is unthinkable. Why, he might even entertain unchaperoned young women and then who would want their daughters to marry him?"

We laughed together at this absurdity. Living with Sid and Gus had made me forget that the rest of the world still adhered to strict rules of conduct.

"So will you allow the matchmaker to select your wife, like a good Jewish son?" Sid asked.

"I could throw the same question back at you, Miss Goldfarb."

"Touché. But one only has to look at me to know the answer. You still choose to live in a traditional area and wear a beard."

"Then to answer your question—I still adhere to the basics of my religion, but only when it does not conflict with reason and the twentieth century. I attend the occasional seder with my family, but see no reason to observe dietary restrictions which were created for a desert lifestyle. My parents think I am lost beyond hope. And you, Miss Murphy—are you still a good Catholic girl?"

"I never was. When I was a small child I used to slip out during the middle of mass to raid the priest's blackberry bushes. There was always too much emphasis on the fires of hell for my liking. I think my God would be more forgiving and have a better sense of humor."

"Then we worship the same deity," Jacob said. "Forgiving and humorous. The world would be a better place if such was the tenet of life."

Gus had already started to wander around the room. "These photographs are magnificent, Jacob. Nell was right. You do have a great talent."

"I'm merely a novice, Miss Walcott. Still learning my trade."

"But you've captured the life of the city perfectly," Gus said. "Come and look at this, Sid and Molly." She held up a large print of some scruffy children, playing among lines of drying laundry on a rooftop. There were scenes in crowded streets, and ominous back alleys.

"Why," I exclaimed, "this is the alley that the Eastmans frequent—and, if I'm not mistaken, those are members of the gang, lurking in that doorway. How did you manage to take their pictures, Jacob?"

"I am amazed that you are so familiar with gang members," Jacob said. "You do lead a dangerous life, Miss Murphy."

"My visit there was accidental, but you must have lingered long enough to set up your exposure."

"I was there with Nell. She was writing one of her exposure articles on the worst slums in the city. This was one of the sites she chose."

"She is remarkably fearless," I said.

"I would rather say foolhardy," Jacob answered. "Sometimes her lack of regard for her own safety worries me."

"And so you go on assignments with her to take pictures, but also to act as her protector," I said.

He gave me a long hard look. "You are remarkably perceptive, Miss Murphy."

"Molly."

He inclined his head. "Molly."

We drank more coffee then Sid got to her feet. "I'm afraid we have taken up too much of your time, Jacob. I am delighted to have made your acquaintance and look forward to inviting you to our future soirees."

"And I will be delighted to accept, Miss Goldfarb." Jacob gave that curiously foreign bow. He escorted us to the door and down the stairs.

"We should hail a cab as soon as you see one, Gus dear," Sid said. "Or we may be late for lunch with the Wassermans."

Jacob touched my sleeve lightly. "Are you also expected at the Wassermans, Miss Murphy?"

"No, I'm not, and when will you get it into your head that my name is Molly?"

"In that case, maybe you would allow me to escort you home."

"Oh, that's not necessary. I'm quite comfortable on these streets and it's broad daylight," I said and watched his face fall. "But if you've a mind for a walk on such a fine breezy day, then I wouldn't say no to the company," I added hastily.

"In that case, I'll grab my hat," he said and bounded up the stairs again.

"I think you've made a conquest there, Molly dear," Gus said quietly.

"Oh, no. It is Miss Blankenship who has his heart. He is merely being gentlemanly," I said, and felt myself blushing furiously.

Jacob and I set off, along Rivington until we struck the Bowery. This broad thoroughfare was full of life on a sunny Sunday. Theaters were just opening, many of them offering plays in Yiddish. Cafés were doing a brisk trade. Jacob paused in front of one small theater that advertised moving pictures. COME AND EXPERIENCE THE WONDER OF THE TWENTIETH CENTURY, the billboard proclaimed. YOU WILL NOT BELIEVE YOUR EYES!

"Now that is something that truly interests me," Jacob said. "Photographs capture a moment, but moving pictures—that is the way of the future, Molly." He looked at me expectantly. "Would you like to go to a performance with me?"

"Now?" I asked. "Why, thank you, Jacob, I'd love to. If you've nothing you should be doing at this moment, that is."

"Nothing better than this. I've been twice already, but the scenes never fail to fascinate me."

"I've heard about moving pictures, but I've never seen them yet."

"Then what are we waiting for?" He took my arm and escorted me to the ticket booth.

We joined the crowd inside the darkened theater where an organist was playing in front of red velvet curtains. I was conscious of Jacob sitting close beside me in the dark, and it disturbed me how aware I was of his presence. Then even this closeness was forgotten. The curtains parted to reveal a screen.

Words appeared on the screen. "Ladies and gentlemen. Prepare yourselves for an outrageous journey of entertainment and delight. Hold onto your seats, folks, and ladies, do not be alarmed. What you see is only an image on the screen. It cannot harm you."

The organ music increased and suddenly an image appeared on the screen. It was an ocean with waves breaking. My, but it was so real, you could almost smell the salt in the air and hear the cry of seagulls. The waves came closer and closer. Suddenly a giant wave came crashing at the screen. I heard screams and several people leaped to their feet. I touched my own face, half expecting to be wet. I could see Jacob grinning in the darkness. "A good illusion, wouldn't you say?" he whispered.

The next scene was of a group of inept policemen chasing a car. This was most amusing and the theater resounded to laughter. Then the car changed direction and drove directly at the camera. Again people leaped to their feet, then laughed in embarrassment when they realized it could not reach them. Then the scene changed again. The title appeared on the screen. *The Kiss.* We were in a lady's boudoir. A young man stole in through the open French doors. The young damsel, seated at her vanity, seemed amazed and delighted to see him. He took her into his arms. They gazed into each other's eyes and then there was a gasp from the audience as his lips fastened upon hers. The scene only lasted for a few seconds and then it faded. The show was over. The audience rose, still muttering in horror at what they had just seen.

"What did you think?" Jacob asked as we were jostled toward the exit.

"It was so real. Almost as if we were there."

"If I ever make any money, I plan to build myself such a camera," Jacob said.

"And make a moving picture called *The Kiss?*" I teased.

He shook his head. "I have other plans. I could take my camera back to Russia and bring back living proof to the world of the cruelties and injustices going on there. I could take it to the Boer War in South Africa and show the world what war is really like. If ordinary people knew what was going on, we could change the world."

"That's a wonderful notion, Jacob, but an awful risk for yourself."

"Someone has to take risks or nothing changes," he said.

We stood blinking in the bright sunlight.

"I almost forgot that it was daylight outside," I said.

"Should we take the trolley or do you feel up to walking?" Jacob asked.

"Do I look like a frail young thing who might faint at any moment?" I demanded.

"No, I'd say that you looked most robust and healthy." His frank gaze made me blush again.

He had barely uttered those words when Nell Blankenship appeared, like magic, from a café.

"Jacob. Molly. What a surprise," she said. Her eyes were fixed on me and her expression indicated that she wasn't overjoyed to see me.

"Hello, Nell," Jacob said. "A lovely day, isn't it?"

"Sid, Gus, and I have been viewing Jacob's photographs. He is very talented," I said hastily.

"He is indeed," she said. "So where are Sid and Gus? I should like to thank them for last night."

"They had a lunch appointment and had to make a hasty departure," Jacob said. "I am escorting Molly home."

"Ah," Nell said. Her gaze passed from Jacob to me and back again. "Well, much as I would like to stay and pass the time of day with you, I also must hurry. I'm due at my parents' home for lunch—my weekly penance and lecture session. Please excuse me." She rushed to jump on an already moving electric trolley. "I'll try to send you news about where your heiress worked as soon as possible," she called as she swung herself aboard with agility. "I'll start on it tomorrow!"

"Do not take any foolish risks, remember!" Jacob shouted as the trolley bore her away.

"Fiddle faddle," she shouted back, laughing.

I looked at Jacob. "Now I feel guilty. I hope she won't think badly of me."

"Why should she think badly of you?"

"Because I was dallying with her young man."

"Her young man? Nell and I are friends, nothing more."

"But I thought—I saw the way she treated you with such familiarity."

"She may well want a more intimate relationship," Jacob said, "but not I. I admire Nell. I think she is the most courageous woman I have ever met. But I would not choose such a woman for my wife. Sometimes she frightens me with the intensity of her dedication and fire."

Why did I feel absurdly happy at this statement?

"I see you are smiling," Jacob said. "Could it be that you've just heard some good news?"

"I can't think what you are talking about, Mr. Singer." I tossed back my hair and set off at a lively trot.

"Jacob," he said, keeping pace with me.

❧ Sixteen ❧

Knowing that a young man was interested in me certainly added spice to my life. And such a fascinating young man too. We had talked all the way home, touching on every subject under the sun. Daniel and I had been comfortable with each other, but we had never really discussed deep matters. Jacob and I thrashed out religion and royalty and socialism and communism and even birth control. I was amazed that I could talk about such things with a man. I had pretty much taken life for granted until I left Ireland. I knew that conditions were unfair and that the Irish were treated poorly in their own country, but I had considered those who fought for change to be rabble-rousers and hotheads, spoiling for a fight. In Jacob I saw someone who cared passionately and believed he could make a difference in the world. When he told me some of the things he had done as a member of the Bund in Russia, I was amazed. He couldn't have been more than seventeen at the time, but he had risked his life almost daily.

After we parted, I went to my room and stood at the window, watching him walk away. "Now that is truly a fine fellow," I said out loud. He wouldn't forget to mention that he was engaged to another girl or lack the courage to break off an engagement to a girl he didn't love. Thinking of Daniel reminded me that I had to write a note to him, purely professional, of course. I took out

163

pen, ink, and blotter and started to write. I asked him for any details of Katherine's death that he could find—the point at which she was taken from the river, estimate of how long she had been in the water, where she might have entered, description of what she was wearing, any dressmaker's labels on the clothes to indicate where they were made, any jewelry, any sign of foul play—bruises, wounds, etc. I almost signed it, "Yours, Molly," until I remembered that I was not his and most probably would never be his. But the thought was no longer as painful. In fact I felt a great lifting of the spirit, as if I had awakened after a long hibernation.

I sent the message to the Mulberry Street police station with Shamey and waited for a reply, knowing it might not be until Monday, if Daniel had his weekend free. The moment I thought about Daniel's weekends, scenes flashed through my mind— Daniel and me strolling by the lake in Central Park, eating ice cream at a soda fountain, Daniel kissing me under the leafy boughs of the Ramble in the park. I knew then that I wouldn't get over him so easily, however diverting the fascinating Mr. Singer might be.

As it happened, Daniel didn't have the weekend off. That evening a note was delivered by a uniformed constable.

I'm writing this at work, so forgive the terse tone of this message.

The young woman you think may be Katherine was pulled from the river below the Brooklyn Bridge. She was spotted from the deck of a docked cargo ship. Since she was in midstream, it is unclear where she fell in. She may have jumped from the bridge, which has become a popular suicide site. Her clothing is recorded as a print muslin dress. No mention of dressmakers labels, laundry marks, etc. No mention of any jewelry (and that would include wedding ring— hence the motive for suicide?). Also no suggestion of foul play.

I'm sorry I can't help you more. I trust that your reason for wanting these facts is to satisfy the curiosity of her family, and that you do not entertain any absurd notion of investigating her

death. I need hardly warn you that you have had several lucky escapes recently. Do not test the fates again.
    Daniel

His lack of information gave me nothing to investigate, I thought angrily as I reread the note. To be truthful, I hadn't expected any jewelry, but she was married, or pretending to be, so the lack of ring was strange—unless someone had removed it along with any other means of identification. Of course, it could have slipped off a cold, dead finger in the icy East River, and I didn't think that the New York police would be above even pocketing a wedding ring. But I had been hopeful that an observant policeman might have noticed an unusual label on her clothing or something that didn't fit the picture. Even if she chose to dress simply, her underwear would still be top-quality English, maybe even from Paris. Ah well, it was too late to do anything about that now. The poor girl was dead and buried. I just wished there had been some proof that this was Katherine Faversham. How awful it would be for her parents, never quite knowing what had happened to her. In spite of Daniel's warning, I hoped that Nell would come up with some small fact that could start us on the road to filling in the pieces of this puzzle.

Monday was another rainy day that found us garment workers huddled together, wet and steaming in the warmth of Samuel's Deli at lunchtime. Rose took the opportunity of speaking to the girls about the union and the plans for a walkout.

"So who's going to feed my kids while I'm on a picket line?" one of the older women demanded. "And who is going to tell my Leon when I get the boot?"

"But nobody should be treated the way we are," I said, joining Rose. "You can't like working in such conditions."

"Of course we don't like it, but we have no choice if we want to feed our families," the woman snapped.

"We have to make them sit up and notice that we have power," Rose said.

"Power, schmower," the woman muttered. "My mother's canary has more power than we do, and it lives in a cage."

"But don't you see," Rose insisted, "if our timing is right, then we do have power. You know how Mr. Lowenstein likes to get his clothes into the store before his rivals. If we walked out on the very day that he wanted us to get busy on the new line, I believe he'd listen to us."

"She may have a point, Fanny," another girl said. "If he's not first in the stores, who would want his shoddy clothing? You know how he skimps on the fabric and it's the cheapest quality too."

"It might be worth a try, Rose. Tell us what we have to do."

Suddenly the girls were all around her. "You tell us when, Rose. You give the word. We'll show him we're not made soft like butter."

It was very exciting. I found myself swept up in their enthusiasm.

"Not a word until he hands us the new designs, eh? We don't want him getting a whiff of what we've planned for him," I cautioned.

On the way back across the street Rose joined me. "What do you think, Molly? Isn't it wonderful? They're all with us. We might even get them to cough up the money for union dues."

"I just hope one of them isn't a traitor," I whispered.

"There's not much we can do about it, is there?" Rose glanced around at the girls hurrying back through the rain, their shawls over their heads. "We can't sit back and do nothing, in case we might be betrayed."

As we crossed the street, a fancy carriage clattered away, drawn by a fine matched pair of black horses.

"That looks like old Lowenstein," Rose said. "Trust him to pay a visit when none of us are there. He probably feels too guilty when he sees what we have to go through for him. But we'll show him, won't we, Molly!"

We came into the workroom, shaking the raindrops from our shawls.

"Careful of getting drops on that fabric!" Mr. Katz yelled.

"Yeah, it might melt if it gets wet," Rose commented and got a laugh.

"That will cost you, Rose Levy," Katz said. "You would do well to remember where you are and who is in charge."

"As if I could ever forget where I am," Rose said. "I'm certainly not in our nice big living room back home in Poland with the porcelain stove in the corner and the grand piano."

"Then go back, if you don't like it here," Katz said. "In fact, maybe you'll like to be one of my first volunteers."

"Volunteers to do what?"

"Mr. Lowenstein was just here," Katz said. "He's got some bad news."

"They didn't have the right brand of caviar for his lunch today," Rose whispered to me.

"The new designs won't be ready as soon as he expected and you girls have worked so well that the orders are up to date. So there's nothing much to do until we start work on the new line— maybe next week, who knows. Until then it's half time for every-body. Come in at seven, home at noon. He'll pay you two dollars a week, which is very generous when there's not enough work."

"Very generous!" one of the girl blurted out. "Does he pay us extra when there's too much work and you keep rushing us to get it finished?"

"You can't put everyone on half time," Rose said. "These girls have families who rely on their wages."

"Like I said, Rose Levy, you could volunteer," Katz said, giv-ing her his sneering grin. "Half the girls could volunteer to stay home until the new work comes, and then the other half would get full wages. It's up to you how you handle it."

"I tell you how we handle it," Rose said, sticking out her chin and putting her hands on her hips as she faced him. "We don't accept his measly offer. We walk out. We shut down this crummy sweatshop and we keep it shut until Mr. Lowenstein listens to us and treats us like human beings. Come on, everyone. Get your things. We're leaving now."

It was fantastic. Every girl followed Rose to the door.

"If you go, don't think you'll be coming back," Katz screamed. "We'll get new girls to replace you."

Rose turned and looked back at him. "Even if you can get them to cross our picket line, do you think you can train them in time for the new line and the rush job? We're going to show you who has power around here. In the end you're going to wish you were nicer to us."

Then she turned again and ran up the flight of steps, out to the street. We all followed her.

"Come on, everyone, let's go to Samuel's to plan," she said.

We crossed the street to the deli.

"I thought we weren't going to walk out until he got the new designs," Golda said. "Are you sure we're doing the right thing?"

"I know it's taking a big gamble," Rose said, "but he was going to put us all on half time anyway. Lowenstein won't want to pay any scabs to work this week because there is no work and our picket line is going to keep new girls away. We must all show up tomorrow prepared to stand our ground around the shop and not let anyone inside."

"How can we do that?" a small, frail-looking girl asked. "Look at us. If Katz tried to knock us out of his way, he could."

"Then we need reinforcements," Rose said. "Let's go to the United Hebrew Trades and see if they can get us some male volunteers to help our cause."

"Good idea," I said. "I'm sure that Jacob will want to help."

"Jacob?" she asked. "You mean Mr. Singer?"

I blushed. "Yes, Mr. Singer," I said.

She looked at me curiously. "And how come you're on first-name terms with Mr. Singer when you only met him last week?"

"He's a friend of my friends," I said and hoped she wouldn't push me further.

Someone was sent to Jacob's house, and soon the word got around so that the Hebrew Trades headquarters on Essex Street was jam-packed when we met there later that day.

"They did it. The girls walked out of Lowenstein's." The word went around quickly. Jacob arrived, so did some of the other men I had met the previous Wednesday night.

"Where is Miss Blankenship? She'd want to be here," someone suggested.

"Should someone take a cab to fetch her?" I asked.

Heads turned in my direction.

"Take a cab? Listen to Miss Rockerfeller here," the girl beside me said, rolling her eyes. "And where should you find the money for a cab? Not in this week's pay packet."

"I only meant because it's so important and she'd want to be here," I said quickly. "And she has money to pay for cabs, doesn't she?"

"She has a telephone at her house," Jacob said. "The University Settlement a couple of blocks away has a telephone that they let us use. Do you know how to use a phone, Molly?"

"No, but I expect they'll show me."

He took out a matchbook and scribbled on the back. "Here is her number. You turn the handle and when the operator comes on the line, you ask for the number. Got it?"

"I think so." I shoved the matchbook into my pocket.

"And I usually give them a dime for the privilege," Jacob said, fishing in his pocket and handing me a coin.

I ran up the stairs from the basement, my heart beating fast. I was so annoyed at myself for making that slip. Of course these girls would never have taken a cab in their lives. Paddy Riley would never have slipped out of character so easily.

I reached the austere building of the University Settlement and went inside. It reminded me of the time I had lived in the hostel run by a bible society. Strict and cold. Not the kind of place you'd want to stay longer than necessary. A distinguished-looking woman took me into a cluttered little office and pointed at the telephone on the wall. "Do you know how to use this contraption?"

"I'll manage, thank you."

She stood behind me, her hands on her hips, watching. It was with some trepidation that I cranked the handle and then heard a voice in my ear. "Number please?" I gave it to her and almost immediately a voice answered. "Miss Blankenship's residence."

"Is Miss Blankenship at home, please?"

"I'm afraid she's not. This is her maid speaking." A slow voice with an unfamiliar drawl to it.

"When are you expecting her back?"

"We was expectin' her back by now. Would you care to leave a message for her?"

I dictated my message, suggesting that she might want to join us as soon as possible. When I returned to the headquarters, fifty picketers had been assigned to the morning shift, with the rest ready and waiting to take the places of those who felt faint from standing too long. The meeting concluded in great high spirits but Nell Blankenship didn't put in an appearance.

❧ Seventeen ☙

I t was dark when we finally came out into the evening rain. I hurried home and not even the downpour was able to dampen my spirits. I was bursting with excitement that things were about to happen and that change was in the air. I was so caught up in the momentous things about to happen that I truly believed I was one of them, not just a girl from comfortable surroundings, playing at being a garment worker. This hit me, of course, when I crossed Washington Square and saw the lights from the elegant homes on the north side reflected in the wet pavement, and then Patchin Place with its own quiet serenity.

I came into my living room to find Shamey and Bridie sitting with their cousin Malachy.

"What are you doing here?" I asked coldly. "I thought I made it very clear to your mother that you were not to come to this house."

"Got a message for ya, don't I," he answered, wiping his nose with the back of his hand before holding out an envelope to me. "The lady asked if anyone could take a message to a Miss Molly Murphy at Patchin Place and I said I knew ya on account of my cousins lived at your house. So I got the job. And she said she'd pay me ten cents and I told her the Eastmans always paid us twenty-five. Then she said, 'Likely enough, but I don't have illicit funds at my disposal.' Regular old tartar, she was. Real snooty like. She looks down her nose at me and says, 'So do you want the job, or shall I ask one of these other boys instead?' so of course I took it."

He handed me the envelope, now somewhat grimy and creased. I tore it open.

The letter had been written in obvious haste and uneven penmanship, which must have meant that she had scribbled the note while still out and about. It also meant, I realized with a slight pang of jealousy, that she must have one of those new fountain pens that didn't leave blots all over the place.

> *Molly—I have had a successful day. Kathy was employed by Mostel's on Canal Street and I've just been given some startling information that I have to check out. Can you meet me at Ormond's Café at Canal and Broadway? I'll wait for you.*
> *—N.*

I looked up to see three little faces watching me.

"How long ago did she give you this note, Malachy?"

"Not that long ago. Maybe an hour."

"Then I must go out again at once. Come on, you and I can walk together."

He glanced longingly and pointedly at the kitchen. I laughed. "All right. I'll make us both some bread and dripping to keep us going. And you two—" I turned to Bridie and Shamey "—had better have some too. Who knows how late I'll be home."

Thus fortified, I grabbed an umbrella and we set off down Broadway. This time we rode the trolley. Malachy was entranced. I don't think he had ever ridden an electric trolley before. When we got off at the Canal Street stop, I glanced around and spotted the lighted windows of Ormond's Café.

"Where was the lady when she gave you this letter? Was it around here?"

"No. Down there a ways." He nodded in the direction of the

172

East River. "Down on Canal, not far from Orchard Street and the Walla Walla."

"Thank you," I said. "Now you hurry off home before it gets too late and your family starts to worry about you."

"They don't worry about me. I can take care of myself," he said with a swagger. Then he grabbed at the dime I offered him and took off down Canal at a lively trot. I crossed the street, successfully dodging hansom cabs, trolley cars, and even the occasional automobile, to reach the café. It was a large, opulent type of place, like a smaller Delmonico's, with lots of red plush and potted palms and chandeliers. A piano was playing a lively waltz. I went in and stood in the foyer, looking around. Several tables were occupied, but I didn't spot any familiar faces.

"Can I help you, miss?" A waiter appeared at my side.

"I was to meet someone here. A young lady. Tall, slim, dark haired. Well dressed."

"There has been no unescorted lady here this evening," he said. "Do you have a table reserved?"

"If we did, it would be in the name of Miss Nell Blankenship."

He shook his head. "Then perhaps you would care to sit there and wait." He indicated a red velvet sofa between two potted palms.

"Thank you." I took the seat he indicated. The clock on the wall said seven thirty. Nell would have expected me to be working until seven, so she hadn't hurried. Maybe she was on the trail of more interesting facts. I wondered what she might have unearthed that was important enough to have summoned me here and couldn't wait. It was amazing enough that Katherine had worked for Mostel's. Amazing, but annoying too. All the time I had worked there, not realizing! If only I had asked the right questions, I might have found out what happened to her myself. This thought made me stop and reconsider. Nell had leaped to the conclusion that Kathy's workplace might have had something to do with her disappearance. Could Mr. Mostel or Seedy Sam have possibly been responsible for what happened to her? I shook my head in disbelief. They were not the most pleasant of men—hard-hearted, greedy, but it was a big leap from treating girls badly to disposing of one of them in the East River.

I heard the clock on a nearby church chime eight and still Nell didn't come.

"Do you think your friend mistook the date?" the waiter asked. "Is there something I can bring to you?"

I ordered a cup of coffee and sat sipping it as long minutes ticked by. I was beginning to feel distinctly uneasy. Why was she so late? And what had she been doing in the vicinity of the Walhalla Hall? It might not have been dark when she found Malachy to deliver the letter, but it was certainly dark enough now—and raining hard again. Not the sort of weather you would choose to dawdle outside, especially not in that neighborhood.

At last I could wait there no longer. I was as tense as a wound watch spring. Something had detained Nell Blankenship and something had prevented her from sending me a second message, letting me know that she had been detained. I wasn't sure what to do. It was now raining cats and dogs out there, the fat, heavy drops bouncing off the sidewalk and forming pools in the gutters. Miserable horses plodded past and cabbies sat, equally miserable with their derby hats jammed down on their heads and collars turned up against the rain. I stood outside the café and stared down Canal Street. I was not foolhardy enough to go snooping down there alone at this time of night. Once bitten, twice shy as they say. Should I just go home and wait for Nell to contact me in the morning? It was, of course, possible that she had had enough of the rain and had gone home herself. If I could find a telephone, I could call her. I still had her number on the matchbook in my pocket.

After some trial and error I located a theater on lower Broadway with a telephone. It was a Yiddish theater and I hoped that the owner would speak English. He did and insisted on making the call for me, not out of kindness, I fear, but rather not trusting me with his contraption. Nell's maid answered again.

"Has your mistress not come home yet?" I asked.

"No, miss, and I'm real worried about her. She never comes home this late without getting word to me. She's always real considerate that way."

"I'm sure she's just been detained somewhere," I said, trying to sound more reassuring than I felt. "Please let her know that I waited at the café for an hour, then I felt I couldn't wait any longer. She knows where she can reach me."

"Very good, miss. I'll tell her, just as soon as she comes home." The poor girl's voice shook. I knew how she felt. I should go home and wait for Nell to contact me, but I couldn't. Suddenly I made a decision. I would go to Jacob. He would know what to do. I made my way up rainswept Broadway and turned onto Rivington Street. I just prayed he'd be home by now and was not still involved in strike planning at the Hebrew Trades headquarters. The door to the building opened easily. I climbed the dark stairway and tapped hesitantly on his door. I had a sudden, absurd hope that Jacob would answer and Nell would be inside with him.

He opened the door. "Molly!" He looked pleased but wary. "To what do I owe this honor so late at night? I thought you'd gone home hours ago. I'm not sure I should invite you in without damaging your reputation." He grinned to let me know that this was a joke.

"It's Nell. I was supposed to meet her and she hasn't turned up. I'm worried about her, Jacob." The words came out in a rush. Quickly I told him what had happened and showed him Nell's note. "I waited in the café for over an hour," I said, "and the boy who delivered the note told me that Nell had been near the Walhalla Hall when she gave it to him. The Walhalla Hall is frequented by the Eastmans gang, Jacob."

Jacob gave a deep sigh. "I've been afraid something like this would happen. She takes the most appalling risks without a second thought. Do you know what she was doing in that part of town?"

"She had discovered that Kathy worked for Mostel's. They are on Canal Street, not too far away, so it could be that she was pursuing some connection there."

"I must go and find her," Jacob said. "You have already done enough for one night. You should go home and rest."

"Nonsense," I said. "I'll come with you. There's safety in numbers."

He smiled. "Although two isn't a very big number." He put his hand on my shoulder. "But it's very companionable." His hand remained there until we started down the stairs.

As we came out into the night the rain had stopped and a damp mist clung around the lampposts and area railings. The mist seemed to muffle all sound so that it felt as if we were alone in a dark world. Only the mournful tooting of ships out in the mist on the river told us that the city was still alive and awake. We cut down Chrystie Street. I kept an eye open all the way for any sign of a building that might be the Eastmans headquarters, but of course they'd hardly be likely to advertise the fact. The street was quiet, respectable, and in darkness. We came out onto Canal, not far from Orchard Street and the Walhalla. The area was dimly lit by the occasional gas lamp and the mist swirled in from the East River so that we moved like two ghosts.

"Here is the Walhalla Hall," Jacob said. "We should ask if anyone has seen her."

The hall itself appeared to be in darkness. Jacob stopped several men coming out of saloons and got only rude comments for his pains. "Whatdaya want another girl for when you've already got one? Greedy, ain't ya?" It was most frustrating and after a while we gave up. There was nobody else on the street.

"We should maybe check the café again to see if she came there after I'd left," I suggested.

"Good idea."

We walked back along Canal Street.

"That's Mostel's," I said, pointing at the looming dark shape. "There is a furniture maker on the ground floors and Mostel's occupies the top three."

Jacob tried the door but it was firmly locked and no lights shone in the building. We walked on to Broadway but the café was closed. So were most of the other businesses around it. Only the theaters were still ablaze with lights.

"Should we try calling her house?" he asked.

"I've tried twice. Her maid sounds very worried."

"Then we must go back along Canal and systematically check each backstreet and alley," Jacob said.

"But what would she be doing there, at this time of night?" I asked, not wanting to listen to the answer that echoed in my own head.

He shrugged.

"There is one possibility." I could hardly make my mouth say the words. "I was almost taken by the Eastmans once, until luckily the police intervened. If she was snooping too close to their activities, then maybe they've got her."

Jacob stared at me with a look of sheer dread.

"But that's something we can't tackle alone," I said hastily as I saw Jacob steeling himself to confront a gang. "We'll have to alert the police. I have a friend who is a police captain. We should let him know right away."

"But we should search the area first," Jacob said. "Just to make sure. If we pass a policeman on the beat here, we can tell him and have him spread the word that we are looking for her." We turned back along Canal in the direction we had come. "Of course, we could be worrying for nothing," Jacob said, trying to sound bright and confident. "Nell could have arrived at your house by now, at my place, at anyplace as the whim took her. It is impossible to know how her mind works. I have been out on assignments with her before and she has been off in all directions, like a dog chasing a rabbit." He attempted a smile and

I could tell it was himself he was trying to convince, more than me.

I wasn't sure what we were going to achieve by searching the area. Clearly Nell wouldn't still be walking around the area alone in the dark and damp. And it wasn't like Hester and Essex Streets and those livelier areas north of here, where shop fronts would still be open and street life still going on. If anyone lived around here, they had their front doors locked and their blinds drawn. I had to run to keep up with Jacob. He was striding out like a man on a mission. We turned up the first side street and then back to Canal. Singing floated to us from corner saloons. Drunken men staggered past us. Dogs barked. Cats slunk into alleyways. We tried the next side street and the next.

"This is a futile project, Jacob. How can we hope to find her this way? She could be anywhere in New York by now. And if someone had kidnapped her, we could be walking right past and not even know."

"Don't say that." He shivered. "I need to feel that I have done everything I can do. We may just meet a street urchin or a woman of the night who has seen something."

"All right. Press on, then," I said gallantly although my feet by now were throbbing. Ladies' shoes are not made for tramping over cobbles for hours. Pointed toes may be all the rage, but they are not designed for comfort. I glanced down enviously at Jacob's big workman's boots.

We passed Mostel's again and searched the area around it, but saw nothing out of the ordinary. We crossed the Bowery and kept going. Two ladies of the night lurked in a doorway. We asked them.

"We ain't interested in missing girls, honey," one of them said. "We only notice if a gentleman like yourself goes past. What's she done, run away from her old man?" They broke into peals of laughter. We trudged on, discouraged.

We were coming to the place where Canal Street changed

direction, after it crossed Division. Surely Jacob didn't intend to scout it out all the way to the East River? Then suddenly we heard the clatter of boots and two small boys ran past us. I grabbed at one, hoping that it might be one of Nuala's boys.

"Here, let go of me, I ain't done nothing," he yelled in fright.

"We aren't going to hurt you," Jacob said. "We're looking for a lady. We thought you might have seen her around here. A tall lady in black, nicely dressed?"

"Ain't seen no one like that," the other boy mumbled.

I glanced down at the object he was attempting to hide behind his back. "What have you got there?" I asked and made a grab for it. He tried to jerk it away and the ostrich plume came off in my hand.

"Where did you find this?" I demanded. "I thought you said you hadn't seen the lady. This is her hat."

"We ain't seen no lady," the first boy said. "We found the hat on the ground. Finders keepers. We was taking it home to our mom."

"Can you take us to where you found the hat?" Jacob said. "Then I'll give you fifty cents as a trade for the hat. Is that fair?"

"Okay, mister. It was down here." They led back along Canal then down an alleyway where the houses from two streets backed onto each other. There were coal bunkers and all manner of sheds and shacks and outhouses and it smelled bad. We picked our way cautiously in almost total darkness.

"Right about here, mister," the bigger boy said. "It was just lying here, just like that. Tom kicked it and we thought it was a dead bird or something and didn't think much of it. But then we saw the ribbon and he picked it up."

"You've been very helpful," Jacob said. "It belongs to our friend. Here's the fifty cents. And if you happen to see the lady we're looking for, tell her where we are, will you?"

"Sure thing, mister." The boys grinned and ran off with their bounty.

Jacob and I stood looking at the hat.

"She wouldn't have taken her hat off in this weather," he said.

"If she was being led away against her will, she might have let the hat fall to the ground as a clue," I said.

Jacob nodded. "She might indeed." The words came out as a whisper. We were both whispering. It was that sort of place. "On the other hand," he went on, "she might be around here— hurt or . . ."

He didn't need to say any more. We started looking. I wished we had a lantern with us. The darkness was almost complete. We peeked behind coal bunkers and sheds and called her name softly.

"She could have been thrown inside any of these," Jacob said, his voice rising in annoyance. "Nell! It's us. It's Jacob," he said, more loudly now.

Then there was a sudden breeze. The mist swirled, the clouds parted, and for a moment the moon shone down, throwing grotesque shadows down the alley. And for a second something sparkled. I ran to it just as the clouds came together again and we were plunged into darkness once more. I bent over behind a large coal bin. Then my hand recoiled as I realized what I was touching. The sparkling object had been a buckle on a shoe and the shoe was still on a foot.

₩₰ Eighteen ₷₰

J acob, over here, quickly!"

He rushed to my side and dropped to his knees among the debris. "Oh, Gott. Oh, Gott. Oh, Gott!" he repeated over and over. "Help me, Molly. Move her carefully, she may still be alive."

I said nothing, but the ankle I was touching was cold. She had been stuffed into a narrow area between the bin and a brick wall and it was hard to get her out. When at last we extracted her, her head lolled like a doll's, her mouth open in a silent yell of surprise. I shuddered and looked away. Jacob put his arms around me. "Don't look. It is too horrible," he said. "Who could have done this terrible thing?"

I stood, twisting her bonnet nervously in my hands, then I recoiled as my hand touched something sticky. The outside of the bonnet was wet from the rain. It was the inside that was sticky. I bent to examine her head. Suddenly a bright light shone on us.

"What's going on here?" a deep voice demanded.

"Thank God you have come, Officer." Jacob got to his feet. "A young woman has been brutally murdered."

"So it seems, sir." The constable came closer, shining the light in our faces. The light was blinding and all I could see of the policeman was the silhouette of his distinctively shaped helmet. "You'd better both step away and put your hands up."

"We didn't kill her," I snapped. "We've just found her. She was our friend. We've been looking for her."

"Put your hands up, I said." The flashlight waved up and down, its beam bouncing from the high brick walls around us. Then the flashlight focused on my hand. The policeman came closer. "What's that on your hand?"

I looked at it. "It must be blood. We found her bonnet first, you see, and the inside is sticky."

More feet came down the alleyway.

"Down here, Charlie," the constable shouted. "I caught the pair of them, bending down over the corpse, they were. Get out your handcuffs."

"Don't be ridiculous," I said as the second officer approached me, handcuffs at the ready. "I have just told you. This is our friend. We have been looking for her all evening because she didn't meet me when she was supposed to. We feared that something bad might have happened to her."

"Oh, and why was that, miss?"

"This is Miss Nell Blankenship, from a prominent family," Jacob said quietly. "You must have heard of her. She writes— wrote articles for the newspapers. I am Jacob Singer. I worked as her photographer."

"Oh, yes. The lady reporter. I've seen her name in the papers. Charlie, run and send a message to headquarters that we've got a murder on our hands. And in the meantime you two stay right where you are."

"We wouldn't dream of abandoning her," I said. "We want to find out who killed her as much as you do. And if you think we had anything to do with her murder, you only have to touch her. She has been dead for some time."

The other constable departed. I was suddenly very cold and hugged my arms to me, shivering. I was very conscious of my fingers sticking together and longed to wash that hand. I still found it hard to handle death and I was overcome with feelings of guilt. If I hadn't asked Nell to help me, she'd never have been in this part of town. She would never have uncovered a fact that cost her her life. It was too much to hope for that she had left any hint as to what that fact might have been. I tried make myself think like an investigator. I got up and started to search the area.

"Hey, where are you going?" the constable asked.

"I was looking for her purse. I don't see it."

"She was probably bashed over the head for her purse. If she was foolish enough to be out alone in this part of town, what can you expect?" the constable said, with the ease of small talk. I decided to remain silent and not let him know that robbery may not have been the motive and she may not have been a random victim.

"What in God's name was she doing in this part of town anyway?" the constable went on. "She must have known it wasn't safe for a lady."

"Nell didn't stop to think about things like that," Jacob said. "When she was onto a story, she took appalling risks. She never . . . she wouldn't . . ." His voice faltered. I reached out and touched his arm.

I was praying, for once, that the police detective who was summoned to this scene would not be Daniel. I really didn't feel up to facing him or the tongue lashing he would obviously give me. However, the detective sergeant who arrived shortly afterward, with two more constables, was a fresh-faced young man called Macnamara. He listened politely as we told him how we had found her after finding the boys with her bonnet. When we tried to describe the boys, I realized that the description fit every street urchin on the Lower East Side. I was angry at myself for not getting their names, nor for searching them further to see if they had other items belonging to Nell in their pockets. Had they found her purse and stuffed their pockets with anything worth stealing?

"A curious fact, that has been worrying me," I said. "The boys had Miss Blankenship's bonnet, and yet the inside of the bonnet is sticky with blood. Doesn't that indicate it was on her head when she was struck?"

The young officer looked at me with interest. "I wouldn't expect a young lady to think of things like that."

"This is no ordinary young lady," Jacob said. "Miss Murphy is a private investigator."

I was flattered that he had leaped to defend me, but I rather wished he hadn't mentioned it. Macnamara stared at me even harder. "Then maybe she can tell me why a well-dressed lady came to be found alone, in this part of the city. Was this some kind of investigation she was carrying out?"

"I rather fear that it was," I said. "Although I have no idea what brought her to this alleyway."

"As for that," Macnamara said, "she may well have been grabbed on the street in full view of anyone who happened to be passing. The types that frequent this area wouldn't think twice about grabbing her and dragging her into the alleyway—knowing that most folk would pretend they hadn't seen anything and pass by on the other side. So if her purse is missing, then we have to conclude that robbery was the motive."

"Which doesn't make sense," I said. "She is still wearing gloves and I think I can see the shape of a ring under the leather. Why not take her jewelry too?"

"Someone was coming and they had to beat it in a hurry," Sergeant Macnamara suggested. "They clubbed her from behind. Her hat came off when they turned her over and they left the hat lying there when they stuffed her into that hiding place."

"Rather careless, wouldn't you say?" I asked. "If the boys hadn't picked up her hat, we'd never have found her."

Sergeant Macnamara shook his head. "Like I said, they were in a hurry to beat it. Maybe she had a nice fat wallet in her purse and that was enough for them."

Another constable arrived to tell him that a morgue wagon was ready to transport the body. "I'll need you to come to police headquarters on Mulberry Street to make statements," Macnamara said. He didn't offer us a ride in the morgue wagon, for which I was glad. "Constable Daly will show you the way."

The original constable escorted us to the end of the alley and then motioned for us to go with him along Canal. As we came to the first cross street I glanced up and noticed that it was Chrystie. Somewhere along that street was the Eastmans headquarters in a building that must have backed onto that very alleyway. I might suggest that line of inquiry when we made our statement.

It was a long weary trudge back along Canal to the police headquarters. We gave them our names and addresses and dictated our statements to a uniformed sergeant. Then we were told to wait. Someone brought us cups of tea which were most welcome. We sat in a small, windowless room, on hard, straight-backed chairs, and waited. Jacob looked around him. "I have been in rooms like this before," he said. "They would always keep you waiting. There would be screams from other rooms. Sometimes I still have nightmares."

I wanted to take his hand, but it still seemed too forward. "I'm so sorry," I said. "I dragged you into this. I can't tell you how badly I feel at this moment."

"It is I who feels guilty," he said angrily. "How could I have let her go alone to a place like that? I should have protected her better."

"You were not her bodyguard, Jacob. And from what I saw she would not have listened to you. She led her own life."

He nodded. "But it doesn't ease the guilt," he said.

"I know. Nothing eases the guilt at the moment. I feel terrible myself. It was I who sent her there."

He reached out and took my hand. I was glad it was the other hand, not the one sticky with dried blood. His hand was as cold as mine. We sat there, clutching each other for support.

"At least they don't suspect us anymore," I said. "For a while I was scared that—"

I broke off as the door was flung open and a disheveled, wild-eyed Daniel came bursting in. He looked as if he hadn't slept in several days. His shirt collar was unbuttoned and he wore no tie. "I hope you are finally satisfied," he shouted. "What have I been telling you all along, and you don't listen. Did you drag her into one of your crazy schemes?"

Jacob rose to his feet. "I don't think that's any way to address this young lady," he said quietly. "She has done nothing wrong."

"Done nothing wrong? She insists on poking her nose into things better left alone," Daniel said. "And who are you?"

"Jacob Singer. A friend of Miss Murphy."

I saw Daniel's eyebrow go up. "Is that so?"

"Miss Murphy came to me when she was concerned that Miss Blankenship had not shown up at the appointed time for their meeting."

"And just what was Miss Blankenship doing in an alleyway behind Canal Street at night?" Daniel spat out the words.

"I have no idea," I said, staring him straight in the eye. "The only matter in which she was giving me help was finding out details about that missing couple. The couple you were helping me to trace. Katherine and Michael Kelly."

"Michael Kelly?" he said, still glaring angrily. "The man who met an unpleasant end after getting himself mixed up with the Eastmans? You sent her to investigate that?"

"No, I didn't. I wanted to find out where Katherine had worked." I was yelling too, now. "I had discovered that she worked in the garment industry. Nell knew all about sweatshops. She offered to find out for me. And she did find the name of the company Katherine worked for. It was Mostel's on Canal Street—which explains what she was doing in the area to start with. Why she stayed around after dark I cannot tell you. She scribbled a note to me to say that she had learned something interesting and was going to follow up on it. That's all I can tell you."

Daniel's bluster had subsided. "And she paid for the inter-

186

esting fact with her life. Is any piece of knowledge worth the life of a human being?"

"Of course not. And I would not have wished her to take any kind of risk," I said. "I had no idea—"

"That's just it, Molly. You have no idea. If you were a cat, you'd have already used up eight of your nine lives. Maybe this will teach you a lesson you won't forget in a hurry. If ever you get another harebrained scheme in your head, think of Miss Blankenship lying there with her head bashed in."

"I really think Miss Murphy has been through enough for one night," Jacob said coldly. "If you don't mind, I'd like to take her home now."

Daniel looked at him, long and hard, then nodded. "Well, I know where to find you if I have more questions," he said. "But I don't think we have a hope in Hades of finding out who killed her."

"You have your informants among the gangs, don't you?" I asked. "You could find out if one of the Eastmans killed her."

Daniel nodded. "I could probably glean that fact after a while, but they'd never tell me what she discovered or who was paying them, so it would be a lost cause. There would be no point in making an arrest or trying to bring anyone to trial. Believe me, I've tried it often enough." He stared hard at me again. "It could have nothing to do with the Eastmans. It could have been as simple as snatching her purse or wanting her shoes. Life is cheap in the Lower East Side, as you have just discovered. As Katherine and Michael discovered too. They are dead, Molly. A lost cause. Your friend lost her life for nothing." He went to say something else, then tossed his head abruptly in the direction of the door. "Go on, then. You can go."

"Thank you," I said as I rose to my feet. As I stood up the room swung around. I teetered and swayed. Daniel and Jacob steadied me at the same moment. "I'm fine, honestly," I said quickly. "I haven't really eaten since midday, and then the shock."

"I'll give you the money for a cab," Daniel said.

"That's not necessary. I have money," Jacob answered. "I'll make sure she gets home safely."

"Then please go and secure a cab for Miss Murphy. I'll bring her out momentarily," Daniel said.

As soon as Jacob had left the room Daniel spun around to me, his eyes dark and angry. "And who, pray, is that gentleman?"

"A good friend, Daniel."

"He didn't think he was just a good friend. I saw him looking at you."

"Maybe more someday, then."

"He is not of your race or religion, Molly. Don't you see that this can lead nowhere?"

"Maybe I am becoming an expert at relationships that lead nowhere," I said. "And I didn't think that you and Miss Norton shared the same religion. Maybe it's not a stumbling block when money and power are involved."

He winced as if I'd slapped him across the face, which, I must confess, I had wanted to do—actually longed to do now.

"This is stupid, Molly," he said. "You don't love him. You can't love him."

"I'll go and see if Jacob has found me a cab, if you'll excuse me."

"Molly—" He reached out his hand to me.

"Good-bye, Daniel," I said, then spun on my heels and fled.

❧ Nineteen ❧

T hat man's behavior toward you was quite insufferable," Jacob said as the cab carried us away at a fast clip clop. "Give these fellows a badge and a uniform and the small amount of power goes to their heads."

I didn't think this was the moment to point out that Daniel, as a detective, wore neither badge nor uniform, and as one of the youngest captains on the force, he wielded a considerable amount of power.

"He has saved me from a couple of awkward situations in the past and was annoyed that I was still trying to pursue the notion of being an investigator," I said, not wanting to go into further explanations. I was starting to shiver as delayed shock set in.

"That doesn't give him permission to shout at you," Jacob said, "especially after what you have been through tonight."

"What we have both been through tonight. I still can't believe it," I said. "Poor Nell. It doesn't seem possible, does it?"

"I find it hard to believe too," Jacob said. "I saw so many terrible things as a young man in Russia, but one does not expect to see them repeated, here in America. She was a fine woman. She could have accomplished much. I should have . . ." He turned away from me.

"You tried to warn her. You tried to warn both of us," I said.

189

"You are blameless in this, Jacob. Don't put yourself through this torment."

Without thinking I reached across and stroked his cheek. He seized my hand and brought it to his lips. "When I first saw you, I thought a bright ray of sunshine had come into my life, Molly. I thought—that could be a girl who would make me laugh and dance and forget all I that I have been and seen."

"I think it will be a while before either of us can laugh and dance again, Jacob," I said, "but we will help each other get through this."

His arms came around me and he held me fiercely to him. I let him hold me close, not sure what I felt, still too conscious of Daniel's angry, worried face in that police headquarters room.

Then Jacob released me suddenly, putting his hands on my shoulders. "I want you to promise me that you will not attempt anything more to do with Nell's death," he said. "Whoever did this is heartless and ruthless. Swear you won't try to track down her killer."

"I promise you I won't do anything stupid, Jacob," I said, "and you must promise me the same."

"I couldn't bear to lose you, so soon after I have found you," he whispered and cradled my head to him again. I lay against his shoulder until the cab stopped at the entrance to Patchin Place.

"Are you sure you'll be all right?" Jacob asked. "Would you like me to come in and make you a hot drink maybe?"

"It's late," I said. "You should get some rest yourself. You look terrible."

"Thank you for the kind words." He managed a smile.

I reached up and touched his cheek, my hand savoring the strangeness of his beard. "We're both exhausted and upset, Jacob. I think sleep is what we need most."

He nodded. "Very well, then. I'll take the cab home and see you tomorrow." He brought my fingertips to his lips, then he was gone.

As I went to open my front door, the one across the street opened and Gus was standing there in a flowing Oriental robe, her hair hidden behind a purple turban.

"Molly, it *is* you. I was painting in my studio and I thought I saw you getting out of a cab with the attractive Mr. Singer. Have you been somewhere exciting? Do come inside and tell all!"

My first instinct was to invent some harmless event that Jacob and I had attended together, but I couldn't lie to such a dear friend.

"Actually, it's been a horrible, beastly evening," I said, and heard my voice shake. "We found a friend murdered." I realized as I said it that Nell had been their friend rather than mine. "Nell Blankenship," I added.

"Nell? Nell has been killed?"

"What's this?" Sid's head appeared behind Gus's turban.

I had no option but to go in and tell them everything. The reliving of the evening was almost as painful as the experience itself.

"How awful for you, Molly," Sid said.

"Me? What do I matter? I'm alive," I burst out. "It's poor Nell! If I hadn't asked her to help me, she'd be alive. I feel so terrible." I sank my head into my hands. "She didn't even like me very much, you know. She saw me as a threat. She was really only carrying out this assignment to please Jacob because she was smitten with him. So I've betrayed her all around."

"Brandy, I think, don't you, Gus?" Sid rose and went for the decanter.

"Brandy in hot milk. She'll need to sleep and it won't be easy." Gus brought out a saucepan and lit the gas.

"Stop blaming yourself, Molly," Sid said as she poured a generous amount of brandy into a glass beaker. "You didn't set out to lure Jacob away from her with your feminine wiles, did you?"

I had to smile at this thought. "No. Of course not."

"And you didn't ask Nell to take on anything you knew to be dangerous?"

"No."

"Then stop blaming yourself." She took the hot milk off the stove and poured it into the brandy. "I know—I knew Nell Blankenship quite well. She would never have been forced or tricked into doing anything she didn't want to do. She went looking for this person Katherine because she was intrigued, because she saw it as a challenge. It appealed to her reporter's instinct. Her choice, Molly, not yours."

"Now drink up and then get a good night's sleep," Gus said. "And if you will take advice from two friends who care for you, you will take this terrible event as a warning. Somebody out there killed Nell Blankenship because of what she discovered. That person is still out there and even more desperate now. So no heroics, Molly. Leave the detective work to the police."

"That's what Jacob just said."

"I knew I liked him," Gus said, turning to Sid for a confirming nod.

"Has anyone notified her family, I wonder?" The ever efficient Sid rose to her feet.

"Her poor maid should be told, at least," I said. "Last time I spoke to her, she was sick with worry. Do you think I should call her at this late hour?"

"I'll do it," Sid said, putting a firm hand on my shoulder. "You go to bed. Do you want us to come with you?"

"No, you've been more than kind, as usual." I got to my feet. "One day I must find a way to repay you."

"Repay us by staying out of trouble and not ending up like Nell in an alleyway," Gus said. Then she gave me a little push. "Go on with you. To bed before the brandy wears off."

In spite of the brandy that warmed my whole body, I lay awake long into the night, listening to bare branches scratching against the window, my mind in a turmoil. It didn't matter that everyone had insisted that Nell was headstrong and impulsive and made her own choices, I was overcome with guilt and remorse. This was the second time that I had let someone else do my dirty work. I had put young Shamey's life at risk and now I had cost Nell Blankenship her life. If I, instead of she, had found out some vital fact about Katherine's life or death, then maybe I would have been lying behind a coal bin tonight. I swore to myself that I would never again involve another person in my investigations and that by hook or by crook, I would find out who killed Nell. I couldn't bear the thought that her death would just be ignored by the New York police.

I sat up in bed and reached for my notebook and pencil. I could hear Paddy's voice in my head—start with what you know. I knew that Nell had discovered that Katherine worked for Mostel and Klein. She had also uncovered another useful piece of information, one important enough that she wanted to share it with me immediately—a piece of information so important to somebody that it had cost Nell her life.

What else did I know? Her body was found close to Mostel's factory. I tried to picture Mr. Mostel or Seedy Sam throwing Katherine into the river, or stalking Nell and luring her down an alleyway. Somehow it was hard to believe. I could imagine the despicable Mr. Katz at Lowenstein's doing a thing like that, but not Seedy Sam, for all his bluster. Then I thought how important money was to Mr. Mostel. If he thought his business was being threatened, he might have paid someone to do away with Katherine. That I could imagine. And who better to get rid of her quietly than one of the Eastmans?

If that was so, there was no way I would ever be able to prove it. I was not foolish enough to go poking around the Walhalla Hall and Chrystie Street again—and I had just promised Jacob that I wouldn't act stupidly. But I could go back to Mostel's, I decided. It occurred to me that this strike at Lowenstein's would give me a perfect excuse to return to Mostel's, especially if Lowenstein did fire some of us for striking. On the other hand, I reminded myself, I would probably not be able to complete my other commission and find out who was handing over Mostel's designs to his competitor. Which would mean I wouldn't get paid.

Item to remember for future reference, I said to myself. Never try to take on two cases at once. Item number two—never get romantically involved with anybody connected with the case. I thought of Jacob's arms around me, his lips against my fingers and the strange, not unpleasant, tickle of his beard. Had Nell guessed that Jacob was falling for me? Had Jacob, ever honest and open, actually told her his true feelings for me? In which case we had both driven her to her death.

I fell at last into troubled sleep, only to be woken by the alarm clock what seemed like minutes later. It was still dark. The wind was still blowing, making the bare branches dance crazily in the light of the street lamp. I stood on the cold linoleum, wondering what I was doing awake at this hour, until I remembered that I had to join my fellow workers on a picket line before Mr. Katz arrived at Lowenstein's.

I dressed in my warmest clothing, looked longingly at my wool cape, then took a shawl like the other girls. I made myself a cup of tea, a thick slice of bread and cheese for later sustenance, and some toast for breakfast. I was just eating it hurriedly when I looked up to see Seamus standing there.

"So you're really going to walk a picket line, are you?" he said.

I had given him sketchy details when I came home the night before.

"I'm afraid so. Those girls need all the support they can get."

"Be careful, Molly," he said. "Those bosses don't play fair. Don't try to do anything too heroic, will you?"

"No, of course I won't." I was touched by his concern.

"You're a good woman, Molly," he said. "I've been feeling so guilty that you've taken us in like this and I'm doing nothing to support my own family. I'm going out this very day to find something. I may not be strong enough to go back down the tunnel yet, but there are other jobs that don't require strength."

"You recover your health first, Seamus," I said. "I can take care of things until you do."

"No, you've made it too easy for me," he said. "Life is not supposed to be easy. We're born to a struggle and we die in a struggle, and it's a struggle in between too."

Trust an Irishman to be poetic at five in the morning!

"I'm going to visit Tammany Hall," he said. "I'm a loyal voter. They owe me something. Surely they'll find a loyal Irishman a job."

"Good luck, then," I said. "Tell the children good-bye for me and make sure they wash their faces before they go to school."

He smiled. "You're a good little mother to them. I was thinking, Molly—when the end does come, for Kathleen, I mean . . ."

"Don't even let that thought cross your mind," I said severely. "She's not dead yet and maybe she's not going to die. And even if she did, I'm not the wife for you, Seamus."

Then I beat a hurried retreat. I had enough on my plate at the moment without having to worry about proposals from Seamus O'Connor.

The streets were still wet from last night's downpour and I picked my way carefully between puddles. I had actually been looking forward to this moment, especially to seeing Katz's face when confronted by a cordon of angry girls. But that was before the events of last night. I couldn't get the image of Nell's dead face out of my mind. I had to do something, at least follow up on the Mostel's connection, but I couldn't approach him until I had gone through the motions of this strike. Besides, these girls needed my support. I couldn't back out on them now.

When I reached Lowenstein's, a knot of excited girls had already gathered, whispering together in the shadows. Rose was among them. She looked up and saw me.

"Molly—over here, quick, we need you," she said. "We're making signs, but we don't write English so good."

They had some squares of cardboard, a pot of black paint, and a large brush.

"What do you want me to say?"

"You'd know the right thing," Rose said. "We can write it in Yiddish and Italian and even Polish, but not in English."

"How about 'Lowenstein unfair to workers! We want better conditions'?" one of the girls suggested.

"We demand better conditions," I suggested.

"That's good. And tell the world we are not slaves, we are free human beings with rights," another girl chimed in.

"And we need a workplace that is warm enough and light enough."

"And a proper water closet that doesn't freeze."

"And a foreman who keeps his hands to himself."

"And why should we work on the Sabbath? My papa wants to throw me out because we work that day."

"He doesn't even let us get home in time for Shabbat on Friday nights!"

The suggestions were coming thick and fast. "Hold on," I yelled. "I only have a few signs here. We just need to state why we are striking and that's because they are unfair."

They nodded and watched as I wrote the messages, then Rose handed them out to several girls. While this was going on the three men who were the cutters and pressers came to work. They needed a little persuading to join us, but when they saw that they weren't going to be allowed inside and that fifty angry girls might set upon them, they changed their minds. Two of them went home and one decided to join our line.

"I watched the police hack strikers to death with their swords in Poland," he said. "That is why I come to America. Now I see if democracy works or not."

Jacob arrived, carrying his camera, and with him the young Russian from the cloak-makers' union arrived and a couple of men I hadn't met before. While the Russian was instructing the girls about passive resistance and not losing their tempers whatever was said to them, Jacob drew me aside. "I've been worrying about you all night," he said.

"And I about you," I replied. "I don't suppose you slept any better than I did."

"Hardly a wink. I could not shake off the awful feeling of guilt."

"Jacob, you shouldn't feel guilty. You admitted yourself that Nell was headstrong. She did what she pleased."

"It's not just that," he said. "I feel guilty that she wanted more than friendship from me and I was unable to give it to her. I can't help thinking that some of her bravado and daring were attempts to make me admire her."

"Love doesn't work that way," I said. "You can't choose when you fall in love. It just happens."

"This is so true," Jacob said, and his gaze held mine.

I smiled uneasily. "We have sterner things to occupy us this morning, I fear."

"Yes. And I wish you weren't involved in this matter, Molly. I don't want you to be involved in more danger."

"How can there be danger?" I demanded. "Look how many of us there are. You have your camera. You can take pictures and get public opinion on our side."

"I intend to, but just in case—could you not go home?"

"Of course not. I'm one of these girls at the moment. I suffered with them in Lowenstein's. Their conditions are intolerable, Jacob. They do deserve better, and they might need a spokeswoman who speaks English."

"This Katherine you seek was a spokeswoman who spoke English," he said, "and look what happened to her. Look what happened to Nell last night."

"All right everybody. To your places," Rose shouted. "And remember, we don't scare easy. We are not going to be bullied, whatever they say. This is America. We have a right to strike here."

"God bless America," a voice from the crowd said and was echoed down the line.

I stepped into the line beside Rose. Jacob and the other men moved off to one side, where they could observe from a stoop. At around six thirty Mr. Katz arrived. He came striding down the street, his black derby at a jaunty angle on his head, and didn't notice the line of girls until the last minute.

"What's this?" he demanded.

Rose dug me in the side. "It should be fairly obvious, Mr. Katz," I said. "We don't like the way Lowenstein's treats us. We're on strike until our demands are met."

He glared at me. "I should have known you were trouble. A rabble-rouser like all the damned Irish."

"It was not I who instigated this strike," I said. "All the girls feel the same. The place isn't fit for a pig, it's freezing cold, you cheat us out of our money by fining us, by charging us to use the washroom, and by turning back the hands on the clock too. Don't think we haven't seen you! And now you want to cut our wages in half because we worked too fast and finished the order. That was the final straw. It made the girls angry enough to walk out."

Katz looked up and down the line. "Those of you who are stupid enough to listen to these troublemakers will find yourself out of a job and right before the holidays too. Just when you'll be needing money for heat. And don't think another firm will take you on, because they won't. So it's up to you. Get inside now and nothing more will be said. Stay out and you're all fired."

"And who's going to make the new season's dresses for you then, Mr. Katz?" Rose asked sweetly. "Won't the designs be ready in a few days?"

"Don't think we'll have any trouble replacing you, Rose Levy. I'll put out the word today and by tomorrow girls will be lining up from here to the Battery."

"They can line up as long as they want," Rose said, "but they are not going into this building. Neither are you."

"You think you can stop me? A few little girls?" He laughed.

"Not just a few little girls," Jacob said as he and his friends stepped from the shadows. "We are representatives of the United Hebrew Trades and the cloak-makers' union. If necessary we will call out more of our members in support. We will provide a ring of steel around this place. So try your best, Mr. Foreman. You are wasting your time."

Katz shot us a look of pure venom, then stalked away again.

"We've won! He's going away!" one of the girls shouted.

"Don't be silly," Rose said. "This is just the beginning. He will be back with Mr. Lowenstein and they will do everything in their power to try to frighten us. But we will not give in. If we can hold out this time, then we'll have made it better for every working girl in New York City."

"Let's hear it for Rose! Rose is our champion!" someone shouted and the line of girls broke into applause.

Daylight came and with it a watery sun, making the sidewalks steam as the puddles evaporated.

"I prayed last night that it wouldn't rain today," Rose said, adjusting the shawl around her shoulders. "Maybe I should have prayed that the sun wouldn't shine. Only in New York can November be as hot as summer if it pleases."

We stood and stood. Passersby shouted out words of encouragement. Mr. Samuel from the deli came across with hot tea for everyone. Clocks across the city chimed out the hours. We drew quite a crowd of bystanders, some curious, some supportive, some mocking. Then around noon the crowd parted to let a long, elegant automobile through. Its hood was down and it was driven by a chauffeur in brown livery. It came to a halt and Mr. Lowenstein got out of the backseat. He came toward us cautiously.

"Girls, girls," he said in a soft, gentle voice. "What foolishness is this? You risk your jobs because some socialist tells you to strike? These Hebrew Trades fellows—they don't have your welfare at heart. They're anarchists, every one of them. They want to bring down the economy, bring down the government. They don't care about you." He looked up and down the line. "I tell you what—I'm going to make you a most generous offer. Any girl who goes back to her machine right now, I'm not even going to take a note of her name, and I keep her on at full pay. The rest of you—out. Finished. On the street. Is that what you want?"

Rose dug me in the side again. I stepped forward hesitantly. "We want better conditions, Mr. Lowenstein. Fair conditions— enough heat in the winter, enough fresh air so we don't get sick, enough light so we don't go blind, and a foreman who doesn't try to cheat us by winding back the clock. That is all we ask. We work as hard as we can for you. We want you to be fair."

Lowenstein held up his hand. "All right. All right. I get better lighting put in, just as soon as electricity comes to this street." He held up his hand to silence the angry mutter that rose from the line. "And any girl who goes back now—I give a dollar bonus."

Several girls stirred on the line. Rose stepped out in front of them. "Not good enough, Mr. Lowenstein. We want six dollars a week, like the girls get at the other shops. And no more paying for the washroom towel and mirror, and no more being fined if we have to stand up to stretch our backs or we need to use the washroom."

Lowenstein looked up and down the line. "You want six dollars, go to one of those other shops who pay this magnificent amount. You are trying my patience. All right, girls. Back to work now if you want your jobs and the bonus I promised you."

One tiny, frail-looking girl stepped out of the line. "Please, Mr. Lowenstein, does that mean that we'll all go back on full wages right now? No more half pay until the new line is ready? My sister and I are the only breadwinners and my mother is sick. We'll starve if I don't work."

I saw that a new idea had occurred to Lowenstein. His brain was ticking: If he kept us out on strike for a few more days, he wouldn't have to pay us a cent. "Full wages when there's work to be done. I don't pay girls to sit twiddling their thumbs," he said. "I guess none of you want to be sensible and loyal. Fine with me. I'll replace the lot of you."

He spun around and stalked back to the car. The chauffeur leaped out to open the door. I noticed then the other occupants of the backseat. They sat together, very chummy, whispering and smiling. One of them was his daughter, Letitia, in her fur-trimmed bonnet. The other was a handsome young man. It took me a moment to place him. As the car drove away, spattering mud from the puddles on those who stood too close, I remembered who he was: He was Mr. Mostel's son.

✨ Twenty ✨

ostel's son and Lowenstein's daughter—did Papa Mostel know about this relationship, given his distrust of Lowenstein? I rather thought not. But Mr. Lowenstein obviously approved. I took this one stage further—here was an obvious connection between the two garment shops, an easy way to pass information. Mostel had told me that he took the designs home at night. How easy it would be for his son to copy them and hand them over to Lowenstein? So it was possible, but it didn't make any sense. If Papa Mostel didn't prosper, who would pay the fees to keep the son at his fancy university? And what son would be such a traitor to his father?

All the same, it was an interesting thought and my first real lead in the case. With all the momentous things that had just happened, I had all but forgotten that this had started with a simple case of stealing fashion designs. It might still be the one case I had the ability to bring to a conclusion.

I let my thoughts wander as I stood on that sidewalk, stamping my feet to keep them warm. It had become cold and windy again, with the threat of more rain. After Lowenstein had left a tremor of fear had gone through the line of girls.

"He's going to fire us all. We'll be out in the street," I heard one girl sobbing.

Rose strode up and down the line. "You're not using your

brain, Gina," she said. "If he doesn't get this place back in full operation in a week, he's not going to win the race to get his new line of clothing into the stores, is he? And there is no way that he can hire and train a whole new set of girls in one week. All we have to do is be strong and wait this one out, and stick together. Right?"

"That's right, Rose. You tell her!" voices shouted encouragement.

We broke for the night when darkness fell. We didn't think that Mr. Lowenstein could do much overnight and the girls were cold, hungry, and exhausted. Jacob put his hand on my shoulder as the strikers dispersed.

"Come and have a bowl of soup and a glass of wine with me. You must be ready to drop."

I smiled at him. "My feet are about ready to fall off. Other than that I'm fine."

He took me to a small café and we had borscht, which Jacob told me was a Russian beet and cabbage soup, served with coarse brown bread and a glass of red wine. I felt my strength returning immediately although that may have been because Jacob was sitting opposite me. He had the sweetest smile and the way he gazed at me from behind those owlish specs was quite heartwarming. We sat chatting until the café owner started sweeping around our feet. Jacob wanted to walk me home, but I could see that he was as tired as I.

"Don't worry. I'll be fine," I said.

"But I do worry," he said. "I couldn't sleep last night. I kept thinking what if they find out the connection between you and Nell? What if they think she told you more than she did, and they come looking for you?"

This was something that hadn't crossed my mind before and I rather wished he hadn't mentioned it.

"Nonsense. They could have no way of knowing that Nell was asking questions on my behalf. I'm perfectly safe," I said, "and I intend to stay that way. I'm heading straight home to a hot bath and bed."

I waved, smiled, and set off with more bravado than I actually felt. He stood on the sidewalk watching me until I reached the corner of the block and turned out of sight. Jacob—an added complication in my life. He was obviously smitten with me. What did I really think about him? He was kind and wise and had a good sense of humor. If I could only shake off my last remaining dreams of Daniel Sullivan, then I could allow myself to fall for a man like Jacob Singer.

Next morning it was back on the picket way at first light. A cold day with frost in the air. The girls stomped their feet and clapped their hands together to stay warm. I wondered how long this standoff would continue. Until Mr. Lowenstein had his own designs completed or he had managed to acquire designs from Mostel's, obviously. In which case I should do something to speed things up.

I've never been known for my great patience. Another of my major faults, or cardinal sins, according to my mother. I would always be the one who dipped her finger in the cake batter or who opened the oven to see if the Yorkshire pudding was rising and thus made it go flat. So by the third day of standing outside Lowenstein's, I was suffering more from boredom than from cold, hunger, or fear.

I knew that I had promised Jacob that I wouldn't pursue Nell's killer, but I was itching to get back to Mostel's again. I told myself that it was only because I wanted to get the business of the designs sorted out and with Lowenstein's out on strike, that could never happen. But at the back of my mind loomed the question of Nell and what she had found out. And Mostel's was the one concrete link I had in the chain of Katherine's disappearance and Nell's death.

I slipped away from the line, on the pretext of finding a washroom, found a nearby stationer, bought paper and envelope, looked longingly at the new fountain pens displayed in the glass counter, then persuaded the clerk to let me use his pen and ink. As soon as I had money, I would buy myself one of those new fountain pens so that I could write notes anywhere—along with the watch that was so necessary to my profession, of course. Having left the store, my head swimming with such grand ideas, I was soon reminded that if I didn't conclude a case soon, I was not likely to have the money for food, let alone luxuries.

The message I had penned was to Mr. Mostel, asking if he could meet me at Steiner's Coffee House on Lower Broadway, sufficiently far away from prying eyes. Half an hour after I delivered it, he appeared at the door of the coffeehouse.

"Miss Murphy?" he said, sitting down at the table beside me. "You have news for me?"

"How can I have news for you when the Lowenstein girls are out on strike?" I asked. "Nor am I likely to find out anything unless they return to work."

His broad forehead crinkled into a frown. "I heard about that. A sorry matter, Miss Murphy. Not that I would shed a tear for Lowenstein, but it's the rest of us that I worry about. Once our girls hear about it, they'll all be getting ideas. We have to nip this in the bud before it spreads to the other garment shops."

"That's precisely why I wanted to see you, Mr. Mostel. How can I complete my assignment and ferret out your spy if Lowenstein's is closed?

"Of course this could be a blessing in disguise," he said. "My new designs could be finished and in the stores while that criminal Lowenstein wrings his hands in despair and his factory remains closed."

I was not happy with this way of thinking. It was an all too probable line of development and would mean that I was not paid. I shook my head. "He told the girls he intends to fire them all and hire new workers if necessary. He'll get those garments into the stores, by hook or by crook. And having all new girls wouldn't stop your spy from slipping the designs to him."

"True." He nodded, his large, melancholy jowls quivering. "So what is the answer, Miss Murphy?"

"I've been thinking, Mr. Mostel, and I've come up with a solution." He leaned closer to me, across the marble-topped table. "You must announce to everyone at your factory that your new designs will be completed, let's say, next Tuesday. Make sure everyone knows this. I have another idea as well—why not make a false set of designs, dresses you never intend to make and sell, and see if your spy takes the bait. Add something outlandish to the design—a big frilly collar, a velvet hood, a gentleman's bow tie—and see if Lowenstein is tricked into making it."

Mr. Mostel rubbed his hands together in delight. "I like it, Miss Murphy. Oh, the joy of getting the better of Lowenstein."

"You must make sure that these drawings are easily accessible on your desk and you are away from your office enough so that the spy is able to sneak in and take them."

"Naturally. Naturally." He was still rubbing his hands and beaming. "And if that fool Lowenstein is stupid enough to make a dress with a frilly collar or a bow tie, you'll make me the happiest man in New York City!"

"Let's hope he takes the bait," I said, "and that we catch your thief. I have to admit that I've found no hint of suspicion so far, but time will tell." That wasn't exactly the truth. An image of Ben Mostel in the back of Lowenstein's car came into my head, but I didn't think it was the right moment to tell Mr. Mostel that I had my suspicions about his son. "You are not personally worried that your employees might follow suit and go out on strike then?"

"My employees? I'm like a father to them, Miss Murphy. Why should they think of striking?"

I bit my tongue and moved to the next topic. "So you've no particular troublemakers at the moment?"

"You saw for yourself. They are happy and content and if anyone wants to make trouble, then I show her the door. I don't tolerate troublemakers."

I took a big swig of coffee and grasped the bull by the horns. "I heard you had an English girl working for you who was a bit of a rabble-rouser? One of the girls at Lowenstein's told me, because she thought I was English too."

His face didn't register any change in expression. "I don't recall any English girl. She can't have lasted long. I leave the hiring and firing to my foreman and concentrate myself on making the profits."

"So your business is flourishing, is it, Mr. Mostel?" I asked sweetly.

"I can't complain, Miss Murphy. It's a living."

"And your son—that was your son who came into the shop once, wasn't it—he plans to follow you into the business one day?"

"My son?" He rolled deep soulful eyes. "You speak of my oldest son, Ben? He plans to break his father's heart, that's what he plans to do, Miss Murphy. We made a mistake with that boy—we brought him up to have everything he wanted, all the things we never had ourselves. And has he thanked us for it?" He shook his head. "My wife cries herself to sleep worrying over him. We scrimp and save to send him to Harvard University, the finest in the land, and what do I hear but that he's failed his latest examinations. All he's interested in is having a good time and going through his father's money. He'll be the ruin of me, Miss Murphy."

"Does he have a sweetheart who might be a sobering influence, Mr. Mostel?"

"Does he have a sweetheart? It's a different sweetheart every week, Miss Murphy. And it's my money that is buying them expensive presents and jewelry and taking them to dine at Delmonico's. He won't hear of a matchmaker. He tells us that he's an American and he lives in the twentieth century and he'll choose himself a bride when he's good and ready."

"It must be a great worry for you," I commiserated, "but I'm sure he'll come to his senses soon enough."

"He'd better. This time I've laid down the law. Any more failed exams and you're not getting another penny from me, I told him. You'll be out earning your living by the sweat of your brow like your father had to. That shook him up, Miss Murphy."

"I'm sure it must have."

He pulled his watch out of his vest pocket and glanced at it. "I must get back to work, Miss Murphy. I've enjoyed our little chat and I like your thinking. I'll come up with some outlandish sketches over the weekend and by this time next week we may have found out the traitor in our midst."

He escorted me from the coffeehouse, bowed, and we went our separate ways. As I walked away I tried to digest all that I had learned. He truly didn't seem to remember Katherine and somehow I couldn't picture him ordering her murder—which meant that if anyone ordered her death it was the foreman, Seedy Sam.

And concerning the other matter of the purloined designs, Mostel's son now stood clearly at the head of my list of suspects. He had opportunity and he had a motive, if he was angry with his father for cracking the whip and stopping his pleasurable lifestyle. It was clear that he needed more money than his father was giving him and I presumed Mr. Lowenstein would come up with a handsome finder's fee. I wondered if he was sweet on Lowenstein's daughter, or if he was also only courting her in an effort to slight his father. However, if he were the traitor in the camp, the designs could move smoothly from one garment shop to the other without either party in the transaction going near the workplace. Which meant I would have no way of catching the suspects, and thus no way of being paid. I'd also have to tread very carefully if I wanted to make an accusation against

Mostel's son. Parents do not take kindly to suggestions that their offspring are not all they should be, however plain this might be to the rest of the world. It occurred to me that I should check up on the infamous Ben Mostel and see if I could uncover any other unfavorable facts against him.

I rejoined the picket line outside Lowenstein's. Nothing much had happened during my absence, except that frail little Fanny had fainted and was currently sitting in Samuel's being revived with a bowl of their best chicken soup. We stood, stamping our feet to keep warm until darkness fell and the icy blast from the East River made us decide to call it a day.

Jacob had a meeting of the United Hebrew Trades and I went home, grateful for a chance to warm up and get some sleep. I came in on a peaceful domestic scene, Bridie in her nightgown sitting on her papa's knee and Shamey curled up at his feet as Seamus told them a story. As I listened, I caught the words and realized that the story was about their mother, Kathleen, and their life back in Ireland. I climbed the stairs thinking of my own half-forgotten life back in Ireland. Was it really less than a year ago that I had lived in a cottage and gone to our plot to dig potatoes in the rain and walked on the cliff tops in the wind and gazed out at the ocean, wondering what would become of me? Never, in my wildest dreams, could I have pictured this.

Major Faversham's letter, along with the pictures of Katherine and Michael, were lying on my bedside table. I really should be writing that letter to him, telling him the sad news of his daughter's demise. I couldn't put it off much longer. I took out paper, pen, and ink, then sat, studying the photograph of Katherine again. The haughty face stared back at me, head held proudly, dressed in all her finery. Such a waste. Just like Nell— two lives that held so much promise, both cut short. Tears of compassion welled up in my eyes.

Then I blinked away the tears and stared harder at the photograph. I had asked Daniel if the body pulled from the East River had been wearing any jewelry and the answer had been in the negative. I took the photo under the gas and peered at it harder, wishing I had a magnifying glass. The locket Katherine was wearing around her neck was very distinctive—it was heart-shaped, and had a flower design on it in what looked like precious stones. My heart started racing. Now I knew what had disturbed me when I first saw Letitia Lowenstein. She had been wearing an identical locket around her neck.

❦ Twenty-one ❧

All thoughts of a hot bath and rest were put aside. I rushed down the stairs again, clutching the photograph, past the astonished O'Connor family and across the street to Sid and Gus.

"Dear God, don't tell us something else is wrong," Sid said, looking at my face. "I don't think we could take another tragedy."

"No, nothing is wrong," I said, "but I wondered if you might own a magnifying glass."

"But of course," Sid said, as if people showed up on her doorstep at nine o'clock every night demanding magnifying glasses. "Come in, do. We were just about to have coffee."

Sid's Turkish coffee late at night was a guarantee of no sleep, but I missed the reassurance of their company, so I accepted and was taken through to the kitchen, where Gus was putting a pot of water onto the stove.

"Molly!" she exclaimed. "Have they found Nell's killer yet? We tried to find out when her funeral will be, but the police have not released her body to her family. What a tragic business for them. We are extremely cut up about it too, are we not, Sid?"

"Positively melancholy," Sid echoed. "Poor Gus has been quite out of sorts since you left and even worse since she heard of Nell Blankeship's death, Molly. You should see the painting she has started—all dark swirls, like deep gloomy pools."

"Don't mind me," Gus said, "I always get this way with the approach of winter."

"Then we must whisk you south to the sun," Sid said. "Florida, do you think?"

My heart lurched at the thought of Sid and Gus going away, then Gus shook her head. "We couldn't abandon Molly, and Ryan will expect us to hold his hand while his play opens in the city. Let's just go out and fill the place with flowers and oranges tomorrow. That should suffice."

"Here is the requested object." Sid handed me the magnifying glass she had found in a drawer. "Are you planning to become Mr. Sherlock Holmes?"

I laughed. "No, I just wanted to examine this photograph more closely." I placed it on the table.

"That is the English girl who you were trying to trace—the one they said had drowned in the East River." Sid peered over my shoulder. "Molly, you are not still pursuing this inquiry, are you? Wasn't Nell also looking into this girl's disappearance when she was killed?"

"Molly—I thought we gave you enough stern warnings," Gus added.

"I promised to do nothing foolish, and I plan to keep that promise," I said. "This is another matter altogether. I wanted to examine the necklace she is wearing. I think I might have seen it in New York."

"She pawned it, perhaps."

I hadn't thought of that possibility. Katherine could well have pawned her jewelry to keep herself and Michael going and Letitia Lowenstein could have bought the locket quite legitimately at a pawn shop. Nothing underhand involved after all.

I put the magnifying glass to my eye and examined the locket. In closer detail I could see that the stones were arranged in a design that looked like forget-me-nots. How very appropriate, I thought. I am not going to forget you, Katherine! And I am going to find out how Letitia Lowenstein came by a very similar locket. I remembered Mr. Mostel lamenting that his son showered his lady friends with jewelry. Had Ben acquired this particular jewel? It was too much of a coincidence that he had come across it in a pawn shop. Yes, Mr. Ben Mostel, I must really check into you, I thought as walked home across Patchin Place.

The next day was Friday, the fourth since our strike began. It was obvious to me that Mr. Lowenstein was going to be content to have us standing out in the street until the moment he wanted work to commence again. Then it would be a case of accept my conditions or I find replacements. Only then would it start to get ugly. I hoped that my meeting with Mr. Mostel yesterday might bring things to a swifter conclusion. If he had announced the unveiling of his new line, as planned, then Mr. Lowenstein would want us back at work by sometime next week. It would be interesting to see when he made his move.

Around midmorning, Jacob came running up, waving a copy of the *New York Herald*. "Look, they printed my photograph," he exclaimed and we gathered around to see. Under the headline GARMENT WORKERS DEMAND BETTER CONDITIONS was a picture of our picket line. Jacob had chosen to focus on the frailest-looking girls. Little Fanny was positively sagging against her picket sign. The girls looked like frozen waifs. The whole scene was most appealing.

"It's wonderful, Jacob," I said. "If this doesn't stir up public sympathy, I don't know what will."

By midday we had had a visit from various reporters, plus some society ladies who were part of the Ladies' League, working for justice and equality for women. They brought hot buns and cocoa with them and promised to approach the big department stores on our behalf, pressuring them into not buying Lowenstein's garments if he didn't settle the strike favorably. This was a big boost to morale and the girls sang as they stood in line— "She's Only a Bird in a Gilded Cage," "Mighty Like a Rose"—all the latest popular songs as well as plaintive Yiddish, soulful Russian ditties, and sprightly Italian ones. The rest of us clapped and stamped our feet. A crowd gathered and cheered us on.

Toward evening the mood of the crowd changed. A group of unsavory-looking men with battered derbys or caps pulled down over their eyes, oversize jackets, and big boots started jeering and hurling insults at us. They pushed past the onlookers and came right up to where they thought the line was weakest, towering over the smallest girls.

"Well, lookee here. Ain't they sweet? Poor little orphan girls out on the street—hey, honey, why are you wasting your time standing in this line for a few measly dollars when you could be making yourself big money if you come to work for me?"

"Work for you?" one of the girls asked. "Do you run a garment shop?"

"Yeah, only my girls take their garments off," the man guffawed. "Ain't that right, Flossie?"

A hard, brazen-looking woman, wearing tight tawdry clothing that proclaimed her to be a streetwalker stepped out of the crowd and stood in front of the girls. "You get paid for lying flat on your back, girls. Make money in your sleep. What could be easier?"

Another flashy woman had joined her, this one in a red velvet gown with an outrageous ostrich feather in a hat which was tilted rakishly down over her face. "Not this one, Floss," she said. "She ain't got what the gentlemen likes. She's flat as a pancake." She moved down the line, standing in front of Sophia, a plump little Italian. "Now you could do very well for yourself, dearie. Nice round little derriere—something for the gentleman to get his hands around."

"And a good pair of water wings in front too, right Floss?" The other woman cackled.

"I'm a good girl. Don't say things like that." Sophia pulled her shawl around her and looked as if she was about to cry.

"If you stand out here on the street, the police are going to think you're one of us," the streetwalker continued, reaching out to tug at Sophia's long hair.

Jacob had started to move toward the confrontation. "Leave these girls alone. They are respectable and don't want anything to do with the likes of you," he said.

"With the likes of us?" the man demanded. "Who are you insulting?"

"I'm telling you to hop it, or I'll call the police."

"Call the police—that's a good one!" The man laughed and looked around. I noticed several policeman standing on the corner watching us.

"Officers, these people are upsetting our girls and trying to intimidate them," I called to constables who stood, arms folded, and grinning.

I saw the louts move in my direction. There was something about one of them lurking at the back of the pack that caught my attention. I had seen him before—one of the Eastmans maybe. Then I had no time for idle contemplation as the biggest and most brutish looking of the bunch swaggered right up to me.

"It's the other way around, girlie," he growled. "Youse is blocking dis sidewalk so that honest folk like ourselves can't get by without stepping in the nasty dirty street. My poor Flossie doesn't want to get mud all over her nice clean shoes, do you Floss?" He turned back to grin at the brazen hussy behind him. "Now move out of the way, or else!"

I remembered now why the men and their actions seemed familiar to me. If I wasn't mistaken, these same bullyboys had been accosting passersby outside the polling booth on election day. They were gangland enforcers and since the Eastmans ruled this part of the city, Eastmans they obviously were. The brute coming toward me was one I hadn't seen before. I faced him, confident that he wouldn't try anything with all these people looking on.

"We're not moving," I said. "We have every right to stand here. Cross over if you want to get past."

"Step aside, or I'm just going to have to push past you." The lout was leering down at me. I could smell his stinking breath, laced with alcohol.

I glared up at him. "Get away from me, you great brute! You don't frighten me."

"Don't say I didn't warn you." He was still grinning inanely.

"Try to push past me and you'll be sorry!" I said.

"Molly!" Jacob shouted. "Just ignore them."

But he was too late. The brute came at me with his shoulder, like a rugby charge. I stuck my foot out and he went sprawling forward, grabbing onto a lamppost to prevent himself from falling.

"Did you see what she did? She attacked me!" he yelled, righting himself against a street lamp and turning on me. "Youse going to get what's coming to you now, girlie!"

He swung at me. I dodged aside but too late. His fist glanced off my face and I staggered backward. He was still grinning at me, looking like a great brutish ape.

"Holy Mother of God!" I exclaimed, putting my hand up to my stinging face. "Now you're the one who's going to be sorry."

I snatched Rose's picket sign and swung it at him. It was only made of cardboard and flimsy wood so that the contact sounded worse than it really was as it crashed against his head. It certainly felt satisfying.

"Get out of here now and leave us alone!" I yelled, raining blows against his head as the sign splintered and all I was left with was a stick of wood.

Then I looked up in relief as blue uniforms finally came into the fray.

"Arrest her, Officer. She is attacking innocent citizens," one of the streetwalkers shouted.

Hands grabbed both my arms.

"Let go of me at once," I shouted angrily. "These louts started attacking us. We were just defending ourselves."

"Not what I saw, miss," one of the constables said. "You're the one holding the weapon. Come on, into the paddy wagon with you."

I was bundled into a waiting wagon, along with Jacob, Sophia, and a couple of other girls.

"This is outrageous," I stormed as the wagon took off at a gallop. "When we get to police headquarters, I'm going to make a big stink. Those policemen just stood and watched while we were harassed."

"Of course they did, Molly," Jacob said calmly. "The whole thing was set up. It's been done a hundred times before. When shop owners want to break up a strike, they hire starkes—strong-arm men—to do their dirty work. They want the girls intimidated so that they go back to work with no fuss."

I grabbed hold of Jacob as we were thrown around by the lurching wagon.

"Then why didn't the police arrest them if they knew what was happening?"

"Because the police have been bribed, of course. They were waiting for the moment when you did exactly what they wanted you to do. You struck one of them."

"Just because a few police are corrupt, doesn't mean we won't get fair treatment when we get to headquarters," I said. "Those starkes were propositioning Sophia, making lewd comments to her. You heard them threaten me."

Jacob was shaking his head patiently. "You are still very naïve," he said. "To tell you the truth, I had been expecting something like this since the very first day of the strike. I had warned you that these bosses do not play fair, hadn't I?"

"But you did nothing," I said. "You didn't attack anyone. Why have they arrested you?"

"Because I am known to them. I am safer in custody and they

hope to break the strike without people like myself around to let the girls know their rights."

"Do you think they will succeed?" I peered through the small back window of the paddy wagon. "I hope Rose is strong enough to keep the girls from giving in."

"And someone has gone to the Hebrew Trades for reinforcements too," Jacob said. "With any luck they just wanted to scare us and think they have done so."

"So Lowenstein hired bullies, did he? I thought I recognized one of them, lurking in the shadows at the back. Could they have been members of the Eastmans?"

"Very possible," Jacob said. "They often use gangs to do their dirty work."

"The police stand by and watch while gang members beat up young women?" I demanded. I was still hot enough to explode. "What sort of society is this?"

Jacob shrugged. "Much the same the world over. The poor have no voice. The rich have the money and power. Money buys anything."

"Then it's a rotten world," I snapped. I looked across at the three girls who had been arrested with us, frail little girls who had done nothing, now clinging to each other in a terrified huddle.

"Don't worry, it will be all right," I said to them. "I'll tell the policemen that you did nothing wrong."

One of them had her hand up to her mouth, sobbing. "My family will be ashamed when they hear I go to prison. My papa, he will throw me out."

"Nobody's going to throw you out. Jacob and I will come and talk to your family and let them know the truth if you want. Once we get to headquarters and we can talk to some uncorrupt policemen, they'll let us go right away, and we'll be home in time for supper, I'm sure."

The girls gazed at me, wanting to believe me. One managed a watery smile.

The wagon came to an abrupt halt, almost throwing us onto the floor. The door opened.

"Okay, you lot. Out you get and no funny business," a voice ordered.

Jacob stepped down first then held out his hand to escort us women down the steps. His calm demeanor was reassuring and he handed each of us down like a society lady, arriving at a ball.

I glanced around as we stepped out into the dark street.

"This isn't police headquarters," I said. "Where have they taken us?"

"I rather fear it's the courthouse," Jacob said.

"Courthouse? They're going to try us as common criminals— without a proper investigation?"

"It looks that way," Jacob said. "Now remember, Molly, stay calm. They'll say things to try and make you blow up. Act like these other girls will—confused, innocent, scared. That's what might work on the judge, not hotheaded and indignant."

"I've never played the helpless female in my life," I said, tossing back my hair.

"No, I don't suppose you have," he admitted, smiling, "but this would be a good time to learn."

"Come on now. Move it. Up the steps." A constable swung his baton to chivvy us along.

"We are not cattle, Officer," I said, "and we do not need driving."

"What have I just been telling you?" Jacob whispered. "This is serious, Molly. If you annoy the judge, you could find yourself in prison."

"Nonsense. You can't send someone to jail without proof that they've done something wrong."

"But that's just what I'm trying to tell you. They will manufacture proof. Now, please, keep quiet and act submissively, I beg you."

"No talking. In you go," The voice behind the cattle prod said.

We were marshaled into a long hallway and then into a small holding room. A clerk was sitting at a high, old-fashioned desk. He took down our names and addresses, then left us with just a police guard.

One by one the three girls were taken out and did not return. Jacob and I sat on the hard bench waiting. It must have been well past my suppertime and my insides were growling with hunger. I was also cold and tired, and just a little bit scared too, if the truth be known. I had always been a staunch believer in right and wrong, and the ultimate triumph of right. Now it seemed that right might not be about to triumph. Should I do what I had sworn never to do again and summon Daniel to my aid? A disturbing thought crossed my mind. He might not wish to go against the official police position.

I had heard, of course, that the New York police could be bribed, but I had never seen it in action until now. I went through that scene again in my mind, those constables standing on the opposite corner, arms folded, smirking, as the louts came at us. I could almost smell that foul breath again and I shuddered. I tried to picture their faces—were any of them gang members I had seen before? Could the police really be working with a gang? That one familiar face at the back of the crowd—where and when had I seen him before? Then it hit me like an ice-cold shower. He was in shadow, at the back of the group, and I hadn't had a chance to see him clearly before the brawl began. In fact I had never seen his face clearly. The only time I had seen it before was on a newspaper cutting from Ireland, standing at Katherine's side as she prepared for a day's hunting. If I was not completely mistaken, the man I had spotted today was Michael Kelly.

❧ Twenty-two ☙

I f Michael Kelly was still alive, and working with the East-mans, then that changed everything. He would probably know who killed Katherine. Was he out to get revenge right now, and did this mean that the Eastmans had no part in her death? Somehow I would have to find him and talk to him. Then I reminded myself that a lot of Irishmen have that sort of face—the typical look of what they call Black Irish. Daniel himself looked not unlike Michael Kelly. And I had only glimpsed him for a moment in the shadows, hardly enough to make a positive identification.

"Miss Murphy." I jumped to my feet as my name was called.

Jacob reached across and touched my arm. "Now remember," he said. "Helpless, innocent, frail. No outbursts."

I nodded, hung my head, and looked coy, making him smile.

I was taken into a drafty, dimly lit courtroom. It was empty apart from a judge, sitting at a high bench, and a couple of policemen. My footsteps clattered on the marble floor as I was led forward.

"Miss Molly Murphy, Your Honor," the bailiff said. "She is charged with disturbing the peace."

The judge peered down at me. He had a cold, beaklike face, like a stone eagle, and I couldn't tell if he might be moved by my youth and frailty. Did he know that I had been framed? Had he also been bribed?

"I understand that you were part of a street disturbance, earlier this evening."

"I was part of a picket line. My coworkers and I are on strike against Lowenstein's garment factory, Your Honor."

"I also understand that you struck passersby with a wooden sign." His voice matched his face in coldness.

"Only after I was struck myself by a very large loutish bully. It was self-defense, Your Honor."

He glanced down. "The witness's statement only mentions your attack with the sign. The complaint says that you were blocking the sidewalk, preventing pedestrians from passing by. When one attempted to pass, you hit him with your sign. So I ask you now, Miss Murphy, did you or did you not attack a person with a sign?"

"Yes, but it was after . . ."

He held up his hand. "I'm not asking what preceded it. This is America, Miss Murphy, not Ireland. You can't just go around brawling in the streets here. We have laws to protect innocent citizens."

"Innocent citizens?" My voice rose. "You call those louts innocent citizens? They were baiting us and you know very well that they were paid to bait us, just as the police were paid to watch them. If this is American law, then I don't think very much of it."

"Nobody asked you to come here, Miss Murphy," the judge said. For an awful moment I thought he was going to send me back to Ireland. "I can be lenient with you and charge you with disturbing the peace. That carries with it a ten-dollar fine and a night in jail. I could also add to it a charge of inflicting grievous bodily harm which would mean a month in women's prison and a hundred-dollar fine. It's up to you."

He paused and frowned down at me, like a parent appealing to a naughty child. "If you swear to me that you will not attempt to disturb the peace again, then I'll let you off lightly this time. However, if I catch you back on the street protesting and harassing innocent passersby, I won't be so generous next time. It will be a month in prison, and I think you'll find that prison isn't a very pleasant place to be, especially not at this time of year."

He leaned forward. "So what is it to be, Miss Murphy? Do I have your solemn word that you will not attempt to disturb the peace again?"

I was not going to have anyone to speak for me. I was not going to find justice in this court. I looked down at my feet, playing the repentant child. "Yes, Your Honor," I said.

"In that case I sentence you to one night in jail and a ten-dollar fine." He brought down his gavel. "Take her away. Bring in the next case."

Hands led me away. I was still seething with anger. If this was America, did I really want to be part of it? The moment I got out of jail, I'd take the first boat anywhere—South America, Africa, Australia. . . .

I was led down a flight of stone steps, then a door was opened with a big key. It felt cold and clammy down there, dimly lit and very unpleasant.

"Another one for you, Bert," the man with me said cheerfully as he presented me at the half door of a small cubbyhole. An elderly, toothless man got to his feet. "What's she done? Killed her old man?"

"Disturbing the peace. She's in for the night."

"Okay. Just a moment while I get the featherbeds in the guest room ready." He gave a wheezy laugh as he shuffled down the corridor ahead of me. An iron door squeaked open. "In you go, honey. All modern conveniences. Bucket in the corner. Breakfast at seven." I was propelled inside with a hefty shove and the door clanged shut behind me.

I looked around, afraid to see with whom I might be sharing this cell. But I was alone. A narrow wooden plank ran along one wall. There was a bucket in the corner. That was it. I sat on the bench and hugged my arms to me. It was miserably cold and I was sick with hunger. I was also sick with anger that I was so powerless. Were those three little girls also in similar cells, I wondered? Was Jacob also locked up here? I longed for the comforting calm of his presence, but I didn't wish him in this place. After what he had been through in Russia, a night in a cell like this must be like reliving a nightmare.

I sat on my plank, hugging my knees to me to try to keep warm. There was no way I was going to be able to sleep on this thing. As my anger dissipated I began to feel wretched and alone. My chosen profession was not turning out to be what I had wanted at all. I seemed to be going to prison with monotonous regularity. And it wasn't as if I was much closer to solving any cases either. When I got out, my next step would be to prove to my own satisfaction that Michael Kelly was alive, and I wasn't sure how I was going to do that safely. If he was still alive, then who killed Katherine and how did Letitia Lowenstein get her locket? Every step forward I took, things just became more muddled.

I started as something scurried across the floor. It was too dark to make out what it was—either a rat or a mouse or a very large cockroach. Either way I had no intention of letting it anywhere near me. I hugged my knees tighter to myself and kept watch.

It was a long cold night. Several times I nodded off, only to wake myself as my head banged against the cold damp stone of the wall. At times voices cried out in sleep, waking me from my doze. And in my half consciousness I saw phantom rats about to eat my toes. I wanted to spend a penny, but not into that bucket, not having to cross that floor.

"It's only one night," I told myself. "I can put up with anything for one night." Then I shifted myself into the corner and touched a spider's web. If there's one thing in the world that I hate, it's spiders. Without warning I started to cry. It was all so shocking and unfair and I was being punished for something I didn't do when I was trying to do was help people . . . I sat there sniveling and feeling pretty sorry for myself until I gave myself a stern talking-to. "Just listen to you, behaving like a proper ninny," I said out loud. "Poor Jacob had to endure far worse than this. They tortured him, they tried to kill him when he was only a boy, and he's come through it all right. He's even brave enough to go on fighting, so the least you can do is stick this out for one night."

Thus fortified I rested my head on top of my knees and fell asleep. At first light I woke to the rattle of something against bars and a mug and piece of bread were shoved through. I drank the hot coffee, and ate all of the bread. Then I spruced myself up in preparation for my release. I was not going to let them see that my night in jail had upset me or dampened my spirits.

An hour or so later old toothless-mouth shuffled up to my door and opened it. "Out you go then, girlie. You're free."

A guard escorted me up the flight of steps, through to the front of the building, and out into the gray morning air. I stood, breathing deeply and watching the pigeons flapping and pecking in the little park opposite. As I came down the flight of steps I saw a figure sitting on a bench in the little park. He got to his feet.

"Molly!" He called and ran to me.

"Jacob!" I was enveloped in his arms.

"Are you all right?" he asked.

"Never felt better. The food rivaled Delmonico's, the bed was softer than at the Waldorf-Astoria."

He gazed at me. "I am in awe of you. What does it take to dampen your spirits?"

I neglected to mention my weeping session in the small hours of the morning. "What's one lousy night in jail?" I said with a good attempt at a carefree smile. "Uncomfortable maybe, but not unbearable. I'm ready to go right back on duty and let them see that they can't crush us so easily."

"You are not going back on duty," he said firmly. "You are going straight home to bed and you are going to stay there."

"But the girls will think I've deserted them."

He put his hands on my shoulders and held me securely. "Didn't you understand what the judge said? The first offence is minor. If you are arrested again for the same offence, it will be off to prison for a long while. People die in prison, Molly—typhoid and any number of foul diseases are rampant. And you'd be sharing a cell with the dregs of society—violent, conscience-less criminals. I am not going to let that happen to you. If necessary I'm going to lock you in your room and take away the key."

"You can't stop me," I said defiantly.

"Molly, you seem to have forgotten. This is not even your fight. It was brave of you to help in this way, but you are not one of them." He was shouting at me now.

"Oh, and you're a lady garment worker yourself, are you?" I demanded. "You could have fooled me."

"I help them because I have the knowledge. It is the business of the United Hebrew Trades to help all unions. I paid your fine, by the way."

"You didn't have to do that. I'm not a pauper." I was still angry with him.

"It wasn't my money. We have a fund to assist strikers who run afoul of the law."

"Then save your money for the real strikers, since I'm not really one of them."

"So your present job makes you a millionaire, does it?"

I couldn't come up with a ready answer to that one.

"Molly," he said quietly now. "Don't be so stubborn. I admire the way you have taken these girls' cause as your own. As I said before, I am in awe at the way you toss off a night in jail as if it were no more inconvenience than a broken fingernail, but when it comes to your common sense—" He shook his head and I had to laugh.

"Come," he said, taking my arm. "First things first. You need a good breakfast, then I am taking you home."

I gave him an embarrassed grin. "If it's first things first, then I need to find a public convenience in a hurry. I wasn't about to use that bucket in my cell."

Jacob laughed and escorted me across the public garden where a wrought-iron-decorated public lavatory was indeed a welcome sight. Then I allowed myself to be led up Broadway, away from city hall, away from Lowenstein's.

"But what about the other girls? Do you know what happened to them? And what about you? Did they release you last night?"

"The three girls were sent home with just a warning, so I understand. I was detained for the night just like you."

"But that wasn't fair, Jacob. You did nothing. At least I hit that great lout."

He shrugged. "I am used to it by now."

"Do you think the those strong-arm bullyboys—starkes, did you call them—managed to break up the strike without us there?"

"We'll find out soon enough, won't we?" he said. "Although I rather think that their behavior last night was merely a warning. They wanted to show us how rough they could get if we keep going."

"All the more reason for me to go back and help."

We stood at the curb, waiting for a milk wagon to pass with churns and harness jangling merrily. "We will not go through this again." He swung me to the right and marched me into a café, seating me at an oilcloth-covered table then ordering coffee and sweet rolls for us. We were both equally hungry and ate in silence until the plate was empty.

"More?" Jacob asked.

I shook my head. "Sufficient unto the day, as my mother always said. Now I'm back to my old self and ready to tackle anything."

"All right, I'll make a deal with you," Jacob said. "We will visit the strike scene and let the girls see that you have come through your ordeal with flying colors. That itself will boost their spirits. Then I will escort you straight home, where you will stay. Understood?"

"For a gentle soul, you can be quite forceful when you want to," I said.

He smiled. "When I care about something or somebody enough, I can be passionate."

We walked close beside each other in companionable silence.

"Jacob?"

He looked up.

"Do you think there is any way to find out about Michael Kelly—without getting involved with the Eastmans, I mean?"

"Straight home," he repeated, "and stay there."

❧ Twenty-three ❧

I fell into a dreamless sleep the moment my head hit the pillow and was not conscious of the hours passing. I came to, like a diver coming up from deep water, to a rhythmic hammering. I lay for a while, trying to remember where I was and what I was doing lying in bed with the setting sun glowing red onto my face. Then I realized that the hammering was someone pounding on my front door.

"All right, I'm coming," I heard Seamus calling.

He opened the door. I heard men's voices and sat up, afraid that the police had come to arrest me again, or, worse still, that the Eastmans had found where I lived. Then men's boots coming up the stairs in a great hurry. I leaped out of bed and reached for my dressing gown. I was only half into it when my door burst open.

"How dare you come into a lady's boudoir," I started to say, then my jaw dropped in astonishment. "Jacob! What are you doing here? Don't tell me that the starkes have broken the strike?"

He was beaming. "I had to come to tell you the good news straight away—we won, Molly. We won!" He took my hands and danced around with me. "Mr. Lowenstein came and told the girls that he would meet their demands—six dollars a week, like the other shops, and finish on Friday and Saturday nights by six o'clock to be home in time for Shabbat, and better heat and light too. They go back to work on Monday morning. It's a miracle."

"It certainly is," I said. I was pleased too, of course, but more skeptical than Jacob. Of course he didn't know about my little scheme with Mr. Mostel. If Lowenstein had found out that he could get his hands on Mostel's designs on Tuesday, then he'd need his shop up and running again on Monday, wouldn't he? And how easy it would be to pay the girls the promised six dollars a week, then manage to dock them that extra dollar in fines. And as for heat and light—he could keep promising those until the cows came home.

But for now the news was good all around. The girls could go back to work. Lowenstein could get his hands on Mostel's designs. I could catch Lowenstein's spy, collect my fee, and go back to sleeping late.

"Come on, get dressed," Jacob said, panting a little after his crazy dance. "We are celebrating tonight at the meeting room. This is not just a victory for the ladies garment workers, it is a victory for all unions. We have shown that we can strike and win in a small way. Next time we can make demands to a whole industry."

"Then go and wait downstairs, if you want me to get dressed," I said, pushing him away. "I'm sure your matchmaker will never be able to find a good match for you, if you've been discovered in a lady's boudoir."

"I think I may have found a good match myself, without any help of the *schadchen*." He gave me a quick glance then closed the door behind him.

I stood staring at the door, my heart beating rather fast. What did I feel about Jacob Singer? I wasn't sure. Oh, I liked him, I certainly admired him, and if I were honest, I liked the way he wanted to take care of me. But marry him? I had never considered marrying anyone but Daniel. Maybe this was the right time to put that foolish notion behind me, once and for all.

The Hebrew Trades meeting room was full to bursting by the time we got there. Music was spilling out onto the sidewalk. A violinist and an accordion player sat on stools in one corner, playing a lively tune, while the rest of the floor was a milling, seething crowd of dancers, all of them girls. The young men stood around the wall, looking on and clapping. The tune ended and the girls, red-faced and glowing, made for the punch bowl.

"Molly!" Rose spotted me through the crowd and made her way to me. "You've heard the wonderful news. Isn't it grand? And all thanks to you."

"Thanks to me? Oh no, I was only one person among all of you."

"But you stood up to those starkes. You made that bully look like a fool in front of all of us. It made them think twice, Molly."

"Then I'm glad I could help."

She slipped her arm through mine. "Come and taste my mama's stuffed cabbage rolls. Best cabbage rolls outside Warsaw, she says. Was prison really terrible?"

"Could have been worse," I said. "I survived, as you see."

"We're all so proud of you." She grabbed a plate and started piling cabbage rolls on it.

"Enough." I laughed. "Save some for the others."

"Look at all this good food. A holiday feast. Everyone brought something—Italian spaghetti and German potato dumplings and blintzes—a grand tour of the world."

We ate and drank and danced some more.

"That young man in the worker's cap is looking at you, Rose," I whispered to her. "Why don't you get him to dance with you?"

"Dance with me?" A look of pure horror, with just a tinge of delight. "If my papa heard I had danced with a man, I'd be turned out of the house. He'd want nothing more to do with me."

"But in America men and girls dance together all the time. What is the harm in it?"

She shook her head. "Not Jewish girls," she said. "Not Jewish men."

"Wait a minute." I forced my way through the crowd to Jacob. "I want you to dance with me," I said.

He looked a little uncertain.

"What—you don't find me attractive enough? Or are you afraid it will get back to the matchmaker?"

He laughed and put one hand awkwardly around my waist. Then he nodded to the musicians who struck up another lively number.

"Can you do the polka?" he asked.

"No, but I'll pick it up soon enough."

We started around the floor. Even over the music I thought I could detect a collective gasp from the Jewish girls—maybe from the Italians too. But after a while I noticed one of the young men leave the wall and ask one of the girls to dance. Soon there were three or four couples. But I also noticed most girls slinking away shyly or flat-out refusing.

Some of the eyes watching us were openly disapproving.

"Those older women are looking at us as if we're doing something highly improper," I whispered.

"In their eyes we are," he whispered back. "A young man and woman are not supposed to touch each other, and a Jewish man and a Christian woman—*oy vay*, that is the worst!"

"I suppose it will take a while," I said.

"It will take a generation, maybe more," he said. "Not everyone is as freethinking as we are. They call this the melting pot, but we haven't yet had time to melt. As of yet, we are still separate ingredients floating around in the broth."

"So are we condemned as hopeless sinners?"

"I'm afraid so, but who cares?" His grip tightened around my waist as he spun me around the floor, faster and faster.

At last a collective tiredness came over the crowd. These girls had been on a picket line since early morning, and they had just run out of steam. The girls started to drift away. I noticed Jacob's eyelids sagging and realized that he hadn't had the luxury of being able to sleep the day away.

"You must go home to bed," I said.

He kept hold of my hand. "Molly, tomorrow is Sunday when I usually try to visit my parents."

"That's all right. You and I don't have to see each other every day."

He swallowed hard before saying, "I was wondering whether you would come with me."

Visiting his parents. This was indeed becoming serious. His eyes were pleading.

"Of course, Jacob. I would be delighted to come with you," I said and watched his face light up.

So at noon the next day I walked down Delancey Street, my arm through Jacob's. Delancey on a Sunday was bustling with life— street peddlers, musicians, the shrieks of children playing tag, and at the far end of the street, the tower of the new East River Bridge reached steely arms out across the river to Brooklyn. Cables were strung across to the far side of the river, but as yet there was no roadway beneath them, so that they looked like the beginnings of a giant spider web in the morning sun.

"This street is busy enough now," Jacob said. "I don't know what will happen when traffic from Williamsburg comes streaming across. The city is already jam-packed with people. We should lock the gates and keep the rest out!"

I looked at him and saw that he was joking. I was glad that he was relaxed and enjoying himself. I was distinctly nervous. Being taken home to meet the family was something I was unsure about.

"They do know I'm coming, don't they?"

"Not exactly, but don't worry. They'll be delighted to meet you."

"I'm not at all sure that they will be thrilled to meet an Irish Catholic girl who goes about unchaperoned in the company of a young man."

"They like to meet new people. My mother doesn't get out

much. She is still unsure of herself in a new country. It will be good for her, also good for them to see that their son is happy and meeting nice girls."

"Meeting nice girls by himself," I reminded him. "Without a proper introduction through the matchmaker."

"We're in America. They'll have to accept that," he said. "Come on. It will be fine. My mother is a good cook."

He led me into a solid brick building and up four flights of stairs to the front door of the Singer household. The door was opened by a small, shrunken man who started in surprise or horror when he saw me standing beside Jacob.

"Hello, Papa. I've brought a friend with me," he said. "This is Miss Murphy. Molly, this is my father, Itzik Singer."

Jacob's father clicked his heels together with the same little bow that I remembered when first meeting Jacob.

"How do you do? I'm pleased to meet you." For once I stammered out the words.

"Come in, please."

He ushered me inside graciously enough. The room was spartan with no curtains at the windows, a rug covering part of a bare wood floor, a simple table, and several chairs. But the table was laid with a white cloth and some good cutlery. Jacob's father called out something in Yiddish and a woman came scurrying through from the kitchen, wiping her hands on her apron as she came. She looked older than she probably was, with a wrinkled, worried face. I can't tell you what color her hair was because it was hidden under a scarf, tied tightly around her head. She stopped, gazing at me with mouth open. Again I couldn't tell if the look was surprise or horror.

"Hello, Mama." Jacob crossed the room to give her a kiss on her cheek. "I've brought a friend to join us for a meal." A rapid conversation in Yiddish followed and I saw her give me a quick glance. Then she managed a smile.

"Please," she said, pointing at the best chair. "I sorry. Not speaking good English yet."

"Can I give you any help in the kitchen?" I asked.

"No thanks, better not," Jacob answered for her. "Just sit and enjoy yourself. Is there any more of that wine I brought you, Papa?"

"Wine? Now? Before we eat? Okay. I get wine."

He brought out a wine bottle and glasses on a silver tray.

"What a beautiful tray."

"We bring—from old country. Many things—must leave behind."

"My parents haven't been here long," Jacob said.

"My son—he send us money for boat," Mr. Singer said proudly. "My wife—she very shy. Not learn English yet. Please excuse."

"Nothing to excuse," I said. "I'll just have to try and learn Yiddish."

Another look of astonishment then he burst out laughing. "Learn Yiddish, she say! That's good."

Jacob's mother appeared again at the sound of the laughter and my statement was obviously repeated to her. She didn't laugh. Any girl wanting to learn Yiddish must obviously have designs on her son—that's what the expression said.

"Sit down, Mama. Drink wine with us," Jacob said.

His mother hesitated then perched on the edge of the nearest chair. She took the glass he offered her.

"Cheers," I said, raising my glass. "How do you say 'cheers'?"

"L'chaim," Jacob said, then nodded in approval over my pronunciation of the word. I took a sip. The wine was red and very sweet, but not unpleasant. "It's good," I said.

Jacob's mother fired another question at him.

"She wants to know where you are from," he said. "I told her Ireland."

Her look indicated that Ireland was only one step away from the moon.

She said something else, making Jacob smile. "She asks if there are Jews in Ireland."

"There are, but I'm not one of them," I answered, and this was relayed to Jacob's mother. I thought as much, the look said.

Then she jumped up and disappeared into the kitchen again. A few minutes later we were summoned to table and Mrs. Singer carried in a platter of fish and a bowl of potatoes. I helped myself cautiously, not wanting to appear greedy and waited in case anyone was going to say a blessing. Luckily, I was right. Jacob's father said some words in Hebrew and then picked up his fork.

"My mother makes the best potatoes with sour cream. It's good, isn't it?" Jacob said.

"Very. And the fish are herring, aren't they? We used to eat a lot of herring at home."

Jacob translated this and for the first time I saw a small nod of approval.

After the main course we had a sweet macaroni pudding, followed by tea and honey cake, then Mrs. Singer headed for the kitchen again. I, wanting to be the good guest and suitable friend for their son, jumped up and followed her.

"Let me help you with the washing up," I said. "I'm well house-trained."

She held up her hands to say no.

"But I'd be happy to," I said as I picked up the dishes and put them in the nearest sink. She gave a cry of horror as Jacob appeared behind me.

"What did I do? I'm not going to break anything," I said.

Jacob said something reassuring to his mother, then gave me an embarrassed grin. "You put the dairy dishes in the meat sink."

It was then that I noticed for the first time that there were two sinks, and two stacks of dishes on the shelf.

"There are different dishes for meat and for dairy?"

He nodded. "And we can't eat them together and there different cloths for washing and drying the dishes. One of our crazy food rules, of which there are many."

"I'm sorry. I had no idea."

"How could you?" he said. "It really doesn't matter."

"I'm sure it does matter," I said noting his mother's distressed face.

Jacob shrugged. "They will have to get the kitchen made kosher again. It's not the worst thing in the world. There are too many religious customs from the old country that are not practical in our new life over here and will probably be lost someday." He brushed it aside with a gesture, but I looked at the stricken face at the sink. Jacob might take his religious background lightly, but I had the distinct feeling that his parents weren't about to toss aside their religious customs in a new country.

"I'm really sorry," I said to Jacob's mother this time. "I wanted to help. I didn't know."

She managed a weak smile. *"Ist nichts."*

"Forget it." Jacob took my arm and escorted me out of the kitchen, before I could break another rule, I suspect.

The atmosphere was decidedly awkward after that and we left soon after.

"They must think I'm a proper heathen." I gave an embarrassed laugh.

"Not at all. They will think you are kind and sweet and very pretty, just like I do. They will learn to love you in time and think that I have made a good choice for myself."

"Whoa—hold on a minute, aren't we rushing ahead a little?" I asked, laughing nervously. "We've only just met, Jacob."

"Some things you know straightaway."

"But we know nothing about each other yet. You have only seen my good side. You haven't had a chance to witness my terrible temper or my stubbornness. And I, in turn, know little about you. For all I know you might snore at night and be prone to fits of black despair."

He was smiling at me the way a father smiles indulgently at his beloved child. "Whatever my faults, I promise to correct them instantly for you."

"But Jacob—"

"Molly, is the idea of marriage so repugnant to you?" He stopped and turned to face me.

"Of course not. Sometime, in the future, I hope to marry."

"Then the idea of marrying *me* does not thrill you with anticipation?"

"I didn't say that either. It's just—too soon, Jacob."

"I'm not trying to rush you, Molly. It's just that I knew the moment I saw you, and it would have been wonderful if you had known too."

"I do enjoy your company, Jacob, and I think you're a fine person too. So let's take it slowly from there, shall we?"

"Of course. Why not? It's a lovely Sunday and we have the day to ourselves. Let us not even think about tomorrow."

He slipped his arm through mine and we walked arm in arm down the street. It was hard to enjoy a free day, strolling in the sunshine when I had so many things I should be doing. I really should be trying to find out whether Michael Kelly was still alive. I should also be looking into Ben Mostel and his extravagant lifestyle. Then I gave in to temptation and put those thoughts aside. Just for once, everything could wait until tomorrow.

❧ Twenty-four ❧

On Monday morning I joined the line of girls waiting outside Lowenstein's. There was an air of anticipation in the crowd. I think some of the girls truly believed that they would go down those steps and find the place miraculously transformed into a place of heat, light, and beauty. It was a freezing cold morning, with ice in the gutters and a wind that cut right through me coming off the East River. Thank God we had not had to face temperatures as bad as this last week or we'd never have held out for four days!

Mr. Katz made a grand entrance just before seven and walked down the steps ahead of us, brandishing the key.

"You should be very grateful you have such a generous boss," he said. "You should be very grateful you're still working here. Me—I would have thrown the lot of you out."

Then he stood in the doorway, scrutinizing each girl as she went in. When it was my turn, he put out a hand and stopped me.

"Not you," he said. "The boss don't want you back. You're a troublemaker."

There was a clamor around me. "But you have to have Molly back! That's not fair."

I was gratified to hear this, but those girls didn't realize how relieved I was never to have to work in that place again.

"It's all right." I turned to face the girls. "Don't worry about me. I'll be just fine. No sense in making a fuss about me. I'll get myself a better job somewhere else."

Rose pushed her way to stand beside me. "No, Molly, it's not all right." She stood on tiptoe and glared at Katz. "If you don't let her come back then we'll all go on strike again."

"Rose—it's all right." I put my hand on her shoulder to restrain her. "The girls have got you and you'll do just famously, so don't worry about me." I gave her an encouraging smile as she looked at me dubiously. "No, honestly. I have a hundred plans of things I want to do. Just make sure you don't let that bully Katz get away with anything. Remember what Lowenstein promised you and make sure he puts in electric light straightaway. And better heating too."

I leaned across and gave her a little kiss on her cheek. "I'll stay in touch," I said. "I'll come to Samuel's Deli at lunchtime to get all the latest news."

I gave Mr. Katz a haughty stare, then I pushed past the rest of the girls waiting on the steps. I was free of Lowenstein's. It felt wonderful. And it was also playing into my plans—I could now quite legitimately go back to Mostel's, tell Mr. Mostel what had happened, and start working there again. That way I could keep an eye on his son, as well as on anyone else who might want to sneak up to his office and come down with his designs. And I could ask questions about Katherine too. Just perfect, in fact. I skipped down Essex Street with sprightly step.

Later that morning I was reinstated at Mostel's. The conditions inside were not much better than at Lowenstein's—cold and drafty and the only heat coming from a couple of oil stoves, one at either door.

"I don't know why the boss was softhearted enough to take you back," Seedy Sam said, looking at me with great distaste. "First you walk out and then you want to come back. You should recognize a good thing when you see it."

"I'll let you know when I see it," I said, eyeing him with the same distaste. Then I breezed past him to take my old place next to Sadie. She looked surprised and delighted to see me.

"How come they took you back?" she whispered.

"My uncle did the boss a favor once. I'm not letting him forget it," I said.

A little later Mr. Mostel himself showed up. "I've been working on the new designs all weekend, girls," he said, waving a briefcase at us, "and I think we've got the goods this time. My new styles will be all the rave. They'll go off the racks like hotcakes. I just need to put some finishing touches and get the sample hands to work on them, and then it's full speed ahead."

At lunchtime the girls crowded around me as we went down the stairs.

"How come you're back again? Mostel never takes anyone back!" Golda said.

"Where did you go, anyway?" Sadie asked.

"I had things I had to do," I said vaguely. "Now I've done them and I need to start earning money again."

"I know where she went." Little Sarah gave me a knowing look. "She went to work for Lowenstein. And I know what she was really doing there too."

"You do?" The alarm must have shown on my face.

"Sure. You're not really one of us, are you?" She stood on the sidewalk, smiling at me, blushing at being the center of attention for once.

For once I didn't know what to say. "What do you mean?" I asked.

"I heard about the strike," she said triumphantly. "Everyone is talking about it. I heard you were sent there to help organize the workers. You really work for the union ladies, don't you?"

"Not exactly," I said, relief rushing to my face. "But I did help organize the strike there, it's true."

"See, I knew it." Sarah looked smug.

The rest of the girls pressed closer. "You helped organize a strike? And did the girls win?"

243

"Yes, they did. They went back to work today with better pay and better conditions."

"And is that why you're here—to do the same thing for us?" Sadie asked, her fact alight with excitement.

"I'm here to earn money," I said.

"Oh sure. Of course you are." Sadie touched the side of her nose and winked at me.

"You tell us how we can go on strike too." One of the girls tugged at my sleeve. She was a beautiful stately Italian called Gina and had been very upset when Paula was fired.

"Strike? Us? Why should we want to go on strike?" an older woman asked. "We have it good here. Six dollars a week and no funny business."

"Good? You call that good?" Gina demanded. "All garment workers are treated like dreck and you know it. It's about time we show Seedy Sam and old Mostel that they don't rule the world."

"This isn't a good time to go on strike, you know," I said hastily. "Mr. Mostel wants to start work on his new designs this week, remember."

"Then what better time?" Gina said. "He wants to get those garments in the stores for the holidays. He'd probably agree to anything we wanted just to keep us working."

"He could also fire the lot of you and hire new girls to replace you," I said. "That's what Lowenstein threatened to do. I don't know why he gave in so quickly."

Disappointed faces looked at me. "Are you saying we shouldn't go on strike like the Lowenstein girls?" one of them asked. "You think we have it so good here that we should all be happy?"

"Of course not," I said, "and I didn't say you shouldn't go on strike. But you have to know what you're doing. It's not as easy as it sounds. You need the backing of the Hebrew Trades and the other garment workers, or they'll make mincemeat of you."

"Mincemeat? They kill us?" one of the Italian girls asked, staring at me with huge eyes.

I laughed. "No, but they'll threaten you. They sent the starkes to attack us and when we tried to defend ourselves, some of us got carted off to jail for causing trouble."

"You got sent to jail? *Oy vay!*"

I looked around the group of expectant faces. "Look, if you really want to organize, you need to join the union. You need to choose your union representatives to go to meetings for you and get advice on how to go about your strike."

"We already had one girl start doing that stuff, didn't we?" Golda asked. "Remember Kathy?"

"Oh sure. Kathy." The name went around the circle of girls.

"Kathy? Was she American?" I asked.

"No, she was English. She talked funny, like you," one of the girls said.

"She was the greatest. She stand up to Sam and she don't take no nonsense from him."

"What happened to her?" I asked.

Blank faces stared at me. "We don't know," Golda said. "She was at work one day and then she got called out of the room and she never came back."

"We asked Sam where she had gone and he didn't know neither," another girl added.

"Did somebody come for her? Who called her out of the room?" I asked.

Several shrugs.

"We're not supposed to look up when we're working," Sadie said. "You know how Seedy Sam likes to take our money from us."

"I work near the door," a bouncy little redhead called Ida said. "I saw her go past and I heard her say, 'What are you doing here?' "

"But you didn't see who it was?"

"No, but soon after that Mr. Mostel's son came in."

"Enough of this," Sadie said loudly. "Kathy's gone. All the talking in the world isn't going to bring her back. Let's go eat. You know Sam is just dying to dock our pay for being late again."

Nobody could disagree with this and we surged down the street to the little café where some girls bought hot drinks to go with their sandwich and others splurged five cents on the daily special. I joined the latter and had a bowl of stew that must have been made from a tough old buffalo. As I chewed on pieces of gristle, I also tried to digest what I had just heard. So Katherine had actually disappeared in the middle of the day from Mostel's, lured from the room by someone who came for her—someone she knew. And another interesting fact had come out—Ben Mostel had come into the room right after Kathy disappeared.

If Michael Kelly was still alive, maybe he would be able to take up the story from that point. Surely he would have found out what had happened to her, especially if he was a member of the Eastmans. Gang members always have an ear to the ground, don't they? So my number-one priority was to find Michael Kelly. Not an easy assignment. I had no desire to follow Nell Blankenship to my doom. Maybe it was now time to shake off all notions of foolish pride and ask Daniel to help me.

That evening when I returned home, I took up pen and paper.

Dear Daniel,
    I witnessed an ugly incident at a garment worker's strike on Friday last. I think that some of the starkes were members of the Eastmans gang, and one of them looked very much like the photograph of Michael Kelly. Since I am forbidden to do any more foolish investigating in that part of town, I wondered if you could find out for me if Michael Kelly is indeed still alive.
    Yours sincerely,
    M. Murphy

On Tuesday morning I hurried to work with great anticipation. Today was the day that Mr. Mostel was going to bring in the finished designs for the sample hands to work on. Today someone might try to borrow, steal, or copy them. Of course, if that someone was his son Ben, then why would he need to do it at the office? He could more easily take a peek at them at home in his father's study—unless the old man kept them under lock and key.

I sat at my machine and worked with an eye on the door until Mr. Mostel came in.

"Here they are—my new designs," he said, tapping his brief-case. "All finished and ready to go like I promised. And they are spectacular, if I say so myself. So different—so chic. You girls are going to be proud just to be working on them." He looked around the room and was met by a lot of blank stares. Of course many of the girls just didn't understand him, but those who did were not showing enthusiasm. Mostel smiled at us. "If you girls work hard and we get the first lot shipped by December first, there will a bonus all around. Then we'll all have a good holiday with something to celebrate, won't we?"

"A good holiday? He doesn't even give us one day off over the eight days of Chanukah," Sadie muttered to me. "He gives us Christmas Day off and what good is that to Jewish families?"

Mr. Mostel went up to his office and then returned. "Sam—I got to pop out for a while," he called down the length of the room. "If the sample hands come in before I get back, tell them the designs are in the top drawer on the right. Got it? They can start work straightaway."

He's certainly laying it on thick, I thought. If I were the spy, I might begin to smell a rat.

"New designs. As if we care," Sadie muttered to me. "A collar is a collar is a collar."

We hadn't been working long when the door opened again and Ben Mostel came in. With his top hat and silver-tipped cane he looked like a peacock in a henhouse.

"Morning, girls. You're all looking very lovely today," he said, picking out some of the younger, prettier girls to grace with his smile. A general titter followed him down the room.

"Your dad's not here, Mr. Ben," Sam called as Ben passed us in the direction of Mostel's office.

"No matter. I just wanted to leave something for him," Ben said.

I was on my feet instantly. "I need to go to the washroom, Sam," I said. "It's really urgent. Can I go?"

"Okay, I'll give you permission this once," he said. "Only don't make a habit of it."

"How come she gets permission when I don't?" Sadie asked.

"Because she ain't running in and out all day like some I could mention, including you," Sam said. He jerked his head to me. "Go on then, if you're going."

I sprinted through the door like a girl who has to go in a hurry. I even opened the washroom door, went in, and closed it behind me, just in case Sam was still watching me. Then I opened it a crack, checked around it, and was up the stairs like a shot. The door to Mostel's office was open and Ben was so busy looking in one of the drawers in his father's desk that he didn't hear me coming.

"Did you find what you are looking for?" I asked.

He spun around with a guilty look on his face.

"Your father has worked hard to give you all the benefits he never had," I went on, "and this is how you repay him?"

"Who the hell are you, and how did you know?"

"I've been watching you, Ben Mostel," I said. I was enjoying this moment, confident that I could run down the flight of steps ahead of him and was within shouting distance of a roomful of girls. "What do you think your father would say if he knew you were betraying him to Lowenstein?"

Without warning he came around the desk and while I was still thinking I might have to defend myself after all, he closed the door.

"What do you want?" he hissed at me. "Is it money? Is that it? All right then, how much?" He reached for his wallet.

I was no longer feeling quite as brave as I had been, but I decided I was still within shouting distance.

"Since all the money you have comes from your father and he is paying me in this Lowenstein business, I don't require to be paid twice over," I said.

Ben looked puzzled and horrified. "My father is paying you to follow me? He must have heard about me and Letitia then. You can tell him he doesn't have to worry—it's nothing serious. Just a bit of fun, you know."

He was talking very fast, his eyes darting nervously like a schoolboy caught at the cookie jar.

"What do you mean, it's not serious—betraying your father to his rival?"

"Betraying?" He laughed uneasily. "Oh, come on, that's a bit strong, wouldn't you say? I only took the girl to supper a few times. I take hundreds of women to supper."

"Only this girl's name was Lowenstein. But taking Letitia Lowenstein to supper wasn't what I was talking about, and you know it. I'm talking about the other matter—your father's designs. You were looking in the wrong drawer, by the way."

"Designs—what designs? I don't follow you."

"Isn't that what you came here for, the moment your father left his office? Had he kept them locked away at home?"

He laughed again, a little more easily now. "I'm afraid I don't see what my father's designs have to do with me and Letitia."

"Oh, so you weren't just about to copy them and slip them to Mr. Lowenstein?"

"Why on earth would I want to do that? My old man might be dashed annoying, but I'm not out to ruin him." He stared at me and I saw the worry grow on his face. "Is that what he believes—that I'm out to betray him? I know he thinks poorly of me, because I'm rather a duffer where money is concerned, but surely he must know—I mean, you must set him straight, miss— uh." He was looking at me like a scared schoolboy again.

"So you're telling me that you didn't come here to sneak a look at your father's new designs then?"

"I had no idea he had come up with new designs. I'm not at all interested in the fashion industry, much to his disappointment."

"Then what were you doing in his desk?" I couldn't help asking.

He blushed scarlet. "If you really must know, he keeps his checkbook in that drawer. I thought I might—uh—borrow one of his checks."

If Ben Mostel was acting then he had better apply for the lead role in Ryan O'Hare's next play. "You're not going to tell him, are you?" He tried a winning smile.

"Not if you replace it immediately."

"Oh, very well, although there will be a certain restauranteur who may not be happy if I don't pay the bill after dinner tonight."

He gave a sheepish smile, half opened the drawer, then looked up at me thoughtfully.

"You say you are working for my father, but I've seen you before, among the girls on the shop floor." Not quite as inane a young man as his father had thought. "So it seems to me that you might not want the fact that you are working secretly for my father to be revealed."

"Most astute of you. So you are suggesting that we have a bargain—I say nothing about your helping yourself to your father's checks if you say nothing about my not really being a seamstress?"

"Exactly."

We looked at each other for a long while in silence. "Very well," I said. "However, if your father ever comments on anything missing from his desk, I shall feel obliged to tell him what I witnessed."

"And if any of the girls comment that you are behaving strangely, I shall be obliged to set them straight."

"I never behave strangely," I said with the ghost of a smile.

"So sneaking up to the boss's office isn't strange behavior?"

"I am supposed to be in the washroom, which is where I am going when you are ready to leave."

"Don't trust me in here alone, huh?"

"Your father tells me you give him a lot of grief."

"My father is a stingy old man who keeps me permanently short of cash. How is a fellow to enjoy life if he has no money?"

"It must be hard to have to go without champagne every now and then, or not to be able to see every new show that opens," I said sweetly, but he caught my sarcasm and blushed again. "So tell me—how did Letitia Lowenstein come by that very attractive, unique locket I saw around her neck?" I knew this was really taking a chance. If Ben had acquired Katherine's locket, it might have been taken from her dead body. This inane, overgrown schoolboy act might conceal a clever killer for all I knew.

This time he flushed almost beetroot red. "So that's what you were getting at all the time! I guess you already know, don't you?"

"I might do, but I'd like to hear your version."

He winced. "Did my father find out and send you to get an admission of my guilt?"

"He may have. So how did you meet Katherine?"

"Who?"

"The girl who owned that locket." I inched toward the door, feeling more secure when my hand wrapped around the door-knob behind me. "But surely you knew that, didn't you? Did you meet her here, at the factory?"

"I've no idea who you are talking about. You know where I found the locket—at the bottom of my father's drawer in his desk here. I wanted some cash to buy Letitia a present and I thought to myself, what does he need a pretty little thing like this for, so I pocketed it—as I think you knew all along, didn't you?"

"Oh yes," I stammered. "I knew that all along."

251

❧ Twenty-five ❧

I don't remember how I came down that flight of stairs again. I sat on the W.C. letting the cold bring me back to my senses. Mr. Mostel after all—that genial man playing the worried father and betrayed employer so well. Had he paid someone to remove Katherine or had she been lured up to his office and dispatched right here? Until now I had dismissed the notion that I was dealing with a highly dangerous man.

"You took long enough, didn't you," Seedy Sam commented as I returned to my seat.

"Sorry, but I'm not feeling too well today," I said, giving the phrase enough meaning to make him refrain from further questions.

At lunchtime I decided that my ill health was a good excuse for staying put and keeping an eye on the place.

"Aren't you coming to eat?" Sadie asked me.

"No, thanks. I've got a piece of bread and cheese in my bag if I feel like eating anything at all," I said.

"Do you want me to bring you something back from the café?" Sadie asked.

"I think it was their food that did it in the first place," I said. "That stew yesterday."

"It was bad. I couldn't finish mine," she said. "I didn't even want to look at it. But I could bring you some noodle soup and a roll. It's very nourishing."

"Thanks, Sadie. You're a pal, but I think I'll survive," I said. "You better get going or you'll be at the back of the queue."

She left. It was completely quiet in the sewing room. Even Seedy Sam had gone to have his lunch with the cutters and pressers downstairs. I nibbled nervously on my bread and cheese. I hadn't had to lie about that one—I really did feel sick. Katherine's locket in Mostel's drawer. One day she disappeared and never came back. And if Mostel got wind that I was snooping, or was involved in starting a strike, then the same thing could happen to me. "Get out while you still can," a voice whispered in my head.

I looked up as I heard footsteps coming up the stairs. The half hour for lunch wouldn't be over for fifteen more minutes and girls were not usually in a hurry to return. Sadie came into the room. She had flushed cheeks from the cold wind.

"Horrible food again. Be happy you didn't order anything. I came back early—couldn't stand the smell," she said. "Now I need to go to the washroom myself."

She went through the inner door without even pausing to take her shawl off. I heard the washroom door close, then another sound that had me up on my feet—it was the creak of floorboards. Sadie was going up the stairs to Mostel's office. I gave her a head start and then I crept up the stairs after her. Mr. Mostel's office door was closed. Cautiously I inched it open. The office was empty. I crept through into the back room beyond which the sample hands occupied when they were at work. Empty apart from bolts of cloth and a couple of forlorn dummies.

Could those creaking floorboards have been the product of my overactive imagination? I could have sworn I heard feet going up the stairs. But she couldn't just have vanished. She must have heard me following her and be hiding, waiting for me to go downstairs again before she looked for the designs. I checked the drawer to see if she had maybe taken them already and was sitting somewhere, copying them furiously. But the folder still lay unopened in Mostel's drawer.

I felt the back of my neck prickle. Where was she? I spent futile minutes turning over bolts of cloth to see if she was behind or under any of them. I was about to go downstairs again when I noticed a door I had overlooked. Mostel's door had always been open as I had come up the stairs, concealing another door to the left of the little landing. This door was not properly shut. I pushed it open and found another short flight of stairs. I crept up it. It was dark and seemed to be leading to some kind of attic storage space. Bolts of cloth were stacked high on either side. It smelled musty. What on earth could Sadie want up here, unless she was doing what Mostel had dreaded and quietly helping herself to a few yards of trim?

Then I heard a girl's voice whisper, "Wait. I think I hear something."

And the whispered answer, "It's okay. They're all at lunch still."

I went up the final steps, around the bolts of cloth, and stood staring at two frightened faces.

"Molly," Sadie stammered. "What are you doing up here?"

"More to the point, what are you doing?" I asked, "and who is this?"

I stared at the other girl. She looked somehow familiar. She was staring back at me, frightened, poised for flight, and yet at the same time defiant.

"Don't tell on us, please, Molly," Sadie begged. "She had nowhere else to go. If they find her they'll kill her."

I came closer, trying to make out her features in the poor light.

"It's all right, Sadie. I should go anyway. It's not right for you to take risks for me," said a very haughty English voice.

"Katherine?" I said.

She started in horror. "Who are you? I never saw you in my life before. How do you know me?"

"It's a long story," I said, "but for now let me just assure you that I am a friend. I'm on your side."

"Did you tell her, Sadie?" Katherine asked.

"Of course she didn't tell me, but don't worry, you can trust me. What on earth possessed you to hide out here, of all places?"

"We couldn't think of anywhere else. This room is hardly ever used, so we thought I'd be safe enough."

"But so close to Mostel. What if he'd discovered you up here?"

"He'd have been annoyed, of course."

"Annoyed. Wasn't he the one trying to have you killed?"

They looked at me as if I was speaking Chinese.

"Mr. Mostel? He's really an old sweetie," Katherine said.

"Then who?"

"Why, her husband and his horrible friends, of course," Sadie said. "She came to me one night in a terrible state and I couldn't think of anywhere else to hide her but here. I smuggled her in early next morning and I've been bringing her food."

"So that's why you've been leaving the café early, and going to the washroom so frequently."

She nodded.

"You've been taking a terrible risk."

"I know," Katherine said, "that's why I should go now, while I have the chance."

"Where will you go?" Sadie asked.

"I've no idea."

"I've an idea," I said. "My name is Molly and believe it or not, I've been trying to find out what happened to you. I've just thought of a perfect place for you to hide out. Go to Nine Patchin Place, behind Jefferson Market in Greenwich Village. Two women live there. Their names are Sid and Gus—don't ask. Tell them you are Katherine and Molly says they should hide you until she gets home. I'll explain everything later."

"Are you sure?" She was still regarding me suspiciously. "Why should you put yourself out for me?"

"I said I'll explain everything later, but for now you have to trust me, Katherine. And nobody would think of looking for you as far away as Greenwich Village, would they?"

"I suppose not."

"Then wrap yourself up in a shawl and get out of here while you can."

We were just about to bundle her down the stairs when the sound of voices rose from below. The girls were back from lunch.

"We'll have to wait until after work," I said. "Sadie and I will work out how we can distract Sam while we get you out of here somehow."

"Don't put yourself at risk for me," Katherine said.

"I wouldn't dream of it," I replied breezily. "Come on, Sadie. Let's get back down there before Sam docks us half our pay."

We rushed down the stairs.

"So where have you two been?" he demanded.

"Washroom again," I said. "We're both sick from the stinking stew we ate yesterday. We're not eating at that café ever again."

Sam just grunted.

"It's like an icehouse in here," one of the girls commented as a group of them came back into the room. "Can't you turn up those stoves any higher?"

"If I do, they'll burst," Sam said. "If only you try working hard enough you'll create your own heat."

"Very funny," the girl muttered.

Machines started clattering again. The afternoon dragged on. Girls clapped their hands together and stamped their feet to bring back the circulation. Sam walked up and down the lines of girls.

"What kind of work are you doing here?" he demanded, stopping beside a machine in the far row. "Those are supposed to be straight lines, not zigzags. Only a blind person would want to buy that garment."

"Maybe I could keep my lines straighter if my hands weren't so cold," the girl he was speaking to said. "The wind comes in through the cracks around this crummy window. I'm so cold I'm one big shiver. I can't take it no more."

"Fine by me," Sam said. "You don't have to take it. Get your things and go. You're out."

"Wait a second." Gina, the tall Italian girl, rose to her feet. She was almost the same size as Sam and she glared at him, eye to eye. "You can't fire her because you don't heat this lousy place well enough for us to do our work."

"I just did," Sam said. "You want to join her—fine by me too."

"This place is too cold for anyone to work properly," Gina said. "It's a disgrace. Look at it. Nobody ever sweeps the floors. Nobody cleans the W.C. No light, no heat. We're treated no better than animals."

Sam was still lounging against the window ledge with a lazy grin on his face. "Like I said, anyone who don't like it can hit the road, anytime."

"Fine," Gina said. "We take you up on your kind offer." She looked around the room. "You said it wasn't a good time to strike now. How much worse does it have to get? Look at our hands. We all got chillblains from the cold. Come on, girls. What are we waiting for? Let's show them." Several girls had risen to their feet. "You can tell Mr. Mostel he better treat us nice if he wants his new designs in the stores anytime soon," Gina said loudly, "cos we're walking out. Let's go, everyone."

Some girls jumped up, cheering, others lagged, looking at each other with scared faces, but in the end they were all on their feet, nobody wanting to be the last out of the door. I had no alternative but to rise to my feet with the rest of the girls. As they all surged forward to grab their bags and scarves from the hooks along the back wall, Sam pushed past and stood in the doorway.

"Nobody's going anywhere," he bellowed in a threatening voice.

"You can't stop us, Sam," someone shouted back.

"You wanna bet?" He leaped through the doorway and slammed the door shut. We heard the sound of bolts being shot. "You ain't going nowhere till I get the boss," he called through the door. "You're going to sit there and stew."

Then we heard the sound of his heavy boots running down stairs.

Girls began to whimper.

"Oh, *Mein Gott*, we're in trouble now."

"He's gonna get the boss."

"He's gonna bring the police."

"We'll all be fired."

"My papa will throw me out if I lose my job!"

The wail rose in different languages, most of which I couldn't understand, but understood anyway.

"They can't keep us in here against our will," Sadie said, pushing through the crush of girls at the door. "It's against the law. Let's see if we can break down that door."

"You heard the bolts. We can't break through bolts," someone said.

A great mass of girls pressed around the door.

"I want to get out. I hate being locked in," one little girl screamed from the middle of the crowd. She forced her way to the door and pounded on it. "Let me out! Let me out!"

"They locked her in jail when she was a kid in Russia, then they shot her parents," someone explained. "No wonder she's scared."

"Henny, calm down." Gina grabbed at her, but Henny fought her off like a wild thing.

"Leave me be. I have to get out—"

There was a crash and the oil stove toppled to the floor. With a whoosh flame raced along the spilled oil, eating up the lint and scraps of fabric in its path. Panicked girls tried to get away, screaming as the flames reached them. A skirt blazed up and screams rose with it. Other girls batted out the flames with their shawls.

"Somebody get water," someone was shouting and girls were already racing for the washroom. I was one of them, but there was nothing in there in which to carry water, except for an old tin mug.

Someone filled it and raced away in a futile attempt to put out the flames with four ounces of water.

"Soak some cloth," I shouted. "We can lay that on the flames to beat them down."

We grabbed at the nearest bolt and tried to tear it, then slopped water over the whole thing, staggering out with it between us, like a battering ram.

But it was too late. Fueled by the debris on the floor the flames had caught at the first tables and the machine oil made them leap higher and fiercer. The whole area around the door was now on fire. Black smoke billowed out and the acrid smell drove us back, coughing and retching. The girls were huddled together like a flock of sheep, herded together and moving this way and that as the flames drove them.

"Maybe it will burn down the door and someone can rush through the flames to get help," a voice suggested, but I couldn't imagine anyone volunteering to rush through those flames that now licked ceiling-high. Wooden rafters were blazing and crackling like a bonfire.

"They'll come up from downstairs to rescue us," I heard someone saying.

"Perhaps they won't even know until it's too late," I said. "Fires don't spread downward. Let's see how we can get out of here."

We ran across to the windows and tried to get them open, but the frames were buckled and they wouldn't budge. Besides, they only led to a daunting five-story drop.

"Come on, up to Mostel's office," I shouted. The girls nearest me surged forward, fighting to be first up the stairs.

"Don't panic. Don't push!" I yelled over the screams and shouts. "We don't want anyone getting trampled."

Stinging, blinding smoke accompanied us up the stairs. With

eyes streaming and smarting we burst into the office. There was one small window to one side. We opened it, but again it was useless—a sheer drop into the well between buildings.

Girls screamed from the window. "Somebody help us!" But they were shouting to nobody in a useless well of blank walls.

We could feel the heat of the flames and the acrid black smoke coming up the stairs behind us now. Girls packed tighter and tighter, not wanting to be the last on the stairs. I tried to herd them back again, out of the office, but nobody was willing to retreat toward those flames.

"It's no good. There's nothing this way. We'll have to try the attic," I yelled, "and if that doesn't work we'll just have to break the windows and see if we can find any cloth long enough to lower ourselves to the street."

"Lower ourselves to the street, are you crazy?" someone close to me screamed.

"Move!" I shouted, trying to close Mostel's office door enough to open the door to the attic hidden behind it, but nobody wanted to risk being shut in the office.

"Help me, Sadie!" I screamed and we literally pummeled and clawed girls out of the way to open the other door. When the girls saw that there was indeed another door and maybe a way of escape, they didn't fight us as much. We opened it and staggered up the stairs to be met by a frightened Katherine.

"What's happening? I can smell smoke."

"Place is on fire. We have to get out," I gasped. We were all finding it hard to breathe by now. The girls weren't screaming anymore, but coughing and moaning and praying. Ave Marias and Hebrew prayers rose simultaneously to the smoke-filled rafters.

"This is not good," one of the girls groaned. "Look at all this fabric. Look at the gauze and muslin. It will burn like crazy. We better get back down again and try the windows."

"Wait," Katherine shouted. "There is a window at the end that leads onto the roof. We may be able to get out that way."

She ran to the skylight at the far end. It was cut into the slanted roof above our heads. "Help me push this table under it," Katherine shouted as I ran to join her. We shoved the heavy table between us. She climbed up beside me and we pushed at the window with all our might. Just when I thought we were going to have to smash it, it came flying open.

"Give me a push." I hoisted up my skirts and dragged myself out. The pitched roof of the attic ended in a broad flat strip of tarred rooftop.

"Come on, it's all right. We can get out this way," I shouted back as smoke licked around my ankles. "Help them up, Katherine. Give us your hands."

"I'm not getting on no roof," someone said but a little girl scrambled onto the table.

"I ain't waiting to be cooked like a chicken," she said and reached up to me. Katherine shoved from below and I hauled her through the narrow window.

"Sit on your bottom and slide down gently to the flat part," I said, then reached for the next one.

One after another we handed the girls out onto the roof until the flat area was jam-packed with terrified, sobbing bodies. Now I just prayed that the roof didn't collapse under the weight of them.

There was an explosion as glass blew out from a window on the floor below us and flames licked upward. Smoke billowed up toward us, making it hard to see.

"Where do we go now?" someone shrieked.

That was a good point. I hadn't had a chance to see how we might get off the rooftop.

"Hold on a minute. Katherine, you get the last few out," I said and slithered down the slates myself, working my way through the crush of bodies. When I reached the end of the roof and turned the corner they followed me, like rats after the Pied Piper. We kept on going down the other side. I had hoped that this roof would join the next building somewhere, but it didn't.

There was a six-foot gap between them. Safety was a few tantalizing feet away.

At the other end of the building there was a crash and sparks shot high into the air as part of the ceiling fell in. A collective scream arose again.

"We're going to be burned alive."

One girl threw her leg over the parapet. "I'm not waiting to fall into that," she said. "I'm ending it now."

Katherine grabbed at her. "Don't be stupid," she said. "We're going to get out of this. Listen—I can hear the fire engines."

And it was true. In the distance we could hear bells ringing as fire engines galloped toward us. I looked at the flames, now licking up from all sides and knew that there was little the firemen could do. Even if they had ladders long enough, how could they put them through the flames to reach us? I stood at the parapet and looked at the rooftop on the next building. It was maybe less than six feet away and stacks of lumber were piled on it. If only I could get across—

Without hesitating any longer I unlaced my boots, undid my skirt, and pulled it off, then off came my petticoat until I stood there in my drawers and stockings. This produced a gasp of horror almost as great as the original flames had done. I climbed up on the parapet and heard screams behind me.

"Molly, don't do it," someone called.

"I'll be fine." I didn't feel fine. I had done some stupid things in my life, including jumping little ravines on the cliff tops, usually on a dare, but that was long ago now and I was out of practice for such stunts. I glanced down. My eyes were streaming from the smoke and all I could see was a blurred mass of upturned faces five floors below me beneath the drifting smoke. If I missed, it would be a quick death and maybe the girl had been right. Maybe it would be better than being burned alive.

I'm not usually a religious person—in fact definitely heathen, according to my mother—but I crossed myself hastily, just to make sure. "Jesus, Mary, and Joseph and all the saints, just help me this time, not for myself but for those girls," I whispered, "and I promise I'll start going to mass again." Then I took a deep breath and leaped. Cold air rushed past me, then my fingers grabbed onto the brickwork, my legs scrabbled, and for a second I teetered on the brink. Another shriek behind me as I hauled myself over the parapet and stood, safe and secure on the other rooftop. I rushed to the lumber and came up with a plank that I thought was long enough.

"Catch the other end," I shouted, standing it up and then letting it fall in their direction.

Hands caught it as it fell. It reached, but only just. I ran back and found a second one, a little longer. Then a third. We had a bridge of precarious planks. I stood up on the parapet at one end.

"Come on, I'll help you," I said.

Nobody moved.

"Look, any moment that roof is going to collapse and you'll all fall into the fire. Is that what you want?" I yelled, my voice harsh and scratchy from the smoke. I rubbed at my eyes and tried to focus as I set my balance.

"Come on, hurry up," Katherine shouted, stepping up to steady her end of the plank.

After what seemed an age one girl climbed up, looked down, shrieked, and hastily got down again.

"Come across on all fours then," I suggested. "Crawl like a baby, only hurry."

The girl tried again, this time hitching up her skirts and clambering across on hands and knees. When she reached safety she burst into tears. Another girl followed and soon there was a stream of frightened animals coming toward me on all fours. I shouted across to make sure they only came one at a time, as once the first girls had succeeded they all wanted to be next.

It was going well until Henny, the one whose panic had set off the whole thing, got to the middle. She looked down, then cowered, frozen on the middle of the planks.

"Henny, come on. Give me your hand," I shouted. "You're almost there. Hurry. The other girls are waiting."

"I can't," she whimpered.

There was nothing for it. I leaned over the side until I could grab at her hands, then I yanked her like a sack of potatoes. On the other side a cheer went up and girls started coming across again. The fire bells came closer until I could see a flash of red beneath us, but I didn't see how they could ever get a ladder up here. Hoses started spraying the lower floors, plunging us into clouds of billowing smoke that made the crossing impossible.

"Idiots!" Katherine shouted down. She started handing girls across to me, shouting at them to get a move on. It seemed to take forever. Every now and then there would be another crash, another roar as more of the building collapsed. My heart was beating so loudly, I'd swear you could hear it over the other noises. We'd never get them all across in time. I became a machine—reach out, grab girl, drag her to safety, reach out again. When I looked around behind me, the square roof was packed with girls. Only the last few remained on the other side.

"Hurry up, the roof's going!" I shouted. "Run if you dare. Hold the plank steady, Katherine."

We knelt on either end. A girl screamed as she ran across, but it was the same half-exhilarated scream that a roller-coaster produces. Another followed, then another. One girl froze. It was little Sarah and she held her lunch bag in one hand.

"Drop the bag, you'll be unbalanced!" I shouted, but she didn't obey. She just stood there, like a statue.

Sadie got up behind her and gave her a mighty shove that sent her staggering across to me. As I caught her she went sprawling. The bag fell from her grasp. Sheets of paper flew out over the parapet to be lost in the smoke. I caught a glimpse of a dress with a high frilly collar, another with a gentleman's bow tie. I turned to look at Sarah but she had melted into the crowd and I had more important things to take care of.

Four more girls, then at last I held out my hand for Sadie and Katherine.

"Well done. You did a marvelous job," the latter said as she stepped down gracefully.

"So did you."

"Good old British sangfroid. We don't lose our nerve like the continentals do." She gave me a triumphant smile as we joined the crush of girls.

Then behind our backs came a great cracking sound. Flames shot up, making us all jump back and brush off the sparks that landed on us. We turned around to see the roof fall in. There were a few moments of panic when it looked as if the fire might spread to our building, but before that could happen a door onto our rooftop opened and a fireman appeared.

"They're all up here, Barney," he shouted. "They're safe."

Weeping and hugging we made our way down the stairs, into the arms of relatives, friends, and well-wishers. Families snapped up daughters and mothers and whisked them away, weeping with joy. I looked around for Sarah. She was hurrying toward the outstretched arms of a frail-looking woman and a girl I recognized—the sister who worked for Lowenstein's. Little Fanny who looked as if she wouldn't hurt a fly. As I started to push my way through the crowd to reach them then I saw them hugging and kissing and I lost my nerve.

One by one girls were whisked away from me. I stared out through a blur of tears feeling suddenly alone and helpless. Then through the crowd I thought I saw Daniel's face and started toward him.

Suddenly I heard someone shouting my name.

"Molly!" I spun around to see Jacob running toward me. "Molly, I've been looking everywhere. Thank God."

I had thought the tears in my eyes were just from the smoke. Now I knew they weren't. I fell into his arms, blubbing. His arms were warm and strong around me and I lay my head against his shoulder, feeling safe.

"This is enough," he said, stroking my hair. "I can't take any more of this. I want you to marry me right away, so that I can look after you."

At any other moment I would have told him that I could look after myself very nicely thank you, but I had to admit it sounded most appealing.

"Your mother won't approve," was all I could think of saying.

"She'll have to learn to accept it, won't she? And who could not learn to love you, Molly?"

I looked up into his face. He was smiling at me with infinite tenderness. To be cherished and protected—what more could any woman want? I felt a warm glow spreading all through me.

"Now we had better get me home before your mother learns that I was on the street in my underwear," I said.

Jacob eyed me. "At least I know that you have good legs before I sign the wedding document," he said, still smiling. "Most Jewish men are not so fortunate."

"How did you know I'd be here?" I asked, as my brain started to clear.

"I've been keeping an eye on you. I had a feeling you'd be doing something else stupid."

"I didn't intend this to be dangerous," I said. "They locked us in. A stove was knocked over and the place was a complete firetrap. It was an accident that could have happened anywhere."

"It wasn't deliberate then?"

"No, of course not."

"But I thought Mostel was responsible for Katherine's disappearance?"

Katherine—I had forgotten all about her. I looked around and saw her sitting on a doorstep, all alone, looking as shocked and bewildered as I had been. I took Jacob's hand.

"Over here," I said. "There's someone I want you to meet."

She rose to her feet as we approached her.

"Jacob," I said. "This is Katherine."

❧ Twenty-six ☙

K atherine?" Jacob looked from her face to mine. "You found her? You mean she didn't drown then?"

"Obviously not."

"Why did you think I had drowned?" Katherine asked.

Spray from fire hoses and flying particles from the fire coated us in a sooty rain.

"The police told us that a woman resembling your picture had been pulled from the East River," I said.

"My picture? How did you get my picture?" She looked completely bewildered.

"Your father sent it to me," I said. "I am an investigator. He hired me to track you down."

The bewilderment was replaced by a look of utter horror. "Then you weren't—I mean, we thought the woman who—"

"The young woman who discovered you?" I said, suddenly putting the pieces together. "Her name was Nell Blankenship. She was trying to find out what happened to you after you disappeared from Mostel's. We suspected foul play, you see." As I spoke it was my turn to go cold all over. I had just taken in the implication of her words. "You thought she was the detective," I said.

She nodded. "We got word from Michael's cousin who also

worked for my father that a woman detective had been dispatched to find us. Naturally we thought . . ."

"So you killed her?" I demanded angrily.

"Not me. Of course not."

"The Eastmans then."

She shook her head, a look of bleak despair on her face. "Not the Eastmans. The man I married, Michael Kelly."

Jacob forced his way through the crowd, stepped out into the street, and flagged down a cab. The driver looked at us in horror. "You're not thinking of putting them young ladies on my clean seat, are you?" he asked.

"They've just been rescued from the fire," Jacob said. "Surely you don't want them to have to walk home in their condition. What if they were your own daughters?" He reached into his pocket. "There will be an extra dollar to aid with the cleanup," he said.

The cabby's eyes widened as Jacob produced the dollar bill. "You're right, sir. We couldn't expect them to walk in their condition, could we?" he said with a grin. Jacob opened the door and bundled us inside. As we drove away I glanced out of the window and again I thought I caught a glimpse of Daniel's face in the crowd.

The cab made its way slowly through the great crush of people. I looked back but Daniel's face had gone. I turned back to Katherine, who was sitting tight-lipped, staring straight ahead of her.

"You say that Michael was the one who killed Nell Blankenship? Couldn't you have stopped him?" I asked as the cab got up speed and turned into the Bowery.

"I had no idea." She hugged her arms to herself, shivering. "My God, don't you think I would have stopped him if I had known what he was going to do? She found out where we were hiding. Michael had done some work for the Eastmans, so they let us hide out in a shed behind their headquarters. This woman came and she asked questions about me. Mike thought that—"

She bit her lip, looking younger and more fragile than her photograph. "He said he'd take care of her. I never dreamed . . . then he came back and told me he'd killed her by mistake and we'd have to stay hidden until we could make a run for it and go out West where they'd never find us."

"What I don't understand," Jacob said, "is why it was so terrible that the detective found you? You are a married woman, after all. Your parents might be annoyed but legally there is not much they can do."

Katherine sank her head into her hands. "You don't know the half of it," she said.

"Don't worry about that now," I said. "I'll hide you where you'll be safe."

The cab driver reined in his horse and poked his head down to us. "Patchin Place did you say, sir? I don't want to take the horse all the way down, on account of how it's hard to back him up again."

"That's fine. We can walk a few yards," I said.

Jacob jumped down first and handed us down from the cab. Katherine looked around her. "This is nice," she said. "It reminds me of London. Quite different from the New York I have seen up to now."

We walked the length of Patchin Place and stopped outside Number Nine. I knocked on the front door. Sid opened it, looked at me, then her jaw dropped open.

"Molly—what in God's name have you been doing to yourself?"

I had quite forgotten that I had no skirt or petticoat on, that I was dirty and covered in soot. Katherine didn't look much better.

"We were in a fire," I said. "We got trapped and we had to climb out over the rooftops."

"Mercy me." For once Sid sounded less sophisticated than usual. "Come inside, do. I'll find the brandy and I'll get Gus to run you a hot bath. What an awful experience for you."

Her eyes moved past me to Jacob and Katherine. "You were in the fire too?"

"Katherine was. I was merely the comforting shoulder afterward," Jacob said.

"Katherine?" Sid's eyes opened wide. "*The* Katherine?"

"*The* Katherine."

"But I thought she had drowned."

"Does everyone in New York know about me?" Katherine asked, uncertainly.

"Only my very closest friends," I said. I looked up at Sid. "I want to ask you a favor."

"Other than a hot bath and a good meal?"

"I want to ask you to hide Katherine for a few days. Her husband is trying to find her and that would not be a good idea."

"Then for God's sake don't stand there on the doorstep. Get inside." Sid grabbed at Katherine's shoulder and yanked her into the house. "Gus, dearest," she called, "you'll never believe who has come to visit!"

Gus came running down the stairs, wearing a painter's smock, brandishing a paintbrush and with a smudge of orange on her nose.

"Molly, what on earth have you been doing to yourself? Are you making a protest against the wearing of skirts, a la bloomer?"

"I had to abandon it in a fire," I said.

"When she jumped from rooftop to rooftop," Katherine said. "She was fearless."

Gus's gaze turned to Katherine.

"This is Katherine," I said.

"The Katherine," Sid added.

"Resurrected from the dead?" Gus asked.

"Never died in the first place. Went underground. Wicked husband," Sid said. "Wants us to hide her."

I smiled at Sid's succinct account. That pretty much summed it up.

"Well of course we'll hide her, but let's clean her up first," Gus said.

"May I suggest brandy for shock first," Jacob said.

"Oh, Mr. Singer. I didn't notice you standing there," Gus said. "Were you part of this amazing exploit?"

"He was there at the fire, looking for me, worried sick," I said.

"You can't imagine how powerless and wretched I felt, watching the building go up in flames and being kept away by the fire crews," Jacob said. "And then she was one of the last girls to come down from the next building. I don't ever want to go through that again."

"He wants to marry me," I said in response to Sid's raised eyebrow.

"And do you want to marry him?" Sid's voice sounded sharp. "Not that I am against the principle of marriage for the rest of the world, but . . ."

"I think I might," I said, smiling shyly at Jacob.

"Could do worse, I suppose." Sid gave Jacob an appraising glance. "At least he won't try to put you into a glass case like a stuffed bird."

"I don't know about that." Jacob laughed. "It may well be the only way of keeping her out of trouble."

"You do have a point there," Gus agreed. "She does seem to attract trouble, I'll agree. Molly dearest, you haven't told us how you came to be involved in a fire in the first place."

We sat at the kitchen table, sipping brandy, while I told the whole story of the fire.

"I must be confused, but I don't quite see how Katherine comes into a fire at Mostel's. I thought she left there weeks ago," Gus said.

"I ran away from Michael and Sadie hid me in Mostel's attic," Katherine said.

"You ran away from your husband because he ill-treated you?"

"No, he didn't ill-treat me, but I couldn't stay with a cold-blooded murderer." She filled in the gaps, including what she knew about Nell's murder. It can't have been easy for her and Sid and Gus nodded with sympathy.

"One thing I don't understand," Sid said. "If you were married, then there's nothing much your father could have done about it, is there? He couldn't have forced you to come home."

"I asked that same question," Jacob said.

Katherine sighed. "I lied about my age. I lied about almost everything to get married. For all I know the marriage isn't valid at all. But it wasn't myself we were worried about, it was Michael. I knew he was with the freedom fighters in Ireland and that was one of the things that made him attractive to me. I thought it was wonderful to be passionate about a just cause. I mean, we English really have no right to rule Ireland, do we?"

She looked at me as if wanting my personal forgiveness.

"It's not your fault," I said. "You were born to it. You didn't choose it."

"Go on about Michael," Sid said. "You say he was a freedom fighter."

"I knew that he loved danger, but I thought that he was also noble and good. After I married him I found out that he loved violence. He had killed a police officer when the police tried to break up a demonstration. He was proud of it. And I found out something else too—he only married me as a way of getting his hands on some money and leaving Ireland in a hurry." She put her hands over her mouth and sat fighting with emotion for a moment, then composed herself again. "I have been such a fool," she said.

"So Michael was scared that he could be sent back to Ireland to stand trial for killing a policeman," I said.

"Of course. And then this second killing. I couldn't abide it any longer."

"So you ran away from him."

"Not at first," she said. "He told me that I'd be an accessory to the murder. He'd tell everyone that it was my idea and that I had egged him on, so I'd hang with him. I didn't know what to do. Then—then something else happened."

"Another murder?" I asked.

"In a way," she said. "One of the reasons I agreed to marry Michael and flee to America with him was because I was expecting his child. I knew how ashamed my parents would be and I couldn't face them. After Michael killed that young woman, I miscarried. It was awful—and you know what Michael said when it was all over? He said, 'Well at least that's one stroke of luck, isn't it? Now we won't be saddled with a brat.' " She gave a big, shuddering sigh. "I had just lost my baby."

Without warning she began to cry, hiding her face in her hands before mastering herself again. "I promised myself I wouldn't give in to self-pity," she said.

I reached out and put my hand on her shoulder.

"Don't worry, Katherine, you'll be safe now," I said.

"You're going to turn me over to my father."

"You don't want to go home?"

"No, of course not," she said. "I hated that life—the boredom was awful. Hunting and parties and then over to London for more parties and inane chatter. I don't ever want to go back to that."

"Your parents are very worried about you. I understand your mother is an invalid."

"When it suits her," Katherine said. "So will you tell my father?"

"Your father is my client," I said. "I shall have to write and tell him that I've found you, safe and sound. What you do after that is up to you, although I beg you to write to them yourself and ask for their forgiveness."

"It sounds to me that the marriage wasn't legal," Jacob said. "And if you're underage, they could demand that you come back to them."

"Then I shall go somewhere where they can't find me until I turn twenty-one. I shall be quite a rich woman then."

"How will you manage until then?"

"I don't know," she said. "I can't think about that now. My concern at this moment is that Michael doesn't find me. I know he's been looking for me."

"He still loves you then?" Gus asked.

"I doubt if he ever loved me. He wants me with him for his own protection. I am a bartering tool—not much more."

"You should tell the police what you know about Michael," Jacob said.

"Turn in my own husband, you mean?" She shook her head. "I can't do that. However he has behaved toward me, I really loved him. I believed him when he said he loved me. I was carrying his child. I can't betray him now."

"Even if he wants to hurt you?" I demanded.

She shook her head. "I'm sure he doesn't mean me harm. He's just frightened at the moment. He doesn't know where to go. He doesn't know whether he can trust me or not." She grabbed at my arm suddenly. "You won't tell the police about him, promise me that. Not until I've decided what I must do next."

"All right," I said. "We will say nothing until you've made up your own mind. But he killed somebody, Katherine. He killed a good woman. You can't expect us to sit by and do nothing. You know in your heart that you have to tell them."

Katherine sighed. "I know. I'm so confused and so frightened—I don't know what I feel anymore. But I did love him once."

"But you are afraid for your life. You can't go on living this way," Jacob said angrily. "The man must be brought to justice."

"The man is a brute. You were quite right to leave him," Sid said.

"Don't worry, you'll be safe here. He'll never be able to find you. Our lips are sealed," Gus added.

"Thank heavens for that. Now we can all relax," Jacob said.

It turned out he wasn't one hundred percent right.

An hour or so later we were bathed, changed, and restored. Sid and Gus insisted on feeding us. After a large filling meal of roast beef, cabbage, and potatoes (the Moroccan phase having begun to wane), Jacob took his leave reluctantly.

"You're sure you will be all right now?"

"You've said that a dozen times. How could I possibly not be all right? I am among friends and my own home is across the street, complete with large male bodyguard. Nobody would think of looking for Katherine here. We will sleep soundly tonight, believe me."

He went then. I crossed the street to my own house and returned with pen and paper.

"I am writing to your father, Katherine," I said. "I will limit my news to telling him that I have found you safe and sound if you will complete the letter yourself."

She chewed on her lip. "But he'll come after me as soon as he gets the letter."

"Then tell him not to."

"You don't know my father. He was used to ordering men around in the army for most of his life. He expects everyone else to salute and obey—wife and daughter included."

"Tell him that you have left Michael Kelly and it appears that your marriage might not be legal—that will make him happy. Then tell him that you are not ready to come home yet, but will keep in touch from now on. He can't ask for more."

Still she hesitated.

"Katherine, if it were your child and you were desperately worried about her, wouldn't you want to get a message from her, saying that she was safe?"

She nodded and sat at the table. She blotted and folded the letter before I could read it and thrust it into an envelope.

"That's done then," she said.

She put her hand instinctively to her throat.

"You used to wear a locket," I said.

She nodded. "My grandmother's."

"What happened to it? How did Mr. Mostel get his hands on it?"

"We needed money. Michael told me to pawn it. I asked Mr. Mostel if I could pawn it to him. He gave me twenty dollars for it. Not nearly enough but it kept us going. Michael drank most of the money away, of course. I wonder if it was still in Mostel's office and it burned in the fire."

"No, it's safe," I said, "and I may be able to get it back for you."

Her face lit up. "Really?"

"I can't promise anything, but I'll try."

She jumped up and hugged me. "Molly, you are a miracle worker."

"I must go home now," I said. "Keep out of sight and let my two trusty friends take care of you. You'll be quite safe with them."

"I'm sure I shall." Katherine looked around her. "In fact I shall be so comfortable here that I may never want to leave."

I smiled as I walked to the front door. I had the same warm feelings about Nine Patchin Place. I hadn't wanted to leave either. My little home across the street still felt like a bleak substitute, but at least I didn't have to worry that Shamey and Bridie were living in an unbearable slum.

I stepped out into the night and pulled my wrap around me as I crossed the street. As I went to open my front door a figure stepped out of the shadows and an arm grabbed me.

I opened my mouth to scream, but no sound came out.

"It's only me," Daniel's voice said.

"Holy Mother of God! My heart nearly jumped right out of my chest," I said.

Daniel stepped out of the shadows into the light of the street lamp. "I had to see you. I've just called at your house but they said you weren't home."

"I was across the street with Sid and Gus," I said. "What do you mean by scaring me half to death?"

"I heard about the fire. I got there just in time to see you in the arms of that Singer fellow. Before I could reach you, you went off in a cab with him."

"I was naturally upset, having just escaped from being burned to death. Jacob comforted me."

"Ah, so that's all it was. That's fine then." The lines of concern had melted from his face. Anger welled up inside me.

"No, that's not all it was. I think you should know that he's asked me to marry him."

He looked at me for a second, then laughed. "Of course you're not going to marry him."

"Oh, and why not, pray? Does the New York police force have jurisdiction over marriages these days?"

"You're not going to marry him because you don't love him."

"How do you know that I don't love him?"

"Because you love me and you can't love two people at once."

"I *loved* you," I corrected. "But I grew tired of waiting. Almost a year has gone by, Daniel, and still you haven't told Miss Norton of my existence."

The flickering light of the gas lamp lit his face. He was wearing his greatcoat with the collar turned up and the wind tugged at his unruly curls. As usual the physical attraction of the man was overwhelming. I fought it.

"The time has never been right, Molly. I work so darned hard that I barely have time to sleep. I have hardly seen Miss Norton for months and when I do see her, the time just goes before I can pluck up courage. I told you it has to be done properly. If I make her feel betrayed, she will stop at nothing until she has ruined me completely and utterly. She might appear sweet but she has a ruthless streak in her nature."

"If you chose such a person to marry—your advancement must indeed mean a lot to you."

"I was a young man when I first proposed to her. She seemed sweet and delicate and all that a man could want in a wife."

"Rich too, of course. And influential."

279

"That was taken into consideration. But I didn't have a chance to see any of her faults until later."

"And now it seems you would rather live with her faults than risk her wrath. That doesn't say much for your character."

"I agree. I have been a hopeless coward where this is concerned. I just beg you, do not do anything rash to spite me."

"If I marry Jacob, it will not be to spite you. It will be because he is kind and caring and honorable and will take good care of me."

"When did you ever need anyone to take care of you?" That roguish smile crossed his lips.

"Maybe I have had enough of trying to fend for myself. And I can help him with his work too. He is making a difference, Daniel."

"And I am not?"

"Of course you are, but Jacob does his work for love, and you do yours for ambition. He could make a lot of money from his photographs but chooses to take pictures to arouse the public conscience. He is actively seeking to better the lot of those poor people who have no voice of their own. It's a noble cause."

"But not your cause. I don't see you as a rabid socialist by nature," Daniel said. "When your enthusiasm wanes, what will you have left then?"

"Mutual respect and affection."

"Is that enough, Molly?"

"It may have to be, Daniel. If you came to me tomorrow and told me that you were free of your engagement and asked me to marry you, I might well consider it, but I do not intend to become an elderly spinster while I sit at home waiting."

"You could always have written to Miss Norton yourself. That would have brought matters to a head."

I shook my head. "Oh no, Daniel. Either you come to me willingly, freely, and with your whole heart, or not at all. It has to be your choice and yours alone. You should go now. The night is cold to be standing outside."

"You could ask me in."

"That wouldn't be proper, would it? Word might get back to my fiancé."

As I went to walk past him he grabbed my arm and swung me around to face him. "Don't do this to me, Molly. Don't taunt me this way."

"I assure you, sir, that I take matters of the heart very earnestly. If you think my decision to marry Jacob is merely to taunt you, then you are wrong. If I commit to him, I commit wholeheartedly, and with full knowledge of what I am giving up."

He grasped at my shoulders, his fingers digging into my flesh. "Don't give up on me, Molly, please."

"Let go of me." I shook myself free. "You're not going to soften me up with your sweet-talking blarney anymore. I'm getting on with my own life without you and I'm doing just fine."

"Apart from almost getting yourself burned to death in a fire, shot at, captured by gangster, and arrested for prostitution?"

"Apart from those, yes."

I looked at him and he started to laugh. I had to smile too.

"I love you, Molly Murphy," he said softly, then he reached out to stroke my cheek.

"Good night, Daniel," I said somewhat shakily, then I fled inside the door before I could weaken. Once inside I stood in the doorway with my hand to that cheek where his hand had been.

⁂ Twenty-seven ⁑

I t was an unaccustomed luxury to rise with the sun the next morning, to dress and breakfast in leisure, and to get a kiss from the children as they went off to school.

"I'm glad you're not going to that horrid place anymore, Molly," Bridie said, wrapping her little arms around my neck. "It was no fun when you weren't here. All we had to eat was dripping toast and Shamey bullied me."

"Well, I'm going to bully you now," I said, stroking her hair fondly. "And my first command is to bring me your hairbrush. You have a knot the size of Galway Bay in the back of your hair. And you, Shamey, haven't washed your neck in a week. Go and do it now."

"Tough guys don't need to wash their necks," he muttered as he made for the scullery.

I waved as they ran off to school.

"They're turning out just grand, aren't they?" I asked Seamus, who had come into the room.

"Thanks to your help. Who knows where they'd have been if we had stayed with Nuala in the tenement? I wish there was some way to repay you, Molly. I'm doing my best to find a job, really I am. I'm seeing a man today at the department store called Macy's. Do you know of it? They say it's very grand. They take on extra help for the Christmas season—carrying packages for ladies and the like."

"You'll be back on your feet soon enough."

He nodded as if he didn't really believe this. "I've only ever been a laborer, you see, and now I don't think I've the strength to swing a pick and shovel."

"You'll find something, Seamus. Don't worry about it. I've just concluded two cases, so I'll have money coming in."

As I said that, a smile spread across my face. Two cases solved. I had become a real detective. I would go and collect my fee today. I thought it only fair to confront Sarah first and verify the truth about those papers I had seen. I had been wrong about things before—just occasionally.

I had no idea where Sarah lived, or Mr. Mostel either. I headed for the garment factory because I couldn't think of any other sensible starting point. As I approached along Canal Street I saw that a small crowd was still gathered around the burned-out shell of the building. Men were dragging out sorry-looking pieces of furniture from the cabinetmaker on the ground floor. On the sidewalk were stacked bolts of waterlogged, singed cloth. It was a sorry sight. I noticed that several of my fellow workers were standing among the crowd, staring at the building as if they couldn't believe what they saw. Then Seedy Sam emerged from the ruined doorway, shaking his head. He spotted me and pointed his finger accusingly.

"It was you, wasn't it? You and that Sadie girl—you started the fire deliberately because I locked you in. I knew you were trouble from the first day."

I marched right up to him. "We started the fire?" I demanded "Is that what your addled brain has been thinking? We were almost burned alive in that firetrap. It was only sheer luck that we got out."

"You probably didn't mean it to burn up the whole building—just drawing attention to yourselves."

"The fire started because one of the little girls panicked at the thought of being locked in and she knocked over one of those unsafe oil stoves. You'll be lucky that you're not arrested after we've told the police how you locked us in."

"Me—arrested?" He stepped away, his eyes darting around the crowd. "I didn't do anything against the law."

"I'd say holding people prisoner against their will might be grounds for arrest," I said, looking at the other girls in the crowd. "What do you think?"

The crowd made angry murmurs.

"I was just doing my duty, doing right by Mr. Mostel."

"I hope that's how he sees it, because I'm on my way to visit him now, and you can be sure I'll let him know how you locked us in—just as we'll be letting the newspapers know all the details too."

He seemed to deflate like a balloon. "I'm just the foreman," he said. "They can't pin anything on me." And he hurried off. The girls looked at me and laughed.

"Are you really going to tell the police and the newspapers?" one of them asked.

"I might. In fact I probably should, shouldn't I? It would make people aware of how badly we've been treated. Maybe some good will come of it." I decided to visit Jacob as soon as I'd settled the matter with Sarah.

"Do any of you know where Sarah lives? The frail-looking girl from Russia—quiet as a mouse?"

"Oh that one." One of the girls nodded. "She lives on Hester. Two buildings from us."

I noted the address in my little book. "And what about Mr. Mostel?" I asked.

"You're going to see him too?"

"I might—just to tell him what I think of him and his fire-trap," I said. "Does anyone know where he lives?"

"Oh sure. We go to supper there every Shabbat," one of the girls said with a laugh.

"He lives on the Upper East Side," someone else said. "Right by the park. Fancy schmancy. I saw him when I went uptown to the zoo once. He came out of a side street, right across from the zoo. He was riding in his carriage with his family. Very grand."

"Thanks," I said.

"Are you really going to see him? You sure have *chutzpah*, Molly. I bet he throws you out." I heard them calling after me as I made my way toward Hester Street. Of all the Lower East Side, Hester Street was the most bustling street of commerce. Pushcarts made through traffic impossible. It was hard enough for a pedestrian to squeeze between them. Everything from fish to old clothes, from the lyrics to popular Yiddish songs to roasting sweet corn, all crammed in along the sidewalk. I picked up my skirts and stepped daintily through the debris. Sarah's building was above a kosher butcher shop and the dead animal smell accompanied me up the stairs. I knocked on the front door. It was Sarah's narrow little face that peeped through the crack in the opened door.

"Molly! What are you doing here?"

"Just come to pay you a visit, Sarah."

She opened the door wide. "Come in, please. This is so nice of you." She led me into a small room, that clearly comprised their living space. On one wall was a shelf of pots and dishes. There was a crude bench and table. Possessions were stacked in orange crates and blankets and quilts were folded in a corner. A pale woman sat in the one good chair, a rug over her knees. In the poor light her skin looked almost gray and was so shrunk around her bones that she looked like a marble statue sitting there. Sarah's sister Fanny sat on an upturned crate at her feet. The place was damp and cold, the wallpaper peeling to show black holes in the walls. It was about the most sorry sight I had seen since coming to America.

"Mama, this is Molly who works with me," Sarah said, then repeated it in Yiddish in case her mother hadn't understood. "She was wonderful. She jumped across the roof, like in a circus."

Sarah's mother said something. Sarah nodded. "Mama says you must have some tea with us. She is sorry we have no cake or sugar."

"Oh no, don't make tea specially for me . . ."

"Of course you must have tea." Sarah filled a pan from a jug, then put in onto a little spirit stove.

I sat on the bench and looked around again. On the shelf and the walls were some fine little charcoal sketches—street scenes and street urchins.

"You must be the artist, Sarah," I said.

"My sister Fanny also draws well," Sarah said. "We had a tutor in Russia who had studied in Paris. He taught us well. He said we both had a gift."

"That must have made copying Mostel's designs easy for you then."

The girls both jumped as if they had been burned.

"What do you mean?" Sarah asked.

"I saw those pages that floated away yesterday. They were Mr. Mostel's new designs. You were going to hand them to your sister to take to Lowenstein's, weren't you?"

Sarah glanced swiftly around the room. "Please. Not here. Mama doesn't know. She doesn't understand much English, but—step outside, please."

I followed her out of the front door. "So I copied his designs," she said, lifting her little chin defiantly. "Serve him right, mean old man."

"But Sarah, he was employing you."

"I was slaving for him," she said venomously. Quite a transformation from the meek little mouse who had worked beside me. "He deserves what he gets. He wouldn't let my sister work with me. He said no families, bad for business, so she had to find work with Lowenstein. Then Mr. Lowenstein found out I was working for Mostel and he tell us he pay good money if we find out what Mostel's new designs look like."

"You must have known that was wrong?"

"Wrong? Ha! I tell you something—I wasn't going to do it. I say to Fanny we are from good family. We do not resort to stealing like common peasants. And that very next day my mother is taken bad. We have to send for the doctor. The doctor wants paying right away. I come in to work an hour late and the foreman says to me, 'If you're gonna come in late again, don't bother showing up.' He wouldn't even listen. So I thought—why not? We did it last season and Lowenstein give us fifty dollars. Fifty dollars—can you imagine? We could buy Mama good food, we could pay the rent and the doctor bills."

"But you were cheating your employer."

"Oh, and he never cheated us? Ten cents for sneezing. Ten cents for going to the washroom, for coming back one minute late from lunch. And don't think we didn't know about turning back the clock hands to get extra minutes out of us. We were cheated every single day, so don't preach to me about cheating." She looked at me, suddenly suspicious. "Why do you want to know this? Are you some kind of church lady preacher?"

I shook my head. "No, I was hired by Mr. Mostel to find out who was stealing his designs."

"So you're going to go and tell him you've found out?"

"I have to."

"And then what? We get arrested and go to jail and our mother will die. That's good American justice. They killed my father and brothers in Russia, you know. We came here with nothing—we left everything in Russia: clothes, jewelry, books, all left behind. Our mother has been sick ever since."

"I'm really sorry," I said. "I'll do what I can for you. I'll make Mostel agree not to press charges, if you promise me you won't do it again."

"Won't do it again?" She laughed bitterly. "I won't be stealing Mostel's designs again because there is no Mostel's. We'll be trying to live on Fanny's six dollars a week and we're going to starve and Mama's going to die."

"I really am sorry. If I could do something, I would. Perhaps another shop will take you on."

"Me and fifty other girls. Oh sure."

"I should go," I said. "Give my respects to your mother. I hope her health improves."

Without saying a word she turned and went back into the room. I heard her telling them in Yiddish that I didn't want any tea.

I felt really sick as I descended the stairs to busy Hester Street. Here, down below that one room, life was going on merrily—housewives bargaining over herrings and chickens, little boys throwing mud balls at each other, a monkey dancing on an organ grinder's shoulder. Should I just forget the whole thing and let Mostel think that I hadn't found his spy? If I made personal judgements about each case that I undertook, I wouldn't be making much money in my chosen profession. I had to learn to keep myself remote. I had been hired to do a job. I had done that job and now my duty was to report my findings to my employer.

I couldn't help feeling like a heel as I rode the Third Avenue El north to the Upper East Side where I had been told Mr. Mostel lived. It was always a shock going from the Lower East Side to another part of the city. The sensation was like Alice falling down a rabbit hole and finding herself in another world. There were mansions facing the park with the occasional horse and carriage waiting patiently outside a front door. A maid was scrubbing front steps. A nanny walked past pushing a high English perambulator. On a street across from the zoo I found a mailman delivering letters. Luckily he was an observant mailman and directed me to East Sixty-third.

I found the house easily enough—an elegant brownstone, four floors high. This was what the sweat of his laborers had bought for Mr. Mostel and his family. It was hard to feel too sorry for his current disaster.

I pulled back my shoulders with resolution and went up the front steps. The door was opened by a stiffly starched maid.

"Miss Murphy to see Mr. Mostel."

"Mr. Mostel senior or junior?" she asked, trying to size me up with a haughty stare.

"Senior. I have been carrying out a commission from him."

"I'm afraid he is not at home at present, but he is expected shortly. If you would care to wait?"

"Thank you." I stepped into the welcoming warmth of the front hall. I wasn't sure that my nerves would hold up to waiting, but it seemed stupid to have come all this way for nothing. I was shown into a small sitting room, obviously a front parlor for visitors as the fire wasn't lit. I sat on a brocade chair and waited. A clock ticked loudly on the mantelpiece, otherwise there was no sound, no hint that a family lived in this house. I wondered about Mrs. Mostel and what she might be doing.

Then, after what seemed an eternity, I heard footsteps on the stairs. The footsteps came toward me and Ben Mostel came into the room. He froze when he saw who was sitting there.

"You. What are you doing here?"

"I'm here to see your father."

Another look of pure terror. "You're not going to tell him, are you? About the checks, I mean. Because I don't make a habit of it and—"

"I'm not here to tell him about what I saw," I said. In mid-sentence I saw my opportunity. "If you can do me a favor," I added.

"A favor? It's no good asking me for cash. As you have observed, I am constantly hard up."

"It's not cash I want. It's the return of that locket to its rightful owner. It belonged to her grandmother and it means a lot to her."

"But I can't ask Letitia for it back."

"If you could maybe substitute another piece of jewelry and explain the locket's history, I'm sure she could be persuaded."

Ben sucked in air through his teeth. "Another piece of jewelry. That means money, which I don't seem to have at the moment."

"Then the promise of another piece. You gave her something which was not yours to give. You helped yourself to what you found in your father's drawer. The piece was only being pawned with the expectation of being retrieved."

"I just don't see how—"

"Then I shall be forced to tell your father what you did. I may also be forced to mention the checks."

He paced nervously. "All right. I'll do what I can. Where can I find you?"

"My card." I handed it to him.

He glanced at it. "Discreet investigations? You're actually a professional dick? So that's why you were snooping around. Detecting what, may one ask?"

"Something I have come to share with your father, as soon as he returns."

As if on cue the front door opened. "Millie—my hat and gloves!" a voice boomed. He spied us through the half-opened door and came through, his hat and gloves still in his hand. "Miss Murphy." He looked surprised.

"Mr. Mostel."

"I'm sorry I wasn't home to receive you."

"Your son was keeping me well amused, thank you." I glanced at Ben whose eyes were riveted to my face.

"At least the boy is good for something then," Mostel said. "Off you go then, boy. With your father out of work, it will be up to you to support the family from now on." Then he laughed at Ben's stricken face.

"Very droll, Papa," Ben said. "Now if you will excuse me. A pleasure talking to you, Miss Murphy."

"And you too, Mr. Mostel. I look forward to hearing your future—news."

Ben nodded and beat a hasty retreat.

"If we really did have to rely on the boy, we'd all starve," Mostel said genially as he pulled up a chair. "Now to what do I owe the pleasure of this visit?"

I took a deep breath, was about to tell him, and changed my mind at the last moment. "I came to express my condolences at the loss of your factory."

He nodded. "A sad business, Miss Murphy."

"It is indeed. I hope you were insured."

"Naturally, but what use is insurance money? I'll have lost the profits from the holiday season by the time I'm up and running again."

"And your workers will have lost their income for the whole holiday season too, which for them will mean going without food and heat."

"That is naturally regrettable. Let us hope they find jobs with other shops."

"You will be rebuilding again, surely?"

"I was only renting space so that decision is not mine to make. I rather think that I will reopen across the bridge in Brooklyn. Plenty of room to expand over there and a workforce ready and waiting."

"And your old workforce?"

"Is welcome to reapply if they care to ride the trolley across the bridge. But I rather think I'll take Mrs. Mostel to Florida for the winter before we make any plans. New York doesn't agree with her delicate constitution."

I studied him sitting there relaxed and smiling, with his tailored suit and its velvet collar and his gold watch chain strung across his vest and I thought of Sarah's one room. My conscience whispered that I should just keep quiet about what I had found out. On the other hand, I was damned if he'd get away without paying me.

I took a deep breath and plunged right in. "I came today because I found out which of your girls was spying for Lowenstein."

A broad shrug of his hands. "As if that's any use to me now, Miss Murphy. Lowenstein will have the Christmas market to himself and *mazeltov* to him."

"I also came to collect my fee."

This jolted him from his complacency. "Your fee? You expect me to pay you now when I have become a penniless beggar out on the street with no income?"

"Enough income to take Mrs. Mostel to Florida for the winter."

"But Miss Murphy, surely you must see that—"

"Mr. Mostel," I interrupted. "Did you or did you not hire me to find the spy in your midst? Did we not shake hands over the deal?"

"We did, Miss Murphy, but circumstances have changed."

"The deal, as I remember it, was for me to ferret out the spy. I have done so."

"Give me the girl's name then, Miss Murphy and I will hand it over to the police."

"You'd have a hard time proving anything, Mr. Mostel. The evidence went up in flames in the fire—the fire started by your inadequate and ancient heating system, I might add."

He spread his hands again, a little happier now. "With no evidence, you expect me to pay you?"

I nodded. "Because I can guarantee that it will never happen to you again."

"Of course it will never happen to me again. I'll be over in Brooklyn."

"And I can tell you how it was done, so that you'll know what to look out for next time."

"Ah." He paused.

"And I think you would like your family to consider you a man of his word," I added for good measure.

Another pause then a heavy sigh. "Very well, Miss Murphy. If you wish to take the last penny from my starving children, go ahead. Ruin me. I'll be sending you a check if you care to present your bill."

"If you'd be good enough to provide paper and ink, I'll be happy to write you a bill on the spot, Mr. Mostel, and then you won't have the inconvenience of having to mail me a check."

He got to his feet reluctantly. "Very well, Miss Murphy. If you'll wait one moment."

I waited and he returned with a portable lap desk on which were paper and ink. I wrote, "To Molly Murphy of J. P. Riley and Associates. For services to unmask a spy at Mostel's garment factory $100."

Mostel stared at it. "Did we agree on one hundred, Miss Murphy?"

"We did, Mr. Mostel, as I think you very well remember."

"Since you say yourself you have no evidence, the job is only half finished, wouldn't you say? Shall we settle on fifty?"

"One hundred, Mr. Mostel."

"You'll be the ruin of me, Miss Murphy." He took out a checkbook then froze with his hand held about the check.

"So how did she do it, Miss Murphy?"

"She was a girl nobody would have suspected—quiet, unobtrusive, so well behaved that when she asked to go to the washroom your foreman never objected. She had a sister who worked for Lowenstein, and she had studied art. It only took her a second or two to copy your sketches. She's a very competent artist, in fact you could do worse than employ her to help you with your designs."

"I'd never employ someone I couldn't trust," he said. "In fact I'm shocked that one of my girls could betray me so easily, after I treated them like a father. It goes straight to my heart, Miss Murphy."

I struggled with wanting to tell him the truth about his factory and ensuring that I received my payment. "If you're going to reopen your factory, Mr. Mostel," I said at last, "may I suggest that you make the conditions bearable for your employees. And relax your rule about not hiring members of the same family. Then they won't be tempted to betray you." Then, as his hand was still poised above that check, "It was one hundred dollars, Mr. Mostel."

I watched as he filled in the check with bold, black strokes. He blotted it then handed it to me. "Don't let it be said that Max Mostel doesn't keep his word."

"Thank you." I put the check into my purse and rose from my seat.

"Good-bye, Mr. Mostel." I held out my hand to him. "It was a pleasure doing business with you."

"Good-bye, Miss Murphy."

He escorted me personally to the door.

❧ Twenty-eight ❧

With a light heart and one hundred dollars in my purse
I jumped on the trolley back to the Lower East Side
and presented myself at Jacob's apartment on Rivington Street.

"Is everything all right?" he asked in a worried voice.

"Couldn't be better. Look at this—a check for one hundred
dollars. You can come to the bank with me and watch me deposit
it and then I'm going to take you out to lunch. But I also have
an ulterior motive—" I laughed at Jacob's expression. "I've come
for help." I breezed past him into the apartment. "I think I should
tell my story to the newspapers—how we escaped from the fire,
as told by a garment worker. It might help raise public awareness
of the abuses in the garment industry. It was a pity you didn't
bring your camera with you that day."

He gave an embarrassed smile. "I did have my little Kodak
in my pocket but I was too concerned about you to remember
to use it."

"Oh, Jacob. You are so sweet." I wrapped my arms around
his neck.

"So when shall we get married?" His hands tightened around
my waist.

"Why rush into something so important? Let's enjoy each
other's company for a while and get to know each other better."

"Very well, although I made up my mind the moment I saw you."

"You were desperate to beat the matchmaker who would have saddled you with a boring, respectable, religious girl," I teased.

He shook his head. "I've never felt this way about a girl before you. I never believed this happiness was possible, Molly. Would it be highly improper to try to kiss you?"

"It would completely wreck my reputation, as you very well know," I said. "But since my reputation is already wrecked by coming here alone, I'll allow you a quick peck on the cheek."

His lips brushed my cheek and I was disturbed by the still strange sensation of his beard scratching me. I moved away, laughing. "Your beard. It tickles."

"Then I'll shave it off for you."

"You'll do no such thing. I think it looks grand. I'll learn to like it." I moved away from him. "Now enough frivolity. I want you to help me write this newspaper article and then you'll know the right people to take it to."

We spent a pleasant hour composing the piece and then walked together to Herald Square and presented it to one of Jacob's contacts at the *Herald*. He seemed excited to get the scoop and asked me more questions and asked Jacob to take my picture.

"I prefer to remain anonymous, if you don't mind," I said. "It's the conditions I wanted to feature, not me."

After that we visited the bank to deposit the check, then had the promised lunch at a nice restaurant. I suggested Delmonico's, but steady and sensible Jacob steered me in the direction of a French café just below Union Square. I insisted on paying, much to Jacob's embarrassment. On the way home we walked around Wanamaker's department store, looking in wonder at the items on the food counter—cans and bottles from all over the world, foodstuffs I had never even heard of—as well as the silk stockings from France and varieties of face makeup. I finally arrived home, tired but content, about five o'clock, having left Jacob to hurry off to a union meeting somewhere.

"Hello, all." I hung my cape on the peg in the hall. No answer. Shamey was often out playing with his friends or earning dimes by running errands, but Bridie and Seamus were always around. I lit the gas in the kitchen then checked around the house. Nobody.

Then I noticed a piece of paper had been pushed through the letter slot. I picked it up and carried it close to the gas mantle to read. It was scrawled in poor penmanship:

> *If you want to see the little girl again Katherine must meet me at the end of Delancey Street at eight o'clock tonight. Tell her to come alone or no trade.*

I stared at the paper, willing the words to say something different. Think, Molly, I commanded myself, trying to slow down my racing brain. The simplest thing to do would be to let Katherine go and trade herself for Bridie. Michael wouldn't harm his wife, would he? But then she wouldn't want to go with him either. If I told the police I would be risking Bridie's life. Michael might kill her as soon as he spotted a police helmet. Or, I could say nothing to Katherine and go in her place. In the dark, with a shawl over my head, I could get close enough to snatch Bridie away, close enough to appeal to his better nature. I'd give him a chance to escape, promise to say nothing until he was safely far away, even give him money for a train ticket.

I wandered around the kitchen in a panic, straightening out the tablecloth, putting a jug back on the shelf, trying to come up with something better. But I couldn't. Nothing really mattered at this point apart from saving Bridie. This man had killed at least twice before. He wouldn't hesitate to kill a child, or to drag her with him as a hostage. And I didn't want Katherine to be a hostage either. But then I didn't want to be a hostage myself—or a dead body, for that matter.

Would I really be in danger, I asked myself. Delancey Street, from what I remembered, was full of life. If I cried out, someone would come to my aid. Shops would still be open at eight o'clock. Workers would be returning from work, saloons would be full. In fact it was a strange place to choose for such a meeting—unless Michael had decided that he could melt into the crowds of the Lower East Side and make it hard for anyone to follow him.

I took my shawl off the peg and wrapped it over my head, hiding that telltale red hair. Apart from that we were about the same stature. If I couldn't get close enough, I'd yell for help. Passersby would grab the child for me. Thus reassured that I was doing the right thing I wrote a hurried note to Seamus and the boy. "Out with Bridie. Don't worry. Back soon. Love, Molly." No sense in worrying them too.

Then I let myself out and closed the front door behind me. It was a damp, cold, wintery night. Fog would be swirling in from the East River which might aid my cause. As I set off down Patchin Place I heard footsteps behind me. I spun around. Katherine was running down Patchin Place after me, wrapping a shawl around her as she ran.

"Wait, Molly. Where are you going?"

"Nowhere. Just out for a stroll."

She caught up to me, her face anguished. "He came here. I saw him. He put something through your letter box. I've been waiting for you to come home. What did he say? Please tell me the truth."

"I wasn't going to tell you," I said, and handed her the note, "but for once I can't come up with a good lie."

She held it up under the gas lamp to read it and gasped. "He's taken a little girl?"

"Yes, Young Bridie who lives with me."

"He had a big sack with him. I never thought—never imagined—what were you going to do? Not the police. He'd kill her."

"If you really must know, I was going in your place. I was

going to try and snatch the child and then find safety in the crowds on Delancey Street. It's sure to be busy at this time of night."

"You'll do no such thing," Katherine said, with that commanding look I remembered so well from the photograph. "I'll go and make the trade. If Michael wants to take me with him, so be it. It's my fault. I chose to run away with him. I made my own bed. Now I must lie in it."

"But you didn't know his true nature then, Katherine."

She gave a rueful smile. "He could be very charming when he wanted to. I'd never met anyone like him."

"But you don't want to go with him now, do you?"

"Of course not. Knowing that he killed a woman in cold blood, and that he felt nothing at all for our lost child, I could never love him again."

"Then let me go in your place."

"Absolutely not. He won't hurt me. I'll be all right, I'm sure."

"I'll come with you then," I said. "I'll be in the crowd behind you and if I get a chance I'll dart out and snatch Bridie. If Michael tries to grab you, scream and make a fuss."

She nodded solemnly. "Yes. All right. In fact I'd be very glad if you'd come with me. I have been living in fear for weeks with no one to turn to. Those awful men Michael latched onto—those Eastman brutes—it was like being plunged into hell."

"I'm sure it was," I said. I slipped my arm through hers. "We escaped from the fire together, didn't we? We can come through this. He'll find out we're not soft and frightened little women—"

"We are Amazons, not to be trifled with." Katherine threw back her head defiantly.

We strode out, matching steps, in the direction of Delancey Street. As I had expected, Delancey was bustling with life as we entered it from the Bowery.

"This is the end of Delancey Street," I said.

"Or the beginning," Katherine pointed out.

We stood on the street corner, scanning the crowds who

hurried past, eager to be home and out of the damp chill. The fog was indeed rolling in, clinging to lampposts and awnings. It muffled the sound of a clock chiming the three quarters. Maybe he hadn't arrived yet.

"We should walk to the other end of the street," Katherine suggested. "That would be more logical. He could make an easier escape down on the docks and there would be fewer people around to witness too."

In my confusion I hadn't paused to consider that Delancey did indeed end in the dockland. It would be easy to hide a small child on the wharf among piles of cargo. It would also be easy to throw a small child into the river without being seen.

"Then let us hurry," I said. "Maybe we can intercept him before he reaches the docks."

We pushed our way along the crowded street, dodging carts, horses, children, and piles of rubbish. The street seemed twice as long as I remembered it. I wished that Jacob had not gone to an unknown meeting tonight. I wished that I had asked for Daniel's help. I wished we weren't so very alone. As we approached the far end, the traffic thinned. There were fewer open stores, fewer lights, fewer people. And thicker fog. A mournful foghorn sounded from out on the river. Then the fog swirled, parted, and closed again and I caught a glimpse of a giant structure rising up in front of me—a giant monster from childhood nightmares, reaching out cruel arms. I stared at the fog as if the thing might be a figment of my imagination. Then I remembered, with a cold sinking feeling that clutched at my gut. That was why he had chosen Delancey over any other street. I was looking at the tower being built for the new East River Bridge.

Katherine must have echoed my thoughts. "It's not built all the way across the river yet, is it?" she asked.

"Just the towers and the cables. No roadway yet."

"No way to get across then. That's good. Perhaps Michael thinks it's finished and he can get out of New York that way."

"Only if he's a tightrope walker."

As we came closer the giant tower loomed above us, the steel girders, ringed with scaffolding, rising into the fog.

"Let's wait here," Katherine said. "I'll stand out in the middle of the street, where I can be seen and where I can see him coming. You wait in a doorway where he can't see you."

I nodded and moved across the street to a darkened doorway. Katherine walked boldly out into the street. I drew my cape around me to stop myself from shivering. The fog had muffled the sounds of Delancey Street so that they came as a distant murmur. It was amazing how remote and deserted it felt here, only a block away from all that life and gaiety.

Katherine walked up and down, stamping her feet against the chill. Then she stopped, her head cocked to one side, listening.

I stepped out from my doorway and heard it too.

"Help me. Somebody help me, please." The little voice floated out of the fog above our heads.

I came out of my hiding place and stood beside Katherine, who was staring upward.

"It's Bridie," I whispered. "Where can she be?"

"Up there, somewhere." Katherine pointed. "It sounds like it's coming from the tower."

"But how—?" I ran around it, peering up at the scaffolding. How could he have taken a small child up there? Then I saw it— a crude staircase made of wood going up between the scaffolding and the tower. It had a gate across it to keep people out but the lock had been forced and the gate flapped open.

"I'll go up," Katherine said. "If Michael's up there, he's expecting me."

"If he's left the child up there, she won't come to you," I said. "We'll go together. Come on."

We held hands and shrank together, taking those makeshift steps side by side. After one flight there was no more light coming up from the street, only an eerie orange glow coming from the city streets beyond. We felt our way up. Eight steps in one direction then eight in the other, back and forth zigzagging up the side of the tower. My legs started to tremble at the exertion. Would these steps never end?

I sensed rather than saw that we had come to an opening. Cold air rushed into my face and I felt nothingness on one side of me. My hand gripped at the cold metal of the scaffolding as wind swirled around me.

Then the voice came again—a small whimper of a terrified child. "Somebody get me down, please."

"She's out there," I whispered to Katherine. But how could she be? I had seen for myself in daylight that there were only cables strung across the river. Then the fog swirled and through the mist I saw that a narrow walkway of planks, about a foot wide, was strung out from the tower, running beside the bottom cable—a fine path for the workmen, I've no doubt, but then they were used to the height. I could only see a few feet in front of me but I could make out the shape of a small person, out there on that path in the fog.

I didn't stop to think. "It's all right, darling. Molly's here. I'm coming for you," I called. I turned back to Katherine. "You stay here and keep watch. Let me know if you hear him coming."

Then I took a deep breath and stepped out onto the catwalk. It bucked and swayed under my feet like a live thing and I clung onto the thin cables that ran beside it, waist high—the only means of support. The wire seemed as frail and ethereal as gossamer. Cold damp air rushed up from the invisible river. I peered into the gloom, trying to make out the bigger shape of a man, but Bridie appeared to be quite alone. Had he lost his nerve and abandoned her then?

"Molly," she whimpered. "I'm frightened. I can't move. The man said he'd be back, but he hasn't come."

"It's going to be just fine, my darling," I said, trying to keep my voice calm and even. "I'll get you down and we'll go home."

Inch by inch I moved closer to her. She was standing sideways, clinging onto that support cable with both hands. I reached her and let go with one hand to put my arm around her and give her a kiss. "See, it's really me and you're safe now," I said. "Now all we have to do is move back slowly toward the tower then we can go home."

"I can't," she whispered. "I can't move."

For a horrible moment I thought he might have tied her in some way, but then she added, "I'm scared I'll fall."

"You won't fall. Look, we'll take tiny steps, holding on, just like this. One foot. Two foot. Do it just like me."

I started to move. I felt the walkway vibrate and sway again under my feet. I was so intent on watching her progress that I didn't look up until Bridie screamed.

Michael Kelly was standing a few feet away between us and the tower. His arm was around Katherine's neck and one big hand was over her mouth.

"There you are, Katherine," he said pleasantly. "What did I tell you? They were as easy to trap as the rats on your father's estate, weren't they now?"

Katherine struggled as he shoved her forward. "I couldn't believe that my own wife would turn traitor on me. What sort of wife is that? You promised to love, honor, and obey."

He had released her mouth or she had broken free. "It was a sham, Michael. You were a sham. You used me."

"You should have come alone like I told you, Kathy, then the child would have been safe. We'd have been off, across the bridge to Brooklyn before anyone came looking for us. Now we have to take care of them first."

It didn't take much intelligence to know what he had in mind. Would it be possible to survive a fall into water from this height? I wasn't sure how high we were, but surely too high to survive a fall. I wasn't even sure if we were over water yet.

"Why do you want me with you?" she demanded "You don't really love me. I'll slow you down."

"Insurance, me darlin'. You're my insurance."

He pushed her closer to Bridie and me. The catwalk swayed

and shuddered. Bridie whimpered again. Then, for the first time in my life I found myself face-to-face with Michael Kelly in the flesh. He was watching me with an arrogant smile at that handsome mouth. Cocky. Sure of himself. Delighted that I had been so stupidly naïve. I tried to make my brain work in an orderly fashion. Maybe I could protect myself, but how could I possibly defend myself and a small child on this gossamer thread so high above the world?

"How did you find us?" I asked, stalling for time.

"Easy." Again that cocky grin. Enjoying this almost. "You think the Eastmans don't run this city? They know all about you."

I felt Bridie's little body brush against me and was terrified that she'd cling onto me, sealing our doom.

"Bridie," I whispered to her. "Hold on very tight to that wire and don't move or let go until I tell you to."

Michael had released Katherine from his grip. "Wait there," he said as he moved past her. "I don't need your help, but don't think of moving. I don't want to get rid of you too, but I will if I have to."

"Just let us go, please," I said in my most submissive voice. "We can't do you any harm. At least let me take the little girl back to the tower."

"You've already done me harm," he said. Then he came at me. The one thing in my favor was that I was ready for him. While I talked I had released one hand quickly to hitch up my skirts enough to move my legs. As he came toward me I held on grimly with both hands and kicked out backward, like a mule. I heard the grunt of air escaping, letting me know that my kick had been high enough to do damage. I had brought one of my brothers to his knees once with a similar move. He teetered for a moment, fought to regain his balance, then as he teetered backward he made a grab for the foot that had kicked him. His hands fastened around my ankle, almost jerking me off the catwalk. I clutched at the wire as his full weight tugged at me. Bridie screamed, the catwalk swung wildly, and then there we were, poised at the edge of eternity, Michael hanging over nothingness and about to pull me with him.

"Let me up again," he shouted. "If I go, I'll make damned sure you all go with me."

My brain was racing, trying to work out how I could pry his hand loose without sacrificing my own balance. In the short seconds that I hesitated Michael grabbed at the planks with his other hand and hauled himself back onto the catwalk.

"You've made enough trouble," he gasped, clambering to his feet. "Why couldn't you have left us alone? I might have spared the child, but not now." He looked past me to Katherine. "When I give you the nod, we throw her down. Ready?"

"No," Katherine said. "No, Michael, I'm not doing it. I'm not helping you again."

"Don't be a fool, Katherine. Don't think you'll get off free. You won't. I'll tell them you begged me to kill that woman. I'll tell them it was you who made me do it."

"Thank you for making up my mind for me," Katherine said. "I would have done anything for you once, Michael, but not now. But then I really loved you once. This proves that you never loved me. Why don't you go, while you still have time? I'll grant you that much."

"You'll grant me? You are in not in a position to grant me anything, Katherine. If you won't help me, I can do it alone. I don't need your stinking help to get rid of a couple of scrawny females. But, by God, you're going to be sorry."

Katherine stuck out her chin defiantly. "I'll help her. It will be two against one and likely enough we'll all go down."

At that moment a light shone out from the tower, cutting an eerie swath through the mist.

"You out there," a big voice shouted. "Police! We know you're there, Kelly."

"Take one step out here and I throw them down—all of them," Michael shouted back.

"We've got sharpshooters aiming at you. We don't need to

take a step," the voice shouted back. "Come quietly or you're a dead man."

Michael grasped at Katherine.

"Come with me, Katherine," he pleaded. "We'll get away. We'll escape. If they catch you, they'll send you to jail. They'll send you home."

"You'd better run if you don't want to be caught," Katherine said evenly.

"Katherine!" He reached out to her.

She knocked away his hand. "Go, Michael."

Michael glanced back at the light, then forced his way past me and Bridie, pushing us aside. I held onto her grimly, thinking he might try to throw us over as he passed, or take Bridie hostage again, but I need not have worried. He was anxious to get away and hardly noticed our presence.

"Hold it right there, Kelly," the voice behind us shouted.

Michael had started to run away, teetering, staggering out along the catwalk that disappeared into the fog.

"Duck down, ladies," the voice commanded. A shot whizzed over our heads, then another. Michael teetered, then, as if in slow motion, he fell and was swallowed up into the night. We didn't even hear a splash.

❧ Twenty-nine ❧

Strong arms helped us back to the safety of the stairway.
Even as I stood on the solid wood of the landing again
I felt myself swaying.

"You're all right now, ladies," the helmeted figure said. "You're
lucky that we got here when we did, and that Higgins is such a
crack shot."

Another constable reached out to scoop up Bridie into his
arms. She cried out in fear.

"It's all right, darling. These nice policemen are here to help
us," I said. "They'll take you down to the ground again. We're
following right behind."

"Just a minute," Katherine said. "I'm feeling faint. I have to
sit down for a moment."

"That's what comes of wearing corsets," I said, helping her
to the step.

"You mean you don't?"

"Never have," I said.

"But don't your insides rattle around? That's what Mother said
would happen if I didn't."

"I've never felt them rattling around yet," I said. "Put your
head down until you feel better."

"Thank you, Molly."

I perched on the step beside her and put my hand on her shoulder.

"It was all so horrible, wasn't it?" she whispered.

"Very horrible," I said. "Especially for you."

"For me? It was you he was trying to kill."

"But you loved him once," I said. "I had no second thoughts about fighting for my life."

"I still can't believe . . ." she began and put her hand over her mouth. "I thought I was so strong and brave but . . ."

"You were, very strong and brave. You had to make some horrible choices out there. Your parents would be proud of you."

"I'm not going back to them," she said, looking up suddenly. She got to her feet. "I'm recovered now, thank you. Let's go down."

As we made our way down the steps a man came up toward us, taking the steps two at a time. In the dim light of the flashlight behind us I took in the unruly curls, the square jaw, and for a horrible moment I thought that it was Michael, and he had somehow survived the shooting and the fall. Then as he came closer to the light I recognized him.

"Daniel!"

"Thank God you're safe," he gasped as he saw me, and he grasped my shoulders as he fought to regain his breath. "I came as soon as I heard." His gaze went past me to Katherine. "You must be Miss Faversham. I'm Captain Sullivan of the New York police. I'm glad to see you safe and sound. What happened to Kelly?"

"Higgins shot him, sir. Fell into the drink," one of the constables said.

"Good work, boys. I passed the little girl at the bottom of the tower. She's with her brother."

"Her brother? What's he doing here?" I asked.

"He was the one who came to find me," Daniel said. "Smart lad, that one. He came home and found the note that Kelly left for you and came to tell me right away. I was out on a case unfortunately, so they sent a constable to fetch me and dispatched sharpshooters straight to the bridge."

"We could have handled it without your men, you know," I said. "Katherine and I had the situation under control."

"Oh, you did, did you?" Daniel gave me a quizzical look.

"Absolutely." I picked up my skirts and pushed past him to descend the final flight of steps.

When we reached the bottom of the tower and came out onto the dockside we found that a crowd had gathered. It took me a while to pick out Bridie, standing to one side, holding Shamey's hand.

"Molly!" they cried and ran to me.

I knelt to hug them both, and couldn't stop the tears from streaming down my cheeks. "You see," I said to Shamey through my tears. "You see how good it is to go to school now? You might not have been able to read the note."

We were laughing and crying at the same time. I looked up to see Daniel watching us. I got to my feet.

"I'd better get these children home now. It's past their bedtime."

"I've a carriage waiting," Daniel said. He took my elbow and steered us though the crowd.

"Don't we need a statement first, sir?" one of the constables asked.

"The morning will do, Higgins. You get back to HQ and make your report. I'll join you as soon as I can."

Daniel handed us into the carriage, then climbed in himself. It was a tight squeeze. I took Bridie on my lap and Katherine balanced Shamey on hers. Daniel was beside me. I was aware of the pressure of his body against mine. Would I never get over these stupid feelings when he was near me? I stroked Bridie's hair and pretended I didn't notice him.

"I suppose it's a waste of time to ask, but what in God's name made you decide to climb a half-built tower with a man like Kelly?" he demanded.

"The answer to that is simple," I said. "He took Bridie."

"You could have come to me for help, as young Seamus here so properly did."

"And when he spotted the first police uniform, what do you think he would have done with her?" I demanded. "Anyway, we had no idea we were going up to a place like that. The note said the end of Delancey Street. I didn't think about the half-built bridge."

"That's one more of your nine lives gone," Daniel said. "I hope it gave you enough of a scare up there to seek a more sensible occupation in the future."

"Something like a companion, had you in mind?" I said, turning away from him. "I find such jobs to be more of a strain on the heart."

"You did very well, Seamus, my boy," Daniel said, leaning past me to ruffle Shamey's hair. "Your father will be proud of you. If you go on like this, I might be able to use you as a messenger when you get a little older."

"Really?" Seamus leaned forward to look at Daniel. "How old do I have to be?"

"You have to have enough schooling so that you can read longer notes with harder words," I said and saw Daniel's smile.

The bright lights of the Bowery flashed past us. A theater performance had just ended and the crowd spilled off the sidewalk forcing our horse to slow to a walk.

"Where can we take you, Miss Faversham?" Daniel asked Katherine.

"She's staying across the street from me, with my friends," I said.

"Ah. Across the street. A good thought," Daniel said. "And may I say, Miss Faversham, or rather Mrs. Kelly, that I commend your bravery tonight. I can only tell you that you've had a narrow escape in more ways than one. The man you married was a dangerous thug, wanted by police both here and in Ireland. Had you stayed with him, you would soon have become part of one of the most violent criminal elements in the city, from which there would have been no escape."

"I realize that," she said, "and I suppose I should be grateful, but it's all been rather a shock. I did love him, you know. You can't just stop loving someone, just like that."

I could feel Daniel looking at me.

"No," he said. "You can't."

Katherine sighed. "I expect I'll get over him with time. I come from tough stock, you know. My father fought in the Khyber Pass." She gave a sad little chuckle. "I'll be all right."

The carriage slowed and came to a halt.

"We're here," Daniel said and lifted the children down, then assisted Katherine and myself from the carriage. His hand lingered against mine. When I tried to pull mine away he was looking at me again.

"Are you going to invite me in tonight?" he asked.

"I think not. The children are tired. But thank you for escorting us home." I gave a correct little nod of the head, equal to anything Miss Arabella Norton could produce.

The children had run ahead to the front door. Seamus opened it and the worried look melted instantly from his face. "Oh, so there you are. I wondered where on God's earth you'd all got to. I've been worrying about you."

"We're all just fine, Seamus. And these children are ready for some bread and milk and bed."

Seamus looked past me to Katherine and Daniel and the carriage at the end of Patchin Place.

"We had a little excitement. No doubt the children will tell you about it in their own good time," I said.

"I've had a little excitement of my own," Seamus said. "I got a job at last. I've been hired by Macy's department store to carry out packages to carriages and automobiles during the Christmas season. And if that works well, they'll keep me on in the stock room."

"I'm pleased for you, Seamus," I said. "Go inside, children.

Say good night to Miss Faversham and thank you to Captain Sullivan."

"Good night, Miss Faversham. Thank you, Captain Sullivan," two voices chanted in unison. "Daddy, you'll never guess what . . ." I heard animated voices as they went into the kitchen.

"I'll be off to bed then," Katherine said. "Thank you again, Molly."

"Do you want me to come with you, Katherine?" I asked.

She glanced at Daniel, then at me. "No, I think not," she said, and walked across Patchin Place to Number Nine.

Daniel and I were left standing together in the darkness. "I must go and fix that bread and milk for the children," I said. "Thank you for bringing us home and thank your men for coming to our aid."

"Molly," he said urgently, "I'll tell her, I promise. Don't do anything rash."

"If you mean marry someone else, it wouldn't be rash. It would be a carefully thought through decision. I don't make promises lightly."

"Promise me that you won't make a commitment to another man until I'm free to ask you myself. If I get down on my knees and you tell me that you choose another man over me, then I'll go away and never bother you again."

I looked up at his earnest face and suddenly laughed. "Daniel—I've a feeling you're full of blarney. You won't tell her. Oh, you'll have great intentions, but when you see her and you realize what you'd be risking and what you'd be giving up, then you'll suddenly become tongue-tied again."

"No, Molly. Not this time. I swear to you. I love you. I can't live without you. I beg you, don't rush into a marriage you'd regret. A lifetime is a lot of years to live with someone you don't love."

"And a lot of years to wait for something that may never happen," I said.

"Just tell me you do still love me and that if I come to you free and available, you'll not send me away."

I looked at him and had to smile. "Oh, Daniel. Like Katherine said, you can't just stop loving somebody. There will probably be a place in my heart for you for the rest of my life. But that doesn't mean I can't find happiness with someone else."

"Not the same happiness we two can have together."

"No, probably not the same kind of passion. But passion often dies, doesn't it? Mutual affection and companionship can last forever."

"You can get those from a dog," Daniel said.

"One thing you should understand, Daniel," I said. "If I marry Jacob, I won't be settling for second best. I would be marrying him because I believe we could be happy together."

"No, Molly. I won't let you marry him. I'll burst into the ceremony and carry you off if I have to."

"Oh, Daniel." I had to smile again. "If you come to me on your knees before I've made the trip to the altar, I might listen to what you have to say. Other than that, I'm not promising anything. Good night, now."

I moved to make my escape but Daniel was quicker. He grabbed me and crushed his lips against mine. I tried not to respond but my body took over and for just a moment I was one with him, pressed against him, the warmth of his body flowing through me. Then I controlled myself and pushed him away.

"That wasn't fair, Daniel. Go home."

"Does he set you on fire when he kisses you? Does he make you feel the way I do?" he demanded.

"There's more to life than kisses." I fled to my front door and slammed it behind me, leaving him standing on the cobblestones outside. Once inside I rested my forehead against the cold oak of the door. Not for the first time I wished I had never met Captain Daniel Sullivan.

The sound of lively children's voices came from the kitchen.

"And then you'll never guess what the policeman did!"

I envied their ability to rebound from tragedy or terror.

The next morning I was awakened by pounding on my front door. I put on my robe and made my way downstairs. Jacob stood outside, a newspaper in his hands.

"I've just seen today's paper," he said, waving it at me as he came into the house.

The headline in the first column of the *New York Times* read, DANGEROUS RESCUE ON NEW EAST RIVER BRIDGE. I scanned down the text. Two young women attempted daring rescue of a child, taken up there by a madman. Situation resolved by fearless, sharpshooting New York police. It mentioned me by name.

"What were you thinking?" Jacob demanded.

"Michael Kelly had Bridie with him. He wanted to trade her for Katherine. I went along to make sure Bridie got down safely."

"You're lucky to be alive. I went to take a look for myself this morning. Those few planks along the side of the cable? That's what you were on?"

I nodded. "And it wasn't very pleasant, I can tell you."

He put his hands on my shoulders. "Molly, please listen to me. No more of this reckless behavior. I can't live, worrying about you every time you're out of my sight. The moment I saw this I thought that I should have been there, I should have saved you."

"I don't intend to make a habit of it, I assure you. In fact I can positively guarantee that I'll never climb up a half-built bridge again." I attempted a laugh. "You don't have to worry about me, Jacob."

"Not worry? Since I've met you a woman was killed by mistake in your place, you were almost burned to death in a fire, and then almost hurled to your death from a bridge. What is there to reassure me that you're not to be worried about?"

"Let's just hope that my future cases are more mundane."

"Let's just hope there are no future cases," he said firmly. "Molly, I want you to give up this absurd idea right now. If you want a job, I can find you one that will challenge you and use your talents. The women's trade union league could use someone fearless and articulate like you. You'd be doing a real service, Molly. Making a difference. What do you say?"

"It's very tempting, Jacob. I will think about it."

"Just promise me you'll stop trying to be a detective."

"But I'm not trying to be one," I said as the realization came to me. "I *am* a detective. I've just concluded two cases satisfactorily. I'll have earned two hundred dollars—not bad for a month's work, wouldn't you say?"

Jacob shook his head, but he was smiling. "Molly. What am I going to do with you? I don't want to let you out of my sight for another moment."

I turned away from him. "Jacob, I . . ."

"I'm sorry. That was stupid of me," he said. "I promised I wouldn't put you in a glass case, didn't I? It's because I care so much that I—"

"Jacob," I interrupted and looked at him this time. "This talk of marriage makes me uneasy. There's something you should know. I like you, Jacob. I admire you and respect you, but I'm not sure that I can love you."

He looked down at his hands. "I see," he said. "Cannot love be learned and grow over time? If our match had been arranged by the matchmaker, we wouldn't even know each other before the ceremony, and yet many such marriages are truly happy ones."

"I'm sure they are, but that would be a risk I wasn't willing to take. I will only marry for love."

There was another long pause.

"Is there someone else?"

"Yes, and no."

"That policeman," he said sharply. "The one who shouted at you." He looked at me for confirmation and I nodded. "He shouted, as I did, because he'd been worried for you. Do you still love him?"

"I'm not sure, but I have experienced what love feels like, and I'm not ready to settle for less."

"Then why did you not marry him?"

"Because he wasn't free."

"Ah," he said quietly. "So are you're trying to tell me that you don't want to marry me?"

"I don't know, Jacob. I really don't know what I want. That's the trouble. I want to be fair to you as well as fair to me, so that if I decide to marry you, it will be because you're my true choice and not because I'm settling for second best. You do understand that, don't you?"

"I understand." He paused, staring past me out of the window. "And I commend you for it. You will let me continue to visit you so that I can woo you and sweep you off your feet?"

I laughed, making him smile too. "You do not need to woo me. You have nothing to prove to me. It is I who has to decide what I want from life and to shake off the ghosts of the past. But I look forward to continuing our friendship and seeing where it might lead us."

His face lit up. "Then I am content."

"Thank you. You are a very dear person." I put my hand to his cheek and leaned forward to brush his lips with a kiss.

"I'll have to get used to that beard, someday," I said.

A week later a letter arrived from Ireland from Major Faversham.

Dear Miss Murphy,

I can't tell you how relieved my wife and I were to receive the letter from you and from Katherine. To know she is alive and well and to discover that she is no longer married to that bounder has lifted our spirits considerably. Of course, we had hoped that she would return to us immediately, but she has promised that she will keep in touch with us via letters and may be coming home soon. Thank you for your splendid work. Enclosed please find a check for twenty-five guineas.

A little over a hundred dollars! I was on my way to becoming a successful woman. I ran across the street and burst into Sid and Gus's house waving the envelope. I found them all at the kitchen table, enjoying the morning coffee and hot rolls ritual.

"A letter from your parents, Katherine. They were so thrilled to hear from you." I stopped. A strange man was sitting at the kitchen table with his back to me. "Oh," I said, "I'm so sorry. I didn't realize you had company."

The man rose to his feet and turned toward me. "Company, you call it? It is I, darling Molly, come home to the bosom of my loved ones." And the dashing, irresponsible, loveable, infuriating Ryan O'Hare stood there, dressed in a black velvet jacket with a large diamond pin in his purple silk cravat.

"Ryan!" I ran to his arms. "How wonderful to see you. We have missed you so much. Have you finally brought the play to New York?"

"It is due to make its glorious opening at the Victoria Theater next week—don't say anything about bad omen in the name. It was the one theater that was free and willing."

"Why should it be a bad omen?" Katherine asked.

Ryan made a face. "I had to leave England in a hurry after the queen was not amused about my satirical play about Her Majesty and Albert." Then that brilliant smile flashed across his face. "I must say it was deliciously wicked. I had the both of them to a T, in all their boring glory. I even gave them plaid sheets on the marriage bed."

"Ryan, you are very naughty, we all know that," Sid said. "I hope your American audiences haven't been equally incensed with your new satire of the American lifestyle."

"My dear, it goes over most of their heads. They laugh uproariously, not realizing they are laughing about themselves. It is too marvelous for words. You'll all come to opening night, of course, as my guests—and to the party afterward. Everyone who is anyone will be there."

"We wouldn't miss it for the world, would we?" Gus said, looking around the table.

I realized with a great flood of relief that this was my normal life now. I could eat long, luxurious breakfasts and take hot baths and go to plays. I was no longer a sweatshop worker. I was Molly, a member of the artistic set of Greenwich Village.

"Let me have a roll and some coffee, please," I said. "I'm positively starving."

"And I have to haste myself in the direction of the Victoria Theater to see about the scenery," Ryan said. "I gather there's an annoying pillar that will have to go. Let us hope it will not bring the house down, literally." He blew kisses and swept out.

Katherine was looking at me strangely. "I may have made a mistake," she said. "I had thought that Jacob was the man in your life, and then I thought that perhaps it was the policeman, but perhaps I am wrong."

"Ryan?" I laughed.

"My dear Katherine," Sid said. "Everyone loves Ryan. Even Ryan loves Ryan."

"Especially Ryan loves Ryan," Gus added. "No, I think that Jacob might not be such a bad choice for Molly after all."

"I've just told him I'm not ready to think of marriage yet. I'm not at all sure I want to marry him."

"Quite right. Too earnest." Sid set a cup of Turkish coffee in front of me. "And think what a hindrance it would be to your career if you wanted to marry. You need time to enjoy life first, Molly."

"You're right," I said. "What is the rush? I'm sure husbands are an infernal inconvenience."

I glanced across at Katherine who was looking pensive, fingering the locket she now wore again at her neck, returned by the repentant Ben Mostel. "I'm sorry," I said, flushing. "How insensitive of us to speak of marriage, after what you've just been through. I expect you never wish to hear the word again."

"Not for a long while," Katherine answered. "But I can assure you I'm not going to be a widow and wear black. As a matter of fact, I am excited about starting life on my own, although I have no idea what I'll find to do with myself."

"We've told you that you're welcome to stay here as long as you want," Sid said. "You can fill the empty nest left by Molly."

Katherine smiled. "You are most kind, but I have to leave New York, just in case my father comes looking for me. He can be very forceful, as I've told you. I will stay in touch with my parents, but I really don't want to go home again."

"Then you must go to Boston, of course," Gus said. "I'm sure we can find something for you there. My family owns half the city. I'll write some letters for you."

"But I don't want to go back to the upper-class life," Katherine said. "Now I've seen how much needs to be done for poor working women, I'm anxious to do more for them."

"Not back to a terrible sweatshop, surely?" I asked.

"Preferably not a terrible sweatshop," Katherine agreed, "but I have to do something useful to give my life a meaning."

Her words struck at my conscience. Was I being selfish if I didn't continue to work for the union? As Jacob had said there was a lot of good I could do. Then Sid sat at the table between us, brandishing the silver coffeepot.

"I commend you, Katherine," she said, "but I have to confess that my morning coffee and hot rolls and my friends, and Gus here of course, are what give my life meaning. I couldn't exist without them."

"Amen to that," Gus said, and raised her coffee cup in salute. I did the same.

*　*　*

Just before Christmas I received a letter from Katherine.

I have settled in Boston. There is a thriving garment industry here as well as a large Irish population, so I feel well at home. Thanks to Gus's connections, I am boarding with several other girls of good family who have started a league dedicated to improving the lot of female factory workers. We have started a branch of the garment workers union in several shops. We have just opened a clinic in one of the worst slums and staffed it with volunteer doctors and nurses. It is challenging, but satisfying work.

Thank you for everything. I hope we may meet again and I wish you well.

Katherine